JASON ANSPACH

NICK COLE

MESSAGE FOR THE DEAD

SEASON 1

BOOK 8

GALAXY'S EDGE

Galaxy's Edge: MESSAGE FOR THE DEAD
By Jason Anspach & Nick Cole

This is a work of fiction. Any similarity to real persons, living or dead, is coincidental and not intended by the author.

 Version 1.1
Hardcover ISBN: 978-1-949731-39-2

Edited by David Gatewood
Published by Galaxy's Edge, LLC

Cover Art: Fabian Saravia
Cover Design: Ryan Bubion
Interior Formatting: Kevin G. Summers

For more information:

Website: GalaxysEdge.us
Facebook: facebook.com/atgalaxysedge
Newsletter: InTheLegion.com

GET SOME
KTF
KTF
KTF

PART I

KEEL

01

Indelible VI
Orbiting the Planet Porcha

The *Indelible VI* hovered above the planet Porcha, its remote docking corridor extended and coupled with the Black Fleet shuttle waiting to receive Exo. Inside the *Six*'s cockpit, Captain Aeson Keel monitored a holodisplay that flashed undulating green text in stylish fonts curated by celebrity designers. A model of a modern shipboard AI text-to-user interface.

"All right, docking hookup is complete," Keel reported to his navigator, Ravi. "Pressure's good. Air is flowing. I'm gonna go see Exo off the ship."

"And you are thinking this is the last stop?" Ravi asked the question from under a sharply raised eyebrow. A triumphal arch. "There will be no more impediments to reaching the Republic's secret fleet?"

And Leenah and Garret, thought Keel. He gave a noncommittal smile as he rose from his chair. "I guess we'll have to wait and see."

He found Exo waiting for him in the ship's lounge. The shock trooper was kitted out in his glossy, black armor, his rifle slung over his shoulder, looking every bit the soldier ready for combat... except for the way he held a forge-vault case to his chest like a lady clutching her pearls as she walked through a dark alley.

Exo nodded as Keel approached. "All right. Now we're gonna get this done. Right, bro?"

"Yeah," Keel answered. "Save the day. Steal some ships. A real good time." He let the sentiment marinate. "You sure you don't want to fly with me? We did good against the mids down there."

"Nah," Exo said, looking around the ship as though he were pricing it out. His tone was politely dismissive, suggesting their destruction of an escaping speeder column had been a fun but ultimately meaningless diversion. A weekend fling and then on to better things. "I'd gotta get back with the other guys. I know them, and other than Bossa, they'll get suspicious if I choose to spend time with someone other than the Black Fleet. Come to think of it, Bossa'll probably get suspicious, too."

"Suspicious of what?"

"Ah, you know." Exo waved his hand, the universal gesture for avoiding a point that needs addressing. Just because. Because you don't want to talk about it. "Black Fleet, Empire, shock troopers... you're outside of all that, Wraith."

Keel gave a fractional nod and a conciliatory frown, conceding the point. He wanted to stress that the Legion was what Exo was supposed to be fighting for—saving it from itself, as Exo had so often announced. Keel wanted to push the point, to get Exo to make a firm commitment that, when it came right down to it, he was still Victory and Legion. But he wasn't sure the bond of the Legion was enough to cover for the trouble that kind of pushing might cause. So he didn't.

Something of that inner thought must have been readable on Keel's face. Perhaps a look that asked what was so bad about traveling in a different ship—or that asked for Exo to at least acknowledge how many times Keel could have wiped out Exo's team of shock troopers and never took it.

Keel had learned how to read a man in his time out on the edge. He had a whole second education beyond what the Legion Academy had taught him. Right now, just by standing in place and being the man he was, Keel was triggering a sort of inner conflict in his former squad brother.

He crossed his arms stoically. Playing the role of a father waiting to hear the reasonings of his son. Giving no emotional or conversational quarter, though it was clearly desired.

Of course, it was Keel's scheming ways that had gotten Exo and his shock trooper team involved in the fight with the mid-core rebels at the Creiswel Bazaar. But not without good reason. The Black Fleet and its shock troopers didn't exactly show up on the galactic stage inviting trustworthiness. If they were willing to sneak-attack Tarrago, wiping out a garrison of legionnaires and countless civilians, they would be willing to put a knife in Keel's back.

"You know it's just squad stuff," Exo said finally. It was a feeble explanation for why he was leaving the ship. Then again, it wouldn't be such a big deal if he weren't also depriving Keel of perhaps the only insurance he had to stave off a double-cross. "Doesn't change no matter where you're fighting. You understand."

Keel rocked back on his heels and rubbed the back of his head. "Yeah, I understand. Just remember, Exo, we were squad brothers first. You, me, Chhun, Masters... and a whole lotta good leejes who didn't get to live long enough to see today."

This seemed to frustrate Exo. "What's your point?"

Keel placed his palms on his chest, looking hurt. "My point," he said, taking care to give his voice just enough of an edge to sound serious, but not so much that he might inflame Exo's considerable temper, "is that you're dealing with an unknown entity."

Exo waved off this line of thinking.

Keel persisted. "I get that the Legion is broken. The Legion, hell, Legion Commander Keller himself, allowed what happened to us on Kublar. They let more and more points in. I get all of that. But we always knew what to expect in the Legion. We knew it was a calculated risk. Agree with the House of Reason's demands for the sake of peace now, and hope things get better in the future."

"Oba," Exo said, shaking his head as he looked down at the deck. "You sound like Chhun."

Keel smiled. "I'm just saying, there was always a point on the horizon where the Legion was going to bring the reckoning. You saw the holos. Saw what they did on Ankalor. The Legion woke up and kicked some ass. And instead of sticking with it and being a part of it... well, you're part of another element standing in the Legion's way. That ain't helping."

"Look." Exo's voice had a cutting tone. He sounded like a man who had been patiently suffering a fool out of courtesy, enduring a long-winded speech by a respected elder, but who now had important business to attend to. "Article Nineteen, whether it's legit like Keller says or whether it's a power grab like the House of Reason says, I mean, I just don't know." He shrugged.

"What? You trust the House of Reason? C'mon, Exo."

"I'm just saying, I bet none of this happens if the Black Fleet didn't show up. Without the Black Fleet, I bet everybody's just waiting to see how much longer they can take advantage of legionnaire deaths. I bet Keller and the House of Reason and the points are all just fine to sit back and watch legionnaires die collectin' taxes—and then sip champagne while Dark Ops teams fix the problems they created. I mean, we lost a piece of our souls with every one of those ops that needed doing,

Wraith. How many people have we killed? No one was in a hurry to stop the dying. It was always just wait and see. Wait... and... see."

"Okay, it's a bet." Keel gave a disarming smile. This was not the time to escalate the conversation into a fight. The ships were docked, and it wouldn't be long before someone among the shuttle's crew would come wondering what was taking Exo so long. It was time to say goodbye. Time to check mags, kit up, and surrender himself to the Wraith, who would do what needed doing. "If I win, I get the scope on your blaster. If you win, you get my seamball holocard collection."

Exo chuckled. "Yeah, I guess we'll see." There was finality in this statement. Like a man at the end of long argument in a sports pub, with nothing left to do but to sit down and watch the game.

Keel motioned toward the docking door. "Once you're on your ship, I'll go ahead and beam you the location of the fleet."

Exo nodded and reached out to open the docking access hatch.

"But hey," Keel called after him. "Make sure your friends over there don't take the opportunity to try and shoot me out of the stars once you've got the hand and the coordinates. I made myself expendable for you, pal. And I generally try to avoid that in life."

Exo shook his head. "Nah, I would never let that happen."

Keel gave a lopsided smile devoid of any warmth or mirth. One that communicated that he knew better than Exo how the galaxy really worked. He held out his hand. "Things tend to go sideways in times like this. And sideways is where you find out just how little you have control over."

Exo shook the hand. "It's fine."

Keel pulled Exo in close. "Your boys go after me again like you did on Wayste, and you're still on that shuttle with them... I can't promise you don't go down with 'em this time."

Exo broke away from the handshake with a downward wrench of the arm. "Said that wouldn't happen." He opened the docking door, revealing the pressurized extendable corridor that telescoped from the Six to the Black Fleet shuttle.

Over Exo's shoulder, Keel could see Bombassa and another of the shock troopers. The two men were only few meters from the door of the Six.

"Come to pay a visit?" Keel said.

Bombassa's helmet was on, his armor fully sealed to protect against the potential rigors of deep space. The shock trooper accompanying him looked jumpy and uncomfortable in a silvery, thin emergency survival suit; his armor was probably still among the wreckage left in the Creiswel Bazaar. Keel didn't blame them for preparing for the worst. These docking connectors were supposedly tested to withstand all sorts of catastrophic beatings, but there were plenty of stories: faulty connections, debris carving out holes that depressurized the connection and sucked hapless souls into open space. It paid to make these trips, short as they were, in a full spacesuit.

Bombassa's voice came from his external comm speakers. "I came to see what was taking so long."

Keel shoved his hands in his pockets and shrugged innocently. "Just saying our goodbyes. You know how it is with old war buddies—always one more story to tell."

"Come on, Bossa," said Exo, stepping over the Six's threshold into the docking corridor.

Keel walked amiably over to the door controls. As soon as the shock troopers turned to make their way back to their waiting shuttle, he sealed the Six's door and headed for the cockpit.

He sat down next to Ravi and did a quick check of the display showing the Six's passive scanners, looking for any visiting star craft. "They make it aboard their ship?"

Ravi shook his head. "They all three are having some sort of conversation outside our airlock door. I transmitted the fleet's coordinates as you requested, and we are nearly free to do as we please."

"After our guests finally get a move on, let's hang around for a bit." Keel checked his sensors again, figuring he looked like an obsessive to his navigator. "I want to see when it'll happen."

"When what will happen?"

"The double cross, Ravi."

Ravi tugged at his pointy black beard. "I confess that I did not obtain suitable readings of the disposition of the shock troopers, Exo and Bombassa excluded, to have a fully realized probability model for such an event. That said, I do not think it probable that Exo and Bombassa will renege on the agreement."

"Not them, but the others. One of them was with Bombassa when Exo was leaving, and he seemed a little too jumpy to be concerned with only a hull breach."

"Hmm," Ravi answered, sounding unimpressed.

"Don't 'hmm' me," Keel said stridently. "He looked like he was up to something."

"If you say so."

"Ravi, I know that look."

The navigator nodded and examined his own displays. "How long will we be waiting for this impending betrayal?"

Keel folded his arms and didn't answer. He knew he'd made the right assessment. The other shock troopers weren't legionnaires. Bombassa and Exo had already expressed their concern that this was the case, and Keel had come to the same conclusion in the time they'd spent at the Creiswel Bazaar. And just because they weren't really leejes, it didn't mean they were schmucks. They were dangerous. Wildcards. Not to be trusted.

Keel didn't trust them by a long shot.

Ravi arched an eyebrow at his display. "The shock troopers have still not moved from their spot."

Keel stood and rubbed his face. "Maybe they forgot to use the bathroom before they left. I'll go see what's up."

He walked back to the airlock and opened the docking connector door. The three shock troopers spun around.

Exo handed the case that was supposed to contain Maydoon's severed hand—but didn't; Keel had made the switch on Porcha—to the shock trooper wearing the thin vacuum suit. "Here," he said. "Take this back onboard the shuttle."

"Aren't you are coming?" The shock trooper eyed Keel suspiciously through the clear viewport mask of his helmet.

"Yeah." Exo looked from Bombassa to Keel. "I just need to talk with our team leader about something in private. Something that concerns Wraith here."

The shock trooper hesitated, opening his mouth as if he had something to say, then closing it back up tight. He turned and moved away so fast that he nearly jogged down the corridor to the shuttle.

Keel's sense of an impending betrayal heightened, but he didn't allow his body language to give away such thoughts. He simply unfolded his arms to motion to Exo and Bombassa that they step back inside. When they had done so, Keel closed and resealed the door to the docking corridor.

"Call me old-fashioned," he said, "but there's something about leaving the door open while in deep space that I don't like."

When no one answered him, Keel let his hand drop ever so gently toward the blaster holstered in his gun belt. "So what's up?"

Bombassa looked at Exo. "Yes, what is up? Because we have a mission to complete, and there should not be further delays."

Exo let out a sigh. "Wraith is concerned that once we have the location of the fleet, plus the hand, he'll be expendable enough for us to cut his throat. I told him that wouldn't happen." He looked Keel in the eye. "And as far as I'm concerned, it won't."

Keel nodded.

Exo looked back at Bombassa and added, "But I think he ought to hear it from you, too. No hard feelings from any of us. No double crosses. We stick with the plan and work together. We stay professional."

Holding his arms out to the sides, Keel said, "Fine by me, Exo."

All eyes were then on Bombassa. Keel knew the big man was the shock trooper team leader. Presumably it was his call to make.

"It is as Exo says," said Bombassa, nodding at Keel. "You will not be double-crossed. You will not be discarded once we have completed our mission. You will be treated with respect and will remain safe. I assure you this on behalf of myself and the soldiers under my command."

Keel smiled and slapped Bombassa on his armored shoulder. "Thanks, pal. I knew you were one of the good ones."

An urgent high-pitched warning sounded over the Six's speakers, flooding the ship. Keel tensed like an athlete ready to make a play. He looked up; he listened.

"What's that mean?" Bombassa asked.

"Nothing good," Keel muttered. He moved toward the cockpit, still looking up, like he was attempting to hear something just outside the ship. "Ravi, what's going on?"

The navigator's voice answered from the ship's all-comm. "It is most unusual, and not in a good way. A Republic corvette painted with the MCR flag has appeared over the planet. They have taken notice of us and are headed in our direction."

"The MCR stole another corvette?" Exo asked, no doubt recalling the last time. The mid-core rebels had managed back then to obtain the smallest and swiftest capital ship used in the Republic navy. It was a corvette named Pride of Ankalor that the surviving members of Victory Company—Keel, Chhun, Masters, Twenties, and Exo—had boarded in order to save the House of Reason from destruction at the hands of delusional MCR and murderous zhee.

And now here was another one.

"Maybe the dealer had some nice incentives," Keel quipped as he raced toward the cockpit.

"We should get back to the shuttle." There was an urgency in Bombassa's voice, one that suggested the big shock trooper was no longer sure whether such a thing was even a possibility.

"The corvette has launched fighters," Ravi reported.

Keel had expected as much. They were probably Preyhunter interceptors tasked with reaching the docked ships before they had a chance to separate and escape. They would certainly arrive before the slower corvette had reached effective firing range.

"Wait." Ravi sounded piqued. "These are... Republican Lancers?"

The hologram had likely had the same expectations as Keel. In any case, Ravi was clearly surprised at seeing an MCR-painted vessel scramble Republic starfighters. Perhaps they had stolen the ship and its complement of snub fighters? Or maybe the crew had mutinied and joined the MCR.

"Something's not right." Keel halted his run long enough to point at Exo and Bombassa. "Stay aboard the ship. If those Lancers start firing, the first thing that'll go is that docking corridor. And then you're both floating outside in the cold."

"What can we do?" Exo asked. He meant to help.

"If you want to get in the fight, you can manually command a burst turret emplacement," Keel shouted back. "Otherwise strap yourself in and pray."

Exo immediately moved toward the Six's aft turret.

Keel knew that Ravi was fully capable of overseeing the turrets from the cockpit, but while the support AI did a better than average job tracing targets and converting locks to effective fire, a legionnaire running the gun platform could do just as well, and maybe better. For all the turrets' predictive algorithms modeling combat, artificial intelligence—in Keel's opinion—had never fully developed the right instincts for combat. That problem abounded in all AI, regardless of its purpose. There was no programming out there that could make up for those gut feelings that so often spelled the difference between success and failure, life and death. Even a top-of-the-line combat targeting system couldn't tell when things were just... off. Or if they could, they didn't know what to make of it. They had a hard time recognizing traps. They had a hard time calculating when a single shot in the course of a battle counted more than all the other programmed auto-fires. They were fine in a target-rich environment, when all it took was selecting their next lock and eliminating it in a full-fledged battle. But there was just too much happening in a fight. Too much that could go wrong. Too much that needed seeing, and then... processing of a variety and sort that humans—with their mix of empathy, emotion, and reason—were simply able to do better. That's why great armies of bots and unmanned ships had never grown to widespread galactic use. They could cause damage, but they couldn't win wars.

Bombassa followed Keel toward the cockpit. "I'll come with you."

Keel shrugged. "Suit yourself."

As they arrived at the cockpit, Keel slid into his captain's seat. The well-worn leather embraced his body. Sitting there felt just right, like returning to a warm bed after getting up on a frigid night. He immediately began adjusting actuators and hurrying through the docking procedures, trying to see if he could salvage the docking tube. He glanced at his sensor array and saw that shields were set to full, with weapons systems armed and ready to go. Knowing his navigator, there were probably already a number of exit trajectories calculated for a hyperspace escape. They'd be able to leave Porcha before the incoming Lancers could even warm up their blaster cannons.

"Okay, Ravi, what looks good?" Keel said after re-routing nonessential life support to thruster standby. "Where we jumping?"

Bombassa reached out with a staying hand. "Jumping? No, no. We have to stay with the shuttle. It takes much longer for them to program jump coordinates, believe me. And if we don't leave together, we'll have to circle around and repeat this whole process because of the hand."

Keel grimaced. He didn't like the idea of being forced to wait around for the relatively slow and unwieldy Black Fleet shuttle to get its coordinates and jump. He let out a sigh. "I'm not gonna stick around and allow my ship to get shot to hell."

"I wouldn't ask you to do that. I'm only requesting that you refrain from leaving the system until the shuttle has coordinates and is ready to jump out. The Lancers will split their attention between the two crafts, and our shuttle is armored enough to handle a beating—for a while anyway. But if we leave it alone, it will be disabled at best, and potentially destroyed. That would mean mission failure for all of us."

Keel thought of the finger he'd ripped off of Maydoon's hand before giving Exo the case with the fake. He knew that the mission would go on just fine without the shuttle. Maybe even better. But that wasn't a card he was ready to flip over for Bombassa to see. Not yet. Discretion, in this case, involved playing along.

"All right," he said. "I'll see what I can do. Maybe we can pull some of these Lancers off of your buddies."

"Good. Thank you."

Ravi looked at the two men with him in the cockpit. "A Lancer is a two-man craft, so they will be firing on us pretty much constantly. Thankfully they are older than Raptors or tri-fighters, and their blaster cannons will not pack quite the same punch."

"Don't forget about the concussion warhead they're equipped with," Keel said, wrapping his fingers around his flight controls. To Bombassa he added, "If your buddies on the shuttle don't get moving, they'll make for an easy target for those."

Bombassa furrowed his brow. "I was in the Legion. I know all this."

Keel grinned. "Just a refresher. You've been with the Black Fleet for a while. Don't know what you might've forgotten, Leej."

"They are in firing range," Ravi announced, as casually as a holonews anchor telling viewers that the night's seamball scores would be on in a few minutes.

Blaster fire seared toward the ships at range, and the green bolts raced hotly through the empty space where the docking coupling and corridor had been.

"Staying on the ship was a good call," said Bombassa.

"I tend to make those," replied Keel with a fractional tip of his head.

The Indelible VI shot away with an abruptness that was matched only by the way it spun and looped through the field of fire. The Lancer pilots and their gunners struggled to keep up with the ship's maneuvers.

Keeping his concentration directly on his front viewport and the HUD overlaid in front of it, Keel asked Bombassa, "How much time do they need to jump?"

Bombassa made a low groaning noise as though he were thinking of his answer and didn't like it. "The jump computers take time. Seems like a lot of time. I don't know exactly how long, but I've heard one of our team who has some minor flying experience talking about how this particular shuttle took its sweet time about going anywhere—whether in hyperspace or anywhere else."

Keel allowed himself to look away from his displays to stare, confounded, at Bombassa. "Do you mean to tell me that you're flying a mission-critical, high-speed mission for your space wizard boss completely under AI?"

Ravi let out a low laugh. "Hoo, hoo, hoo."

"Pilots are a precious commodity and could not be spared at this particular juncture in the Black Fleet," Bombassa replied. "We do fine running an AI." He sounded hurt, perhaps even taken aback.

Keel rolled his eyes. "Some empire." He lurched the Six to the left, corkscrewing into a long loop that threaded down past a Lancer that had been trying to come up on an intercept path to get a shot at the ship's belly. Ravi sent out torrents of blaster cannon fire to pound at the Lancer—and ultimately ignite its gases in a brief explosion.

One down. But the Lancers were plentiful, and Keel didn't think he and Ravi would be able to take them all, at least not without sustaining significant damage to the shield array, and possibly losing an essential drive function. If that happened, they would need to stop for repairs—and Keel didn't like the idea of jumping to another star port. He didn't want to keep Leenah and the rest of the crew waiting any longer than they already had. Nor did he like the idea of flying a damaged Indelible VI into the heart of a hidden and purportedly lethal fleet.

"Ravi, can you get some verification that they at least started the process of getting out of here? Some idea of how much longer we have to keep this up?"

To this point all Bombassa's shuttle had done was move about like a pig on ice, following a straight trajectory with no evasive action of any kind. The AI was apparently programmed to trust its thick hull and powerful shielding to protect it from the Lancers' oncoming attack. It was all but useless in the fight.

Ravi's fingers danced across his console. "I confirmed that they have the coordinates. It's only a matter of time. Shall I ask them when they think they will make the jump?"

Before Keel could answer, Ravi gave a concerned grunt.

"What is it?"

Ravi shook his head. "All of the fighters have stopped pursuing the shuttle. And technically speaking, I do not see why they would do this."

"We're famous," Keel said, a broad smile on his face. "They probably realized who this shuttle was running with."

Bombassa pointed at an oncoming fighter that was spitting death directly into the shields in front of the cockpit. "Lancer!"

Keel casually pushed down on his flight controls, causing the Six to loop gracefully, while Exo sent blaster fire into the offending starship.

Unfazed, Keel continued, "I mean, it's been a pretty eventful few months. You can't tell me word of what the Six has done hasn't spread at least somewhere in the galaxy."

Ravi frowned. "I do not think that is it. I am going to do a digital monitoring of the recent aggregate holo-news."

"You're going to watch the news in the middle of a dogfight, Ravi?"

Bombassa leaned forward. "Do you need me to do something?"

A volley of blaster fire raced across the Six's shield array, causing the cockpit to tremble and shudder.

Keel looked back and locked eyes with Bombassa. "Yeah. Pray."

Bombassa leaned back into his seat. "That's not reassuring."

Ravi was perfectly still, his fingers no longer dancing across the Six's console, his eyes no longer perusing the various screens and heads-up displays. He remained like this for several seconds before coming back with a quick shake of his head, as if returning from a trance. "Oh dear."

The ship rocked from another direct hit to the shields.

"'Oh, dear,' what?" said Keel as he attempted to swing the Six in front of a spiraling Lancer and also get Exo positioned to take a shot at another one that had been hounding them, dodging in and out of the Six's periphery.

"It would seem that the Black Fleet shuttle now appears to be flying in formation with these MCR Lancers. It has been possibly captured?"

"Already?" Keel didn't think that was possible, but he had to focus on evasion for the time being. Still, he had a funny feeling the worst was yet to come.

02

"I'm sending them instructions, but they aren't responding to me." Bombassa spoke through gritted teeth. He'd been trying to reach his team over S-comm.

"What do you mean they aren't responding?" Keel boomed, louder than he'd meant to. "You're the team leader, aren't you?"

"Yes, I am the team leader." The annoyance was evident in Bombassa's voice. "But they are not returning my call over S-comm."

Keel rolled his head and looked up at the cockpit roof in a motion that seemed to say, *Great. Just great.* He hit the comm and tried the other shock trooper on board. "Exo! Your boys back on the shuttle listening to you?"

"I got nothing on comms from them either. But I got Lancers stacked eye-high!"

It was clear that the Lancers no longer viewed the shuttle as a threat. Instead it was being used as cover. They swooped around it, formed up behind it, and launched wave after wave of attack patterns, trying to get the better of the *Indelible VI.* So far, Ravi, Keel, and Exo had prevented the Lancers from doing any real damage, but Keel's patience was wearing thin. The only reason he was even still out here was because the shuttle needed some time to escape. But if the shuttle wasn't even at risk...

"Ravi, what's the story? Can they receive their little S-comm transmissions?"

"I have no confirmation that the messages from Bombassa or Exo were received, Captain. However, a sensor sweep indicates that there are life forms on board. They're not dead. They're either ignoring or unaware of the attempts to reach them."

Keel frowned. "Maybe they're sleeping."

Bombassa was speaking quietly into his comm, still trying to reach the shuttle. He didn't appear to be having much success.

The big shock trooper looked up and asked, "How much longer, best case scenario, do you think you can stay out here in the fight?"

Keel gave a quick look at his instrument panels and heads-up display. The Lancers were older fighters. Better than Preyhunters, but still nothing too difficult. Not like going up against Raptors. The real trouble was the Republic corvette the MCR were in control of. It had been moving in their general direction the entire time, and Keel had been forced to keep the *Six* close to the shuttle, which meant he was almost in firing range of the corvette's big guns. And while he wasn't particularly worried about those bruisers scoring a direct hit—MCR gunners were terrible—the added incoming fire could make the situation volatile enough that a Lancer might get a lucky shot. Or, barring that, the reverse might be true, and in dodging Lancer fire, one of the heavy turbo blaster batteries might zing close enough to cause some serious electrical ionization.

"I don't know," he said. "Five minutes? Maybe ten if we really put some distance between us and the shuttle. But hey, if you were good with leaving those guys behind, we'd already be gone."

Another series of laser blasts darted out in front of the cockpit. The enemy pilot was leading his target far too much. Keel drifted the ship in the hopes that Exo could pick him off.

Ravi chimed in with a calculation for Bombassa to consider. "I anticipate our odds of leaving without serious damage decrease five percent for every minute we remain."

"There you have it," Keel said.

"If we leave," Bombassa said, sounding like he was talking to himself, "we would have to storm the hidden fleet. I don't feel particularly good about attempting that. We need the bio-key."

Keel was about to let Bombassa in on his secret, just to see if it might get them out of the fire, when the big shock trooper held up his hand.

"Wait. I'm getting something on the S-comm."

Ravi and Keel exchanged a look.

Bombassa spoke into his comm, his bucket still off. "Why haven't you answered any of my hails?"

Leaning close to Ravi, Keel said, "Tap into that for me. I wanna hear what the guy on the other end has to say."

Ravi did as he was asked, and the S-comm transmission was relayed over the cockpit audio. Bombassa looked up, obviously surprised by the amplified sound of his own voice, and just as obviously annoyed that Keel had this ability to listen in. But he didn't protest.

"Sir," came the reply from the shuttle, "we have orders to work with the MCR element here and ensure that the fleet is obtained for Goth Sullus and the Republic. Those orders include eliminating all outside elements. Sir, I need to be sure that you have taken control of the ship you're now on."

Keel didn't have to tell Ravi to take over flight controls of the *Six*. The navigator did so immediately, allowing Keel to whip around with his blaster drawn. He leveled it at Bombassa's head. "So that's how this is going to be?"

Bombassa shook his head. "I would never—"

"What the hell?" It was Exo's voice, carried over the S-comm to the cockpit's audio system. "Are you out of your kelhorned minds? I gave my word."

The voice from the shuttle seemed not to care. "Sir, understand that I need to hear within ten seconds that you have either seized control of the ship or are in the process of subduing the ship and killing its crew, or I will open fire with the rest of this MCR element."

Ravi spoke quietly. "We are ready to make the jump, Captain."

Bombassa cleared his throat. "That is *not* going to happen," he responded to his subordinate over comm. "We gave our word as legionnaires. That still means something."

"Not to us," replied the voice from the shuttle. "To hell with your Legion, and to hell with you."

The *Six*'s cockpit rang out with alarms.

"They fired concussion warheads!" yelled Ravi, though Keel already knew this from the tone and pitch of the alarms. "*All* of them!"

"Punch it, Ravi!"

The *Indelible VI* disappeared into the folds of hyperspace, leaving the missiles without a target.

The ship came out of hyperspace by an asteroid Keel recognized as RX-17732. It was a big one—larger than some moons he'd visited—and on its surface were the ghostly remains of an abandoned mining colony. Places like this were scattered throughout the galaxy. Keel had come across this particular rock a few years previous, while smuggling rare Kuta fish packed on ice to an old freighter that served as a floating restaurant specializing in taboo meals, always jumping just ahead of Republic authorities. The hold of the *Six* stank for weeks after that job. Keel vowed never to haul seafood again, no matter how lucrative the dark market rate.

"Okay, Ravi, bring her down onto the mining station's platform." Keel got up and motioned for Bombassa to follow him out of the cockpit. "The three of us need to have a little talk about where we all stand."

"Four of us," corrected Ravi. "I'm coming, too."

"Sure," Keel said, hitching up his gun belt. "But that's just semantics. I already know where you stand."

Ravi said nothing.

"Wait. You *are* with me, right, Ravi?"

"Yes, yes." Ravi finally broke and grinned. "I was just wanting to see your reaction."

Keel furrowed his brow. "How's this for a reaction?"

"Hoo, hoo."

Sticking a finger in the hologram's face, Keel said, "Keep it up and you'll see a whole other reaction that you're *not* going to like."

"The two of you," Bombassa said, "seem at odds, for being partners."

Keel turned to face the shock trooper. "Your soldiers tried to kill you. You don't get to comment."

Ravi laughed again.

"Oh, ha ha," Keel said. "Don't push it. I'm not in the mood."

"Oh? Are you not in the mood?" Ravi wrung his hands as though distressed. He looked out the side viewport window as the ship descended, landing on autopilot. "Well, this is different. Usually you are the very model of amiable likability."

"I don't have time for this." Keel stepped out of the cockpit, trusting Bombassa to follow him. He reached the lounge at roughly the same time as Exo.

"That was a quick jump," Exo said. "Something wrong?"

"Yes, something's wrong!" Keel threw his arms wide. "Your buddies tried to kill us!"

"He meant, is something wrong with the ship," Bombassa offered.

"Yeah, like the hyperdrive breaking again?" Exo said.

"Oh." Keel crossed his arms. "No, nothing's wrong with the ship. She's fine. But that doesn't go the same for your little Black Fleet, or

Empire, or whatever else your space wizard leader wants you to call his little outfit."

Exo held out his arms apologetically. "Look, Wraith, I don't know what's going on. I don't know what got into them."

"Nor I." Bombassa seemed burdened. It was as though the actions of his crew—his *former* crew—were a personal failing.

Keel held up a hand to indicate there was no offense taken from either of them. "You want my guess, your team was probably Nether Ops and got the order from the Republic to cozy up to the MCR and take over the mission. That, or your magic star warlock fearless leader got impatient waiting around."

Exo and Bombassa exchanged a look.

"I guess Nether Ops *might* have wormed their way into the Black Fleet," Exo said.

Keel retrieved his armor from his quarters and sat on a bench to put it on. "Well, once Ravi gets the ship cycled for de-boarding, we'll be able to get an idea of just what's going on in the galaxy. Because it seems to be a different place than it was while we were still at the bazaar." He strapped on his chest plates and looked up at the two shock troopers. "But nothing changes for me. I'm still going to find that fleet, and I'm still getting back my crew."

"Something has obviously changed for *us*," Bombassa said.

"I hear that." Exo rotated his arm in a circle as though his shoulder was sore. "Like, I mean, double crosses aside, how you gonna be able to even get to the fleet? You said you needed Maydoon's bio-signature. Well, that's on the shuttle, right? So I'd say all our plans have changed."

Keel gave a lopsided grin. "Not exactly..."

"What do you mean, not exactly?" Bombassa straightened himself, as if to show off his full, imposing height.

"Don't get excited, big guy." Keel invited Bombassa to relax with an easy roll of his wrist. "In my line of work, it pays to make yourself... *indispensable*. It also pays not to trust anybody. I didn't trust your group a lick, and now we can all be glad for that."

Exo quickly put two and two together. "You mean to say, the hand you gave me back on Porcha..."

Keel allowed himself a wide smile. He was proud of what he'd done. "Yeah, that case just has some burnt-up old MCR hand I found. *But*... I did snap off a finger off the real commodity."

"And that'll be enough?" Exo asked.

"Oh, sure. It'll be enough to get us where we need to go. In fact, all you need is a very small sample size. Just a few hairs, really. That's just basic bio science."

Ravi cleared his throat, but didn't otherwise remind the professorial Keel that *he* hadn't known that back when they'd first recovered Maydoon's hand.

Bombassa remained silent and brooding. Keel decided it would be up to the big man to determine whether he and Exo would provide backup on his rescue mission, or if Keel would have to go it alone.

"So what's it gonna be?" Keel asked. "You two are good in a blaster fight, you're former Legion, and at least one of you I trust with my life."

"I say we go with Wraith," Exo said.

Keel nodded emphatically. "Yes. Good call. But there's no pressure here. I can always let you get away from it all by dropping you off on some rock somewhere." He looked around. "Like this one."

Ravi spoke up before Bombassa, who looked perturbed, could reply. "I think you will have a better perspective from which to answer this question once you become aware of some of the goings-on in the galaxy. You are aware of Article Nineteen's declaration, but there is more."

Ravi caused a curated selection of holo-film to play on the lounge's big screen—a series of clips detailing various turning points that had contributed to the current galactic turmoil. In particular, it included reporting on the Legion's take-no-prisoners invasion of Ankalor; Legion Commander Keller's formal invocation of Article Nineteen and subsequent execution of a zhee warlord; and the House of Reason, now seemingly led by Delegate Orrin Karr, denouncing and declaring invalid the Legion's use of Article Nineteen. Karr promised "unified resistance" against the Legion's "naked grab for power," which the House would make possible by immediately ending all hostilities between the Republic and the MCR, so that the two groups could form a peaceful alliance. Both sides promised the support of loyal planets.

The three soldiers watched the clips Ravi presented to them. They seemed to share a certain awe over the obviously monumental events taking place in the galaxy.

But Ravi wasn't done. He'd saved the big one for last. The game changer.

Orrin Karr's declaration that the House of Reason would seek a peaceful alliance with Goth Sullus's Empire.

Ravi froze the view on an image of Goth Sullus himself. As Keel looked at it, his arms dropped from his chest and hung limply at his sides. Shaking away his shock, he approached the holoscreen.

"That's..." he began. "I mean, he's wearing Rechs's armor. That's Tyrus Rechs's armor. Cleaned up a bit, but it's the same suit of Mark I Legion armor. I know it is."

"Yes," agreed Ravi. "That was my analysis as well."

Keel wheeled around to face Exo and Bombassa, both of whom looked just as shocked and disconcerted as he felt. "So *this* is your big savior of the galaxy? A guy who, the first chance he gets, throws in with the House of Reason to oppose Article Nineteen?"

Bombassa gave a low growl. "This was... *not* what I would have expected. All throughout training, the cries shouted by our generals were 'Death to the Republic.' But it would now seem that the Republic was merely a stand-in for the Legion. I do not understand why else this decision would have been made. I do not understand why the Black Fleet would align itself with the House of Reason."

Ravi twitched his mustache. "I know something of Goth Sullus. More, I suspect, than anyone else in the galaxy, save perhaps two. I find it likely that the House of Reason is seeking allies against the Legion wherever they may be found. As for Goth Sullus, his purpose is domination—though he has convinced himself otherwise—and I would surmise that he is seizing the opportunity to get close to Utopion and the House of Reason not in order to destroy the Legion, but in order to topple the Republic and place himself at its head. So, I am saying he has not done such a betrayal as you imagine, Exo. Though the real betrayal may yet still happen."

Exo shook his head. "Nah, man. See, all this means is more fighting. More leejes getting killed. This is exactly what was *not* supposed to happen. We were supposed to go in and take Tarrago, get those shipyards pumping out destroyers so the Black Fleet could dictate terms for a new order in the galaxy. Something that the Legion could look to and say, 'Okay, that's it. We've had enough of the House of Reason. The Republic is dead and beyond saving.'"

His jaw clenched tightly, Exo shook his head. There was a savage anger behind his eyes. "This was *supposed* to save lives. To undo all that was done under the shadow of points. And now it's the Legion against the entire galaxy. It's all *worse*."

Keel shrugged apologetically. "Yeah, well, that's why they say not to put your trust in princes. Look, Exo, I'm not telling you what to do here. But I *am* saying that you can still be loyal to the Legion. Even after throwing in with the Black Fleet. You can still help the people in this galaxy. The ones who count, like Chhun and the rest of Victory."

"I thought you said you didn't really stay in contact with them."

Keel raised his eyebrows. "Well, I mean, you know... we talk. Sometimes. It's not like I have them over for dinner or anything."

Exo frowned in a manner that suggested he didn't believe Keel was telling him the whole truth, but he didn't press it. "Fine. I'm in to help however I can. After we get your crew?"

"Absolutely."

"I'll help, too," Bombassa said.

"The galaxy is changing at a rapid place," said Ravi. "We should consider what it is we truly desire before taking action." He pulled up images of the pitched battles taking place all across the galaxy, on diverse and scattered planets. Legion against MCR. Legion against Republic. Soon the three men were engrossed in the display. Keel chewed his thumb nervously. Exo looked agitated, as though he wanted to jump into the screen and join the fight. Bombassa looked on somberly. The big shock trooper seemed to Keel to be almost regal, and it was clear why the man had been placed in command of his unit, even if his soldiers had turned on him.

"Ravi," Keel said at last. "You think you can get a bead on where Victory Squad is in all of this?"

"I believe I can find that out, yes. You are perhaps thinking they may need a rescue? Because your plate is rather full of those at the moment."

Keel wasn't sure what he was thinking. Except that the galaxy had gone completely to hell, and that every friend he had, save Exo and Ravi, was in a predicament. "I don't know," he admitted. "I just want to keep an eye on them. Case this all goes south. Far south. This is the biggest confrontation the galaxy has seen since the Savage Wars, and I don't think either side is going to show the other much mercy. Not after what Keller did to the zhee, and not with the way the Republic is backed into a corner."

"Perhaps the time to move is now," suggested Bombassa.

Keel kept his focus on Ravi. "Is there anything worthwhile on this mine, Ravi? Seems like it's been forever since we visited."

"You are thinking of asteroid RX-17732. But that is not where we are."

"So where are we?"

"We are on a similar asteroid, one that was in close proximity to our troubles at Porcha and made for an easy jump. I apologize for not clearing this with you beforehand, but since the asteroid was left to you, I thought we may as well visit it."

Keel raised an eyebrow. "*Left*? Like in a will? By who?"

"Tyrus Rechs."

Silence fell over the lounge. Bombassa and Exo both gave Keel a look of wonder.

"Yes, I knew him," Keel said.

Ravi continued. "Its deed belongs to a proxy corporation Rex owned. One of many. He seems to have thrown it in as part of your payment for... services rendered. When I was cycling through your statements, reconciling after the last job, I saw that it was included. Initially I thought the old man was trying to get out of paying the full credit amount by giving you a deed and overestimating its value—a quite common tactic among scum and bounty hunters. However, this deed was given *in addition* to the full payment received."

"Is it worth anything?" This was not really the time to count his credits, but Keel couldn't help himself.

"It was initially a cooperatively held mining colony. It failed, but records do not indicate why. Only that Tyrus Rechs took ownership decades ago. Based on shipping manifests, it never went back into operations. Rechs likely used it as a waypoint or remote base of operations."

"Swell. I own Tyrus Rechs's clubhouse." He had to admit that did have a little cachet, even if it had no monetary value. "Listen, Ravi, I've got a crew to rescue. Let's get moving." Keel turned and headed for the cockpit.

"Captain Keel," Ravi said. "Please wait."

Please? That got Keel's attention. He turned back around.

Ravi pursed his lips, causing the curl of his mustache to do a little dance. "We are reaching a point of monumental importance in the galaxy."

Keel gave a get-a-load-of-this-guy look to Exo and Bombassa. "I'm so glad you're here to tell us this, Ravi."

"I was not finished. This is the reason why I have remained when the rest of my people have moved on."

Keel's ears perked up. He knew what this was—knew the importance of it. Ravi was going to say his piece. Was going to fill in the backstory. "Sorry. Keep going."

Ravi nodded. "There are forces beyond the edge—incomprehensibly far beyond the edge—that have forever toiled for ruin and destruction. My people, the ones you call the Ancients, experienced these forces firsthand. That is why we fled this galaxy, leaving for you only mystery... and me."

Keel was speechless. Ravi, an Ancient? He didn't know what he had expected, but it wasn't this.

Ravi continued. "Goth Sullus obtained a power known to my people. *Older* than my people. He imagined he would use it to stop this threat. But that power has consumed him, though he does not realize it. And now we all stand in the breach."

Exo stepped toward the hologram... or whatever Ravi was. "So you're saying Sullus... that *stuff* he can do... the mind tricks and telekinesis. It's some kind of ancient magic?"

"I am saying that the forces that made the Ancients flee this galaxy, leaving it to be inherited by you, are nearly at our doorstep. I am saying that the destruction of the galaxy is upon us. My task was to find the one could put a stop to this destruction. I fear I may not have done so in time, for Goth Sullus is not the answer."

Keel teetered on the brink of believing what he was hearing and writing it off. It was the absurdity of the whole thing that tipped the scales to the latter. He scoffed. "Spare me the hooey, Ravi. Did something get into your programming? You're an AI. A sophisticated AI, sure, but you're still just an AI."

Ravi smiled. "Do you really think so? Despite the many, many times I have shown myself to be independent of this?" He swept his arm in a motion that seemed to encompass the entirety of the *Indelible VI* and all the time he'd been together with Keel. "I am more than that, as you know. And in one way I am like you, Captain Ford—Keel, Wraith: I take on the appearance of that which will most help me achieve my purposes."

Ravi was up to something, Keel was sure of it. For the sake of Exo and Bombassa—their unease was palpable—Keel was playing this off as some coincidence, but he had no doubt that, eventually, Ravi would have found a way to maneuver them to this location. He wondered whether Tyrus Rechs had even really left this asteroid to him in his will, or if that was just an excuse Ravi came up with.

He gave a wry smile, large enough for all to see. "Okay, agree to disagree, Ravi. Let's get back to what's outside and how it fits into your plan to survive the galactic apocalypse. We come here to Tyrus Rechs's secret hideout, bury ourselves deep in the asteroid's mines, and hope that when the galaxy comes crumbling down, we're still safe? Deep down in the dark?"

Ravi frowned, clearly annoyed.

Pressing on, Keel said, "I'm sure it's a fine plan, Ravi. I have no doubt that you've figured the odds and this is what's best for everyone. But I'd still like to rescue my crew before settling into a doomsday bunker."

"This is not what I am saying," Ravi said with obvious petulance. "I am saying that we should learn whatever we can about Tyrus Rechs. In my research I have come to the realization that he, too, was more than he let on."

"Aha!" Keel wagged a triumphant finger in the air. "You brought us here for a reason. 'Closest jump point,' my last charge pack. Fess up. I trust you, Ravi, but these guys might not, and it feels a bit like we're dragging our feet here when we need to be heading for the fleet."

Exo and Bombassa were watching the exchange like spectators at a tennis match. But Keel could see that they felt he was speaking up for them, arguing on their behalf. Good. He needed them.

Ravi's face grew impassioned, almost severe. "Captain Keel. There are so many variables in what we are about to undertake, beginning with the rescue of Prisma and the rest of the crew, that I cannot even begin to reasonably say what we should expect our chances of success to be. So yes, you are correct: this was not the closest jump point. But it was the *correct* one. This is where we must now be. Do you really believe that Tyrus Rechs gave you this asteroid as a mere accident? An oversight? No. You do not believe that, and neither do I. I did not spend my time away attempting to clear my mind. I studied all that had happened to us since we first took the job from Lao Pak, and that included extensive investigations into Tyrus Rechs. He *wished* for us to be here. I do not know what we will find, but I am confident that visiting here will be worth our time."

Keel stared at Ravi for just a moment, then sent him a quick, surreptitious wink. "Let's go then."

03

The landing lights of the *Indelible VI* were the only thing guiding Keel and his makeshift crew through the pitch black that was the asteroid's surface. There was no distant sun, no particularly brilliant star twinkling down... just a hunk of rock drifting in the darkness of deep space.

Apparently, it hadn't always been that way. The massive landing pad the *Six* settled on was large enough to handle a deep space hauler and the supplies it carried with it—and presumably it had once served just such a purpose. But now the pad and runway were dark, their illumination strips probably no longer even functional.

The paved runway led from the landing pad to a large facility built into the asteroid itself. It was still in good condition, with no dips, bumps, or divots. On either side of it, every thirty meters or so, stood metal light poles—also nonfunctional. The visitors used the ultrabeams mounted on their blaster rifle rails or buckets to find their way. The devices' thick beams of light were like giant swords cleaving the dark, which greedily reclaimed its secrets the moment the lights were pointed in another direction.

Keel directed his ultrabeam to the top of a light pole on his left. The chamber containing the biochemical light source—the type purported to shine for centuries—was broken wide open. "Looks like someone shot all these lights out."

"Remind me to thank them," said Exo, his ultrabeam shaft jumping erratically as the blaster rifle it was mounted to moved up and down from the march. "This place is creepy as hell."

Bombassa sounded unconcerned. "It's just dark."

"It is not the dark itself that should concern the hearts of men," Ravi called out from the forefront of the group. "But rather what hides within that darkness."

"I don't like either one," Exo said.

Keel swept his light on either side of the path, looking for trouble. The asteroid was rocky, the roadside composed of jagged boulders the color of iron ore. Ahead, at the end of the runway, were the mining colony's massive double-blast doors. There were no welcome lights left on.

"We are inside fifty meters of the primary doors," Ravi announced. "Slow your pace. There will be defenses set up."

"Was that outlined in the will?" Keel asked.

"Common sense if one thinks like Tyrus Rechs."

"Tyrus Rechs," Exo repeated. "Kind of hard to believe we're standing where he stood. Guy was crazy."

Keel probed the darkness, shining his light into the distance. "Maybe. Now he's just dead." His ultrabeam fell upon an abnormality. It was so sudden that Keel passed it by, stopping his sweep a second after it fell back into darkness and bringing his light back to bear on it. A pale, organic-looking thing. "Hey, I'm gonna go check something out."

"Famous last words," said Exo, but neither he nor Bombassa made any attempt to stop him.

Keel walked to the edge of the roadside, his steps sure and easy thanks to the magnetic connection of his boots to the runway. But as he stepped onto the asteroid's rocky surface, he had to half-hop, half-skip in the asteroid's low gravity.

The anomaly was, as Keel had suspected, a dead creature. It was like some hellish dog, shaved and naked aside from a hairy tuft around its neck, shoulders, and chest. Its claws appeared to be made of granite, and its skin was tight enough to reveal the bones and muscle underneath. Its head was elongated, with cavernous eyes, and its vicious-looking maw contained ridiculously sharp teeth. Its long, lolling tongue was pointed at the end like an arrow. Keel was impressed by the thickness of its cranium, which looked to have evolved to apply maximum bite pressure with the knife blades it had for teeth.

A gaping hole in his head revealed brain matter. Gore matted its fur.

"Whatcha see?" Exo called over.

Keel motioned for Exo and Bombassa to come and have a look of their own. The shock troopers were soon standing at his side, their own lights shining on the grim discovery.

"Oh, dude, that's messed up," Exo said.

Bombassa stared. "I've never seen a creature like this before. It must be able to withstand the vacuum of space without any protection."

"There's probably a team of Republic biologists that would love the opportunity to look into it," Keel said. He shined his ultrabeam in the distance. "But I'm glad I don't see any more of these things. Wouldn't want to get caught by one out in this gravity."

As Keel brought his ultrabeam down, it landed on another anomaly only yards away. A gloved hand.

"Uh-oh."

The hand led to an arm and then a body. Blood covered the owner's survival suit, which had a deep hole chewed into it. Part of the poor soul's rib cage—still covered in gore—was exposed to the coldness of the asteroid.

Bombassa shook his head. "It looks like this miner fell afoul of the creature. Perhaps she shot it in the struggle."

Ravi appeared between the soldiers' ultrabeams and the macabre spectacle, causing all three men to jump in surprise.

"Dammit, Ravi!" snapped Keel.

Ravi inspected the carnage and wrinkled his nose in distaste. "One wonders whether this unfortunate miner died of atmospheric exposure, once her suit was ripped open, or from her chest being subsequently torn apart. Either one alone would have been sufficient."

Exo let out a whistle. "I'm gonna add 'exposed to the vacuum of space and then eaten alive' to my list of ways I do *not* want to die."

Keel was keenly aware that he was gripping his blaster pistol tightly. Exo and Bombossa had their rifles at the up and ready as well. Keel's HUD showed no life signs beyond the men with him, but that didn't convince him that there were no more creatures out there. And no sense taking chances.

"Ravi," Keel said, his voice almost a whisper, "are you picking up any other life signs? Anything from *Six*?" He looked back at the ship, standing like a lone sentinel in the distance, half expecting to see some four-footed devil dogs scurrying past its landing lights and into the surrounding shadows.

"No," Ravi replied. "There is nothing alive out here but us."

"All right," Keel said, without relaxing his grip on the blaster. "Let's head on inside the colony building. You think Rechs left a key under the mat?"

Ravi headed back toward the runway. "There is a key of sorts, yes."

The others moved back toward the runway with much less ease than the hologram. When they reached it, Exo bounced up and down, clearly happy to once again have magnetic stability under his feet.

When they were within fifteen meters of the great blast doors—massive enough to fit the *Six* through it, if Keel felt the need to attempt the maneuver—Exo said, "Hey Wraith. Why don't you have your holographic friend go on ahead? Just in case there's any trouble at the door. Asteroid predators and defensive turrets won't hurt him."

"Yes, this is fine," Ravi said, already moving ahead to approach the doors.

A pair of linked N-50 auto turrets came online, waking from a slumber at the hologram's presence—or perhaps at the sound of his voice. But their visual targeting scanners must have been confused by Ravi, because after their barrels converged on the hologram, they began to sweep from left to right, as if scanning for other targets.

"Good thing we stayed back," said Keel.

Ravi turned. "These would not fire without giving you an opportunity at least to prove that you belong here by providing the proper passkey—which I have acquired, by the way. I do not think Tyrus Rechs would have been particularly fond of being shot at his own doorstep, and judging by the age of this mounting, I do not think that these turrets are capable of linking to a particular bio-signature."

"Well, I'd rather not take a chance on what you do or do not *think*," Keel said.

"I also think," Ravi continued, as if Keel hasn't spoken, "they are waiting to fire after a predetermined amount of time, should the right passkey not be given. And, to be clear, you are already well within their range."

"Then hurry up and give the passkey!" Keel said emphatically.

Ravi turned to face the massive doors. "Reina."

The guns nosed down in slumber, and the airlock blast doors began to slide open. They were tremendous, and the way they opened in utter silence, due to the lack of atmosphere, only added to the eerie feeling of the asteroid's surface. Ravi walked inside, his holographic robes shimmering. The lights of the shock troopers' ultrabeams shone on him, giving him a look of opacity.

Keel and the others hustled behind him, all business. They took cover inside the sizable airlock, looking outside as if awaiting pursuers.

"You could land a shuttle in here," Exo said, staring up at the ceiling.

He wasn't exaggerating, and Keel wouldn't be surprised if the airlock had been used in just that way. The maneuver would require a talented pilot—or autopilot—but it would save the miners a walk out on the surface. Of course, the truly big space haulers would have landed back where the *Six* was and waited for heavy freight haulers to come out and offload them. The airlock was big and wide enough for those pieces of equipment too. It made Keel feel small.

Bombassa walked over to the airlock's manual close, pressed the smooth command screen, and stepped back as the two great blast doors sandwiched closed again. Though they made no sound, Keel could feel the reverberation across the deck as the two colossal impervisteel doors clamped together.

Only then was there any sound. A hissing as the airlock began filling with breathable atmosphere.

"Welcome back, Tyrus."

The voice was synthetic, clearly an AI and emanating from a localized speaker system.

"It has been fifteen years since your last visit. Please wait while I complete pressurization of the airlock."

The hissing sound continued.

"Feels anticlimactic," Keel said as the party waited like passengers taking a speedlift from the top floor of a Utopian tower all the way down to the lobby.

The hissing ceased.

"Pressurization complete. You may now enter. Interior air quality is at or above minimum Republic environmental standards. You are free to remove any breathing or vacuum protection devices."

The interior airlock door swished open, revealing the inside of the mining facility.

"Holy..." Keel dropped down into a shooter's crouch, his blaster rifle at the ready. Exo and Bombassa gave shouts of alarm and raised their own weapons.

Scattered throughout the building's interior were scores of the vicious four-legged creatures they'd witnessed outside.

As the shock of the sudden sighting gave way, Keel saw that none of the creatures were moving. They were on their sides, their tongues resting on the deck, or lying awkwardly on their backs, legs frozen in the air like slaughtered animals left in a field. All had massive gunshot wounds of the type associated with a high-powered blaster pistol. Except these openings showed no signs of burning typical to blaster fire.

The explorers waded inside the great facility, which looked like a loading bay or great hall that bristled with several doorways. Many of the dead creatures were concentrated around a massive, eight-wheeled all-terrain cargo loader.

"I am still not detecting any other lifeforms," Ravi announced.

"All dead," observed Bombassa, looking around at the dogs.

"Looks like someone with a slug thrower did the damage," Keel said, keeping his own blaster pistol at the ready in spite of Ravi's all-clear. He stepped gingerly over the dead animals. "A powerful one at that."

"Tyrus Rechs?" Exo asked.

Keel nodded. "I guess the old man wasn't much for cleaning up after himself."

"I expected to see more dead miners," said Bombassa, looking from left to right in the great room. "Especially after seeing the one outside."

"Maybe they all got gobbled up down in the mines, or farther out on the surface," Keel suggested. "Or maybe they escaped and the one outside got left behind."

Exo kicked one of the beasts, causing it to roll from its back to its side. "Or maybe Tyrus Rechs dusted everybody and everything here, but only bothered burying the humanoids."

"I don't think so," said Keel. Though he hadn't known Tyrus long, or particularly well, the old bounty hunter had struck him as the sort of person who was *capable* of such a thing, but principled enough not to do it... not without cause, at least. "But I'd say it was definitely him who made this mess. Just look around. There isn't a missed shot anywhere. No impact marks on any of the walls... nothing."

Given the number of dead monsters scattered about the area, that *was* impressive. Whatever hand cannon Rechs had used to kill the beasts off, he'd done the job with one shot per kill. Again and again.

"He was that good?" Bombassa asked.

Keel changed course to investigate the cargo loader. "Yeah, he was. Almost as good as me."

The tires of the great vehicle were each the size of a man. Looking up, Keel saw rectangular portholes along the sides, but they were darkened and impenetrable to his gaze. At the front of the vehicle, attached to the main body, was a cab, looking like a pyramid tipped on its side, its windshield partitioned into two square panes of glass. Even from his perspective down below, Keel could see that these were splattered with blood. He could also unmistakably see the bloody handprint streaked down the glass, leaving five trails of dried blood all the way down.

"Well, I think I found what happened to the other miners." He gestured the others over. "I'd say that the miners tried to lock themselves inside this rig, hoping they'd be safe in there until another ship arrived. Except one of the beasties must have gotten inside before they could seal the thing up."

"Should we open it up?" Bombassa asked.

"Not if we don't have to," Keel replied.

Ravi gave a threat assessment. "I am not detecting any life forms inside the vehicle. There is a ninety-nine percent chance that whatever was in there slaying the miners has died during the time elapsed. Tyrus Rechs probably arrived here well after the colony's inhabitants had faced their own personal holocaust. You can go in if you'd like."

"If it's all the same to you guys," Exo said, motioning toward a doorway marked "Armory," "I'd rather not take a detour to visit any halls of horrors. Especially with the deadline we're under?"

Keel nodded in agreement. "Sure. Why don't you and Bombassa check out the armory and see if there's anything of value? I doubt they'll have much actual weaponry, but they may have some explosives or high-powered laser cutters we could use."

The two shock troopers nodded, and jogged for the armory.

Keel looked to Ravi. "So what now? Did Rechs leave some sort of treasure map? X marks the spot, and all that? What should I be doing here other than being glad Mama didn't raise me to be a space miner?"

Ravi shrugged his shoulders. "I have no idea, Captain Keel. I merely said that this place was left to you, and suggested it was worth investigating. I made no promises as to its importance or any valuable information you might find. It was simply a—"

Keel waved off the navigator's explanation. "All right, all right. There's the command room up ahead. See if you can find out exactly what happened and how Rechs fits into it all. Maybe you'll find something useful. But let's not waste any more time than we have to."

Ravi arched an eyebrow. "We could leave now, if it is what you truly desire..."

Keel spied another door off to the left. It had something scrawled across it in freehand. He stepped closer until he was able to decipher the words, written in standard.

I didn't forget nothing.

"I'm curious now, Ravi. Fifteen more minutes won't kill us. I'll check out this room over here. Now hurry up, huh?"

Ravi gave a nod and went on his way, leaving Keel to inspect the room whose inscription, he knew deep down, had been put there by Tyrus Rechs himself.

04

The "Forget Nothing" room was small, and it felt to Keel as though he'd walked into a personal office and workshop. There was a table, devoid of anything except an old mug and water-stained rings marring its finish. A workbench with bristled cleaning rods and grime-covered boxes overflowing with spare parts and springs. A stool. And no other furniture.

Keel looked around appreciatively. This was obviously where Tyrus Rechs maintained his weapons. Keel had a similar setup on board the *Indelible VI*, and he used it frequently.

He tipped a box with his finger and peered down into what looked to be a collection of replacement barrels for slug throwers. Other boxes contained spare trigger assemblies. Keel picked up a wire cleaning brush, crunching its bristles between his gloved fingers. He shook the rod in the air like a stylus between his fingers. There were probably enough spare parts on this bench for Rechs to have built himself five or six working pistols if he felt the need.

That wouldn't be a bad idea, Keel thought to himself. *Carrying a slug thrower, just as another option*.

It was a pity that time was so short, but maybe after he'd gotten his crew back, he and Ravi could swing by again.

Keel picked up an oily rag that sat on top of a green metal box. Faded white letters stenciled on the top read ".45 acp D-U."

"Hello," Keel said to himself as he unclasped the lid and opened the box.

Inside were heavy depleted uranium bullets set in cartridges designed to load in a slug thrower. There were at least a thousand rounds in the box.

Keel looked around the room. "It would be nice if the old man left something that I could use with these."

He spotted some sort of galactic coat rack mounted to the wall. It was probably where Rechs hung up his armor, or at least took off his bucket. Hanging on one of the pegs was a nylon strap with an assortment of miscellaneous gear. An ultrabeam, multi-tool, and a synthetic pistol holster, the type designed to tuck into a waistband, allowing the wearer to conceal the weapon.

And sure enough, the holster still had a slug thrower nestled inside it.

Keel removed the gun. He turned it over in his hands, rubbing his fingertips across the polished action. It was so much heavier than he remembered from the last time he'd held one. He'd fired slug throwers before—but mainly old Savage War surplus. He'd never seen a seen a weapon like this. It looked similar to the big hand cannon that Tyrus Rechs had carried on his person. Was this gun the brother of the one Rechs carried? Maybe a backup? Could it even fire? Or had the old man left it here as a project to finish at a later date?

Keel pressed a button at the top of the grip, just behind the trigger. An empty magazine slid out. Keel caught it as it dropped. He set the weapon on the table and began loading it from the ammo box. The spring in the magazine protested with each additional bullet he pressed into it, like a dinner guest who'd had enough courses and wasn't pleased about being force-fed. This process was so much more time-consuming than slamming in a new charge pack and being ready to go. It made Keel feel like he was some kind of an ancient historical reenactor preparing for a weekend excursion to bring to life an archaic battle like Bull Run Harbor.

When the weapon was fully loaded, Keel picked a spot on the wall and lined it up in his sights. The slug thrower was heavier than his Intec, but it felt good in his hand, well-balanced, solid and weighty enough that the recoil should be relatively light. That was a good thing. Getting several shots on target with a pistol was of immense value.

Keel became aware that he was allowing himself to get lost in thought. He hailed Ravi over his comm. "Find anything yet, Ravi?"

"I am only now beginning to review the facility security holos and footage. Thankfully the data is microcompressed, which allows for fast review; however, even at so fast a pace—"

"What? Are you watching from the beginning? Just rewind until you see what happened."

"I was saying that while I can review what is there quite swiftly, it seems that Tyrus Rechs only kept an archive dating back over a rolling six-week period. All footage older than that is scrubbed. However, I am communicating with the facility AI to see if it might not be able to rummage up something."

"Okay. But let's make it quick, huh?"

"Understood. How about you? Have you discovered anything interesting?"

"Maybe." Keel examined the hand cannon. "Found a new souvenir."

"Oh. Yes, good. I was hoping that we would be able to stop at the gift shop before leaving. Anything of value for the mission at hand?"

"Nothing yet, smart mouth, but I'll let you know if I find something. Wraith out."

Keel moved back to the bench. It was time to leave. He looked at the ammo crate. It was heavy, but worth taking along, especially if the slug thrower could function reliably enough to be taken on ops. He spied an old bandolier with loops big enough for the old-style shotgun shells, and frowned when he didn't see a matching weapon.

A distant bang sounded outside the open door—it seemed to have originated from far across the great entry room. He moved to the doorway and saw Bombassa and Exo removing crates from the armory and stacking them up outside.

He pinged the shock troopers over the com. "Finding anything interesting?"

"No, not really," Exo replied. "For an armory belonging to Tyrus Rechs, this place sucks."

"It is little more than former ammunition crates and rocket crates all loaded down with spare parts," Bombassa added. "Anything to make it heavy."

That was strange. But, in the time Keel had known him, Tyrus Rechs had proven to be a sort of a weird guy. "Well," Keel said, "the old man was loaded. So if it seems like he stacked up a bunch of junk, maybe go through it. Might just get us all rich. Maybe he's got something good hidden and just wants to keep any nosy visitors away. You need a hand?"

"No. We got it."

Keel was ready to go and help anyway. Until he caught the faint flash of a green light emanating from beneath the cluttered workbench. It blinked from an area that had been covered with rags and boxes. He hadn't noticed it before; perhaps he'd uncovered something by mistake while poking around.

He moved items aside until he revealed the source of the flash: a mound-like device, the light blinking up from its center. He attempted to pick it up, but it wouldn't budge. It had no markings of any kind. Just a single button.

Keel pressed the button.

The base emitted a disjointed chime, which Keel interpreted as a prompt. The green light continued to flash, as if listening.

"Uh..."

The light flashed again, indicating to Keel that it indeed *was* listening. It was processing the sound of Keel's voice.

Keel remembered the passkey Ravi had used to shut down the turrets and open the airlock blast doors. "Reina."

He swallowed, hoping he hadn't just activated some kind of diabolical self-defense system that would now end his life.

Nothing happened for several seconds. The light just flashed and flickered, as though it were communicating in some visual code. Then the flickering intensified, and the device projected a figure suspended above the workbench.

Tyrus Rechs.

Keel took a subconscious step backward as he looked up at the bounty hunter. Well, a projection of him.

"Good. You remembered her," said the holographic projection of Tyrus Rechs—from the chest up.

Keel tilted his head inquisitively. "Rechs?"

Sometimes holograms like these were tied into artificial intelligences that did their best to map the minds of those who had created them. It was possible that what Keel was looking at was an AI simulation of Tyrus Rechs. But it soon became evident that this was simply a recording.

"In case you haven't figured it out yet, I'm Tyrus Rechs. Which means I'm you. Of course, if things are so hazy that you don't remember that, well, all of this might be an exercise in futility.

"But let me give you the refresher course just the same. You are Tyrus Rechs. You're a bounty hunter. Or at least, we were when I recorded this. Maybe that's changed now. Things do that. They change. Either way, you're in a profession that enjoys killing. And you like to kill, Tyrus. That's why you keep doing it—why you keep killing so many people. Just in case you're wondering.

"Now, before you were Tyrus Rechs, you were *this* man."

The reflection shifted, and Keel furrowed his brow at the sight of General Rex, the famed legionnaire who had led the Republic to victory in the Savage Wars—and who had then fallen from the graces of the House of Reason. There was no way this was the same guy. Same name, sure. But Keel had always assumed "Tyrus Rechs" was just the man's chosen bounty hunter name. His real name was probably something unimpressive and forgettable—like Ford—and so he'd adopted the great general's name for the sake of reputation. Out here on the edge, things like that mattered. But for the two Tyruses to *literally* be the same person? Rechs would have to have been—Keel did the math in his head—almost a hundred years old when Keel met him. And he certainly hadn't fought like someone that geriatric.

The holorecording shifted back to the familiar projection of the man Keel knew as Tyrus Rechs before continuing. "Before disappearing, you were General Rex. You ended the Savage Wars. You were also General Reeves in the middle of the Savage Wars. And someone else before that, going all the way back to whatever your real name was before the Savage Wars even started." The holo of Rechs laughed. "To tell the truth, I've faked my own death and started over so many times, I'm not even sure who I really am.

"What I'm saying, in any event, is that you've been around a long, long time. And today, for the first time, I realized that I couldn't quite remember all of those long, long ago times. I can't quite bring to mind who I was over the centuries, or what I was doing."

The hologram motioned to some unseen object behind Keel. "This is going long. You may as well make yourself comfortable."

Keel looked around, then pulled up the stool.

"I asked myself this morning why I wasn't General Rex anymore. I liked being General Rex. Why wasn't I leading a company of legionnaires? Why wasn't I on the battlefield?

"I had to sit down and really think. After about five minutes or so of hard, concentrated thought, I remembered. And then I got scared and figured that if I didn't stop everything and do this now, it would happen again. And maybe the haze doesn't clear up so quick. And maybe I only *think* it cleared up all the way, but I still forget some key pieces of information.

"So I sat down to record this in case you ever happen to come back to this rock after who knows how long. Maybe when you're forgetting and want something that can guide you along the way."

Tyrus Rechs pauses and looks straight down. He looks weary. "Hang out on the edge. Wait. Does that ring a bell? If it doesn't, you should be terrified, Tyrus Rechs. Or whatever your name is right now. Probably Terrence Rods, with the amount of originality we have." He laughed again. "Hang out on the edge. Wait. You remember Casper, don't you? I hope so. He was a good friend who wanted too badly to be a good man, and so he stopped being a good friend. Then he stopped being a good man. And he went off to do the things that all three of us swore would never be done."

Rechs held up a finger, pointing at his supposed future self. "You made a promise to each other. You promised that if any of you tried to take that power, if any of you tried to harness it, no matter how good your intentions... no matter how bad the galaxy got... that if *any* of you tried it, the others would hang out on the edge and wait for them to come back.

"And then they would kill 'em."

Rechs let out a long sigh. "Well, Rechs... That's why you're a bounty hunter right now, hanging out here at galaxy's edge. Taking souls. Bringing justice. Amassing a fortune because there's nothing else to do. No way we'll ever spend it all, but at least when he comes back, we'll be ready for whatever."

Keel became aware that he was holding his breath. He gulped in air, and felt somehow embarrassed for listening in on this most private of messages. The Tyrus Rechs of the hologram looked like he had tears welling in his eyes.

"It's important you don't forget this, Tyrus. If you let Casper live, the galaxy will suffer. If you let that power leave its ancient resting place, the galaxy will be enslaved. It's your duty to the galaxy to stop that—isn't that why you started the damned Legion? And it's your duty to Casper when he shows up—isn't that why you call him friend? You have to kill him. Hang out on the edge. Wait."

The holographic image moved, as though the cam recording Rechs followed him in the motion of standing up. "Don't forget, Rechs. Don't forget nothin'.

"All right. That's about all I had to say."

Keel stood up, expecting the transmission to end.

"Oh, there is just one more thing. Those little beasties—you probably noticed their carcasses all around—well, they've got a pretty good nest. They're millennial hibernators. Can sleep for centuries without food. I was able to block up the nest and keep them trapped by stacking up just about every everything I could find over in the armory. I actually debated putting this message pod over in the armory itself because I had so much trouble stopping them the first time around. You know, as a warning. But if there's one thing that I know isn't going to change about you, it's that your first order of business when getting back is going to be to clean and strip your weapons for the next time. Dirty weapons are like unfaithful friends. Never did anybody any good.

"Oh, and if you're looking for more ammunition, it's in the mess hall. Nothing but trouble is left in that armory. KTF, Leej."

05

Keel stood dumbfounded for several seconds as the hologram of Rechs faded away. The weight of it all, everything that the old man had spoken of... it took time to sink in. He had to shake off thoughts of this "Casper," who Keel felt certain was Goth Sullus—what other man possessed an ancient, dangerous power? who else had Rechs been more determined to kill?—before the immediate danger posed to Bombassa and Exo struck him full on.

"Guys!" Keel shouted across the expanse, forgetting his comm. "Stop!"

"What are you yelling about?" Exo replied over the comm.

Keel ran into the great loading bay, the ammunition can under one arm, the slug thrower in his free hand. "Put them back! Stack 'em back up!"

But Exo and Bombassa were already running out of the armory. They slammed the door shut behind them.

"Something's in there, Wraith!" Exo shouted. "Inside the armory!"

"A lot of somethings," Bombossa added. "And they sound angry."

"Yeah, that's what I was just shouting about," Keel said as he joined them. "I found an old data recording from Rechs, saying that those crates were put there to block in more of those creatures. They've got a nest back there, and he trapped them inside somehow."

Bombassa scowled and shook his head. "And now we have un-trapped them. When we removed the stacked crates, we spotted an opening behind the armory that appears to go into the mines themselves. We were discussing going in to investigate when we heard howls."

Keel switched on his comm. "Ravi! We have company!"

The navigator's voice responded calmly. "Yes, I can see it on the mines' closed-circuit holo-cams. The armory is swarming with the creatures."

Exo was holding down the armory door's emergency close button so its automated sensors wouldn't open the door in response to the movement on the opposite side. Loud thuds were already sounding as the creatures pounded on the door. "Wraith, I don't know if I can let this button go!"

"Ravi," Keel called again. "Can you seal the door to the armory?"

"I can, yes. It may cause other complications."

"Do it. We need to start falling back."

The navigator appeared in the midst of them. "You can let go now, Exo. The door is sealed."

Keel sized up his holographic companion. "Glad you could join us."

Bombassa bounced with nervous energy, his body leaning toward the airlock exit. "I think it's time for us to get out of here."

Ravi nodded. "Yes, I agree. However, this will prove much more problematic for you than it will for me. All the doors in the complex are on the same circuit, so when I shut off the automatic open for the armory, I also shut off the auto-open for the airlock. This was part of a design intended to lock down all doors in the event of a security breach."

Bombassa gripped his rifle. "That doesn't make sense. There would have to be some kind of manual override to get in and out of the airlock in case of an emergency."

"Yes. They installed it inside the airlock itself. And you will not get inside the airlock while the doors are locked down."

"So we got no choice but to open all the doors and then hold the line," Exo said. "Unless we can drive out of here in the big cargo mover?"

Bombassa jogged over to it and tried the mover's door. "Locked tight. Anyone got a cutting torch?"

"We fall back to the airlock blast doors," Keel said. "Ravi, you lift the lockdown and open the doors. We'll hold off any ghouls that come our way until we can slip inside and close things back up again. Then we're home free to the *Six*."

"Sounds like a plan," said Exo.

They hurried to the blast doors and took up firing positions.

"Okay," Ravi announced. "I'm reactivating the auto sensors and opening the blast doors."

The mammoth gears and mechanisms required to open the massive airlock doors groaned in protest, warming up in a slow grind. The armory's security door slid open much more quickly, and almost instantly the first creature, cautious but malicious-looking, padded out into the open.

A single shot from a Bombassa's blaster rifle struck the beast in its neck. It dropped to the deck, dead.

Keel had set down the ammunition can so he could hold his new slug thrower in one hand and his blaster pistol in the other. His rifle was slung over his shoulder. "Well, at least we know they go down easy."

More of the creatures poured out. Their eerie, high-pitched squeals pulsed in Keel's ears.

Ravi took several steps forward, his phantom sword appearing in his hand, and the beasts ran toward him. Four of the monsters jumped at him in tandem, but Ravi swung his weapon through all four in a single stroke, sending eight dog pieces back to the deck.

Those four were only the beginning. Based on the howls, Keel estimated there must be hundreds more packed into the space beyond the armory. The narrow doorway the beasts had to pass through was the only thing preventing them from completely overwhelming the large bay, and even so, at least two dozen had already spilled through.

Another trio leapt toward Ravi. He cut down one, but the other two avoided his blade and passed through Ravi's holographic figure. They shook their hoary heads in confusion, apparently wondering why their jaws had clasped on nothingness instead of the firm flesh of a man.

They didn't stay bewildered long. They turned their attention to the three armored men standing at the blast door, which was inching open at a glacial pace. It had opened maybe a quarter of the way wide enough for one of them to slip through.

Exo and Bombassa converged blaster fire on one of the two beasts, sending it tumbling down. The other kept running. Keel aimed his slug thrower and fired. The massive hand cannon recoiled much more than he was used to, but not so much that he couldn't line up a second shot in case he needed it.

He didn't. His first shot was on target, proving that the gun's sights were true. The blast had caught the creature mid-jump, sending it spinning in the air like a rotary blade. When the beast hit the ground, a massive hole just underneath its left eye poured blood onto the deck. An even larger hole gaped on the other side of its skull.

"Damn," said Exo.

Impressive as the shot was, Ravi's blade was doing most of the work, slicing through the creatures as they poured forth. But even Ravi could not be in all places at once, and more and more were coming around the holographic defender. Keel, Exo, and Bombassa dropped the squirters as they slipped through, divvying the targets between them. But each wave of beasts fell a little closer to their line.

"We will be overrun before long," Bombassa said.

Keel glanced back at the door. "One of you give that door a try," he said. "It might be just wide enough to squeeze through."

"Exo, you first," ordered Bombassa.

"On it."

Exo turned his body sideways and began pushing his way through the still-widening gap. He grunted from the exertion. "Why's this thing gotta take so long to open?"

"This is probably because the temporary power shutoff drained any warmup the doors had, and they are now opening from the first square," Ravi said, talking while he sliced more of the beasts.

"Just focus on killing, Ravi," Keel shouted.

Exo pushed his body harder into the narrow opening, but his armor wouldn't yield enough for him to slip through. He was half in and half out, an arm and a leg in the airlock, the other exposed. "I can't get in. I'm stuck."

"Keep pushing. And keep firing," Bombassa said.

Exo had wisely kept his hand holding his blaster rifle on the side of the door with all the action, and he awkwardly lined up a shot. The blaster bolt went well south of its mark, striking the beast in its hind leg.

Keel quickly adjusted for the miss, sending a blaster bolt from his Intec and finishing the job. "Just shout as soon as you're through, Exo. Then we'll follow."

"And so will they," Bombassa said gravely.

"It's your optimism I like most about you," Keel said as he lined up another shot.

Ravi was finding fewer targets now. The creatures seemed to have realized that the navigator was a distraction rather than a target, so Ravi could no longer merely position himself as a stable sentry, but was instead reduced to chasing down individual beasts with his sword held high above his head.

"What do you suppose they eat when there aren't hapless miners around?" Keel asked.

"Not what's in my thoughts right now," Bombassa replied. "But I hope they're not too hungry."

Keel gave a fractional nod. It was perhaps best not to dwell on such things. There were too many targets and too much danger. They could count on their armor to protect against teeth for a while if they were completely overrun, but not forever. Enough of those creatures would be able to hold them down, pry off the individual pieces, and feast on the exposed legionnaire meat inside. Armor was good for a lot of things, but right now it had Keel feeling like a flay-lobster being prepped for dinner.

The snarling pack was closing in. One of them made a desperate lunge at the defenders, opening its jaws wide as it flew toward Bombassa, and the shock trooper raised his arm to fend off the attack. A crunch sounded, and for a moment Keel wondered if the beast's jaws had actually broken the armor plating on Bombassa's forearm.

Either way, Bombassa didn't cry out. He calmly—and powerfully—held the beast aloft, swinging from his arm like an attack dog trained to never release its bite unless ordered. Bombassa pressed his rifle barrel into the creature's stomach and rapid-fired two successive blaster bolts. The devil dog yelped in pain, sounding more ferocious than hurt. But it let go and fell dead at Bombassa's feet.

"I'm through!" Exo shouted.

Keel pointed a finger at Bombassa, shooting another beast with his free hand. "You go next!"

The big shock trooper didn't argue. And the door must have finally picked up its pace, because despite having a torso notably thicker than Exo's, Bombassa quickly squeezed through the gap into the airlock.

Keel followed suit, shooting with both the slug thrower and his blaster pistol, dropping as many of the advancing creatures as possible as he backed through the opening. One of the beasts leapt straight at him, snapping its jaws mere inches from Keel's face before he sent a bullet through its brain. "Exo! Shut the door! Shut the door!"

Exo was at the emergency controls. "Already on it."

"What about Ravi?" Bombassa asked.

"He'll be fine," said Keel, still firing through the doors, which had reversed direction and were now slowly closing up. "Changing packs!"

Keel slammed home a charge pack in his blaster pistol before rejoining Exo and Bombassa in killing as many of the creatures as possible. They seemed inexhaustible, but now that they could attack only through one narrow opening, the three soldiers held them off with ease.

Then Keel's slug thrower clicked dry, and a sinking sensation lurched in his stomach.

Oh, no. The ammo box.

He'd left the can outside.

He lunged toward the opening and sent an arm through to feel for the valuable bullets.

"What are you doing?" shouted Bombassa.

"Forgot something!" Keel groped blindly until his hand found the ammo case. "Got it!"

But as he hauled it inside, one of the creatures leapt forward and clamped its jaws around his head. Keel brought up both feet against the closing doors and wrenched himself backward. The doors had caught the creature in mid-jump, wedging it in place, and as Keel slipped free and fell back, the beast hung helplessly suspended above the ground.

"That was close," Exo commented.

Keel realized just how stupid of a move he'd made. He had felt the doors closing on his arm as he'd reached through. He could have gotten stuck himself, like the animal. That would have forced Exo and Bombassa to either let his arm get crushed or reverse the direction of the doors, potentially risking their lives. Something about being around Tyrus Rechs's old stomping grounds was making him reckless.

Bombassa's rifle was aimed at the struggling beast, but he didn't fire. He seemed frozen in wonder at the spectacle before him. The timing for the little beasty was... really bad. As the doors continued to close, the thing let loose with a painfully high-pitched scream. Then its ribs cracked audibly, and the howls stopped, replaced by a breathy gurgling sound that issued from its maw. It probably didn't have lungs, per se, seeing as how it survived on a rock with no atmosphere, so the noise was just whatever gases were in its inner cavity being forced out.

Finally Bombassa snapped out of his reverie. "We should put it out of its misery." He pressed his weapon's stock against his shoulder.

"Suit yourself," Keel said, switching out a fresh charge pack and then opening the ammunition can to reload the slug thrower. "But I'm not wasting the ammo. We still got a whole 'nother fight before us."

Bombassa considered, then unsheathed his knife and drove the blade into the beast's skull. It stopped struggling. Bombassa cleaned the creature's black, viscous blood off of his knife using the fur behind the beast's neck. "A mercy kill doesn't automatically mean spending ammunition," he said.

Keel gave a snort.

The door closed with a resounding thud, severing the beast and leaving its front half at the feet of the soldiers. Its blood dripped down the door like some sort of pneumatic leak.

"And with that happy image," Keel said, kicking the beast's severed body away from them, "let's wait for Ravi to rejoin us. Make sure to reload before we run for the ship."

"Run for the ship?" Exo asked. "Why? Seemed like the only one of those things out there was long dead."

"I seriously doubt that they don't know how to get outside," Keel said. "And something tells me that now they know that food's on the table, the pack is excited to chow down. I don't think they'll give up easily. They're probably heading back through the tunnel you guys opened up when you moved those crates."

Bombassa let his rifle hang on its sling and crossed his arms. "You are suggesting that this is our fault somehow?"

Keel shook his head and held up his hands in a calming manner. "Don't get excited. Just stating a fact, not casting blame. I'd have done the same thing as you. I just wouldn't have panicked when I heard something coming, so the tunnel would have been blocked back up."

Bombassa held out a finger to protest.

"He's kidding, Bossa," said Exo.

Ravi materialized within the airlock.

"Oh, hey, Ravi." Keel sounded as if little more had happened than a chance meeting at a kaff shop. "That was some impressive sword work. Kind of makes me wonder what else you've been holding out on me. I can't count the number of scrapes where having an invisible ghost swordsman would've really changed the odds."

Ravi arched an eyebrow. "There is a time, and there is not a time. Now is the time, but it was not then."

Keel stared blankly at his navigator. "Sure."

"Incidentally," Ravi said, pacing the massive airlock, "you are right to believe the creatures are not finished trying for you. The moment the doors closed, they turned at once and went back into the mines. My communications with the facility AI suggested that the miners all died shortly after finding a nest of these beasts. The mine itself only functioned for a few months."

Keel inspected his armor for damage. His HUD informed him that all integrity levels were satisfactory, and his oxygen scrubbers provided him a full supply. "How's everybody's suit integrity?" he asked.

"I'm good," said Bombassa, likewise giving himself a once-over.

"Yeah, me too," Exo added.

Keel hoisted the ammunition box under an arm. "Well, let's open the door and make for the *Six*. Ravi, can you get her guns online and tell her to pick off any smaller targets? I don't want anything waiting around for us to arrive—or to follow us up the ramp like those miners in their cargo loader."

"Yes, that will be fine."

Everyone stood still for an awkward moment.

Keel threw out his arm. "So we gonna draw straws, or can someone open the door? My hands are a little full."

Exo activated a sequence across the control panel, prompting the now-familiar AI voice to announce, "Beginning depressurization."

The air slowly left the room, sucked into the same vents through which it came in. Soon the hissing faded, and the airlock fell silent. A rumble beneath their feet announced that the large exterior airlock doors were beginning to open. These doors moved much more efficiently than those on the other side of the airlock, and within seconds they were facing the asteroid's lifeless exterior. The light from inside the airlock spilled out onto the runway.

Keel gripped his blaster. He'd half-expected the creatures to be waiting just behind the door. But as the massive entry spread wider, all that was visible beyond the region immediately outside was sheer and total black.

"Ultrabeams," Keel said, flipping on his own and mentally chiding himself for forgetting to have it ready before the doors opened. He'd felt... *off* since his encounter with the ghost of Tyrus Rechs.

Exo and Bombassa swept their lights outside, illuminating the door's two defensive N-50s, which were actively looking for targets.

"Yo," Exo said. "Those aren't going to open up on us once we go back outside, are they?"

Ravi stepped forward into the darkness. "No. They are now under a temporary override to withhold fire. They will not fire on any targets, though they continue to scan."

With Ravi's assurances, the men slowly crept outside and onto the runway. The lack of atmosphere made it impossible to hear anything, even with the enhanced audio of their buckets. Keel checked his HUD. It showed no signs of life except for him and the shock troopers. It dawned on him that the HUD hadn't shown any of the creatures inside as life forms, either.

The galaxy was full of mysteries like this.

Something—intuition, or a survival instinct—told Keel he needed to turn around and look up. He did so, shining his ultrabeam onto the rock face just above the doors where the mining facility had been dug in. The bright beam lit up several sets of glowing eyes.

"They're right above us!"

Keel raised his blaster and sent forth bolts that glowed in the darkness. He killed beast after beast, but this only seemed to rally others. Glowing eyes appeared from all around, and devil dogs jumped down from rock face to rock face, moving steadily toward the men. There were hundreds of them.

"Run!" Bombassa yelled, already following his own advice.

Neither Keel nor Exo argued with the big man. They followed him in an all-out sprint. With four legs chasing you, it was always best not to let up your own pace.

"Ravi! Tell those turrets to start shooting!"

"There is at least a thirty percent chance the turrets will lock on to one of the three of you, which would have a fifty-nine percent chance of causing serious injury or death."

"I don't care if it's a seventy percent chance!" Keel shouted, still running for the ship. "Turn them on!"

Immediately the area began to flash with the red hue of blaster fire spurting from the N-50s. Keel glanced back over his shoulder to see the area in front of the airlock doors already littered with carcasses.

"Told you it would work," he crowed.

When the fleeing men came within twenty meters of the *Indelible VI*, Ravi lowered the ramp before Keel could request it. They weren't out of danger yet. The turrets had done a superb job of ripping the pack apart and thinning its numbers, but several of the little monsters had escaped from the N-50s' effective firing range, and they were coming on hard.

"Hurry up inside!" Keel shouted, hoping to spur Exo and Bombassa on to one final surge of speed that would bring them to safety.

Keel reached the ramp first, dropped his ammo box, drew his slug thrower, and began to use it and his blaster pistol to pick off pursuers. Bombassa's long strides brought him to the ramp next. Keel continued to fire away with both weapons.

Exo sprinted past him onto the ramp. "Okay, Wraith, we have you covered."

Blaster rifle bolts streaked by Keel noiselessly, lighting up the asteroid's surface with red flashes of lightning. And it occurred to Keel just how easily he had set himself up for a double cross. Was this another symptom of being off his game after hearing what Rechs had to say about the galaxy? Or was it that he trusted the two former legionnaires? Fighting with Exo again was like being back with Victory Company.

He turned and ran up the ramp, his magnetic boots carrying him awkwardly into his ship, while Exo and Bombassa maintained a steady rate of converging fire on the animals. The burst turret under the *Six* dropped down as well, spraying death at the swarming creatures, and finally the ramp raised, bringing Exo and Bombassa on board. The interior airlock doors slid open, and Keel pulled off his helmet, breathing in the cool air of his ship.

"Okay, Ravi, vacation's over," Keel called on his way to the cockpit. "Time to get us off this rock."

Ravi was already waiting for Keel in his navigator's seat, going through the ship's emergency takeoff sequence. "We have time. The burst turrets caused the predators to retreat. Even if they hadn't, I do not suspect they would have been able to get on board."

Keel plopped down into his captain's seat. "If it's all the same to you, I'd rather we didn't stick around." He set his slug thrower on the middle of his dash console and grimaced. "Of all the luck! Wouldn't you know it?"

"Know what?"

"I left the ammunition can outside." Keel kicked his foot against the floor and leaned back frustrated in his chair, biting a fore knuckle. "I hope I can find some slugs the next time we visit a night market. Not that we'll have time for any more trips before we reach that fleet."

Ravi didn't look up from his console. "You will be thankful to know, then, that Bombassa picked up the forgotten item as he boarded the ship."

Keel smiled. He was happy to hear that. "Good. So let's take off and make the jump. We'll rescue our people, and then we can all disappear into the galaxy."

"I am not sure that this plan of 'disappearing' reflects accurately the desires of the two shock troopers."

Throwing a boot up on the dash, Keel leaned back and laced his hands behind his head. "Eventually, they'll see the galaxy my way, Ravi."

06

Indelible VI
Ungmar System, Hidden Location of Doomsday Fleet

The *Indelible VI* zoomed toward a blue dwarf star in the Ungmar system. "Are you sure it's in there?" Keel asked. "You're sure?"

"It is well hidden, is it not?"

"Well hidden? Ravi, if you hadn't told me it's there, I'd think the coordinates were wrong." He glanced at his navigator. "As it is, I'm still not entirely certain."

Ravi huffed.

The Cybar mother ship—authorized and built by the House of Reason in the hopes of serving as a final line of defense; sought by Goth Sullus for his conquest of the galaxy; and operating independently of all of them, according to Ravi—would have been impossible to find without not only exact coordinates, but blind faith in spades. No one in their right mind would fly into a superheated blue dwarf. But when the Six's external sensors showed acceptable heat and radiation readings, it became obvious that this "blue dwarf" was not the real deal.

"What's that up ahead?" Exo asked. He was sitting with Bombassa in the seats behind Keel and Ravi.

Drifting lifelessly just before the blue dwarf was a series of broken and destroyed starfighters, as well as the ruin of a black-tipped transport shuttle.

"Looks familiar, huh?" Keel asked. "I'll bring the Six underneath her. See if you can get a view of the cockpit."

Bombassa's face showed consternation. "That is our shuttle. They came ahead of us while we stopped at the asteroid."

Keel threw a lopsided grin that doubled as an amused look of patronization. "I know. Bad idea, right?"

"And this was their fate because they didn't have the right bio-signature aboard?" Bombassa asked Keel. "Because you gave us a fake hand."

"I believe that is an accurate assessment," said Ravi.

"It wasn't a fake hand," Keel snapped. "Just not the hand you wanted. The guy who owned it probably found it satisfactory enough."

"I just find it unsettling that this would have been our fate if we had taken the case you gave us, and shown up here without you."

"You didn't," Keel said.

"But if something had happened to you, we'd have had no way of knowing..."

"And if I was king of the galaxy I'd sit on a throne of good looks."

Ravi's mustache twitched. "I would have said cynicism."

Keel gave his navigator a withering look. "Would you have, Ravi?" He turned back to face the shock troopers. "The point is, you're with me, and you're fine."

"No," said Exo. "The point is, you set us up."

Keel threw his hands out like he'd been cut off while waiting in line for a docking platform. "I bought insurance against what seemed to be extremely high odds that your little band of brothers would double-cross me." He settled back into his seat and added, "And, spoiler alert, they did."

The ship floated closer to the blue dwarf that contained the Cybar ship.

"They have accepted our landing request," Ravi announced, "and I have the autopilot following a fixed path to the selected docking bay."

Keel folded his arms. "By the way, you can thank me any time for rescuing you from that shuttle and the idiots who got it blown up."

"Thanks, I guess." Exo smiled, but not in an amused sort of way. If he had any hard feelings, he apparently wasn't going to dwell on them. "Look, I appreciate how often you're right about things like this. Always have. But don't try to play me like that again."

Bombassa seemed more forgiving. He let out a sigh. "Yes. Thank you. It would seem you possessed a better understanding of the situation than we did. I did not expect such treatment."

Keel smiled and facetiously acted embarrassed. "Oh, don't mention it." He winked at Exo and said, "And Exo, the next time I have to trick you, I'll tell you beforehand."

Exo smiled and shook his head. "You changed out here, man."

"Blame Owens. I do."

The Indelible VI pushed into the blue star, which washed the canopy with a beautiful panoply of burning gases, and Keel began to dole out smuggler's wisdom.

"You survive outside of the Legion by not trusting anybody. You guys were thinking like soldiers, so you didn't see it. I was thinking like a paranoid smuggler—and I was right. I learned early on after I left Victory Squad that thinking like a soldier all the time was a good way to get yourself killed."

"Poetic," Bombassa quipped.

"That's me."

Amid the swirling illusion of the "blue dwarf," a massive capital ship came into view. Its sheer size and... alien build brought a silenced awe over those now seeing it for the first time.

"Man..." Exo managed. "That thing's just gonna let us fly right on board? It looks like it could shoot an entire fleet out of the stars all by itself."

Ravi nodded. "It is controlled by a Republic AI consortium that, in my estimation, has been compromised by the very Cybar technology with which it was designed. But our possession of Kael Maydoon's bio-signature will initiate a boarding sequence beyond the control of this AI. It has to let us board. However... once we do, it will send an administrator bot to capture you."

"And we don't want to be captured," said Bombassa.

"I would not recommend it."

Keel snorted and shook his head. "You think we'll be able to get to the brig and get my crew out without having to fight off an army?"

Ravi nodded again. "In my last visit, the Titan presence was severely restricted. I believe you will be assisted from within. Still, time is of the essence."

Looking back at the shock troopers, Keel said, "Glad I just have to perform a rescue instead of trying to hotwire the thing. That still your plan?"

"I..." Bombassa began. "I was unable to reach my handler. However, I believe those who turned against us were Nether Ops spies. We will complete our duty to Goth Sullus."

Like hell you will, Keel thought to himself. Tyrus Rechs's message was still fresh in his mind. Exo and Bombassa would either come around to his way of things, or this starship would be their final resting place. Keel hoped for the former.

The Six moved steadily toward the Cybar docking bay. Keel rose from his seat and adjusted his gun belt. "Well, the three of you can stay here and talk until we land if you like. I'm going to go jock up and get ready to KTF."

"No," Bombassa said, rising as well. "There has been enough talking. Now we act."

Keel, Exo, and Bombassa waited at the bottom of the *Indelible VI*'s ramp for the bot they knew was going to attempt to ensnare them.

It was slow in arriving.

So the soldiers looked around the massive docking bay of this once-hidden ship. It looked like most Republic capital ship bays they'd ever stood in, except for being completely empty. Ravi had told Keel that the ship that had brought Prisma had been ambushed and destroyed. That must have been in another bay... or the bots on board had done an amazing job of cleaning up. There wasn't a blaster scorch anywhere to be seen.

In fact, everything was swept clean and kept tidy. It felt regulation perfect—but lonely, too. Like they were the first to set foot on a ship that had drifted alone through space for centuries, with nothing on board but custodial bots continually buffing, shining, and dusting in a preprogrammed search for approval from masters who had died long before.

"This place gives me the creeps," Exo muttered, giving voice to a feeling that Keel shared.

"Good," Bombassa said. "Use that. Stay alert, expect trouble."

"I do that even when I'm not creeped out," Exo replied.

A personnel-sized blast door opened, and out came a gleaming personal admin bot.

"Looks like trouble is coming," said Keel. "See this, Ravi?"

"Yes, I see it. As I understand things, this is how the trap begins."

"Well, this time the tables are going to be turned. C'mon."

Keel stepped toward the bot, trusting Bombassa and Exo to follow him. He brought the party to a stop twenty meters from the craft, not quite to the halfway point between the ship and the personnel door.

The bot came to a halt in front of them. "Hello. I am CAT37. I will escort you to a confirmation terminal. This way."

Bombassa stepped forward to initiate the plan he had cleared with Keel. "We are representatives of the Galactic Republic, not mere inspectors. The House of Reason has deemed that now is the time to activate this fleet. We are under orders to deliver it to Utopian."

The bot paused and looked at all three of the armored soldiers. "I confess that I certainly knew this day would come. However, you will still need to access the confirmation terminal. This way."

"Get many visitors?" Keel asked, casually following the bot.

"Oh, no. No one has been here in a very long time."

"What about all the wreckage we saw outside?" Exo asked. "What about that?"

CAT37's servomotors locked and brought it to an abrupt halt. It turned to face the men. "I'm afraid I don't know anything about that. I am just here for administrative duties and to provide humanoids with creature comforts, as you might say." Its optical processor lights flashed. "However, I do speak with this vessel's Defense Mind from time to time. Just to have someone to talk to. Custodial bots are all so dull. You may be interested to hear that there has been no shortage of pirates looking to make a tidy sum from salvaging a forgotten and quite lucrative capital ship left alone in the middle of nowhere."

The stinking bot is lying to us, thought Keel. Bots weren't supposed to be able to do that, except for the Nether Ops models. But with Nether Ops, what wasn't a lie?

CAT37 continued. "I suspect if you saw ships, it was likely more of the same."

"Fair enough," Keel said, motioning for the bot to continue on. "You were going to show us the confirmation terminal?"

"Yes, of course." CAT37 turned its back to the three-man delegation. "Right this way."

Keel looked from Bombassa to Exo, then unholstered his blaster, aimed it at the bot, and separated the bot's head from its metallic body with one squeeze of the trigger.

CAT37 crumpled like a heap onto the deck.

"Okay, Ravi, which way do we go?" Keel looked around. He expected to hear klaxons and sirens, but destroying the bot appeared to have triggered no alarms.

Ravi was quick with an answer. "There is significant jamming at the moment. Nothing that I cannot overcome with time, but enough that the three of you should not allow yourselves to be separated. You will be unable to communicate with one another, unless it is through the ship."

"Okay, we'll take that under advisement," Keel said, looking at Bombassa and then Exo. "Wander off at your own peril, kids. So Ravi, which way do we go?"

A schematic of the docking bay and the surrounding areas of the ship appeared on all the legionnaires' HUDs, with a path indicated. "Follow this route," Ravi said. "It is a straight shot from the docking bay to the detention block—perhaps this level was designed for a rapid transfer of prisoners."

"On it." Keel moved through the docking bay with his rifle up, scanning for targets. Exo and Bombassa followed him, similarly alert. They reached the door Ravi had painted on their HUDs, which slid open without prompting.

The trio hurried through and moved with a quiet purposefulness down a wide corridor. They moved from ceramic bulkhead to ceramic bulkhead, covering one another using small-unit tactics.

Bombassa spotted the first hint that the corridor down which they traveled had been a place of trouble. "This area looks like it's been scrubbed clean, but look." He pointed up at a series of burnt black blaster bolt impacts that formed a dotted line about a meter above their heads. "Somebody was either firing at something very tall—probably one of those Titans Ravi told us about—or they were firing from farther down the corridor."

"Impacts look pretty deep." Keel gave a fractional shake of his head. "It's nice to know someone was shooting wildly at a thing that was about to kill them."

As the legionnaires continued forward, they saw no more blaster burns. Neither did they see any guards or sentries. Nothing to detract from the sense that they were raiding a ghost ship.

And maybe that was all it was. Who knew whether Prisma, Leenah, or anyone was still alive?

Keel shook that thought from his mind. *Ravi must know they're all right, or he wouldn't have brought us here.* The risk of being here was incalculably high—far too high for simply recovering corpses. Ravi would have computed those odds, would have told Keel it wasn't worth risking his life for. But here they were. So Keel continued on in confidence. His navigator was many things, but wrong was rarely one of them. They would find at least one survivor. Probably Prisma.

The girl was the one Ravi seemed most keen on recovering. There was something there. A connection. But then, it seemed Prisma had a connection with everyone. Everyone except for Keel.

"I'm starting to feel like we got all dressed up for nothing," Exo said. "Not that I'm complaining."

Ravi's voice came in clearly over the comms. He must have overcome whatever jamming had been sent his way. "You are nearly at the detention block. I would very much like to accompany you, Captain, however, I do not think it would be wise for me to leave the ship. Its AI is not strong enough to protect itself."

"Its AI is nuts," answered Keel. "Don't worry about it, Ravi. Just make sure we're headed to the right spot."

"You are," Ravi confirmed. "You will first enter a guard control room. Several rows of cells emanate from it like spokes from a wheel. I am trying to locate cell numbers for you."

The door to the detention block swished open as they neared it, revealing the central guard area. A set of three stairs led up to a raised platform with a circular security desk. Standing at the desk, looking down at a holoscreen, was a sleek-looking bot. It was a standard humanoid size, but with an airstream-like head fixed with a single glowing blue optical receptor. Its appendages lacked weapons, making it look more like an admin bot than a war bot. But a blaster pistol was magnetically attached to its hip.

In unison, the three legionnaires raised their blaster rifles. But in that instant, it occurred to Keel that the guard had taken no notice of them. It merely clicked and whirred its fingers, swiping the console in front of it as if no one else were in the room.

"Hold up," Keel said, bringing his fist up and trusting in the discipline of his comrades.

They held their fire. They'd all been through the same virtually endless close-quarters training. More than learning how to storm a room, they had learned how to distinguish hostile targets from benign. And each of them must have come to the same conclusion that, though armed, this bot wasn't an immediate threat.

Keel made a slow move to the bot's side. Exo remained by the entry door, and Bombassa mirrored Keel's movements toward the bot's opposite side. All three men kept their rifles trained on the bot, so that if it should attempt something, they could destroy it in a field of converging fire.

The robotic guard still took no notice of them.

Keel spoke softly over his comm. "I'm going to get a closer look."

"Don't touch it," Bombassa warned.

"Wasn't planning on it. Just want to get a better view of whatever this thing is looking at."

With his rifle still pointed directly at the bot, Keel positioned himself to peek over its shoulder at its security console.

The bot was cycling through several holo-feeds. Images flicked past, showing one holding cell after another. All of them were empty.

Then the feed shifted to what looked like some sort of medical laboratory. The mutilated corpse of a man lay dead on the table. His legionnaire-like armor was spread carelessly about the floor. Keel gritted his teeth.

The screen returned to the holding cells and continued to cycle. More empty cells, and then—

Prisma.

He had to resist the urge to call out for the bot to stay on that image. But he knew better.

She sat with her legs tucked beneath her on the impervisteel floor. In front of her was some sort of small object, a marble or pebble. It was rolling back and forth across the ground, seemingly of its own accord.

And then the image was gone. The feed moved on. After several more empty cells and empty corridors, Keel was about to move away. But then Leenah appeared. She was lying peacefully on her side on a bunk in a detention cell. Whether peacefully asleep or peacefully dead, Keel couldn't tell.

He really, truly, wanted her to be all right.

Exo's voice came over the comm. "What do you see, Wraith?

Keel looked up, feeling like a spell had been broken. "This is the right place. For whatever reason, the bot's just cycling through holo-feeds. But I've spotted two members of my crew. One of them for sure is alive. The other one... I think she's alive, too."

"We go get them?" Bombassa asked, gesturing at the oblivious robot with his blaster rifle. "Perhaps this bot is merely programmed to mimic a humanoid guard. Its purpose could be to make this area of the ship feel more familiar to biologics."

"As in, it isn't even sentient?" Exo said.

Keel knew Exo was using the term in the limited capacity with which it was generally applied to droids. None of them were truly sentient; none were capable of making their own decisions independent of programming guidelines. Giving AI that much power was widely thought to be likely to initiate the downfall of civilization. But the most sophisticated bots possessed the illusion of free will—what passed for sentience in most circumstances.

Keel backed away from the guard bot. "Whatever it is, I don't want to leave this thing at our backs."

"What do you suggest?" Bombassa asked, moving around the security desk to stand by Keel, his blaster still pointed at the bot. "It may be programmed to trigger an alarm if interfered with."

Exo shifted from foot to foot. "We either dust the thing, or one of us can stay here and watch it. But I agree with Keel. No way we leave this thing at our backs."

Keel removed his hand from his rifle's foregrip and extended it toward the bot. "Maybe there's some kind of shutoff switch."

"Captain Keel, don't do that!"

The sudden warning came from an external comm. The voice was familiar.

"Garret? Is that you?" Keel felt a flush of hope that the coder was alive. He'd taken a liking to the skinny, awkward kid.

"Yeah! It's me. I found my way into a control corridor when everyone started getting shot. Then I accessed the systems and dug in deep like a subspace tick."

Keel tried to speak, but the kid kept going.

"I haven't figured out how to release anyone from their cells yet. You have to do that manually, and I haven't worked up the courage to try going where you are now. Where would we run to, anyway? Mainly I'm just keeping myself invisible. The Titans—those are the really big war bots—walk right by me and the others. So that's good, because if I can figure out a way to get Leenah and Prisma free, they can probably reach my hideout—"

"Your 'hideout'?" interrupted Keel. The kid was talking as though he were playing pirates in the backyard.

"Yeah, that's what I call where I am now. Nothing comes by here at all. So anyway, I thought I might've determined a way to get Leenah and Prisma out, but so far nothing has worked. I've started experimenting with the concept of strategic denial of—"

"Garret! Save it for later, buddy." Keel knew the kid could see him, since he had obviously seen him reaching for the bot, so he waved his blaster rifle around. "I've got a blaster. I can get them out."

"Well, um... that's not entirely true." There was a pause, as though Garret was waiting for permission to continue.

Keel let his head fall. "And why is that?"

Before Garret could answer, Bombassa hissed into his comm, "Who is this you are speaking to?"

"A member of my crew. Real tech wizard. You'd like him, what with swearing loyalty to space wizards and all."

"Sorry," Garret said. "Hang on... Okay, I've re-routed my voice to reach the secure comm on all of your helmets. I guess you guys are friends of Captain Keel's. I'm Garret. Nice to meet you. Anyway, I'm getting carried away. I can tell you everything that I know so far, and maybe you can formulate a plan that will get them out with it. But I don't think just opening the doors without a clear route of escape is a good idea. As best I can read from the systems, if those doors are opened by anyone other than one of the interrogators—the bots or the replicants, either one—the Titans will come out in force and swarm the entire prison center."

Keel didn't bother to ask what the code slicer meant by "replicant." The word, like "Titan," was self-explanatory. The bots on this ship certainly weren't named abstractly. "Okay, so we'll come to you and figure something out. They look unharmed."

"They're fine, I think," said Garret.

"So where are you?"

"Not far from you, actually." A new map appeared on the legionnaires' HUDs. "If you head down this corridor—it's marked W-3 overhead—you'll come to a maintenance hatch that's partially open. Go inside and then walk aft along the guts of that corridor. Don't take any of the forks, and you'll get to the room that we're all hiding in. More of a way station in a passage, actually. You see—"

"Who is 'we'?" Exo asked.

Keel nodded approvingly at the question.

"Well, there's Skrizz, but he's always off wandering. He should be back soon. And also parts of KRS-88... as much of him as I've been able to reassemble. And the only other is a legionnaire who came in with Ms. Broxin."

Keel wasn't thrilled to learn that anyone on the Nether Ops team working with Andien Broxin was still mingled with his crew. They were the ones who had caused this trouble in the first place. "Okay. We'll head your way. But tell that leej you're with not to try anything funny if he wants to keep on living."

"I don't think he would."

"On second thought, don't tell him anything," Keel said. "I don't want him to even know we're coming." Keel motioned for Bombassa and Exo to move out. "We're on our way now."

"Good." There was obvious relief in Garret's voice. "I was worried that one of the visitors to Prisma would drop in on you. Usually they come around now."

The kid might have led with that fact, Keel thought.

He moved away from the security bot. It still scrolled through holo-feeds, oblivious to everything that had happened around it. It occurred to Keel that this, too, was probably thanks to Garret. That didn't surprise Keel in the least. The kid had a real way with tech.

Exo lead the trio along the pathway provided by the code slicer. He found the loose panel and pulled it aside. "This looks like it."

"I'll go first," Keel said, already stepping through.

When they were all through, Exo pulled the access panel back into place.

The men had to walk single file down the narrow corridor. Tubes of conduits ran alongside them, occasionally feeding into wall-sized connector hubs with glittering status lights shining like stars in the sky.

"Look down," Keel said.

A dry trail of blood ran along the floor. Up ahead, it turned off onto a side passage.

"Should we follow it?" Bombassa asked.

They reached the intersection where the blood trail diverged from the main passage. "Garret said not to go down any of the forking passageways," Keel said, "but he may not know about this. Let's follow it."

"Could be war bots..." Exo warned.

"Bots don't bleed."

They took the side passage. The way Keel saw it, they could always double back and find Garret later. Besides, ever since the code slicer had mentioned replicants, Keel had felt disinclined to fully trust him. If androids were involved, Keel could only trust the people he had come in with. There was no way of truly knowing whether the Garret he had spoken to was an android setting a trap for them.

His stomach dropped as he realized the same applied to Leenah and Prisma. He could rescue them, only to discover that the real Leenah and Prisma were already dead and dumped into the ship's incinerators.

He would have to trust that that wasn't the case.

It occurred to him that he hadn't heard from Ravi in a while. He hailed him on the comm but received no reply. Keel noiselessly informed the others, through legionnaire hand signals, that he'd lost communication with Indelible VI.

As the three men continued to follow the bloodstained tributary from the main access corridor, the side passage widened enough to allow Exo and Bombassa to walk side by side, Keel still in the lead.

And then they found the source of the blood: the corpse of a moktaar. The monkey-like humanoid looked as though he'd been systematically butchered. Cuts of flesh were carved from his legs, and some of the strips continued all the way up to his abdomen.

Bombassa leaned down to inspect the corpse. "He was butchered after his death. And it does not appear he died from a blaster wound." The big shock trooper pointed at two massive puncture marks at the top of the unfortunate creature's head. "This is a predator's bite. Perhaps the machines take on the evolutionary features of galactic carnivores for close-quarters battle."

Keel stared down at the butchered body. "Doesn't explain why he was cut up into steaks."

"He part of your crew?" Exo asked.

"No," Keel said, shaking his head. "Never saw him before. Must've come in with Nether Ops."

Bombassa pointed farther down the corridor. "Do we keep going?"

"I'm torn," said Keel. "Garret might have some answers... but I don't like the idea of leaving whatever killed that moktaar unaccounted for."

"I think we should turn back and meet up with this other legionnaire and your code slicer."

Keel didn't have a better idea. "I guess this guy's not going anywhere."

They went back the way they came and resumed the course on the map Garret had provided them. After a time, Keel's visor identified a heat signature ahead, glowing from around a corner in the darkness.

That could be Garret, or it could be someone else. If it was the legionnaire, there was a chance that he'd start shooting.

Examining the map on his HUD, Keel identified a nearby side passage that appeared to loop back to this main corridor farther ahead. Using hand signals, he indicated the plan to Exo and Bombassa. He would take the side corridor, while they would move on ahead. They'd converge on the unknown party from opposite sides.

The side tunnel was narrow and round like the inside of a tube, and Keel had to duck to keep from bumping his head, but it followed the path he'd expected, looping around back to the main access corridor. As he emerged from the tube, his bucket's audio receptors picked up voices in mid conversation.

"I don't care who you say you are." The voice speaking was unfamiliar. "Take any more steps in this direction and I'll dust you."

"We come to rescue you and that's how you react," Exo shouted back. He was getting hot. "Nah, bro. That don't work."

Bombassa offered a calmer answer. "This is hardly the way I expect a rescue party to be treated."

Keel peeked around a bend in the corridor and saw Garret, pressing himself into some sort of tech station alcove, attempting to make himself as small as possible. Just beyond Garret was the man who must be the legionnaire. He was seated, his bucket off and his armor partially missing. In his hand was a service blaster pointed at the bend in the passage beyond which Exo and Bombassa apparently stood. The guy was built like a hover tank and looked every bit a hardcore leej.

"I'm in position," Keel whispered into his secure comm. "You guys stay hidden behind that corner. Distract him, ask him his name."

"What's your name?" Bombassa called out.

The legionnaire steadied his grip. "Irrelevant. Now this is how we're gonna do this." He used the age-old total command diction every leej was taught in training. "You two are going to put your weapons down and slide them into the open where I can see them. Then you stick your hands out, and when I give the word, you're gonna come out nice and slow. You do that, and I know you're friendly and we can talk. You try anything else, you're dead. How's that sound?"

Keel crept down the corridor while the legionnaire spoke, approaching him from behind. He passed Garret in a flash, and pressed the muzzle of his blaster rifle into the legionnaire's head before the code slicer could even let out a surprised gasp.

A whine sounded from Keel's blaster rifle, indicating that the weapon was primed for a max discharge. "How about you drop your weapon? Or should I just go ahead and take your head off? Either way, this little game of back-and-forth ends." The voice of Wraith transmitted through Keel's bucket was clear, cold, and terrifying. "How does that sound?"

The legionnaire slowly put down his pistol and raised his hands.

07

Bombassa and Exo cautiously aimed their weapons at their new prisoner.

"So what?" the legionnaire asked, looking at the approaching shock troopers. "You all with that Black Fleet? Gotta admit, I was hoping you really were leejes." He let out a resigned sigh. "Will you at least make it quick?"

"We don't have to make it anything at all," Keel said as Exo came near and took away the man's blaster. "Just had to make sure you weren't a liability before we brought you along with Garret."

The legionnaire looked up at the skinny code slicer. "Why didn't you tell me you knew these guys? At least let me know they were coming?"

"Captain Keel told me not to."

The legionnaire trying to look back at Keel in his peripheral vision. "I take it you're Captain Keel? Name's Hutch."

Garret stepped out of his alcove and began a data dump of information. "When everything went crazy and the Cybar—that's what the Titans call themselves—started shooting, Hutch helped me." Garret pointed at the legionnaire as if there might be some doubt about whom he was speaking about. "I mean, he covered for me, shooting the sentries and crawlers while I was getting everything squared away inside the system. The crawlers—think robotic spiders—and all the other machines work for the ship's AI mainframe, something called CRONUS, which is the ship's AI but way beyond what you'd expect. Anyway, Hutch kept them at bay until I could keep the bots off of us for good. See, CRONUS doesn't have total control of the tech—the fail-safes the House of Reason built in, like the bio-validations, are unreal. And with Prisma on board—she has the genetic passkey, which overrides what CRONUS can do. But see, and this is really interesting, if there's a certain alarm that occurs high enough in the threat hierarchy, like a prisoner escape or an attack by another capital ship, CRONUS gets more control. So I can get around what he wants right now, but if you let Leenah and Prisma out, it probably changes and I'll have to work to override, using

Prisma as my passkey authorization to code real-time around whatever CRONUS attempts."

A silence fell over the group.

"You done?" Keel asked. "Not just coming back up for more air?"

Garret rubbed his arm nervously. "Yeah. Sorry."

Keel eyed the partially assembled frame of a badly damaged war bot off to one side. "Is that Prisma's?"

"Yeah. I was trying to put it back together. It's actually quite an interesting—" Garret glanced up at Keel and cut himself off. "I could fill you in on what I learned about Nether Ops's role in all this...?"

"Yes, let's cut to that," Keel said. He pointed an accusing finger at Hutch. "You're *not* Legion, because the Legion weren't the ones who took my crew."

It wasn't a question, but it was clearly an interrogation. Keel wanted to get to the bottom of what he already suspected. He wanted to hear whether this Hutch would give up his charade of being just another legionnaire and play it straight. If he didn't... well, then Keel had little use for him.

Hutch rolled his neck. "There's some right and some wrong to what you're saying." He risked getting shot by slightly shifting his body to get a look at Keel. His eyes went wide in surprise, and then he quickly compressed them into uninterested squints and faced forward again. But he'd given his tell. He'd recognized Wraith. "I am Legion in an official capacity. I'm in the system, on the books. I just do jobs for the Carnivale."

"The Carnivale?" Bombassa said. "And what is that exactly? Because it cannot be what it sounds like."

"It's one of the branches of Nether Ops," Garret said. "Sort of the laughingstock of the community. If you follow the dark channels or can decrypt the agent-to-agent instant messaging used on the Republic's government net, all the operators go on about how worthless..."

Garret trailed off, withering under the heat of Hutch's harsh gaze.

"It's like I said," Hutch continued. "I'm on the books as Legion. But I'm always in transition, assigned to units that don't quite exist. Nether Ops uses me and my team whenever they need a Legion-like team to handle a mission. This was one of those missions."

"Andien Broxin was with you," Keel said.

Hutch shrugged. "Sure. She was some hotshot operator that got transferred to the Carnivale."

"They call that the 'kiss of death' in the ops community," piped in Garret.

Hutch's furrowed brow silenced the code slicer. "So anyway, she's playing all naïve—probably didn't trust my team—and we get sent to grab the little girl. Maydoon. Something about her being the way to control the fleet, like Beanpole said."

Hutch looked at the ground and picked his callused fingers. "Things went bad. Really bad, really fast. The worst I've ever seen—and I've seen lots. My guys are good. Dark Ops good—better, actually. The Titans chewed through us like nothin'. Literally ripped some of us apart and made me watch through my bucket, before it was destroyed." He looked at Garret, and there was genuine gratitude in his eyes. "Little buddy here kept me from gettin' dead. Or worse."

Bombassa started a conversation over their secure comms. "We cannot trust him. I have little tolerance for those who work with no accountability, whether points or these deep state special operators. In my experience, it all ends up the same. They amass the debt, and leave others to pay the bill. He will turn on us."

"Probably true," Exo said. "But if things get as nasty as they're warning us they might, another gun in the fight might be useful."

"I agree," said Keel. "We can keep him ener-chained unless things get bad. We can probably trust him to at least fight on our side until we reach the ship. And if he doesn't play nice, we leave him on the ship for the bots to find."

"You guys decide whether to kill me or not?" Hutch asked, no doubt fully aware that the men were speaking secretly through comms.

"They won't kill you, Hutch," Garret assured him. The code slicer looked from Exo to Bombassa, then to Keel. "Captain, you won't kill him, right?"

"No," Keel said, slinging his blaster rifle over his shoulder and retrieving a pair of ener-chains. "But we're also not taking any chances with Nether Ops."

Hutch let his hands be bound in front of him without resisting, merely watching as Keel attached the binders in the crisscross pattern that prevented all but the most dexterous from slipping free. "Fine by me," he said. "No shame in being taken in by Wraith."

In the spectral tones of his bucket, the sound of Wraith, Keel said, "If anything happened to my crew because of you, you might change your tune before we're done."

"Um, should we wait for Skrizz?" Garret asked. "He kind of comes and goes, but he's definitely still alive. I saw him maybe six hours ago. He's actually been bringing us food. Mainly raw meat that he says he found in some kind of refrigeration unit. It's always at room temperature by the time he brings it to us."

Exo laughed over the private comm. "Dude," he said. "They're eating the monkey man!"

Keel made a face inside his bucket.

Exo switched from comm to external audio to ask Garret, "So do you cook the meat? Or do you eat it raw? Because that's pretty badass."

Exo laughed over the comm again as Garret's face brightened up. Keel could tell that the code slicer was eager to explain. The kid seemed to have an irrepressible desire to let people know how he'd figured out the solution to a problem. Probably the result of some sort of search for approval. Maybe Mom and Dad hadn't taken as good care of Garret as they might have. Maybe all that time as an outsider had left him wanting to show that he belonged.

Whatever it was, something about the kid made Keel feel protective. He interrupted Exo's mock moktaar noises. "Cut him some slack," he said over private comm.

"Oh, it wasn't hard," Garret explained, oblivious to the laugh Exo was having at his expense. He pulled open a workstation pane, exposing a complicated web of wiring. "So if you expose one of these black wires—you have to pull it out of the flex-conduit first—you'll get a raw electrical current. Only it packs a punch. So I siphoned off the flow to other functions to get just the right amount of juice flowing to cook the steaks without burning them. They turned out pretty nice."

"Good job, kid," Keel said. The way Garret beamed at the compliment made Keel feel suddenly old. "Now when can we expect Skrizz? I don't want to leave the wobanki behind, but I will."

Garret closed the panel back up. "Well, uh, it's like I said earlier. He comes and goes. Does a lot of exploring. I kind of think he's trying to figure out a way to get Prisma out of her cell."

"It would seem we are about to beat him to it," said Bombassa. "Can you give us a rundown of what hostile bots are on this ship?"

"How much time ya got?" Hutch said, his face hard. "I've gone up against war bots in the past." He nodded at Keel. "You know the type, don'tcha, Wraith?"

Keel remained silent.

"Sure you do. Some pirate or backwater warlord who thinks he's a planetary king, maybe a drug dealer or Senate-appointed leej who starts believing in his own PR... they start hiring their own private militia. And then they get paranoid, thinking all those hired guns can just as easily be turned on them. So they spend the big money in the dark places, and they get the bots that no one's supposed to have anymore. The big ones designed to wade through entire companies of Savage marines back in the day."

"So... war bots," Exo said. "Got it."

Hutch shook his head. "Not just war bots like the one Garret's been tinkering on. A big war bot like that only managed to slow down these Titans. These things are hunter killers with tri-barrel N-50 blaster cannons that will cut you to ribbons. And then there's the spiders, the crawlers, coming in swarms to try to flush you out into the open so Big Brother can turn you into a meat stain splattered against the deck."

Keel observed the familiar thousand-yard stare of a man nearly broken by what he'd seen in combat.

"The House of Reason built a completely synthetic version of just about every military asset you can imagine," Hutch continued. "Garret checked through the data inventories. Bot pilots that can fly modified Republic starfighters; smaller ships flown autonomously by a hive-mind AI; bots that serve as security like the one you saw back at the cell blocks. They got frontline bots that take all the hits, humanoids with blaster rifles, sent in to draw fire away from the Titans." Hutch looked up, a gallows-like mirth in his eyes. "They even got their own little version of Dark Ops: delicate, jet-black bots designed to move undetected to take out high-profile targets. Those were hunting us for a while, when we fell off the grid. Garret kept 'em off us, but they're still out there."

"Yeah," Garret said. "It's actually really bad."

Hutch nodded. "I came to bring this ship to the House of Reason. But it's functional and independent. The ship itself. The AI that runs the place. This ship is capable of performing every military action you'd expect from a super-destroyer, and can probably do it better. And the assets on board..."

Bombassa was stern and serious, his arms folded as he took in this information. "And you are confident of this? How do you know?"

Garret cleared his throat. "It seems like everyone on the *Forresaw*—that's the ship that brought us here—figured this was a typical fleet. Ten or fifteen destroyers, carriers, corvettes, stuff like that. But as I dug in and observed CRONUS's text logs, it's more than that. He knows I'm looking, and he's... well, he's showing it to me. It's like he's bragging."

"Bragging?" Keel said. "This is an AI we're talking about. You're telling me whoever programmed it thought that displaying the tendencies of a braggart would be good for a Republic fleet?"

"See, that's what I thought," said Garret, a professorial finger held up in the air. "But this AI, it's like what I did with the missiles. It's completely free. This CRONUS has developed its own personality and is far beyond the point of no return. It's bragging because it's proud of what it's done—and what it's done is modify the initial work order to expand this fleet into an entire armada."

The gathering fell silent, and then Garret punctuated his point. "You guys. I think that... I think the AI has built something large enough that, if deployed at the right time with the right subterfuges, it could take over the entire galaxy."

All eyes were fixed on Garret in disbelief.

Keel was the first to speak. "Well, I have good news," he said, his voice rich with sarcasm. "See, Bombassa and Exo figure they learned how to control murderous AIs in their post-Legion training. So what *they're* going to do is take over the fleet and hand it to their space wizard boss who will then... What was it guys? Save the galaxy?"

Neither of the shock troopers answered.

Garret shook his head urgently, as though this idea terrified him. "Oh, no. No, no, no. You can't... you can't do that. I don't know what's keeping the ship from leaving its hiding spot—maybe it's tied to Prisma or waiting for something to happen out there; CRONUS absorbs all the holo-feeds—but we don't want it to go out into the galaxy. I mean, it's all I can manage just to stay hidden from CRONUS." He looked at the shock troopers. "You can't possibly *control* him. That's crazy talk. If you want to save the galaxy, figure out a way to blow this place up."

Bombassa and Exo exchanged a look. Then the big shock trooper said, "And how would you propose we do something like that? *Assuming* we believe you. Our intelligence comes from the highest sources in the Republic, and they state that simply showing up with Maydoon's bio-signature will require the fleet AI to do whatever we tell it to."

"Yeah, your intelligence comes from Orrin Kaar," Garret muttered.

"Wait, what?" Keel said, putting his hands on his hips.

"Yeah, what?" echoed Hutch.

"Delegate Kaar is working with Goth Sullus," Garret said absent-mindedly, as if this were a minor aside to the real business of talking tech. "A buddy of mine intercepted all their transmissions during the Battle of Tarrago. They're working to take over the Republic. I was gonna tell you, but then we got kidnapped and I forgot until now."

"What the hell!" exclaimed Exo. "How is the Black Fleet working with the stinking face of the House of Reason?"

Garret shrugged as if the answer to that question wasn't one he really cared about. "Anyway, yeah, your data is old. It's accurate insofar as that's what was *supposed* to happen. I mean, that's why Ms. Broxin had to bring Prisma here."

"Kid," Keel said, still feeling the shock of what Garret had told them. "You're spilling all sorts of secrets that people would literally kill you for knowing right now."

"Sorry," Garret answered, and he sounded as though he meant it. That he wasn't trying to cause trouble. He was just... sharing data. "All I'm trying to say is that your friends are operating on a demonstrably false set of data. If what they were saying about the bio-signature was true, we wouldn't even be here. Andien and Hutch would have brought the fleet to Utopion already."

"And my entire team wouldn't be dead," Hutch added.

"This..." Bombassa said, holding a hand against the side of his bucket. "This is a *lot* to take in right now."

"Listen," Garret said, nervously shaking his leg. "I think this has the potential to be so bad that the options are to run far away—and by that I mean disappear like the Ancients—or blow this ship up while you're inside of it."

"I vote for running away," said Keel.

Bombassa crossed his arms. "Let me guess," he said to Garret. He sounded conflicted, like he still hadn't quite abandoned all hope of completing his primary mission. "You have some kind of special virus that we can upload for you. And then everything self-destructs."

Garret blushed. "What? No. If I had that, I'd have just uploaded it myself. No, you're the soldiers, you figure out how to blow up a destroyer from the inside. I mean, I'll be honest," he said, looking at Keel, concern in his voice, "when I sent that message to you right after we landed, I was really thinking that you would come with more... guns."

"What message?" Keel and Hutch asked in unison.

"Shut up," Keel barked at Hutch. "Garret, I didn't get any message. I had to figure all this out on my own, and then I came as fast as I could."

Garret looked thoughtful. "Huh. I put it through thirty-six encryptions and then sent it through a transvers static burst designed to show up as a social media notification on one of my dummy accounts."

Keel stared blankly through his helmet at the coder.

"You know," Garret said. "The one I set up for you to check in case I ever had to send you any dead-drop notes."

"I have no idea what you're talking about."

Hutch chuckled and shook his head. "Blow it all to hell or get out of here. Either one works for me. My orders were to secure the fleet—but after seeing what I've seen, I agree with Garret: that can't be done. So the way I figure it, I'm free to do whatever is necessary to deny use of the fleet to anyone else. Including itself."

"We're not doing *anything* until I get the rest of my crew," Keel said. "Or at least Leenah. And since she likes Prisma so much, the girl, too."

He looked down at the partially reassembled but still badly damaged remains of KRS-88. "Can he be of any use?"

Garret shook his head. "Not anytime soon. I've been trying to splice him back together, but for now he's just a basic mainframe. I think I got the power supply set up quick enough so that its memory core wasn't corrupted—he'll still know who he is. Maybe a few hiccups, but otherwise... yeah. But I need more components to get him worth having in a fight."

"He's a big, heavy liability is what he is," Hutch said. "If something can't help us in a fight, it's only going to slow down our leaving."

Keel shook his head. "Prisma is a handful. If she thinks we're leaving her bot behind, things'll go slower than if we just lug him around."

"So what?" asked Exo. "She's a *girl*. Why you flying around with a little girl in the first place? Anyway, pick her up and *make* her come."

"You don't know this girl, Exo," Keel said. "Or the way she seems to be able to get otherwise rational people to do whatever she wants. I seem to be the only exception to that rule, but trust me when I say that our lives will be much harder if we try to leave the bot here."

"So what do you propose?" Bombassa said. "Do I put on a backpack and carry this thing across the ship?"

"Not if we're going to blow the ship. It would slow you down too much. Someone else can get the bot back to the *Six*."

Bombassa sighed. "We are *not* going to blow the ship up. At least not until I've had a chance to confirm what your technician said. Look at this from my perspective, Keel. Your crewmember has been kidnapped by someone diametrically opposed to my mission. And now he's friends with his kidnapper—the psychological endearment of a captor. I can't just take that at face value."

Keel didn't want to argue, he wanted to rescue his crew. And he didn't have a counterargument to give. "Fair enough. So here's what we'll do. Hutch stays with us. Garret, nothing is preventing us from moving freely, so you make your way back to the docking bay on this level. Ravi is waiting there in the *Six*. You can drag the war bot behind you."

"I can't pull that much weight!"

"Then just carry the parts you need and you can build the rest later."

Garret nodded. Apparently that was something he could handle.

"Good," Keel said. "You get to the ship and make sure you're plugged in and doing what you can. In a quarter hour, we'll release Leenah and Prisma. Then we'll all meet you back at the ship."

"How about him?" Exo asked, pointing at Hutch. "Leg looks a little banged up."

"I can walk okay." Hutch slowly rose to his feet.

Garret bundled the war bot's parts with some spools of wire he took from a surplus terminal. He had only selected the parts of the bot he felt were crucial to salvaging KRS-88—parts that weighed considerably less than the giant as a whole—but he still struggled to move it.

"Kid," Keel said, amused at the effort. "There's a hovercart back at the detention center."

"Oh. Okay. I'll go get it and bring it back."

Exo grabbed the bundled parts and dragged it along. "I'll help you get to the cart," he said. "Then you can go from there. It ain't that heavy. I'll wait for you guys at the detention center."

Maybe Exo felt bad about laughing at the kid's expense.

Keel watched the two depart. "All your crew is KIA?" he asked Hutch.

Hutch frowned. "Yeah. Only ones I'm not sure about are Broxin and Ruh-ro, ship's first officer. A moktaar."

"Yeah, he's dead." Keel hoped the Nether Ops agent wouldn't ask for details. "Andien... I know her. She helped me out more than once, but I don't appreciate what she did to me. I definitely don't appreciate her taking my crew."

Hutch shrugged.

"Look, pal, the only reason I'm not holding you accountable is because I figure you were just following orders."

"That I was," Hutch said, limping forward a step. "Truth is, I actually took a liking to the kid. Same with her pink-skinned guardian. Quite a looker, that one."

Keel frowned from behind his bucket and addressed Bombassa. "We'll get Leenah out of her cell first. She knows her way around a blaster—better than the kid at least. Then we spring Prisma, and I head back to the ship with my crew. You and Exo are still free to join us."

Bombassa acknowledged the offer with only a nod.

"Well, how bout it?" Keel asked.

"I think... maybe."

08

Keel, Exo, and Bombassa were stacked outside the prison cell that held Leenah. Hutch stood at a distance. Thanks to a datapad given to Keel by Garret, the door would open with the simple press of a button.

Other than losing contact with Ravi, things had gone surprisingly smoothly. But how much longer would that last? An unauthorized removal of prisoners wasn't exactly an off-grid activity. If this CRONUS thing was blindly groping for them all, this would certainly tell him where the mice were hiding.

A chrono timer in Keel's HUD told him that the full allotment of time given Garret was up. Hopefully the kid was safe with Ravi and protected by the bristling guns of the *Indelible VI*. At least *he* could get out. Though Keel didn't think Ravi would leave him if things started falling apart.

"Okay," Keel said, his finger hovering over the datapad's unlock button. "Here we go." He pressed the screen and tossed the device to Hutch, who caught it easily even with the binders on.

The cell door shot straight up into a recess between the thick walls.

Leenah lifted her head sleepily from her bunk. "Do I get to talk to Prisma?" she asked, seemingly only half-awake, her voice like a dream.

Keel rushed in, with Exo behind him. The room was all clear. He removed his helmet so that she could hear his real voice. "I was hoping you might want to talk to me a bit first."

Leenah looked up, and her eyes grew wide with surprise. "Aeson!" She sprang from her cot, threw her arms around his neck, and pressed her head against his cheek. Her soft pink tendrils-for-hair brushed against him. Then she laughed—a joyful noise of freedom—and rapidly kissed his cheek and lips and forehead, not missing an inch of his face.

"Oh, I get it now," Exo said, his voice carrying that edge of filial teasing Keel had come to know from their time together in Victory Company and their Dark Ops kill team.

Bombassa peered into the cell. He remained stern, sober and serious. "There'll be time for reunions later. For now, we should continue on. You still have another crew member, do you not?"

As if remembering herself, Leenah pulled away from Keel. "Prisma!" Her violet eyes searched Keel imploringly. "She's still here. They sent me to talk to her sometimes. To keep her happy, I think. We can't leave without her."

"Wasn't planning on it," Keel answered with a smile. "You were my first stop, though."

Leenah stepped through the doorway and stopped at the sight of Hutch. "I didn't think anyone else survived. They told me that Prisma and I were the only survivors."

"Looks like the little robots learned how to lie," Hutch spat out bitterly. "I'm alive. So's your catman—somewhere. Your little coder friend made it too. Everyone else is good and dead. Bringing you here was a costly mission."

"We didn't ask to come," Leenah snapped back.

Hutch only grunted in reply.

Bombassa held out a blaster pistol to Leenah. "Wraith says you know how to use one of these."

Leenah took the weapon tentatively, but then seemed to calm her nerves. She checked the weapon to make sure it was on safe, and tucked it into the belt of her coveralls. "I know the way to her cell. But we need to be careful. I've tried keeping track of time, and right now feels like when they come if they're going to ask questions." Without even waiting for an acknowledgement, she started off down the hallway.

Keel followed, looking at her longingly. Wishing that he could freeze time so he could tell her that... that he cared about her. And in a way he hadn't felt since... maybe ever. He blinked the thoughts away. It was no wonder that Chhun hadn't approved of what he'd seen happening. But it had come on like an unexpected summer storm. This was how he felt about her; there was no getting around that. Which meant she was a liability. Not one that needed taking care of, but the sort that needed to be taken into account. Keel already knew that if it came right down to it, he was capable of doing all sorts of stupid things for this Endurian princess. Things that might cost him his life. And maybe... the lives of others.

"You mentioned something about 'them' coming around now," Bombassa said. "Your friend Garret said something similar. Who is it you speak of? The big war bot Titans?"

That was a good question. One that Keel should have asked.

"No," Leenah said. "I haven't seen any of those since the shooting started. The ones that come by our cells are more servile and graceful.

The type designed to interact with humanoids. I guess the best way to describe them is like a really advanced personal admin bot, if that even makes sense."

"I don't see what there is to figure out," said Exo. "We see any bots on the ship, we blast 'em. Pretty simple when you think about it."

"KTF is the only thing that ever made a lick of sense to me in this galaxy," agreed Hutch.

Leenah stopped outside a brig door. "This is it," she whispered.

Keel motioned for Hutch to give him back the datapad.

The Nether Ops agent only grunted, "I got it." He pressed a button, and Prisma's cell door shot upward... as did every other door in the corridor. "Uh-oh."

Keel stormed into the room and took in the scene in a second, a skill pressed on him by endless training in Dark Ops. Prisma was seated on her bunk, her legs hanging off its edge, swinging casually. Kneeling in front of her was another Endurian. One who looked from head to toe, down to the last stitch of clothing, exactly like Leenah.

The door had opened in mid-conversation, and to Keel it sounded like this room's Leenah was saying, "Tell me again how you make it move."

Both Prisma and Leenah swung their heads to look at Keel. He placed the sights of his blaster rifle on the head of this room's Leenah. It was a snap decision, but one that he didn't doubt for a second. He squeezed the trigger. Two blaster bolts struck the kneeling Leenah directly in her temple.

An alien, digital sound issued from her mouth as her body fell over, lifeless. Keel advanced on the target, Exo close behind him.

Blaster-scorched holes in the target's head revealed an adamantine-like skeleton and various circuitry. This must be one of the robotic replicants Garret had mentioned.

It began to move.

Keel unholstered Tyrus Rechs's slug thrower and sent two bullets into the bot, one into its head and one where its heart would be. The depleted uranium bullets left massive holes in the machine. It ceased moving.

The sound of the shots was deafening in the small room. Keel's ears rang intensely, and he wondered why he'd left his bucket off. Prisma covered her ears and screamed.

Leenah, the real Leenah, rushed into the room to comfort Prisma.

"I thought she was you," Prisma sobbed, holding on to Leenah tightly. "I couldn't tell that she wasn't. I should've been able to, but I couldn't."

Leenah held Prisma's head against her chest and stroked her hair as she helped her off the bed. "It's all right. But we have to get you out of here."

Prisma looked down at the destroyed replicant and then to Keel. "You came for me."

Keel's ears were still ringing. Leaving his bucket on his webbing had been a dumb move. Exactly what he'd told himself not to do. But he'd wanted Leenah to see his face. And he had wanted Prisma to see it, too. He remembered how frightened she'd been when he'd rescued her the first time, when Tyrus Rechs blew himself up on Tusca.

"Yeah, well," Keel said, "I guess it was the right thing to do."

Prisma screwed up her face. "That doesn't sound like you at all."

"Cute." Keel put his helmet back on. "Don't push it, kid."

He stepped outside. The other cells were, of course, empty, but he was relieved that there were no klaxons blaring or the sound of footfalls from advancing guards or war bots.

"It's like nobody running this ship even cares," he mumbled to himself. He turned to verify that Prisma and Leenah were still right behind him, trying to drive away the thought that they, too, might be replicants.

"Why did you shoot the fake Leenah?" Prisma asked. "How did you know?"

"Lot of reasons," Keel answered.

"I'd kind of like to know too," said Leenah.

Keel counted on his fingers. "First, I found you in your cell. I doubt they sent the replicant in there whenever you visited Prisma. Second, when you kissed me—"

"Ew, you kissed him?" Prisma said.

Leenah blushed a deeper shade of pink.

"Yes," Keel said. "She liked it, too."

"Pretty ballsy to shoot your girlfriend, bot or not," Hutch called out.

Keel ignored him.

Prisma was holding a marble in her hands. She stuffed it into a pocket and held out an open palm. "Someone give me a blaster."

"We don't arm children to fight our fights," said Bombassa.

"I know how to shoot," Prisma insisted. "Tyrus Rechs taught me. Shoot with your mind, not with your hand. I'm not afraid to kill someone."

"Then that is all the more reason why you should not have a weapon," Bombassa said, moving away from the little girl in an attempt to make that the conversation's last word.

But Prisma was undeterred. She followed Bombassa, speaking loudly. "They're not just going to let you go. They only kept Leenah alive because they knew if they didn't I would never speak to them again. They're afraid of me, and they want to know things about me. Things I don't even know about myself. Things I've never even heard of. But... maybe Ravi knows." She considered her last words. "Is Ravi here?"

"Back at the ship," Keel said.

Exo pinged Keel over the comm. "Dude, you weren't kidding about her."

"Tell me about it."

"They're going to try and stop you from getting me off of this ship," Prisma said, still following her rescuers. "I know they will. It's because I can kill them. All of them. And they know it and it scares them, even though they're machines."

Keel stopped to look at the little girl. The way she was talking made him uncomfortable. He had been wondering whether she might have been a replicant, same as the one in the room with her, but there was no way a bot would go on like this.

"Little girl," Exo said, rolling his shoulders as if to take away the strain of his webbing and combat kit. "You're starting to freak me out. Why you gotta be like this?"

Prisma balled her fists on her hips and craned her neck to look up at the shock trooper. "Because it's the truth. They're afraid of me. They weren't afraid of my father, but they *are* afraid of me."

The team was nearing the guard control room at the center of the detention block, where the frozen guard bot kept its holo-feed vigil.

"We're almost out of here," Keel said, hurrying his pace. He was starting to grow uneasy about this whole situation. "So if you could just save all your prophecies for later, like when we're safely on the ship, that would be much appreciated. Generally, these kill team mission are quiet affairs."

The words seemed to mean nothing to Prisma. "If I can't have a blaster then what about Crash? We have to find him! I can't leave him, he's my friend!"

"Garret's probably already got him loaded up on the ship," Keel said, annoyed. He paused and softened his tone. "Which is where we should be. The sooner we get there, the better. And I think it will go a lot easier if we don't shout out our location to the machines you keep saying are going to try to kill us all."

Keel looked at Leenah, who gave an appreciative nod.

"Okay," said Prisma. She picked up her pace. "I still think I should have a blaster. Tyrus Rechs would let me have a blaster."

"I'm not Tyrus Rechs."

Leenah placed a hand at the center of Prisma's back. "You don't need a blaster. We'll protect you. We'll take care of you."

Prisma didn't argue. But neither did she stop complaining. "What about Skrizz? Is he on the ship with Garret, too?"

Nobody said anything. They just looked from one to another, waiting to see how this particular complication would be dealt with.

"He's not dead, is he?"

"He's alive," Leenah said somewhat hesitantly. "But he's been coming and going on his own, and we don't know where he is right now."

Keel winced at these words. They were the truth, but it would have been a lot easier to just tell the kid that her bot and her cat were waiting for her on the ship. She'd get over it. Eventually.

"What? We can't leave then!" Prisma stopped moving and made a show of planting her feet.

Keel's head dropped, but his shoulders didn't sag. He turned around and walked a few paces to stand right before Prisma. Exo and Bombassa inched forward at the front of the column, scanning for any signs of trouble. Hutch, his hands still bound, wore a smug, amused smile.

"Prisma," Keel said, dropping to a knee. The girl pressed against Leenah. "He's a cat. He'll find his way to the ship before we leave."

"He's not a cat, he's a wobanki. And I saw him get lost plenty of times in his own ship when he was with Hogus!"

Keel looked up at Leenah and asked, "Who's Hogus?"

Leenah gently squeezed Prisma's hand. "He's the star freighter captain who took Prisma to find Tyrus Rechs. Skrizz was his co-pilot."

"He's dead now," Prisma said matter-of-factly. "Got shot by a legionnaire when he was trying to take advantage of people."

Keel stood up. "Thanks for the review. Skrizz will be fine, but I'm not so sure about the rest of us. Now, I'd like to use both of my hands to shoot bad guys, but if I have to use one of them to carry you, I will."

Exo's voice sounded over the comm. "Hey, sounds like someone's coming."

Keel lowered his bucket's audio output and said, "Someone's coming. Keep quiet."

"Give me a weapon," Hutch demanded.

"Me too," said Prisma, doing her best to sound just as hard as the Nether Ops agent.

Leenah pulled Prisma behind a bulkhead at the side of the corridor as Exo and Bombassa moved forward incrementally to intercept the threat.

They could all hear metallic footsteps at the corridor intersection ahead of them. An artificial voice removed any doubt they might have had about what was out there. "Is someone in the cell block?"

The voice sounded like it belonged to some sort of robotic police officer. Keel couldn't say why he thought that, only that he did. But that was the thing about bots: brilliant people spent lots of time modulating voice controls, programming mannerisms, and sculpting appearances to give off just the right feeling for the job. Keel guessed it was the same guard they'd encountered previously—that he was no longer frozen at the station. He was making the rounds.

The guard bot turned the corner. Its servos went silent for a second before it reached for the blaster that was attached to its side. Exo and Bombassa fired in unison, each shock trooper striking the bot, one at center mass and the other a headshot.

The machine flew apart in a shower of sparks. Clearly this was not a model meant for fighting wars.

Everyone stood, rigid and tense, waiting for an alarm that didn't come.

"Starting to think this is all too easy," Keel said.

"Maybe they're just watching," said Hutch, scratching the side of his face with his bound hands. "These things are messed up. Back before Garret was able to keep us hidden, one of them was talking to me. Hacked its way into my bucket. Forced me to watch on my HUD my buddies getting ripped apart. Tortured to death. These aren't your everyday average machines. These things are malevolent, and I wouldn't be surprised if they're just getting a kick out of seeing how far we can make it before the world comes crashing down."

"Sounds like a good reason to get out now," Bombassa said, looking nervously around the area.

"So you don't wanna try to take the ship?" Exo asked. "Because I'm good with that."

Bombassa shook his head. "I am beginning to agree that such a plan is untenable. Call it a bad feeling."

"Come on," Keel said, retaking the lead and carefully looking around the corner the bot had come from. It was all clear. He motioned for the others to follow. The guard control room at the hub of the prison complex was empty.

"It is a straight shot to the docking bay from here," announced Bombassa. "Are we ready to make the move?"

"One sec." Keel moved to check the holo-feeds, hoping to find some clues as to what—if anything—might be waiting for them. Aware that Prisma and Leenah were looking over his shoulder, he cycled quickly past the feed that showed the grotesque image of the of the tortured and dead legionnaire, but he wasn't fast enough. Both Prisma and Leenah gasped during the half second the image appeared. "Sorry about that."

Finally, Keel found a wide view that showed thumbnails of each cam feed. The interface was similar to those used on Republic facilities, and his intuition on how to back out from here and find more blocks of security feeds worked. Soon he was looking at an ordered list of every security station throughout the ship. He began opening them, quickly scanning the multiple thumbnails, backing out, and repeating.

Everything looked empty, but the sheer number of barracks, hangars, meeting rooms, galleys, and restrooms made Keel assume that the fleet had originally been built for a humanoid crew. If that was the Republic's intent, then what had happened? Was it CRONUS that had chosen to form a bot fleet instead? It was chilling to think that the AI had begun constructing war machines of its own initiative.

"This boat is empty wherever I look," Keel called out to the shock troopers. "Let's move to the docking bay and get aboard the *Six*."

"Everything looked nice and clean when *we* got here, too," Hutch said ominously. "But it turned out it was just the bots waiting for the right time to spring an ambush."

"Seems like the bots have had plenty of 'right times' to try to hit us," countered Exo.

"Is there anything waiting for us in the hangar, perhaps?" Bombassa asked Keel.

"No," said Keel. "I checked that too. The *Six* is still parked where we left it, with no one else around."

"Good," Leenah said, smiling. "I wouldn't want her to get a scratch."

Exo laughed. "So let's go already—"

A voice that sounded like thousands of whispers came from the corners of the guard control room.

"Abandon all hope-hope-hope-hope..."

The last word seemed to echo, refusing to leave the ears.

Immediately, weapons were up. Everyone turned slowly, trying to see where the voice was coming from, but there were no visible speakers in the walls.

Prisma wrapped her arms tightly around Leenah's waist.

The hushed voices repeated. "Abandon all hope-hope-hope..."

The screen Keel had been watching fritzed and flickered, and then what looked like a spectral, disembodied skull with glowing red eyes superimposed itself in front of the holo-feed displays. The ghost's mouth gaped wide, as if speaking, and the words issued across the room again. "Abandon all hope-hope-hope..."

Keel's first instinct was to blast the monitor, but stopped as the ghost in the machine addressed him directly.

"Wraith, alias Aeson Ford. Victory Kill Team. Alias Aeson Keel, Operation Righteous Destiny. Abandon all hope-hope-hope..."

Keel took a step back from the screen. "What is this?"

Prisma, still squeezing her arms around Leenah, whispered the answer. "It's him. It's CRONUS. He's coming for us."

"Let him come!" shouted Exo as he looked around the room, sending out a challenge.

The specter replied, "Sergeant Major Caleb Gutierrez. Imperial Shadow Squadron Alpha. Operation Indigo. Abandon all hope-hope-hope..."

The room went silent for a moment, then the voice continued.

"Chief Warrant Officer Two Okimbo Bombassa, Imperial Shadow Squadron Alpha, Operation Indigo, Operation Reliance. Abandon all-hope-hope-hope..."

"Nether Ops Agent Hutch Makaw, Operation Black Heart, Operation Left Turn, Operation Golden Prince, Operation Severe Wing. Abandon all—"

Keel blasted the display, sending white-hot sparks flying in every direction. The voice went silent. "That was getting tedious," Keel said. "Everyone, move. We're leaving."

"The machine was trying to distract us," Bombassa observed.

"Yep," Keel agreed. "Whatever's coming is already on the way, so be careful when that door opens."

"Aeson," Leenah called. She was struggling with Prisma, who was refusing to move. "Help."

"No!" Prisma shouted. "Not without Skrizz! They'll kill him!"

"Kid," shouted Hutch, "they'll kill all of us if we don't get going!"

"Then just leave!" Prisma retorted. "I don't care if they kill me! I don't! But I won't leave him!" The little girl began to sniffle and sob. "I don't want anyone else I care about to die."

09

Keel looked at Prisma and shook his head. "Not this again. We're going to carry you. You're not that big."

"Go ahead and try!" Prisma shouted.

"Hutch!" Keel called out. "Your hands are free. Pick her up."

The Nether Ops agent shrugged his shoulders. "Wouldn't be the first time I had to drag a member of your crew kicking and screaming."

He walked over to Prisma, a slight limp still evident, and lifted her effortlessly, his big arms tucked underneath hers, holding her tightly against his chest. "Time to move, little girl."

Leenah put a staying hand on Hutch's bicep. "Be careful with her."

"No problem."

Bombassa and Exo were at the door that led out of the guard control room and back to the long hallway down which they'd originally come. Exo poked his head out, then quickly pulled it back in as a burst of blaster fire sizzled through the open door, sending showering sparks where it impacted on a far wall. "Looks like the party really is starting!" Exo screamed.

"Bots!" Bombassa shouted, also taking cover from the open doorway. "Two big ones. *Really* big. They just came out of the walls and are coming our way."

Prisma was squirming and kicking in Hutch's arms. The Nether Ops agent grunted through speaking. "Those sound like the Titans. Bad news."

"Let me go!" Prisma screamed. She opened her mouth and bit down on Hutch's gloved hand.

Hutch inhaled in pain. "Knock it off, you little brat!"

"Wraith!" Exo called between bursts of return fire. "What's the plan? We gonna try to push through?"

"We can't stay here!" Keel took one look at the struggling mess that was Prisma, Hutch, and Leenah, then moved toward the entryway. He peeked out to get an idea of what was coming toward them.

The bots were at least a foot taller than KRS-88. In one hand, each bot held a white shield, the type used by riot police, only much bigger—tall as a man and twice as wide. In the other hand was what appeared to be a tri-barreled N-50. Those guns were capable of taking down a light-armored combat sled or an unshielded starfighter, let alone a tiny boarding party.

Keel shook his head. There was an ancient look to these modern war machines, like something plucked from antiquity and made new. Three red eyes—optical sensors, to be more precise—glowed maliciously from the shadows of their helmets.

Bombassa fired several blaster bolts, all of which struck the Titans' shields and deflected skyward, extinguishing overhead lights or burning out along the ceiling. Only miniscule scorch marks were left on the gleaming white shields.

The bots leveled their tri-barrel guns at the doorway and sent forth another burst of fire. All three men defending were forced to duck back inside.

"We can't let those guns get on us inside this room," Exo said, holding the top of his bucket as blaster bolts streaked past him.

Bombassa changed out a charge pack. "So we push."

"Suicide," Exo said. "Wish I had an AP rocket."

Keel turned to check on Hutch and Prisma. Prisma was still struggling. For a kid, her energy reserves were really something.

"Let's try a flashbang," Bombassa said, pulling one from his belt. "Those scramble bots' sensors pretty well. Not as good as an EMP grenade, but I don't think any of us are carrying those."

"Good call," Keel said. "Most bots' audio-visual sensors just can't handle the stress of an ear-popper."

"Ear-popper?" Bombassa said.

"Banger," Exo clarified. The term varied from company to company. "We always called 'em ear-poppers in Victory."

Bombassa nodded, thumbed on the activation, and tossed the grenade into the hall. "Banger out."

It clattered to a stop at the feet of the two advancing Titans and exploded an instant later. The ship-shaking blast reverberated through the deck all the way to Keel and the shock troopers, and the brilliant flash of light that accompanied the boom made the well-lit security room feel dim by comparison.

In spite of the limited time the three had spent together, years of experience resulted in Keel, Exo, and Bombassa cooperating seamlessly as they rolled out and brought their weapons to bear in the corridor. Exo and Bombassa peppered the bots with blaster fire, striking them repeatedly in their helmets as the machines attempted to bring systems back online. Each shot caused a Titan's head to rock like a boxer who'd let his guard down. Smoke rose from the giant bots' chests and necks.

But they didn't fall.

Keel set down his blaster rifle and pulled the slug thrower from its holster. The bots were coming around now, raising their shields against the salvo of blaster fire.

"We need to get closer!" Keel yelled. The distance lessened the impact of the blaster bolts. Unless they were firing with N-18s or their own N-50, which they weren't, they might have to deploy another ear-popper to finish the job.

Keel lined up a bot in his sights as he charged down the hallway. He squeezed the trigger, and the big projectile weapon added to the cacophony of noise with an ear-splitting bang. The bullet slammed directly in the middle of the bot's three red optical eyes and shot out the other side, leaving a gaping hole.

The bot shuddered and shook. It didn't fall, but it did freeze up, as though it had turned to stone.

"That worked," Keel said to himself. He sprinted back to regain the cover of the room.

The remaining bot seemed to be adjusting tactics. It raised its shield, hiding its optical sensors behind it, barely allowing one glowing eye to peer out. The big tri-barreled N-50 poked out from behind the shield and began firing again. The bot lumbered closer, and the three defenders were forced to hide themselves from the onslaught.

"Don't wanna see what a platoon of these things could accomplish," Keel said, unholstering his blaster pistol so he held a weapon in each hand.

"Perhaps there is no platoon available," answered Bombassa.

Keel remembered the way the voice had declared a death sentence for each of them. *Abandon all hope.* It had been playing with them. Mocking them. Keel realized that this AI—CRONUS, whatever—was more human than any AI had ever been before. It was *enjoying* the spectacle and pageantry of a life-and-death drama of its own orchestration. Killing was a way to make a point: that all resistance, and all the strivings of biological life for that matter, was futile. It wanted to instill fear in the hearts of its prey. And, perhaps... respect?

And what would it be willing to do to the galaxy to achieve both?

In that moment of reflection, Keel made up his mind to do whatever it took to stop these things from wreaking havoc across the galaxy.

"I'm gonna use another ear-popper," Exo said, retrieving one of the grenades from his belt.

"Go ahead, Exo," said Bombassa.

"Popper out!"

The weapon erupted, and the three soldiers re-engaged.

But the Titan's tactics changed again. It hid behind its shield. Perhaps the ear-popper disoriented it enough to hold it in place—for now—but it continued to fire its blaster.

This wasn't good.

Keel thought for a split second about what to do next. It occurred to him that the bot wasn't sweeping or varying its fire; it was holding the weapon in a fixed position, as though its arm was rusted in place. Perhaps the ear-popper had been more effective than it first appeared.

Taking a deep breath, Keel rolled out beneath the blaster fire. It sizzled and cooked the air just above him. Those endless low-crawl exercises under energy-wire and through blood and mud during Legion Basic Training were what kept Keel alive. He crawled farther into the open, then rolled until he hit the corridor wall. As he sprang up, he fully expected the bot to move its arm ever so slightly to its left, and cut Keel in two.

But it didn't. The bot seemed only now to be regaining its senses.

Slug thrower in hand, Keel sprinted down the hall in an effort to get a clear shot at the bot's head.

The Titan was definitely more alert now. It began shifting its bulk to prepare for the charging Keel.

Keel jumped, hoping to find himself landing behind the death machine. But the bot thrust its shield at Keel, striking him square in his sternum and pinning him against the wall.

Keel grunted from the pressure the powerful machine was putting him under. If it weren't for his armor, he would be flattened. For a moment, he could do no more than watch as the Titan brought its ponderous tri-cannon N-50 to bear.

Then with a mighty heave, he wrenched his arm free of the shield, nearly dislocating it in the process. He leveled the weapon directly against the Titan's helmet and pulled the trigger.

Again, the machine didn't fall. It merely went offline, leaving Keel trapped between the wall and its shield. Keel tried to push himself out of the predicament, but the machine weighed far too much for him to move it without any leverage.

Blessedly, nothing else was coming for him.

"Little help, guys," Keel said through clenched teeth. The pressure of his armor being forced against his body was catching up to him.

Bombassa and Exo ran forward with care, their rifles up, looking for potential targets. When they were satisfied they were all clear, they took hold of the bot and pulled, while Keel pushed against the shield.

The Titan rocked backwards far enough for Keel to slip free. He quickly moved away before the big bot rocked back into its frozen place, its shield into the wall with a resounding thud.

"These machines are well-built," Bombassa said, panting. "Most war bots I've encountered, especially the smaller, new-market models popular with merc outfits, collapse like dead men when you shut them down."

"Yeah, this is heavy machinery," Exo said.

Keel rubbed at his ribs through his armor. "Tell me about it. Let's go get the others and move while we're clear."

Back in the guard control room, Prisma was still struggling and frustrated, but some of the fight had left her. Hutch continued to hold her tight, and despite her spirt, her body was still only that of a girl; there wasn't much she could do against two hundred and fifty pounds of hardened killer.

Leenah was talking soothingly. "It's okay, Prisma. If you calm down, I'm sure you can walk and Hutch won't have to carry you so tight."

"No! Because Skrizz!" It was the cry of someone who knew enough of the world to hate death, but still had a youthful hope that—this time—things wouldn't be that way. For as much as this little girl had experienced, she still carried an innocent naïveté.

Keel felt a protective urge well up within himself. He felt as though, if he could protect Prisma, he, by extension, would be protecting that which was good in and of itself.

He spoke softly to the girl. "Prisma, you have to go right now. There's no way of knowing how many more of those machines might be coming. You can't stay here. You have to go."

"Not without Skrizz!"

It was clear from the Hutch's expression that he'd reached the end of his patience. "Does anybody got a med pack facilitator? Let's tranq her and go already."

Keel saw Prisma's eyes go wide in panic at the suggestion. He watched the dawning realization across her face that if this happened, they would leave without Skrizz.

"No!" Prisma shouted, struggling. And then she stopped. "No," she said again, softly this time. She closed her eyes.

Then...

"No!"

Her voice carried with it all the power of a concussive bomb. Hutch flew backward, his ener-chains broken. Leenah was also sent flying, crashing shoulder-first into the side of a duty station. Keel had to take several steps back to keep from tumbling end over end.

Prisma dropped straight down from where Hutch had released her and landed on her feet. She looked around, saw Leenah clutching her shoulder, and ran over to her. "I'm sorry! I'm so sorry!"

Leenah groaned and struggled to get to her feet. Keel rushed to her side and lifted her up.

"It's okay," Leenah said, her voice pained. "I'll be all right. How did you...?"

"I don't know," Prisma said. There was real fear evident in her voice. "I think... I think this is what Ravi was teaching me."

"Damn," Exo said. "If you can do that, we don't gotta worry about running out of ear-poppers."

Evidently the shock trooper was more adjusted to seeing something like that than Keel was. Maybe the space wizard stuff wasn't exaggeration.

Keel put a gentle hand on Prisma's shoulder. "Do you think you can do that again? If you have to?"

Prisma held her arm at the elbow and looked down, her hair flopping in front of her face. "I... I don't know."

Keel dropped to his knees and pulled off his helmet. "Listen, Prisma. What matters to me right now—more than anything else—is getting Leenah safely off this ship along with you and everybody else. These are your friends, and these are my friends. I won't let anything bad happen to them. And that includes Skrizz."

Prisma blinked away tears.

"Prisma. If you promise me that you'll do whatever it takes to get Leenah safely to the ship, and that you'll listen to Leenah, Exo, and Bombassa—if you promise me that—I will go and find Skrizz."

A look of fear crossed Leenah's face. She slumped back down, still appearing woozy. "Aeson... no."

Keel continued undeterred. "I promise I'll look everywhere."

Prisma stared at Keel, and then gave a weak smile. "Maybe I was wrong about you."

"Probably not." Keel laid his blaster rifle in Leenah's lap. "Leenah, take this and give it to Hutch *only* if you don't think there are any other options. But don't let yourself trust him. Nether Ops is bad news."

Hutch, who up until now had lain sprawled across the floor, seemingly blacked out, now sat up and rubbed the back of his head.

Leenah shook her head. "Aeson... don't."

"Wraith!" Exo said. "This is a bad idea, man. You shouldn't go off on your own."

Bombassa had moved beside Hutch and was now replacing the broken ener-chains with a fresh pair. "I agree."

"Thanks a lot, pal," Hutch grumbled.

Bombassa ignored the comment. "We need to stay together, Wraith. We need to get to your ship and leave this place."

"Sorry." Keel winked at Prisma. "Already promised." He bent down and kissed Leenah, then donned his helmet. He left the room before further protests could be made, but spoke with the shock troopers over the comm. "Listen, guys. You need to get to the ship, and you need to be ready to go, even if it means going without me."

"For a stupid wobanki?" Exo said.

"Not for Skrizz. For everybody. This Cybar AI needs to be stopped. I don't know if I'll find Skrizz or not, but I'm blowing this ship up."

"And how will you do that?" Bombassa asked.

"Same as back on Tarrago," Keel answered.

"What's that mean?" Exo asked.

Keel sighed. "Seeing as how this is probably the last time we'll see each other alive, I'm gonna come clean. Exo, I never stopped working for Dark Ops. I've just been out in the cold. I'm sorry I lied to you. My job ended up being to find your boss, the space wizard. And when I did,

Owens called me back in—to help Chhun blow up the shipyards. And then… well, then they wanted me to do more. And I wanted to be done. And when Nether Ops kidnapped my crew, that's when I broke off for good. I found you. You know the rest."

When they didn't reply, Keel asked, "Anyone trying to follow me?"

"Nah," said Exo. "They're looking at us."

"Get 'em out of there," Keel said. "And Exo… it was good to fight alongside you again. I'm glad I had the chance."

"Yeah. Me too."

10

Bombassa led the team past the frozen, hulking Titans without incident. But they'd traveled the corridor for all of thirty seconds more before the next wave of trouble came for them.

The ceiling opened up twenty meters in front of them, and out poured spider-like bots, each the size of closed fist. They swarmed down the walls and onto the deck, scurrying toward the crew in a great mass of legs and glowing yellow eyes. Each tiny machine had six optical sensors.

Bombassa and Exo opened fire, sending hot blaster bolts into the clustered mob. Even Leenah, using Wraith's blaster rifle, joined in. The bots flew easily apart, with each shot ripping through several machines before burning out on the deck. But there were so many of them. The surviving bots swarmed over their fallen comrades like circuit-chewing bullet ants.

"Unless the kid wants to pull another trick like she did in the guard room," Hutch shouted over the noise, "you're going to need another gun in this fight. Leenah, give me a weapon!"

Leenah's face flinched with annoyance as she sent another blaster bolt into the group. Clearly she was uncomfortable using the high-powered rifle. But she might have been even less comfortable handing it over to Hutch. She looked down at Prisma, who was standing slightly behind her. "Prisma, can you?"

Prisma planted her feet and squeezed her eyes shut in concentration. She bit her lip before slouching her shoulders and letting out a long exhalation. "I can't do it. I'm sorry. I'm trying, but I can't."

"A weapon!" Hutch shouted.

Bombassa pulled a flashbang from his belt and primed it. He hesitated, knowing the harm it could cause to those not wearing sensory-protecting buckets. He and Exo could carry Leenah and Prisma if it came to that, but he didn't think they could also get Hutch. And Bombassa didn't want to leave the former legionnaire to the mercies of the Cybar.

Leenah pulled the blaster pistol from her belt and handed it to Hutch. "This is a loan."

The Nether Ops legionnaire managed a two-handed grip even with his hands bound. But he didn't immediately shoot. Instead he fiddled with the weapon's power settings. When he did shoot, his blaster bolts appeared faded and less intense. The bots fell all the same.

"Changing packs!" Exo called out. He deftly removed the charge pack from his blaster rifle and slammed another one home as the others continued to fire.

"Lower the intensity!" Hutch shouted at the shock troopers from behind. "You can still kill these things on the lowest setting. Dial it down and hit 'em with full auto!"

Exo and Bombassa exchanged a look and then did as suggested, lowering the output of their weapons to the minimal setting, a level that would just barely stun a humanoid. They fired single shots into the bot swarm, and sure enough, the fragile machines fell.

With their weapons on this low of a setting, they could keep up the barrage for a long time without the need for a pack change. But that didn't help with the main problem: the sheer overwhelming numbers of the spider things. And still more were pouring from the ceiling.

"They keep coming, and they ain't shootin'!" Exo shouted. "Means they need to get in close to do their damage."

The disabled bots' bodies were tumbled every which way, with some revealing their underbellies. Beneath each spider was a needle and a container of green liquid. Like venom. "They probably seek to inject some sort of neurotoxin," Bombassa said. "I think we can go through them if we act quickly!"

"Dude, what?" Exo said.

Bombassa offered no further explanation. "Leenah! Prisma! Come behind us right now and jump on our shoulders." The big shock trooper lowered himself until Prisma could put her arms around his neck. Then he stood up, holding her on his back. "I'll go first."

"We're actually going to try to run through them?" an incredulous Exo shouted.

"Yes! Now grab Leenah and go!" Bombassa took off, charging toward the swarm.

"Who's carrying me?" Hutch called out after him.

Still firing, Exo looked at the man. Hutch's legs were armored, though much of the upper equipment was long gone. "You're good to go from the waist down, man. Just run fast and hope the critters can't high jump."

Exo swept Leenah into his arms and took off.

Hutch slid his feet on the deck like a bullitar preparing to charge. "Yeah, comforting."

Bombassa continued to fire on the machines as he approached, and then burst into them, kicking, punching, and crushing them beneath his feet as he plowed through like a sky speeder in a snowstorm. Exo followed, sprinting for all he was worth. He could see the bots flying around as Bombassa passed safely through the mob, and he did his best to stick to the gap the big man had made. Occasionally crunching a fragile bot beneath his feet, he ran, lungs burning, his breath fire, until he knew he was well clear of them.

Finally, he slowed and looked back to see how Hutch was doing. The Nether Ops agent was a good distance back, moving through the machines, but the bots were crawling all over him. As Exo watched, Hutch dropped his weapon and swatted a bot off of his neck. Then he dropped to his knees, clutching his neck, while more bots swarmed his exposed flesh.

Exo put Leenah down, and Bombassa did the same with Prisma. The big shock trooper growled at Hutch's misfortune.

"Never leave a leej behind," Exo said stoically. He removed an ear-popper. "Better get clear of the blast." He waited for them to disappear around a corner of an intersecting corridor, hoping that there weren't more monstrosities waiting for them. Then, with a seamball infielder's sidearm throw, he sent the grenade straight down the center of the thoroughfare, directly into the swarming spider-bots.

It exploded in a blinding flash and a teeth-rattling boom.

Exo sprinted for the carnage, his weapons stowed. Most of the bots were curled up like dead bugs that had been smacked by a rolled-up tube of paper. Others were still writhing, their delicate legs wriggling. Hutch lay unconscious in the midst of them, and had several puncture marks visible on his neck, face, and arms. Thin trails of blood trickled from the needle wounds.

"No way he's going to make it," Exo mumbled. He grabbed hold of the man's webbing anyway and dragged him toward the others.

Bombassa met him halfway, and helped pull the load toward the docking bay doors. "We'll have to leave him if we run into any further trouble."

"Yeah."

This was the one faithful rescue Hutch would receive by virtue of his having once been a legionnaire. Performed by men who themselves were no longer in the Legion. It was something Hutch could never have hoped for from his peers in Nether Ops.

Exo wondered whether, if Hutch pulled through, he'd know that. If he'd realize that it was the Legion that had saved him. And the thought made him question whether he himself had a place in the Legion. Especially if what Wraith's code slicer had said about Goth Sullus was true.

These thoughts consumed Exo as he ran, pushing himself to his limits. Redlining.

The party reached the doors that bore the welcome text: "Docking Bay E-6." The doors slid open to reveal an even more welcome sight: polished black deck plates, empty of bots, leading to the *Indelible VI*, which sat unmolested, right where they had left it, already lowering its ramp.

They ran toward it. This was a miracle. It was better than it had any reason to be.

Exo would take it.

Bombassa was nearly to the *Six*'s ramp when a set of transparent doors on one side of the docking bay opened, and an industrial-sized rack of bots slid out. The machines unfolded their frames, stepped down from the rack, and began walking in lines toward the lone ship. As the rack rotated, more bots stepped off.

They were Titans, and each row seemed to comprise a fire squadron. They moved in small units, each with three shield bearers in the front and three more behind, all of them armed with the tri-barreled N-50 blaster cannons.

Ravi hailed them from the ship. "Where is Captain Keel?"

With Prisma and Leenah already on board, Bombassa and Exo hurriedly pulled Hutch up the ramp and set the Nether Ops agent down just inside. He looked dead.

"Wraith went to find the wobanki named Skrizz," Bombassa replied. "He said to wait only as long as it was safe to do so."

"This does not sound like him," answered Ravi.

The *Indelible VI* began to send streams of quad burst fire from its turrets. Bombassa stepped back out to observe and lend his own blaster rifle to the encounter. The *Six*'s guns were powerful enough to send the shields held by the Titan vanguard flying in all directions, often with the bots' arms still attached.

The Titans had now been joined by a number of swift-moving smaller bots, built like typical humanoid soldiers and carrying what looked to be modified N-6 blaster rifles. While Ravi concentrated his fire on the Titans, Bombassa took shots at this second group from the ramp.

"You will be of more service on board," Ravi said calmly. "It is my wish that you and Exo take manual control of the topside and belly turrets. Do not be stingy with your firing. The *Indelible VI* has enough charge to hold off this onslaught for a considerable time. Longer than your body is capable of staying awake, even with illicit stimulants."

Bombassa ran up the ramp. "Exo, get up on the topside turrets. I'll take the belly."

"You got it."

"I think it will be better if you control the belly turrets from the cockpit," Ravi said to Bombassa. "I have more for you to do."

When the shock trooper changed course, Ravi continued. "In the event of an emergency, I have instructed the ship's AI to send concussion missiles into anything heavier than a Cybar Titan. They likely have main battle tanks available, judging by the vehicle doors in this bay. But other than in that circumstance, the ship's AI will only have access to weapons systems if you grant it. Simply say the word and it will be done. But I urge you not to cede control unless you absolutely cannot handle it on your own; I have a concern that the Cybar might be able to influence the *Six*'s AI."

Leenah's voice came over the ship's open comm. "I've got Hutch in the medical bay. Exo helped me move him."

"Good," Bombassa said, recalling his own time spent in that bay after Keel had turned his ship's guns on Bombassa's team. How times had changed. "Are you checked out as a medic?"

"Not really. A little. I mean, I know how to turn the machines on."

"Enough to tell if he's even alive?"

"Yeah," Leenah said. "I hooked him up to the monitors. He's alive. Barely."

"Good enough. Have the machines sedate him. If those bots didn't kill him outright, there's no telling what he might do when he wakes up."

"Okay, I'll get on it. And then I'm going to the shield arrays. They might need my help."

Bombassa reached the cockpit, just as Exo's voice burst across the comm.

"Lots of contact!" Exo reported, the sound of his turrets blazing in the background.

Ravi seemed unfazed. He gestured for Bombassa to sit, and began to lecture as soon as Bombassa had done so. "I will show you how to control the belly turret from here." He pointed to a control screen. "This is your fire control. You can adjust pitch and rotation here. It is all very standard. The main cannons are linked, but you can toggle off for individual fire should you feel the need. I have the *Six* on repulsor standby. So if you are a good enough pilot, you can rotate and focus the forward main cannons—those are fixed—on anything that comes your way. They are quite powerful. Currently, I calculate an eighty-nine percent probability that these blast doors," Ravi pointed to a pair of large impervisteel doors at the opposite end of the massive hangar, "are where the next wave of Titans will emerge. If that happens, engage with your turrets before they unload."

Bombassa nodded compulsively, taking in everything the hologram was throwing his way.

Ravi continued. "I currently have the ship oriented so that the main cannons can fire on the largest door in the docking bay—big enough for HK-PPs—as I calculate a seventy-seven percent likelihood that main battle tanks or similar heavy vehicles will be employed from that location, if they are an available asset. If this proves to be the case, it is of paramount importance that you fire the moment that those doors begin to open."

Bombassa continued to nod. "Right. Why are you telling me all this?"

Ravi didn't immediately answer the question. "Garret has accessed the primary database through the *Six*'s computer, and is fighting the AI from there. He kept the Cybar ship from overwhelming you on your retreat to the docking bay and is working to mitigate the attack you are now facing. Listen to what he says, though he is not a soldier. This has the potential to keep you alive more than anything. Do you have any questions?"

"Just one." Bombassa had deduced the reason Ravi was telling him all of this. "Where will you be going?"

"I'm going to save my friend."

The hologram disappeared.

11

Keel had moved about five hundred meters past the corpse of the butchered moktaar when he caught sight of the first roving Cybar Titan on patrol.

Something about the machine's helmet looked familiar to him. An image danced in his mind… something he'd seen in a military history course while studying at the Legion Academy. It seemed like that was many lifetimes ago. And in a way, it was. That was before Victory Company. Before Kublar. Before Dark Ops. Before the mission that had brought him out to the edge of the galaxy.

Back then, in those classes, he'd had no idea who Captain Keel was. Who he would be. He hadn't met Leenah. It was as if the memory belonged to someone else. But it *was* him who had sat ramrod straight at the study desk in an Academy dorm room, diligently studying. Reading all the footnotes that everyone knew wouldn't show up on the exams, because there was just too much to know. With so much history recorded—even accounting for all that had been lost or jumbled before the stabilizing effect of the Great Migration—there was simply too much information for a humanoid brain to contain.

But he'd absorbed what he could. And now, on this strange ship at the edge of the galaxy, the look of the Titan twigged something in the back of his mind. Something ancient. Keel remembered a digital image of some sort of ancient pottery—a black vessel. Crudely painted, in gold lines, were two men, both naked. One was lying on the ground, and the other was thrusting a spear into the vanquished warrior's side. And the helmet that the victor wore… it looked a lot like the helmet of the enormous machine that had lumbered into the access corridor, up ahead of where Keel now hid.

Keel took comfort in knowing what his slug thrower could do to one of these beasts. He also had two ear-poppers, should he need them. And he felt that if he overloaded his charge pack to expend everything with a single shot, that would do the trick as well. Maybe he could even squeeze two lethal shots out of one pack. But that would come later.

For now, he waited, crouched in the shadows. The Titan had turned down the corridor away from Keel, in the same direction Keel was traveling. He didn't think the things could see through the backs of their heads, but he wanted to be sure the thing was truly facing away, unable to spot him in its peripheral vision.

As the bot trudged on, Keel coiled his body, ready to spring out, close the distance, and send a single bullet into the thing's head. Then he'd continue on in his attempt to reach the ship's core. Because that was his primary goal. He hadn't yet put much thought into finding Skrizz.

And so it was a surprise when the wobanki grabbed his arm with his powerful paw.

Skrizz held up his other paw, mimicking the human body language that called for silence. The motion pushed up his lip and revealed glistening, sharp fangs. Keel kept silent, wondering what the big cat was angling toward. He knew Skrizz wasn't just a killer, he was also a survivor. Keel had no doubt that it was Skrizz who had killed the moktaar—because he was hungry, and also, in all likelihood, because he simply wanted to.

The clomping of more bots coming down the hall, toward the two fugitives, told Keel why Skrizz had held him back. Had he jumped out, he would have been spotted for sure.

Skrizz and Keel pressed themselves farther into the shadows. Even when the three Titans turned at the cross-corridor where the other Titan had entered, they remained hidden. Finally, when Keel's enhanced audio receptors no longer detected any noise beyond the wobanki's near-silent breathing, he spoke.

"Thanks," he said, his audio output at the lowest possible level.

"*Chetta.*" Skrizz pointed at the ceiling.

Keel looked up. Above him was an open hatch, or maybe just a removed ceiling panel. He understood: that was how the catman had snuck up on him.

But the opening was a good four meters overhead. "I don't think I can make that jump, Skrizz."

Skrizz nodded in understanding, crouched into a compact ball of muscle, and sprang straight upward into the opening. He tucked up his legs and landed on his feet inside the ceiling. It was an impressive leap, like some sort of ridiculous box jump.

The catman stood up so that his tail dangled down out of the hole, but Keel knew better than to jump up and use it like a rope. He waited until Skrizz peered back down and lowered his paws. Then Keel holstered his blasters and leapt straight up for all he was worth.

He just barely caught Skrizz by the wrist.

The wobanki pulled him up through the opening.

They were on some sort of sub-floor between the ceiling and the next deck. Keel looked around and whispered, "Are we okay to talk up here?"

The reply was an affirmative growl.

"I came here with Ravi and a couple of friends to get out whoever I could find," Keel explained. "We rescued the prisoners. Prisma and Leenah, should be on my ship right now. Garret too. And Hutch."

The catman seemed to show relief on hearing Prisma's name. She had apparently figured out how to tame this apex predator. "*Hezra no salassa Hutch.*"

"I don't like him either, but he's with them. As a prisoner."

Skrizz yowled like an alley cat. "*Prisma hoshazz ne...*"

"I said she's fine." Keel shook his head. "You her pet now?"

Skrizz hissed a denial, but his heart didn't seem in it.

What was it with people and that little girl? Was Keel the only one immune to being suckered by her? But then... wasn't he going ahead and recovering Skrizz after all? Keel was doing exactly what Prisma wanted, as if he'd actually *meant* what he promised.

The wobanki jabbered about the docking bay and the fastest way to arrive.

"Yeah, about that..." Keel couldn't quite believe what he was about to say. "You should go and rejoin her. I promised Prisma that I'd find you just to get her to leave the cell block. She wouldn't budge otherwise."

By the expression on Skrizz's face, it was clear the aloof catman was touched.

"Thing of it is," Keel continued, "I can't come with you."

Skrizz purred a question.

"Sure I want to stay alive. Trouble is, living isn't really an option here. Skrizz, I can't let whatever's controlling this ship get set loose on the galaxy. And right now might be my only chance to stop it. A chance that the Republic or Legion may never have again."

"*Cha Skrizz hassa Keel halach?*"

"No, I'm not going to make you come with me. But I *could* use your guidance. Garret said you've been exploring the ship?"

The catman spread his arms wide and brought his tail up over his head to indicate just how much of the ship he'd personally explored.

"Good. In that case, can you point me to the ship's reactor? I'm going to blow it."

The wobanki's ears flattened. Clearly he didn't like this plan. This suicide mission.

"By the time I actually do it, you and Prisma and Leenah and everybody else will be safe in hyperspace."

This didn't seem to alter Skrizz's opinion of the plan. But he didn't try to talk Keel out of it. He simply asked whether there was anything he could do. He said that he hadn't forgotten how Keel rescued him back on Tusca, when the remote caller for the *Obsidian Crow* ignored his commands, nearly stranding him.

"Yes," Keel answered. "There is something you can do for me. If you ever see Chhun again, tell him that Wraith says he didn't forget nothin'."

Keel moved with Skrizz for what his HUD recorded as nearly a mile through the ship's overhead ducting and ventilation. All Keel had asked was to be pointed in the right direction, not a guided tour. And yet, when he brought this up to the wobanki, Skrizz would only reply that the route was on his way, and he would break away when the time was right.

"*Secha ret na lazzasse?*"

"Yes," replied Keel. "I do enjoy the company."

They came to a stop shortly thereafter. Skrizz pulled open a floor panel, revealing a four-meter drop down into an empty corridor. Or at least, what *looked* like an empty corridor. They waited several minutes to be sure there were no nearby sentries.

Skrizz dropped feet first through the opening and landed in a silent crouch on the deck below. Keel lowered himself until he hung as if from a pull-up bar. Then he dropped as well, landing almost as silently, except for the small clatter his armor made on the deck.

This corridor was different from any of the ship Keel had seen so far. It extended a long way, with no doors or side passages. But it was really just the one wall that struck Keel as if it didn't belong. It was a gray that looked like primed impervisteel, and it had a slight convexity to it. The opposite wall was an ordinary white, making the impervisteel stand out all the more.

As Skrizz beckoned for Keel to follow him down the hall, Keel knew that the wobanki had no intention of heading back to the docking bay. Not yet. Somewhere in its predator brain, it knew the same truth as Keel. The catman might not stick around to see everything go boom, but he had the sense to help Wraith make it happen.

The two walked for what seemed like forever.

"This trip ever end?" Keel asked.

The wobanki purred to assure Keel that, yes, it did.

Keel shook his head. "As long as you know where we're headed."

The corridor didn't seem to have a purpose beyond continuing on and on. There was not a single blast door or exit. No duty stations. Nothing. There was nothing to look at, other than the slightly convex impervisteel gray wall.

He put his hand against it. "Is this a... ship inside a ship?" He didn't know what else it could be.

"*Tu harata.*" Skrizz thought so.

The more Keel looked at the inner wall, the more convinced he became that it had once been the exterior hull of a Republic vessel. He studied it for clues. Soon, smooth, bulbous pockets began to show, and he pegged it as a corvette. That was interesting. Why, in building this Cybar capital ship, did they make use of a corvette hull to fashion an interior wall, deep inside?

"Those shapes there?" Keel said to Skrizz, pointing at spherical bubbles in the impervisteel that looked like metal warts against the otherwise smooth hull. "Those are deep sensor arrays. The Republic installs them on special corvettes used for deep space exploration."

The hull's gray was soon broken up by large strips of painted matte black. Keel realized that this wasn't a change in paint colors; this was part of massive letters on the side of the hull. The painted words went from floor to ceiling in the four-meter-tall corridor, the tops and bottoms of each letter cut off, leaving only the middle for Keel to decipher. He stepped back until he was pressing himself against the opposite wall, getting as wide a view as possible. Comprehension locked into place, and his heart skipped a beat.

"*Deluvia*," he read aloud. "That's the *Deluvia*?"

The wobanki purred an affirmative, and then yammered on several qualifiers. Skrizz hadn't gone inside the ship. He'd only seen these identifiers and the dry-dock exit hatch behind the last letter, which was where he was taking Keel now.

Keel gripped his pistols a little more tightly. The *Deluvia* was a byword. "Dead like *Deluvia*" was an expression used to describe total destruction and annihilation. A situation where all was lost. *Deluvia* was an exploration vessel that had famously gone out beyond galaxy's edge to see what—if anything—was beyond the great dead zone at galaxy's end. And when the ship returned after spending a decade beyond the edge, no one was on board—even though all the escape pods were operational and accounted for. Holo-security footage released to the public was equally haunting: endless footage of a ship empty of all life, with maintenance bots keeping it pristine. There were rumors that a censored three-second clip showed a horror of death and destruction, but officially, the cause of the crew's disappearance was unsolved.

A mystery.

Deluvia was supposed to have been decommissioned and scrapped. But here it was.

Skrizz came to a halt at the *Deluvia*'s dry dock hatch and turned to face Keel.

"You're telling me that this ship's reactor is inside the *Deluvia?*" Keel said.

Skrizz purred yes.

"Well. Then this is where we part ways." Keel left no room for discussion. He wanted Skrizz to get back to the *Six* while he still could.

But the wobanki stood unmoving by Keel's side.

"Look, Skrizz. Thanks for getting me this far. You saved me a lot of time. But I told the kid I'd get you to safety. This is a one-way trip."

The catman didn't budge an inch. "*Het nolo zet na hracha.*"

Keel sighed. "Yeah. You and me both. For Prisma, then."

Keel waved his hand in front of the dry dock's access pad. It prompted him to enter a security key. Using a Dark Ops master pass designed to open all Republic ships, Keel entered the code.

After a moment, the pad chimed, and the *ka-chunk* of the magnetic and physical locks echoed down the corridor. Keel looked from side to side, expecting to see Cybar war machines pour in from both directions. But none were to be found.

He turned to address Skrizz, and found that the catman had disappeared. He shook his head. "Wobanki. Make up your mind."

The interior of *Deluvia* was absolute blackness. No lights came on. Keel activated the ultrabeam built into his bucket and stepped inside.

He stood on a typical on-ramp for personnel use. Lifts were lined up at the far wall—some for people, others for gear and freight. Old-fashioned ladders and stairways went up and down into the inky darkness, waiting to be used in the event of a power failure. A number of signs provided directions to the various sections of the ship. The curious part of Keel wanted to follow the signs to the bridge to see if he could find out what happened on this ship once, long ago. But the legionnaire part of him had a mission to complete.

He began descending the stairs toward the ship's reactor core. For the *Deluvia* to be powering this massive ship around it—as strange as that sounded—its reactor core must have been modified, expanded. It likely would have to take up the bulk of the *Deluvia* itself. Keel hoped that meant he wouldn't have to travel much longer.

An incoming comm chime sounded in Keel's bucket. It sounded almost too loud in the absolute still darkness of this forgotten ship. But the identifier was friendly—and unexpected. It was the *Indelible VI.* Or at least it said it was. A race spawned from a malevolent, awakened AI would likely have the ability to take control of comms. And if they could create replicants...

He would remain wary.

"Go for Wraith." He sounded all business. Entirely neutral. No concern, no optimism.

"Captain Keel. Er, I mean Wraith." It was Garret. Or a convincing impersonation of him. But again, when dealing with a self-aware AI, how hard would it really be to synthesize an organic's voice?

"Identify yourself," Keel said.

"It's me, Garret."

"I don't know a Garret. Get off this channel."

Keel was interested in the response. This would be where a machine might get tripped up.

Might.

"Yes, you do." Garret sounded wounded. That was a good sign. "Garret. I'm... I'm the coder. We're friends."

Keel wouldn't exactly put it *that* way. But he was satisfied with the reply. "I remember you."

"Good. Because I don't know what to do next."

"What do you mean by that? Do whatever Ravi says."

"That's the thing... he left."

"He left?" Keel almost shouted.

"Yeah. Once everybody made it back to the ship, he told Bombassa that he was going to go find you."

Great. This is what having a navigator with a conscience does for you.

Keel had been counting on Ravi getting everyone to safety. Well, it would just have to be someone else. "Leenah can fly the ship in a pinch. Tell her to get out of here as soon as Skrizz shows up. He's on his way." *I think.* "Should be a few more minutes with as fast as the cat moves."

"I don't think she'll do that."

"She's gonna have to," Keel said, moving farther into the blackness of the ship. "And I need you to do something else for me."

"What?"

"Tell me what you know about the *Deluvia*."

There was a pause. "I don't know. I mean, I guess I know as much as anyone else. I went through a phase, around when I was about twelve, when I really got into ghost stories. Unconfirmed paranormal sightings, things like that. So yeah, the *Deluvia*, I researched it a lot, especially about the supposed missing footage. But there really isn't much to know. I'm sure you know as much as I do. Why are you interested in the *Deluvia*?"

"Because I'm standing inside it right now. It's right at the center of this Cybar death trap—Skrizz thinks it serves as the reactor for the whole shebang. I was just wondering if your little forays into the AI's databanks told you anything. Maybe give you a clue about why this ship would be built around some old ghost story."

"That's... incredible," Garret said. He paused. "Hang on..." Keel could hear the code slicer's fingers tapping on a display. "So, as you know, I've had a lot of time to explore the Cybar system, and I've encountered a lot of references to something called *mother*. Whatever it is, it's held in high regard. At first I thought it was some part of the AI, or some process, but then I encountered a reference that referred to it spatially. Like mother is physically at the center of the ship."

Keel had reached a lightless stairway landing. "Yeah, well, I can't say for sure, but I feel like I'm pretty close to the center."

"So... do you think maybe *mother* is the *Deluvia*? I mean, it's a pretty big leap, but..."

"Could be," Keel said, still making his way down toward the reactor. This was just casual conversation. Small talk to pass the time until he knew that everyone would be leaving safely. In the end, it didn't matter why the *Deluvia* was here. Keel was going to blow it all up. And himself with it.

Still, he was curious.

"But if it *is* important to them," Keel said, thinking out loud, "then how come there's nothing here to guard it? I mean, I needed a Dark Ops passkey, but otherwise I just walked right in."

Garret's tone grew serious. "Just because you don't see something doesn't mean it's not there. Which is why you should get out of there. I shut down a lot of the ship's defense capabilities, but it's a constant battle with CRONUS for the upper hand. And if you trip a trigger protocol, that'll automatically give CRONUS more power. I feel like stabbing at the heart of the ship—at *mother*—might qualify as a trigger."

"Relax," Keel said dismissively.

Ravi's voice came from the darkness. "Garret is right."

Keel jumped. "You almost gave me a heart attack."

"Yes, I am sorry for doing this. But you understand how it is. One does not know you are standing there, and so you wait, but they keep talking and still don't know, and then it becomes awkward and eventually you just have to say something."

Keel shook his head. "Listen, buddy, I appreciate you coming for me, but I've punched a one-way ticket to blow up this ship. You need to get back to the *Six* and get everyone out of here."

"You are blowing yourself up?"

"Figure I'd give the galaxy a two-for-one deal. Overload the reactor and take out the Cybar and me. Although I never really saw myself as much of a problem. More of a feature."

"Captain Keel, there is less than one one-hundredth of a percent chance of success in this... *plan* you have just described."

Keel swallowed. "That bad? Well. Still, I gotta do it."

"Captain Keel, do not think the desperate nature of the situation is lost on me. But I know something you do not. I have been in this galaxy for a long, long time. I have spent thousands of years trying to find a person who could bring about the turning of the tide, so to speak. For a time I thought that person might be you. But Captain Keel... it is not."

"Thanks for the vote of confidence."

"This is not an insult. I confess I am relieved it is not you who will be tasked with halting the coming darkness. It is almost surely a death sentence."

Keel didn't know whether to laugh at his navigator or bid him farewell.

"Come back with me to the ship, Captain. Before it is too late. Your purpose is not in stopping the Cybar and those who inhabit them. Your purpose is—"

Keel wanted to ask just what Ravi meant about "those who inhabit them," but their discussion was cut off by a clunk sounding in the distance. An ominous sound. Metal banging against metal.

Keel found himself nodding. "Yeah... maybe you're right. Maybe we should go ahead and get back to the ship."

"Guys," Garret said, sounding like he'd just remembered he'd left the oven on. "I don't think my code is working anymore. Either you triggered a new protocol or..." He spoke almost to himself. "Has he been toying with me? Could that...?" His voice resumed its urgency. "Point is, ship's defenses are active. *Very* active. I'm talking, very, very, very—"

"I get it," Keel snapped.

He gave a quick scan down the stairwell with his ultrabeam. Several flights beneath him, the light proved Garret was right. A swarm of bots, of all varieties, was climbing the stairs.

"Back up!" he commanded Ravi.

But as they raced back up the stairs, they encountered four man-sized combat bots, a scaled-down version of the Titans. Keel quickly shined his ultrabeam into their receptors, hoping to dazzle the sophisticated hardware, and unleashed blaster fire from one hand and bullets from the other. The man-sized bots dropped over the guardrail and tumbled into the darkness below.

But more machines were coming down from above. Many more.

Ravi swept forward like an avenging angel, slicing through their ranks, severing heads and arms. The doomed bots attempted to track him, to make some sense of what was happening, but he was a whirlwind. A ghost. He made a path through the machines, and Keel bounded eagerly through it.

At the *Deluvia*'s dry dock, light spilled in through the open portal. More bots were converging on his position, seemingly coming out of the walls. Some were on the ladders, some climbed down the stairs, and some, thankfully, were being sliced to pieces by Ravi's ethereal blade. All of them seemed to be moving slowly, though—as if they were sore. Or... old? Keel wondered how long they'd been waiting here in the heart of the ship, and whether a bot suffered from slow, creaky joints if left in storage too long.

Funny the kinds of things that popped into his head while he was fighting for his life.

He regained his focus, selecting targets and pulling triggers, sending bullets and blaster bolts into the heads of nearby bots. He never once slowed his pace. He was running like a man who'd found himself too far out at the tide change, and was trying to outrun the creeping waves.

Ravi was even faster. He continued his rampage forward, creating a mostly clear path from Keel to the *Deluvia*'s open hatch. He turned back and took on the bots that pursued Keel from behind. "Keep going!" the navigator shouted as he passed Keel by.

Keel ran, firing at the stray bots who closed in before him, wondering when the shot destined to take him down would strike him between the shoulder blades.

That shot never came. Keel approached the opening that led back into the long corridor of the Cybar ship. Years of combat told him to stop and perform a quick check of his surroundings—to not rush out this door without knowing what waited on the other side. But he had no choice. Ravi was still furiously hacking at the bots, and more were literally coming out of the walls. He had to keep going.

He holstered his blaster and tossed an ear-popper through the *Deluvia*'s open door.

And he kept running, reaching the opening only seconds after the grenade exploded. That close, the bright light was enough make him feel as though he'd stared at the sun for just a second too long, and that was even with his visor's auto-dimmer working to protect him.

In the corridor, he found three large Cybar Titans waiting in ambush. Fortunately they had been dazzled by the flashbang. He shot two of them in the head, execution style, as their servos whined and struggled to regain combat effectiveness. He aimed the slug thrower at the final bot—and heard the click of a dry fire.

Keel hurriedly reached for his blaster pistol, cursing as he drew it back from its holster. But the bot flung its arm up in a defensive posture, hitting Keel's arm and sending the blaster flying. It slid across the deck and stopped a good twenty-five meters away. Keel wonder if his radius bone was broken, even with the protection of his armor. He squeezed his fingers into a fist. Everything seemed to be working... but that hurt.

The only reason Keel wasn't already dead was that the big war bot was too close to make use of its long tri-barreled gun. That gave Keel the briefest of openings. He pulled out his backup weapon, a vibro-knife capable of cutting through just about anything, and plunged the blade into the bot. It sank down into the space between the machine's helmet and shoulders, all the way down to the weapon's hilt.

Sparks flew, and an electrical charge pulsed through Keel's arm. Warning signals on his HUD told him the suit was doing what it could to channel and ground the power surge. Rather than let go, Keel clenched the weapon harder, fishing it around, hoping to do enough damage to save his life.

The Titan wrapped a massive claw around Keel's waist and lifted him off of his feet.

"Gah!" Keel shouted in pain as the Cybar squeezed his pelvis and abdomen mercilessly. He felt like a sliph chick being crushed in its shell. Whatever impact the knife was having, it wasn't enough to slow the bot down. He started to see black spots, even as his armor pumped purified oxygen to his brain.

Things blurred. Sounds grew muffled. Keel was distantly aware of Garret's voice asking... something. Always so curious. He would miss that kid.

He would miss Ravi, too. He liked Ravi. He should have been better about telling him that.

A sudden sensation of falling reached Keel an instant before he crashed onto the deck. The pressure had abated somewhat, and he looked around, his senses slowly returning with each sip of air.

The Titan's arm still gripped his waist, but it was completely severed from the bot's body. With a grunt, Keel pried the clawed hand apart until he was able to push away its hold. He pulled in air in great gulps now, which brought on an uncontrollable coughing fit that splattered his helmet's visor with spittle. He felt the urge to vomit, which was not something he wanted to experience while wearing a bucket. He took rasping breaths until the urge subsided.

Finally, he stood and regained his bearings. The *Deluvia*'s door was shut, and Ravi stood over the destroyed Titan.

"Ravi." Keel's voice sounded rough even through his bucket's external audio. "Sometimes you're all right."

It was the best compliment he could manage.

12

Keel reloaded his slug thrower and retrieved his blaster pistol. The exterior of the *Deluvia* was as quiet as it had been when he'd first arrived with Skrizz. "Well, Ravi. Got any bright ideas on how we get out from here?"

Ravi nodded. "Yes. Fight."

Keel frowned. "Usually you tell me the odds with a statement like that."

"Usually, yes. But your species has a tendency to surrender to 'fate' in the face of overwhelming odds, so there is sometimes a strategic advantage to withholding that calculation. It can sway the likelihood of success by as much as one and a half percent."

Keel shrugged. "Even though I'm a legionnaire and you specifically know how well I do with my back to the wall?"

Ravi led Keel farther down the corridor. "Of course I include all factors in my calculations, so I have taken into consideration your particular attributes, Captain Keel."

Keel waited to see if his navigator would supply him with an actual number. The silence was telling. Keel decided he couldn't wait any longer. "Really? That bad?"

Ravi's eyes twinkled. "I will say that the odds of escaping are better than those facing you had you attempted to destroy the ship as you originally intended."

"Forget I asked."

"Technically you did not ask," Ravi said. "You hinted. This is not the same."

They came upon an exit in the corridor, on the wall opposite the *Deluvia*. Other than the door into the ghost ship, this was the first door Keel had seen in the long corridor from the moment he'd first entered it with Skrizz.

He checked both his weapons. "Well, here we go." He activated the door.

A swarm of small, spider-like bots was waiting to greet them.

Keel leveled his blaster, but Ravi pushed forward, sweeping his blade through the bots. "Through these, we must run," he said.

Hot on his navigator's heels, Keel dodged the bots that attempted to jump up on him. Ravi had once again done a remarkable job at clearing a path for him. But one spider-bot had avoided the holgram's blade. It stood in Keel's path, swaying from side to side like an athletic defender trying to halt Keel's progress. Keel kicked the bot and sent it soaring past Ravi's head. Still in mid-stride, Keel aimed his blaster pistol and shot the machine on its downward arc, sending a shower of sparks and ruined machinery to the ground.

He gave a whoop of self-admiration. "Did you see that, Ravi?"

"Yes, very impressive," said Ravi, though he sounded anything but impressed.

The corridor they ran down was unremarkable, white overhead lights shining on black floors, all going by in a blur as they ran, covering as much ground as possible. They passed a row of speedlifts, twenty on each side. For a moment, they were unimpeded, but only for a moment. At an intersection up ahead, a murderous cadre of bots, in all shapes and sizes, awaited.

"This way!" Ravi called, taking a hard turn into a crossing passage.

Keel followed the hologram as they cut left and right, taking a snaking trail of halls that seemed to him like a maze. All the while, he tried not to think about what might be chasing them.

A Titan appeared ahead in the narrow corridor they moved through, practically filling the space. Ravi didn't slow. He surged forward, slicing the machine in two.

How do you stop something like that? Keel asked himself. And then it occurred to him that he couldn't. Ravi was raging through the ship like a force outside of nature. Only a similar force could stop him—or Ravi would have to stop himself. If Ravi really was the last of his species, and this species had fled the galaxy *despite* being capable of this...? What did that say about the "black wave" that was coming?

Keel didn't have long to think about it. The bots were everywhere now. He understood now why the odds were so low. Without Ravi, he wouldn't have stood a chance of getting back to the ship.

And what if there was no ship to return to?

Keel needed to call the *Six* and let them know to wait a while longer. He ran past two nimble Cybar warriors, smaller than the Titans, perhaps two meters tall, and casually blasted one with each hand as he went by. Then he opened his comm.

"*Six*, what's your status? You still docked?"

"Wraith!" answered Garret, sounding near panic. "It's pretty crazy outside the *Six* right now. Leenah's going to get us out of here, finally. She's heading to the cockpit now. The shields failed *twice*!"

"No!" Keel shouted.

"She got them back up—"

"No, I mean, don't leave!"

"I thought you said—"

"I know what I said!" Keel followed Ravi onto a balcony that overlooked a sort of courtyard. A gilded personal admin bot stood by the balcony rails, and Keel shouldered it off—just in case. It tumbled stiffly to the ground two floors below. "Ravi and I are on our way. Don't leave without us unless you absolutely, positively have to!"

Ravi engaged a Cybar Titan that had emerged from a ceramic panel in the wall, sending maintenance bots scurrying for cover. The navigator cut off the Titan's arm, and the arm, along with its white shield, fell to the ground with a heavy clatter. Keel sent a bullet at the bot, boring a hole through its armor chest plating.

The Cybar looked down, stunned but unharmed.

Keel had meant to shoot the bot in the head. But Ravi had been standing in the way and had thrown Keel's aim off. Or that's what he told himself. He was growing tired.

He fired again, and this time his aim was true. The bot locked up with its legs bent mid-stride, tottered, and fell to the ground with a thud.

Keel continued running, clearing the machine in a single hurdle. His lungs were aching even with his suit doing all it scientifically could to keep him at peak performance. His legs didn't feel so hot, either, and there was a coppery taste in his mouth. It was probably just from the run, but he worried it was damage caused by the squeezing he'd endured outside the *Deluvia*. He couldn't say for sure, but with the pain that stabbed him with every breath, he worried a rib was cracked. This was agony, pure and simple. The likes of which he hadn't experienced since Legion Selection School.

Garret had held his tongue—he must have sensed the action, and that Keel was in no position to talk—but now he resumed the conversation. "Okay, so I tell Leenah that now you're coming and that she *shouldn't* take off?"

The sound of the *Six*'s burst turrets raged in the background as Garret spoke. Things were hot in the docking bay, positively torrid. Keel wondered just how long they could hold out.

"Right," Keel confirmed, struggling to keep his breath even. "Don't take off unless you absolutely have to. And then, when the time comes, wait another five minutes. Wraith out."

"Okay," Garret said meekly. "I'll let everybody know. Hey, is Skrizz with you? We haven't seen him yet."

Keel muted his comm and let out a sigh. What did Garret think he'd meant when he said, "Wraith out?" He needed to be focusing on running and shooting the machines that kept trying to kill him, not talking to the kid.

"Wraith, are you there?"

"He left a while before I did and I haven't seen him since," Keel panted.

"Oh, okay," Garrett said as though he were wrapping up a casual conversation with his parents. "Well, I'd better let you go."

No kidding, Keel thought to himself. This time he didn't bother with a reply. He was growing aware that his reserves were fading.

"Ravi," Keel said, resenting the level of exertion it took just to speak the name. "I can't keep this pace up forever."

The corridor they moved through appeared like so many of the others, and Keel had no idea where they were. Ravi was doing most of the work of tearing through the bots that appeared before them, but even so, each fallen bot was a new obstacle Keel needed to sidestep, spin around, or jump over.

"Yes, I understand your physical limitations, Captain. However, stopping in this situation would mean almost certain death. There will be no reprieves."

Keel didn't reply. He wouldn't use any energy unless it was to propel him forward one more step or kill the enemy. He dug deep. He KTF'd until even his fingers felt utterly fatigued and useless. When the slug thrower was out of bullets, he holstered this most useful of weapons, and jumped over another Titan. He didn't get as high as he needed to though, and he clipped his foot. He stumbled on his landing but managed to maintain his balance and keep running forward. He slammed a new charge pack into his Intec blaster pistol, leaving the empty behind.

Ravi took a hard left around a corner, and Keel followed, his fatigue sending him drifting to the right. The move saved his life, as arcs of blaster bolts soared from behind them in this crossing corridor, slamming ahead of where he'd just been.

He glanced back over his shoulder as he ran. Two squads of the smaller man-sized bots with the N-6 variants were in hot pursuit. But these were matte black. And they were fast.

Faster than Keel.

They would catch him.

"Ravi! Any more blind corners coming up?"

Ravi look back at Keel, and then to the corridor ahead of him. It seemed that he was vacillating between turning to face the pursuing attackers and pressing forward to wade through the prepared defenses standing between them and the *Indelible VI.*

Keel pulled a time-delayed charger from his webbing and cupped it in his hand.

Ravi's gaze fell on the device. "Not a corner, but the blast door ahead will work as well." Ravi nodded ahead at an open quad-paneled blast door.

Why any of the doors were working was a mystery. Keel imagined it was Garret's doing; the kid was still frantically working on their behalf. But then again, maybe it was the AI. Maybe this CRONUS was enjoying all of this.

Keel was not.

"A blast door will do," he huffed. The question was, would he be able to find the extra energy he needed to outrun the explosive's blast radius?

He activated the delayed charge with his thumb and dropped it onto the floor as though discarding a ration pouch. And then he ran until he felt as though his legs might refuse to carry his body another step. If and when that time came, Keel promised himself he would crawl.

But his legs held, and he shot through the blast door like a sprinter crossing a finish line, moving too fast to hit the brakes, having to just... keep going. And maybe continuing to run was the best move. If Ravi didn't close the door, he would need to get away from the blast or risk being cooked inside of his armor.

The charge boomed, and Keel instinctively dove, looking over his shoulder as he did. A ball of flaming havoc enveloped the matte-black Cybar operators and continued to billow forward, advancing toward the still-open blast door.

Ravi was manipulating the controls, and the door panels were closing swiftly. The flaming explosion hit the door just as it was nearly shut, and a pressurized jet of explosive fire roared through.

Keel flattened himself against the deck. The blast shot over his head, burning out in the corridor's ceiling until all that was left was thick, black smoke.

An alarm sounded, and the corridor filled with a white anti-flame chemical. The same type as in the inferno-quenchers some legionnaires carried in their kit to put out localized fires. Keel's bucket warned him of the rapidly diminishing oxygen levels outside, making him thankful for the technology in his heavily modified Dark Ops suit.

Ravi was already continuing on. "The ship is not much farther."

Maybe Ravi was telling the truth, and maybe he was just giving Keel something to keep him going. Keel was so tired and turned around, the *Six* could be the next door over and he wouldn't know it. But he decided it would be best to tell himself that the run was far from over. That he would be sprinting for miles more. That he would run until his heart exploded if that's what it took.

"I believe Garret has gained some additional control," Ravi said, sounding impressed. "He seems to have sealed off our location to the bots."

That was a good trick. It was how Victory Team had survived its mission aboard the *Pride of Ankalor*. Most of them at least. A rogue Nether Ops agent had carefully manipulated the ship's systems, allowing the kill team to save the day.

Bringing up your life's history, Keel thought, *is probably a sure sign in times like this that you're about to die.*

Another part of Keel's psyche answered, *Would that be so bad*?

He struggled to his feet just as a Titan battered through a small personnel door off to one side. He took a single shot with his blaster pistol, nearly depleting its charge pack. It worked almost as well as the slug thrower, deactivating the bot.

Ravi was busy with more of the spider-bots that had poured out of a quick-courier panel. He eviscerated the machines to the last.

Keel had killed his tens of bots, but Ravi had killed hundreds. Keel considered shaking his head in amazement, but was too tired.

They reached another blast door. The panels opened as the pair approached, and there, on the other side, was the blessed sight of the docking bay, and the *Indelible VI*.

Less welcome was the sight of all the *Six*'s weapon systems firing frantically at a slew of Cybar, which seemed to be giving the *Six*'s shields far more than they should possibly be able to handle.

Leenah must be working overtime.

"We have arrived," Ravi announced.

"I see you," Bombassa answered, and it dawned on Keel that his navigator hadn't been talking to Keel, but rather the crew of the *Six*. "I can lower the ramp, but how will you reach it before we're boarded and overrun?"

Keel and Ravi stood at their place by the blast door as unseen observers, but the ship was indeed pressed on all sides by Titans and other combat bots. The only way to it was through so many bots that even Ravi couldn't clear a big enough path. But with the bots punishing the ship's shields, something needed to be done. Now. And Keel knew what that something was.

The *Six* would need to take off.

Without him.

A roar sounded, and a concussion missile streaked away from the *Six*. Keel followed the trail of smoke to the eruption of a main battle tank that had been emerging from an adjoining bay. The tank was thrown three feet into the air, and as it landed, its burning wreck blocked the bay it had been exiting.

"Not many concussion missiles left," Bombassa growled over the comm. "We need a plan."

And then Keel had an idea. Through burning lungs, he gasped out an order. "Clear... the... deck!"

"What are you telling me?" said Bombassa.

Still wheezing from exhaustion, Keel found himself only able to repeat himself. "Clear... the deck!"

Leenah's voice filled the comm. "He's telling us to turn around and take off!"

That wasn't the entirety of what Keel was saying. Clearing the deck, in featherhead terminology, meant taking off before everyone had a chance to get clear of the repulsor thrusters. Those too slow would find themselves cleared of the deck by the force of the ship's departure. But that was only the first part of Keel's plan. They would need to come back after that.

He didn't have the time or wind in his lungs to spell it all out. He'd have to trust Leenah to see the entirety of what he meant. "Yes... do it!"

More fire was exchanged between the *Six* and the war machines as the Naseen freighter lifted gently off its landing struts and rotated until its thrusters were facing Keel and all the bots ahead of him.

Pushing his body against the wall a few feet left of the door he and Ravi had just come through, Keel braced himself.

The ship's thrusters brightened into a purified blue, and the *Indelible VI* rocketed out of the hangar bay. The backwash sent even the Titans flying backwards head over feet. Several of the machines slammed into each other at high speed, sending broken parts in Keel's direction like shrapnel. A Titan that had been right next to the *Six*'s thrusters spun like a top and flew straight through the nearby blast door, missing Keel by far too close of a margin. And then more bots flew his way. One of the smaller machines slammed into his armored thigh. It hurt so bad he had to fight the force of the repulsor-wind to look down and make sure his leg was still attached. The thin bot was destroyed, but Keel's leg appeared intact.

Buffeted by the warm repulsor wash, Keel felt his temperature increase, even as his armor attempted to counteract the effect. Thankfully the wind passed him by as quickly as it came.

He looked around.

Bots were scattered across the docking bay, hanging from catwalks or lying deactivated against the walls where they had impacted. But many of them were already slowly rising back to their feet. Keel bounced on the balls of his feet, a rush of adrenaline bringing back his energy. "You can come back any time..."

The *Indelible VI* was visible through the docking bay's shielded exit. The ship did a quick loop and then reentered the hangar, dropping its ramp and orienting itself so Keel could run aboard. Its landing struts pulverized a Titan that had been struggling to its feet.

Keel assumed Leenah was the one flying it. She handled the ship gracefully; her mechanical genius translated itself quite well to handling flight controls. He willed himself forward through sheer, stubborn determination, legs protesting with each step. He needed time to build up into a jog and then a limping run. The effects of the bot that had crashed into his armored thigh were evident. He supposed he was lucky to be walking at all.

Ravi had the luxury of feeling no fatigue. He was wreaking havoc on the bots that attempted to reinsert themselves into the battlefield. But the bots were recovering quickly, and there were soon too many for him to handle alone. It seemed the ship had an inexhaustible supply—which didn't bode well for the rest of the galaxy.

Cybar raised themselves to their full menace and sought to oppose Keel as he made his breakaway. He responded with lethal blaster shots, dropping them by the wayside. But his already-depleted charge pack was soon empty, and he had no more charge packs. Nor bullets. He felt for more grenades. None of those, either. His knife was still embedded in that Titan back at the center of the ship. He was almost completely out of options.

But he wouldn't go down until he at least found out how well the machines could take a punch.

He kicked one of the guard-model bots in its hips, and managed to topple it over. But in doing so he lost his momentum, which allowed a Titan to block his path and raise its tri-barreled N-50.

Keel felt so weak now. His strength was utterly sapped. He felt faded and slow, decrepit almost. And though he knew that he was about to fling himself at the machine in the hope that he'd escape the shots, bounce off, and then run around it—anything to stay alive—a part of him wondered whether he wouldn't be happier to just stand there and let the bot make all the pain he felt go away.

A ferocious streak of fur, claws, and predatory teeth flew in front of Keel. Skrizz. He threw his considerable size and strength into the massive Titan. The bot actually rocked backward from the impact, and it registered in Keel's mind just how dangerous the big wobanki truly was when angry.

Skrizz dug his claws deep into the bot's circuitry, tearing relentlessly at the machine's neck as Keel sprinted around the melee and headed straight for the ramp of the *Indelible VI*. He had no doubt that the nimble Skrizz would be able to extricate himself from the fight and rejoin him.

As Keel reached the ramp, he spun around to see Skrizz darting back and forth in front of the big Titan. The wobanki dexterously dodged left and right, then finally leapt high in the air, directly over the war bot and toward the *Six*.

The jump was impressive. But not impressive enough.

The Titan reached overhead as Skrizz soared, grabbing the wobanki by the ankle and slamming him back down. Keel searched for Ravi, but the navigator was occupied and must not have seen what was happening. The war bot plodded toward the stunned wobanki.

"You need a weapon," Keel told himself, looking around the ramp for something—anything—that might save Skrizz's life.

"Here." It was Prisma, and she held an N-18 long rifle, which looked comically oversized in her hands.

Keel grabbed the weapon and turned to see that Skrizz had found the wherewithal to kick the Titan's N-50 away. The war bot raised its free hand and prepared to slam it down on the prone wobanki.

The air cracked as Keel squeezed the rifle's trigger. A blaster bolt plunged directly into center mass of the Titan's great frame, putting a hole clean through it. Sparks flew as the machine froze and tumbled forward, threatening to land on top of Skrizz. But the apex killer had recovered enough to undertake a backward rolling somersault before springing to his feet and avoiding being crushed. It was all so smooth and effortless that Keel couldn't help but be impressed. Skrizz reversed his momentum and ran on all fours toward the waiting ramp.

Leenah began to take the ship up even as Skrizz loped toward it. Exo and Bombassa continued to send relentless bursts of turret fire into the bots, and somehow the *Six*'s shields glimmered and absorbed the Cybar assault.

Skrizz leapt up and landed with both feet on the ramp. He and Keel ran inside, and the captain hit the manual close, sealing the ship.

"*Tu hessa chenra Keel.*"

"Thanks," answered Keel. "But let's call it even."

Skrizz purred in gratitude.

Ravi materialized beside them. "I think it is time for us to leave."

Keel agreed. There was still some flying that needed doing, especially if starfighters were scrambled from another bay. "I think you're right."

Leenah shouted over the cockpit comm. "Will you get up here and get us out of here?"

"Yeah," Keel called back. He tossed the N-18 back to Prisma. "Glad you had that on hand," he said, running for the cockpit.

"I wanted to be ready in case they came on board!" Prisma shouted after him.

Keel smiled.

"Incoming starfighters!" Bombassa shouted. "From all over!"

Keel burst into the cockpit to find the *Six* facing a full-pitched assault force of what were probably AI-controlled starfighters. Leenah ceded the pilot's chair to Keel, who quickly dropped into his seat and squeezed his hands around the flight controls. Bombassa was controlling the weapon systems from Ravi's navigator's seat.

Ravi should be here, Keel thought.

But he wasn't, and there was no time to worry about it. He threw the ship into a sharp fork, rolling downward in tight spirals and evading a flurry of incoming blaster cannon fire. "Okay," he said to Bombassa, "I can give you targets of opportunity while I keep us from getting shot, but you have to take them the moment you see them. Don't worry about depleting charge, this baby can shoot all day and a night."

Bombassa grunted, "Yes, Ravi told me."

"Wonderful," Keel said, jinking left and providing Bombassa a perfect kill shot. "Get the nav computer working on jump coordinates. I don't care where to, just make it fast!" It occurred to him that Bombassa was probably inexperienced when it came to this part of piloting a spacecraft, so Keel added, "Actually, I *do* care where—make sure you've got safety protocols on. I don't want us to jump into the middle of a star."

The big shock trooper nodded and focused on his nav controls.

Keel's instrument panel showed nearly forty hostile starfighters inside effective firing range. Streaks of green blaster canon fire were everywhere. The shields flickered, and the ship shuddered with each glancing blow. With the beating they'd already taken, their only hope was getting out of there by making a jump to hyperspace.

Bombassa cursed and hit his nav panel.

"Don't hit her!" shouted Keel. "What does it say?"

"Failure to pre-identify transponder," Bombassa read from his display. He looked over at Keel. "What does that even mean?

Keel shot out a finger to indicate a target of opportunity racing across Bombassa's weapons screen. "Take that one down!"

Bombassa returned his attention to his burst turrets, sending blaster cannon fire just wide of two passing ships, but disintegrating a trailer starfighter.

"Nice work," Keel said. One was better than none. "The message means that you picked a Republican-controlled system that requires security clearance for entry. The typical nav won't let you jump unless you pre-broadcast a transponder so they know who you are the moment you show up."

"How do you do that?"

"Give 'em a fake transponder code from the collection?"

Bombassa looked from left to right, as if they would be on the dash itself. "Where are they?"

Keel pulled the ship up into a loop. "How 'bout we just pick another system?"

"Okay." Bombassa sounded flustered. He was as cool as anyone Keel had ever seen when it came to combat, but figuring out astronavigation while in a dogfight was a new experience, and it was showing.

Keel felt relief when Ravi appeared in the cockpit. "I can take over from here, Mr. Bombassa, and I thank you for your work."

"No arguments from me," Bombassa said, removing himself from the navigator's chair.

"Why don't you head back and take manual control of the other burst turret like Exo?" Keel suggested. "You're a hell of a shot."

"Gladly," Bombassa said, heading aft.

"Okay, where are we?" Ravi asked as he looked over his console.

"*We* were getting out of here," Keel snapped. "Where were *you*?"

"I was reviewing with Prisma her experience on the ship."

"And that couldn't have waited?"

"No. It could not." Ravi's fingers danced across his display. The *Six*'s canopy lit up again with flashes of near-misses impacting against the shield array. "How does the sanctuary in En Shakar sound? Or perhaps the Ryteer Nebula?"

"The nine hells sound fine so long as we're out of *here*!"

Ravi nodded. "En Shakar it is. We are ready."

Keel reached forward and squeezed the hyperspace controls, sending the *Six* slingshotting into hyperspace. The Cybar ship and swarming starfighters were left behind.

Safe in the folds of hyperspace, Keel leaned back in his seat, feeling completely spent. He could barely muster the energy to pull off his helmet and let it drop at his feet. His hair was soaked in sweat. "I feel terrible."

Leenah rose. "Med bay is occupied, but I'll take you to your quarters."

"That sounds nice," Keel said.

"Yes," Ravi said. "You should be inspected for any injuries you may have sustained."

"Yeah." With Leenah's help, Keel rose like an arthritic man out of his easy chair. "Just need to sleep for a few days first."

PART II

THE BATTLE FOR UTOPION

13

Seventh Fleet
Republic Naval Station
Bantaar Reef

Bantaar Reef was a maelstrom system. Long ago some runaway stellar body had smashed into several of the outer moons of the massive gas giant that watched over the Republic's premier naval station, and ever since then, time, gravity, and physics had equalized the destruction of the system into a slow dance of micro worlds and massive asteroids that formed what everyone called "The Reef."

The Republic's fleet headquarters lay inside the crescent-shaped remains of an ancient moon. Tall defense towers and sculpted imperv-isteel buildings merged into the remains of the fractured worldlets and large tidal-locked chunks of rock. Below the surface of these floating rock cities lay massive parks, gardens, and even farms twinkling from opaque domed covers. Docking ports extended their spindly boarding arms for smaller corvette-class vessels to connect, while in the distance the massive, bulbous, almost football-shaped carrier Freedom rode in slow orbit alongside the rest of its spreading escort fleet.

The augmented Seventh Fleet was the only sizable group of Repub Navy ships standing between the upstart, aggressive Black Fleet and the core systems of the Galactic Republic—including, of course, the crown jewel world that ruled the galaxy: Utopion. Where the House of Reason lay.

Control of Utopion was control, at least for the moment, of the entirety of the Galactic Republic.

And even though the current state of affairs looked bad for the House of Reason and the government of the Galactic Republic, the media and news networks were still solidly in support of a House of Reason–dominated galaxy. The rumored reports—that Republic intel services had been conducting a decade-long deception about their true number of fleets—were being suppressed as slanderous gossip. One prominent ship enthusiast, who had long maintained that the Republic did not actually have the amount of ships and fleets it claimed to have, had even been disappeared by a Nether Ops team.

Now, in the subdued lighting of the Fleet Operations conference room at Republic Intelligence Command, X sat across the table from the admiral who'd been defeated at the Battle of Tarrago: Admiral Landoo. A former protégé of X's who had gone legit had arranged this off-the-books meeting. The only people present were X, Landoo, and the compact and muscular man who'd been tapped as X's new assistant. The latter stood in the shadows behind X, quietly listening to the conversation.

"I understand," X began slowly, composing himself. He'd just slammed his flat palm down on the table. The truth was, he was losing control. Of himself, and the situation he was trying to craft.

Some voice inside his head whispered, When did you really ever have control, old boy?

And...

What was your original game anyhow?

I know what the end game is, X replied inside his own mind. Reminding himself who, exactly, was in control. He was. He still was. For the moment. He still had a few more hands to play in a game he'd started long ago.

"I understand, Admiral," he began once again. This time much more calmly. "That your fleet is ready to go head to head against the Black Fleet. But have you asked yourself what options are left to the rest of us if the outcome isn't favorable? In other words... what if you lose?"

Admiral Landoo simply stared back at the man, knowing the question was rhetorical by tone—and by the fact that they had been over this subject already.

"I will tell you what happens if you lose," continued X as though he were lecturing in some academic setting. "Utopion falls because there is no one to defend it, contrary to the House of Reason's news network campaign. We both know yours is the only fleet standing in the way of Black Fleet. And on the other hand, if, somehow, miraculously, you win... well, even then, because of what the House has done with respect to all their backdoor double-dealing with the zhee and... other interests... you will still need to fight the Legion, because Article Nineteen is still in effect and is being pursued with extreme prejudice. And battered and wounded as you no doubt will be after having faced the Black Fleet... the outcome of that second battle is not in doubt. Either way, Admiral... you will lose to someone.

"The only question left within your calculations is: where? As in, will you lose to the Black Fleet at Tarrago, keeping the terrible hardships of battle away from the House of Reason—or will you lose on Utopion's front doorstep to the Legion when they assault the capitol? The funny thing is, it matters little to anyone other than you and your fleet—because to tell you the truth, the side trying to save themselves and only themselves doesn't much care where you die. The House has already factored in your defeat, Admiral. They've already hedged their bets. They just didn't bother to tell you that before you went out to die for them."

Landoo seemed not to follow this bit.

"For whom are you fighting, really, Admiral?" said X when he saw that his arcanely masked allusions were lost on her. "The people who are busy hanging the blame for Tarrago around your neck? Or the citizens of the Republic whom you swore to defend?"

Still Landoo said nothing. Because that part, what the old man was saying, was true. She knew it, even if she didn't want to admit it. Everyone knew there was the House of Reason, and then there was the Republic—whose best interests the House of Reason was supposed to have at heart. Wasn't that really the reason why the galaxy was in the state it was in? Wasn't that the Black Fleet's core grievance? Or rather, its reason for being. Goth Sullus and his upstart Empire saw themselves as the most swift and decisive answer to all the swampy insider politics and perpetual back-scratching that allowed the powerful to stay in power.

"You have," began X, letting go of the argument that had preceded this and warming to his theme, "much more in common with the Legion than you do with our masters at the House. Honestly, Admiral, what has the Legion done, just like you and your Navy comrades, but die in a thousand foreign places trying to save the Republic from itself? And all for what? To be mostly forgotten unless the galaxy needed an object for its scorn. In which case the House of Reason was always more than willing to allow you and the Legion to take the blame for its misadventures. 'Don't be mad at the people who sent the Legion to die,' we've heard the House of Reason payroll activists and journalists opining... 'Be mad at the Legion.' And all so the members of the House of Reason can get a little bit richer off each conflict. For them to take a little bit more control with each supposed defeat. To—"

"The Legion revolted, sir!" said the admiral stridently. "They crossed the line that should not be crossed, whether they had the right to do it or not. And now they're out there wiping out whole races like they've got some divine right to be adjudicators of us all."

"They were pushed!" shouted X. His voice echoed off the dull walls of the conference room.

He caught himself. Composed himself. Leaned forward.

"They were pushed, Admiral," he said quietly. "Pushed with their backs right up against the wall to invoke something that was their right all along—and the right thing to do in the end. Let's just say this Empire, whoever they really are, and this Goth Sullus, whoever he really is, go belly up in the next few days. Just folds up shop and disappears out along the galaxy's edge like everyone wants him to. Let's just say that, Admiral. And furthermore, let's also say the Legion says, 'Oh, sorry. Our bad. Article Nineteen? Got that one wrong. Jumped the gun on wanting to hang you all as traitors and such. House of Reason is back in charge and we'll be good little boys. We won't decimate any more of the protected species who seem to be behind every bombing behind the lines, who seem to be orchestrating this week's campaign of terror that cost us a transport full of schoolchildren.' Let's just say all those things, Admiral. What then? In six months, the House will have you court-martialed for incompetence at Tarrago. Then you'll be glad for what the Legion has done. You'll only wish they'd succeeded.

"You see, Admiral, the only reason they, the masters of the House of Reason, can't court-martial you now is because somewhere in that nest of stuffed cuckoos that call themselves the House of Reason—and isn't that a joke if you ever heard one—someone knows that switching horses mid-stream is still as bad an idea as it ever was. Bad because you're the last fleet standing between the Republic and what appears to be, for all intents and purposes, a despotic tyrant. And so they're more than happy to let you go out and throw this fleet away against a superior force if it gets them a better deal in the end. Buys them some time so they can shift assets around, and hope you do enough damage that some kind of early offer of truce looks like a deal.

"I'll even stun you, Admiral. I'll say they'd actually like to see you win with your little torpedo ship strategy. That would at least allow them to stay in total control for a few days more. And what with the massive amount of credits they make on the slimmest of margins... that means a lot of money. And money is power.

"But don't hesitate for a second in thinking they won't cut a deal with this tyrant, whoever he is, to save not just their necks, but their slice of the pie. We already have back channel information at Nether Ops that this is happening as we speak."

Landoo closed her eyes, peeved. Tired of all the games. To her, flying her fleet out to meet the Black Fleet in battle was the only thing that should've mattered.

But X was right. Of course the House was betting both for her and against her.

Except it wasn't just her. They might think like that, but she did not. She was responsible for those who served alongside her. She was always betting on them. That was the sacred expectation that formed the bond between commanders and their troops.

"I won't go over the strategy with you again," Landoo began. "I took this meeting because of your past and the recommendations that came from those close to me. I said I would listen to what you had to say. And... frankly, all I'm hearing is that I still have only one choice—with two lousy outcomes. Die at Tarrago, fighting the Black Fleet as the House of Reason wishes me to, smashed against the orbital defense gun—or die facing the Legion afterward. And yes, I agree, either way I'm going to lose a lot of ships. And people."

She paused, and X took this to mean she was conceding all the points, or at least his most recent one.

"But I took an oath to defend the Republic," she continued. "Yes, we're probably going to go down in defeat to either the Black Fleet or the Legion—I get that. But I took an oath. And I'll see it through. One way or another."

"There's another way, Admiral," X whispered softly in the ensuing silence, leaning his long frame across the table at her conspiratorially.

The admiral merely rolled her eyes in tired fatigue. There was, to her, no other way. As of now.

"You took an oath to defend the Republic," X said.

Landoo nodded once.

"So did the Legion."

A door opened at the far side of the room, though the parameters of the meeting had specifically stated they were not to be interrupted. In fact, X was not even supposed to be here. He and his assistant had come by a private ship that had already jumped away.

The admiral's attaché walked quickly along the table, and X wondered if some Dark Ops team was about to storm the room and arrest them all.

Could he really trust Keller?

Should Keller trust you? replied that inner voice.

The senior naval officer whispered in the admiral's ear. Her eyes went cold. Like she was seeing some nightmare unfolding that she'd seen one too many times already. Except that it was a nightmare she'd sworn to fight with her last breath.

"Go to battle stations. Tell my shuttle to stand by for departure back to the carrier."

The aide left the room.

Admiral Landoo turned her chair so she could look out at the starfield. In the distance they could see the bright sudden star flares of inbound jump signatures.

"It seems that the Black Fleet has chosen to engage us here, now. Which seems to make everything we've discussed irrelevant."

Across the station—and of course across all the stations within the Bantaar Reef Naval Base, and across all the decks of all the ships of the mighty Seventh Fleet—battle stations was being sounded. Crew were racing to their stations. Pilots to their ships. The whole of them would go out to give battle, even if the outcome was meaningless in the grand scheme of things. Perhaps none of them felt the way the admiral did. Perhaps they still believed there was a chance to win. Somehow. Some way.

The admiral gathered up her tablet and made to leave.

X caught her by the arm.

"We can beat them, Admiral. But not here. Not now. With the Legion's ships, and the Legion itself, we can meet Sullus in a winner-take-all battle."

The admiral snorted, and her eyes showed naked contempt for X.

"Winner take all... listen to yourself. It's like some game to you, whoever you really are. Well, let me tell you. I lost twelve ships at Tarrago. It's no game. It certainly wasn't to the dead. And as far as the Legion is concerned, the last time I checked, they were at war with us. The Republic. And then there's the fact that I'm a point. I heard they were rounding up all the points and shooting them. Yeah, I get it—my rise to the rank of admiral was influenced heavily by not only my connections but my gender. But that wasn't my choice. I've ignored those games and striven to be worthy as a warfighter nonetheless."

She laughed, bitterly.

"The Legion wouldn't have anything to do with me."

The call to battle stations was rising. Deflectors were shimmering to life across the fleet. In moments the Interceptors would lift off the decks and race out to meet the inbound Black Fleet. Soon, many of the living would be marked down as the dead on some report that added them up as mere numbers.

X gestured, and his assistant stepped forward.

"May I present Major Owens of the Legion," said X. "He has come with an offer directly from Legion Commander Keller. I think you should listen to him. I believe there is another way through all this."

14

Audacity
Seventh Fleet Arrival Docks
Bantaar Reef

The Audacity had made port at Bantaar Reef less than six hours before the attack. Now, as klaxons sounded across the docking platform and inner hangars, Raptor crews raced to the flight line, and Repub shuttles loaded with command crew raced up toward the myriad of ships surrounding the massive carrier Freedom, the crew of the hammerhead corvette felt estranged from the impending show.

It had been a slow crawl getting here. Unsure which systems were still under Republic control, the former prisoner-of-war crew had relied on a series of indirect jumps out of Black Fleet-held space. Upon entry into the Bantaar system, inbound for approach to the Reef, Captain Desaix had sent a priority message to Admiral Landoo with details of his crew's escape and return with a new, hijacked ship—the original Audacity having been shot to pieces at the Battle of Tarrago. But in the few hours since their arrival back into the Repub Navy fold, there had been little back-and-forth between the crew of escaped prisoners of war and the armada currently readying itself to retake Tarrago.

And now battle stations were erupting.

"Guns up and targeting across all ships," announced sensor operator Jory Monccray, one of the escapees from the prisoner barracks at Tarrago.

It was Jory and Rocokizzi, a gunner's mate from one of the destroyers that had been blown to bits at Tarrago, who had painted over the ship's old Black Fleet name and re-christened it Audacity, at Desaix's instruction.

"Three Black Fleet battleships inbound, sir," Jory continued over comm from the bridge. The tension was clear in his voice.

By no one's standards was the corvette Audacity even near ready to engage in operations. Desaix and Rocokizzi were currently back in the hyperdrive containment center, putting the destabilized energy injector console back together. It had never worked the way it was supposed to. Major Thales of Repub Artillery was assisting, if only by handing them tools and new interface cards as needed. Most of the bruises Thales had received from the beating he'd taken at the hands of Black Fleet shock trooper interrogators had healed—mostly.

Desaix popped his head up out of the open well he was working in. "Put this thing back together," he said to Rocokizzi.

Rocokizzi, though a gunner's mate, had an affinity for, or rather a fascination with, taking things apart. He also had some adeptness at getting them back together.

Some.

"Deep sensors indicate they're tracking three full wings of tri-fighters inbound, sir." Jory's voice was coming over the ship's general comm and echoing around the nearly empty ship. Though the vessel generally crewed out at two hundred and fifty personnel, Desaix and his fellow former prisoners of war were operating it with only seven. In addition to Desaix, Jory, Rocokizzi, and Thales, they were also accompanied by Corporal Casso, Atumna Fal the Raptor pilot, and Jidoo Nadoori the admin and protocol officer.

Thankfully, Thales had a passion for finding out how many systems he could automate.

"Where's Atumna?" shouted Desaix as he ran shirtless up the main access passage that led to the bridge.

"She went on station to grab some food."

Smart girl, thought Desaix.

Food, throughout their long and sneaky trek through the Black Fleet-occupied systems, had been a source of constant concern. The corvette hadn't been carrying much in the way of supplies and stores when Desaix's crew hijacked her, and they had torn though rations quickly. At a stop on New Rigel, they'd actually had to hunt food and fish. The voluptuously curvy Tennar had of course gone diving, coming back with several of what they ended up calling "lobstrosities"—a local three-clawed carnivorous lobster crossed with a sea scorpion. It tasted excellent when grilled and served with a local heavy cream butter that hinted at sage and mesquite. But that had been their only good meal of late, and this was particularly difficult on the Tennar, whose high metabolism put her in a state of near-constant hunger.

So it wasn't surprising that upon arriving at Bantaar Reef Atumna had gone straight to port supply to get as much food as she could.

Desaix's only worry was whether she'd make it back to the ship now that all hell was breaking lose. What if someone recognized her as a Raptor interceptor pilot and reassigned her to some newly formed ad hoc squadron that was going up against those inbound Black Fleet battleships? Then Desaix would have lost his pilot.

And he was just getting used to the little crush she seemed to have on him.

Halfway up the corridor, Jidoo Nadoori exited the admin and protocol offices ahead of Desaix. Those offices were completely devoid of any computers, workstations, or other equipment generally required for admin and protocol types to perform their functions, but Jidoo had a single tablet, and with that she had set out to download all the forms and required paperwork that allowed a Repub starship to participate in fleet operations.

"Captain!" she shrieked. "Good news!" She seemed oblivious to the impending attack on the station. "I filed all the required forms for boarding an enemy ship of the line and transferring your flag. We are officially in the system! Now I can—"

Desaix ran right past her.

When he arrived at the bridge, he hunched over Jory's sensor station. "Show me!"

Jory ran his hands across the controls and brought up images of the three gray battleships. "They're coming in on three different approach vectors. It looks like they're trying to attack from all sides. The fleet won't be able to run. Which, as I gather from a whole bunch of panicked comm operators, was what they've been planning for weeks. Retrograde was gonna be the big trick attack. Apparently that's all out the door now."

A chime sounded, and Jory slid his chair along the row of operations stations. "Incoming message," he said, working the controls. "Comm activated."

The image of Admiral Landoo appeared. She looked like she was calling in from a transport shuttle.

"Captain Desaix. I don't have time for pleasantries, but I'm glad you survived Tarrago and managed what I can only imagine was a rather daring escape. The crew of the Freedom owe you their lives. You'll have to tell me all about it sometime—if there is a next time when which we meet.

"Switching to the business at hand. I'm attaching your ship to a Nether Ops representative who is headed your way as we speak. You are to get him out of here at all costs and take him where he wants to go. His mission is vital to the safety of the Republic, and I'm putting your ship and crew at his disposal."

Desaix was about to respond when she added, "Landoo out."

Republic Headquarters Shuttle Deck
Bantaar Reef

As command teams and squads of marines scrambled for ships and battle stations, X trailed Owens and Landoo to her shuttle. Owens made his case as they walked, and X loomed silently over both of them, seemingly distracted, but completely involved.

The battle group surrounding the massive super-carrier Freedom was already ejecting Raptors, as well as a squadron of last-gen Lancers that had been brought out of mothball to replace the losses from Tarrago. The Lancers would serve their purpose, but scrounging up enough fighters was a secondary problem compared to scrounging up enough qualified fighter pilots. Far too many pilots had been killed at Tarrago, and still more were lost at a dozen other running battles with the Black Fleet as system after system fell. The House of Reason refused to ever cede any of their precious physical assets—every one of which some member or another had a personal stake in—without at least some military resistance, and often this involved using a fighter escort to buy time so that wealth and assets could escape. All of which led to unnecessary losses in terms of the only asset that really mattered: men.

"That's not my plan," shouted Landoo at Owens over the sudden whine of a heavy shuttle flaring for landing. They had arrived at the hangar deck, and had to wait as shuttles queued up. The deck operations officer held up three fingers at Landoo—her shuttle was apparently third in the queue—while talking over his comm. He was probably running all the shuttle traffic, which looked to require all the concentration he could handle.

"My plan to defeat the Black Fleet is what's known as a Kaufman Retrograde," Landoo said. "It's old-school ranged defense. They want our carrier bad enough, they'll try and chase her down—and the armada will run from the attack fleet while firing ranged torpedoes and extreme long-range battery fire at their lead pursuing vessel. It's death by a thousand cuts in the end. We'll wear them out as they try to catch us."

Owens shook his head, which seemed to irritate Landoo.

"Admiral, respectfully," Owens began, "I realize I'm not a naval commander, nor do I pretend to know anything about ship-to-ship warfare. But I've been in enough battles to realize that, even now, tactically, they've figured you out."

He gestured upward. Within the massive dome that rose over Central Command's busy shuttle hangar deck, giant displays provided a real-time disposition of forces via live feeds and a constantly updating tactical display. The admiral's mouth made a small 'O' as the enemy elements closed in on Bantaar Reef Naval Station from all points of the galactic compass.

"As you can see, Admiral, they're not giving your armada any one direction to run. Make for any heading, and they'll pin you down in a direct ship-to-ship engagement until they can mass their forces effectively."

X stepped forward.

"This isn't the battle, Admiral," he said. As though he were telling her her book report, or school project, just wasn't up to snuff. Instead of pointing out that she was about to kill tens of thousands of personnel in yet another loss to a foe that had defeated her once already, X merely highlighted that she had the wrong answers to the right questions.

The admiral stared at X. And X saw the horror and fear grow in her eyes as she realized she'd been outflanked from the get-go.

The Legion is right, he thought to himself. These point officers are weak. And it wasn't even their own fault. They'd been bred this way. Bred to think politically before they think tactically. To be average instead of above average. To be cautious instead of bold. To survive as opposed to kill.

And yet X knew, as every ship armed their guns and set their sights on the incoming enemy, that there just wasn't enough time to regime-change Landoo and take her fleet away from her. Good, bad, prepared, or incompetent... she was the commander of the Seventh Fleet.

"It doesn't matter," Landoo hissed. "I'm not paid to win. I'm paid to do what I'm told. And I've been ordered to engage the Black Fleet in a winner-take-all battle. Sure, it's not the way I'd fight this engagement, but few plans survive contact with the enemy."

She turned to Owens.

"That's what you legionnaires say, isn't it?"

Owens remained silent.

X spoke instead.

"With an augmented force of Legion destroyers, we can force that battle at Utopion. I can give you your winner-take-all contest, Admiral, and the Legion will fight alongside you, regardless of Article Nineteen. Their war isn't with the Repub Navy. It's with the House of Reason." He paused. "Don't throw everyone's lives away in a battle on bad ground just because someone like Orrin Kaar with no skin in the game wants to see if you can last long enough to get him a better percentage. He knows you can't win. He's just hoping you'll hurt them so badly that there'll be some kind of deal he can weasel his way into—on the other side of a starfield of smashed and broken corvettes and destroyers. "

"I..." began Landoo, then stopped, shaking her head.

Owens pressed the advantage. "Your job isn't to protect the House of Reason—as much as they might see it that way." He was giving her the straight truth, whether the point admiral liked it or not. It was too late to be anything other than genuinely, and brutally, honest. "Your job is to protect the Republic. Same as the Legion."

Landoo held up a hand, indicating she'd heard enough. Or needed a moment to think. Her shuttle was coming in.

Owens met her gaze. "General Keller assures you he will meet you at Utopion to defend the Republic to the death. You have my word, Admiral."

She opened her mouth to say something. Then closed it.

"Please," said X.

Finally, Landoo spoke. "What would you have me do?" It was less a request for instruction than it was an expression of how helpless she felt in the face of approaching destiny.

X sensed his moment and pounced.

"Jump now, Admiral. Jump away and leave Bantaar Reef. Make for Utopion and present a united front, with the Legion, against this Goth Sullus. Strike one final blow that will knock him down, mortally wounding his little upstart empire. Do that, Admiral, and we might just save the Republic. Together."

Admiral Landoo's shuttle was down. Her command team began to make their way out onto the pad. The traffic controller approached, still talking into his comm, and tapped her on the shoulder.

She stared murder into X's old rheumy eyes.

X watched her, looking for something. Then he nodded once to himself, satisfied at what he'd found.

"XO!" shouted Landoo over her back.

One of the command staff officers came over to her at a quick trot. "We're board—"

Landoo cut him off. "Recall all fighters. Tell the fleet we're jumping out. Set our destination for Utopion."

"Yes, Admiral." The XO saluted and left.

Landoo turned back to X.

"Are you coming with us? Or do we get to be killed without the pleasure of your company, old man?"

X smiled.

"I need a ship, Admiral. A fast one. Something expendable and not needed for your operations. I've got a little game I want to run on this Goth Sullus. So I'll also need a daring crew that's been in a pickle or two."

Landoo smiled with her mouth, but there was nothing but pure spite in her eyes.

"I know just the ship. Audacity just came in from Black Fleet space. She's docked at thirty-seven. I'll alert her commander."

15

Imperial Fleet
***Terror*, Third Wing Interceptor Command**
Approach to Bantaar Reef Republic Base

Lieutenant Commander Kat Haladis limped away from the digital sandbox showing the opposing forces in and around the crescent-shaped asteroid field that surrounded the massive gas giant known as Bantaar Reef, home of the Seventh Fleet's headquarters. Within the center of the crescent lay the prize: the Republican super-carrier she'd almost gotten at the Battle of Tarrago. It was surrounded by more than ninety smaller vessels, ranging from destroyers to frigates to auxiliary carriers, along with a wide array of special-duty corvettes.

Within the hour they would all be nothing more than an expanding debris field.

And she hated the thought of it. Because she wouldn't be flying, or fighting, in this battle.

The flight surgeon wouldn't clear her for duty. Until her leg could be reconstructed and cybernetically augmented, she had been relegated to command and control duties aboard the bridge of the Terror.

And so now she stood, watching. Little more than a spectator.

First Wing departed off the battleship Imperator and swept in, shooting up the outlying turret defenses along the tidally locked asteroid belt. Turret fire was heavy, but insufficient to slow the attack. Third Squadron managed to take out the reef's torpedo storage bays for a main supply depot, and the result was an apocalyptic bloom that lit up half the reef and destroyed the small planetoid that was home to Ordnance Command.

Second Wing was next to hit the naval station. Escorting the torpedo bombers in, they would try to take out the carrier escorts and their screen of Aegis-connected ships.

Republican interceptors would...

But they weren't.

They weren't coming out to engage beyond the defensive perimeter.

Kat picked up her comm. "Wolf Leader," she called, irritated because the whole left side of her body was on fire with the nerve pain that had plagued her since she'd ejected from the burning wreckage of her fighter at Tarrago.

Second Wing's flight leader came back over the comm. "Wolf Leader here."

"Wolf Leader, this is Siren Six." Siren was the designator for Terror's command team. Six was the identifier for Interceptor Operations. "Tactical says those bandits are not engaging your attack."

"Negative, Six. We're inbound and hot on the escorts. Bombers ready to drop."

"Sitrep on bandits?"

There was a pause as the signal flared and washed out in a sudden storm of static.

"Thirty seconds to release, Six. The bandits seem to be clearing jump exits and escorting shuttles. Keeping Third away from the slow movers. Repeat, they are not engaging."

Kat ached to be out there in her tri-fighter dialing in her blasters and going head-to-head against the Repub fighter pilots. Instead, forcing her face to betray none of the pain her body felt, she set down her comm and limped out into the main darkened central nexus of the battleship's Combat Information Center.

Captain Vampa, the raven-haired commander of Terror stared, hands folded, down at the massive tactical display of the unfolding conflict around Bantaar Reef. "Time to main gun range solution?" she snapped at some unseen figure in the dark.

"One minute, thirty-nine seconds."

Kat approached her commander.

"Captain," she began.

Vampa didn't turn. Instead she remained intent on the battle unfolding in miniature beneath her eyes. As though she were forcing her will to become a real thing out there in the desperate duels for firing position as pod-mounted blasters flared and enemy ships took strafing fire, responding with lethal doses of volley fire from their PDCs and aft batteries.

"Enemy bandits are not engaging, Captain."

"And...?" replied Vampa. Her voice was dry and sarcastic.

In the short time she'd served aboard Terror after returning to duty, Kat had discovered that the commander had no other setting. And yet despite Vampa's thinly veiled contempt, her crew adored her to the point of sycophancy. As did much of the fleet. Because what the captain lacked in personality, she made up for in skill. It was her maneuver at Tarrago that had put hot fire among the Seventh's destroyer screen and ruined their flank.

"And..." continued Kat, feeling suddenly self-conscious in front of this tall and beautiful woman whose body and face hadn't been ruined in combat, "I think they're not going to give battle. They're going to jump out of the system."

As an officer, it was Kat's job to deal out the tactical truth as she saw it, no matter what people thought of her or what the consequences were. The Republic played those games. Imperial officer training had beaten that out of her.

Captain Vampa turned slowly.

"That... assessment," she said coldly, "would be at odds with the overall tactical strategy Admiral Rommal has assured us the Republic will follow. Intel from General Ordo indicates they'll try to run and gun. Lure us into one of their stupid retrogrades they've been training for. Thinking we're dumb enough to play their silly little games."

"I understand, Captain," replied Kat. "But my pilots are telling me their interceptors are clearing jump exits and escorting shuttles aboard the larger ships. It looks like an exit. If they were going to retrograde on us, ma'am, their interceptors would be buying time to let the big ships put some distance between us and them."

Beyond the dark windows of the bay, out there among the Seventh, a frigate's engines ignited, causing a bright flash that looked like the time-lapsed life and death of some star not long for the galaxy.

Vampa inhaled, then breathed out sharply through her nose. She searched the woman standing before her. Obviously Kat Haladis was a capable pilot. She'd been one of the heroes of Tarrago. She'd even received a medal from the emperor himself, along with that giant shock trooper Vampa wouldn't mind getting to know. The woman did know fighter ops.

"Recommendations," said Vampa.

Kat moved toward the display and called up the sand table gesture controls. "We can move here," she said. "That would cut off the jump exit for much of the fleet. But we've got to alter course now."

Vampa had altered course at Tarrago. In so doing, she'd saved the battle—by bringing her waist guns alongside the Republic's main super-destroyer for effective broadside fire into her escorts. She'd also gotten a severe reprimand, due to the fact that Terror's deflectors had been knocked out. And she hadn't received a medal from the emperor like the girl in front of her had.

That had irritated Vampa. She was competitive, and very ambitious.

"Noted," said Vampa. She turned her back on the interceptor ops coordinator.

Kat stood, waiting for something further. But when it was clear nothing else was forthcoming from her commander, she returned, or retreated it seemed, back to the interceptor ops node.

Three minutes later, as the Imperial noose closed about the neck of Repub forces at Bantaar Reef, the Repub ships leapt away into hyperspace, darting off like bees into the nether of faster-than-light travel.

Seventh Fleet Arrival Docks
Bantaar Reef

Owens had to commandeer a heavy lift speeder to get him and X down to the docks. Already other stations were going up in sudden destruction as ghostly tri-fighters swept in across the base. But Landoo's acquiescence to X's plan had saved the day. Beyond the glass enclosures, the last of the shuttles were docking on the big ships of the Seventh, and moments later those ships were leaping away to hyperspace.

As X and Owens neared the dock where the corvette Audacity still held position, the once-busy base of Bantaar Reef seemed an abandoned place that might never be occupied again. Stores and other essentials had been discarded pell-mell by those seeking to board their ships. Owens pulled off the main passage and headed through the massive arch that led to the hangar and dock. More equipment lay scattered here, never fully loaded before the abandon station order was given. It was all such a waste. Owens felt as though he were driving through what the future of the Republic would look like if the Legion lost.

At least they left base power on, he thought. If they'd killed that, then the atmospheric force fields would have failed, and boarding the corvette would have taken a lot longer. Especially if someone had decided to depressurize the station as a parting gift.

"You're sure this is going to work?" he asked X.

X nodded and re-crossed his long legs.

"Remind me why," Owens pressed. The plan they'd hatched with Keller had gone beyond the shadowy world of Dark Ops dirty work, straight down the rabbit hole into Nether Ops insanity. But Owens was the item, and X was the salesman selling the must-have shiny.

"A war of attrition wears out the Legion a lot faster than the Republic," began X in almost scholarly tones. "All the Legion knows how to do is fight. And they do it well. But a war has so little to do with fighting and so much more to do with resources. And the House of Reason has a deep bench of players from across the Republic only far too willing to supply them with enough to wear the Legion out. Forcing a battle at Utopion gives us the chance to knock both sides out at once—and it gives the Legion a chance to fully implement Article Nineteen. It's not a great chance, no. But it's our only play as far as I can see."

Owens spotted a man guarding the cargo deck with an N-4. Even though the man had no armor, his bearing and vigilance tagged him clearly as a leej. Owens pulled up alongside, and the legionnaire hustled forward to escort them aboard.

"Corporal Casso, sir," he said, recognizing Owens and saluting.

"What're you doing here, son? Where's your unit?" Owens asked as they followed the corporal into the depths of the Audacity's hangar deck.

Casso reached a comm station and held up one finger. "Got 'em," he said. "Cleared to depart."

A moment later the portside cargo doors began to seal off the open deck.

Casso turned back to Owens. "Captured at Tarrago. Assigned to the gun. Escaped with this crazy bunch, and no one's bothered to tell me where to report. I did make sure Legion HQ knew I'd escaped, sir."

"That's fine. Things are a bit chaotic right now. Stick with me and I'll get you back in a unit."

"That's all right by me, sir. Looking forward to some trigger time. Very much so."

X cleared his throat and asked to be taken to see the captain immediately.

Beyond the cockpit windows of the bridge, tri-fighters were streaking in to strike other stations. Just as an explosion rocked the planetoid the *Audacity* was docked to, as a curvy, orange-skinned Tennar slipped past Owens, casting her doe eyes up at the powerfully built legionnaire as she slid into the pilot's seat.

"So," said Desaix. "Where are we taking you?"

"Tarrago," stated X simply.

"We're not going anywhere if I don't clear mooring lines and get a departure clearance from control," said Atumna over the din of electronic chatter.

"Tarrago?" Desaix stood between X and Owens on the flight deck, his stance suggesting complete resistance to moving the ship one parsec back toward the prison they had just escaped from. "We just came from Tarrago."

A Black Fleet bomber streaked past the bow, and a massive explosion rocked the station beyond the hangar deck.

X, as usual, wasn't having a bit of anything that didn't serve the byzantine maneuverings only he saw within his mind. "Good, then you'll be familiar with the route. I can see why the admiral selected you, dear boy. At first I thought I was being fobbed off on an under-crewed ship of the line that wasn't—most likely, mind you—going to survive escape from the system currently being overrun by that madman Goth Sullus and his bunch. So wheels up, Captain, or whatever it is that you do to get this bucket flying in the right direction."

Desaix also wasn't having any of it.

"Why, exactly, would we want to go back to the prison planet of that... madman, as you call him? Just so you know, the original Audacity was blown out from under me at Tarrago. We... uh... requisitioned this one," Desaix added with a hint of pride.

"We stole it!" said Atumna. "Classic combat hijack. Like in the movies!"

Beyond the cockpit window, fires engulfed a turret battery. A moment later it detonated in spectacular fashion. Across the comm screen and the front HUD projection, words in big block ghostly projection appeared: "Catastrophic Breach in Progress. Abandon Station. Abandon Station. Abandon Station."

"Need to disconnect now! Seriously," cried Atumna as the vibration of the explosion shook the Audacity's violently.

"Disconnect now. Take us out, Atumna!"

The Tennar's slender tentacles flew across the controls. As soon as the ship's AI gave the signal that mooring lines had been cleared, she grasped the engine control throttles and put the Audacity in motion.

Desaix slid into the co-pilot's seat and ran a systems check. He set the nav comp to begin the calc for a jump to Tarrago.

"You were about to tell me why we want to go back to that madman," he said to X as he input trajectories and selected the best possible debris-field-free jump exit points.

"Why... to talk to him, dear boy," X murmured drolly as he strapped into the navigator's chair directly behind the captain. A moment later he had his pipe out and was stoking it to life. Owens found a seat at the rear of the bridge.

"You can't smoke on a starship," Desaix muttered.

"So I've heard," said X, puffing the burnished dark wood pipe. "But you've got bigger problems to worry about than an old man and his pipe."

He was right. As the Audacity cleared Bantaar Reef's defensive perimeter, it was immediately clear that one of the big battleships was moving in to cut off the jump exit point for the under-crewed corvette.

Audacity
Bantaar Reef

The *Audacity* was a fast corvette, but she wasn't a tricked-out light freighter or blockade runner. Under impulse, she wasn't nearly as fast as the interceptors screaming past her hull as she tore away from Bantaar Reef.

"Engaging," said Rocokizzi over the ship's comm. He was down in Battery Control, running a jury-rigged fire control station that allowed him to take command of any battery on the ship while keeping the rest on auto-engage. The only problem was that auto-engage—a feature much touted by the House of Reason as an improvement that favored the high-production corvettes over their more heavily crewed capital ships—rarely managed to score a hit.

Three tri-fighter interceptors came in fast at the corvette, strafed the dorsal deflector, and ran up a line of bright fire that almost knocked out the reactor shielding. Power flickered on the bridge, and emergency damage control automation announcements sprang to monotone life with urgent warnings of impending disaster.

Desaix shut off the master control alarm systems.

Ahead the massive battleship loomed into view.

"Watch those main guns, Atumna," warned Desaix. "At this speed, we won't be able to avoid an ion shot."

"Got it, Captain. But we can't back off if we're gonna make the jump window."

X noted the harried, almost green Repub protocol and admin officer braced against the bulkhead entrance to the bridge. She looked as though she was about to say something, but then, as Atumna rolled the Audacity over on her side to avoid hitting another ship, the woman stumbled away from view, and it was clear that she was seeking some place to be privately sick.

X raised his eyebrows in a kind of mirthful satisfaction at this.

"Oh-three master portside power management bus offline," reported Jory from comm. "She's telling me we have a fire on board."

Captain Desaix looked back at Owens. "Can you handle that, Major?"

Owens nodded and stood.

A wave of tri-fighters swept in like a swarm of angry insects, blasters raking the forward deflectors. Panel warning indicators shrieked indignantly at the damage. Atumna took her hand from the engine throttles and re-routed emergency reserves to the damaged array then cranked her head over to the left to check the aft display as more fighters streaked down the length of the spindly hull.

"Watch those fighters, Rocko!" she shouted over the comm. "They're going for our engines!"

Over the bridge speakers, Rocokizzi's voice came in hollow and booming. "Well, they're in for a surprise then." Targeting sensors pitched urgently in the background, indicating the guns he was running were cycling through their loading and engagement status.

Now it seemed to X, looking placidly out from the hydra of straps he'd ensconced himself within in the navigator's chair, that the Audacity was diving in toward the forward split hull of the immense Black Fleet battleship ahead.

"I say..." began X. "You rather do drive this thing like a fighter as opposed to a ship of the line, don't you, little girl?"

"Window?" shouted Desaix.

"Still good, Captain," replied the Tennar, her entire body bent forward over her control station, her beautiful head staring at the ship ahead in fierce concentration.

A moment later the ship was racing up the length of the battleship's forward section as though it were just hundreds of feet over some technological dust-gray moon. Turrets, power domes, and other structures flew past the cockpit windows.

"Engine overload!" groaned Desaix. He stood to deal with the warning sensor indicators on the power management panels.

"Don't worry, sir!" shouted Rocokizzi over the bridge speakers. "That's just me! I dialed in a reactor pulse to confuse their targeting sensors. Power's stable. Keep drivin' on, Captain."

Beyond the cockpit windows, matte-black and gray tri-fighters raced out ahead of the suicidal corvette. Some turned, or suddenly swerved, attempting to get the corvette to break off from her track to jump, but Atumna held course. She rolled the massive ship in a full one-eighty and gave all batteries near perfect engagement windows on the tangos swarming her hull.

A deflector screen ululated its imminent collapse.

Over comm, Casso said something about the fire on deck three spreading into the aft sections.

In a monotone, the jump computer promised an impending successful solution.

Atumna whooped triumphantly as the Audacity streaked off the starboard edge of the battleship and found her window. The Tennar pushed the jump throttles full forward, and the Audacity was gone.

Bound for Tarrago.

16

Audacity
Hyperspace En Route to Tarrago

As the Audacity dashed through hyperspace, whatever repairs could be effected were made. The fire on deck three had done some damage, causing a need to re-route a few systems, but for the most part, much of what was damaged was cosmetic.

Desaix was alone on the bridge, taking dog watch, when toward dawn, X wandered in with two cups of coffee and sat down in the navigator's chair. With the help of Jidoo, Desaix had assigned the major and X officer's quarters, hoping to get them out of his way. Now it appeared the old man had sleep problems and wanted company.

Which was the last thing Desaix wanted.

The truth was, in Desaix's mind, the original Audacity had never been holed in a dozen places back at the Battle of Tarrago. In his mind, he had simply edited out the part where his original command got shot to pieces, boarded, and ultimately scuttled. He had done his best to forget being frog-marched to the brig aboard the Imperial ship in manacles.

It was humiliating. To say the least.

He knew editing all that out wasn't good. Knew he might be suffering from some kind of PTSD. But there was a war on, and there wasn't time for anything else. So... this new corvette was the Audacity. His Audacity. His ship as it always had been.

What had he really expected on return to Repub space? That was the thing that had occupied him for most of the dog watch. He'd expected...

A hero's welcome.

A plan to crush the Black Fleet.

A fight.

Instead he'd found a desperate Navy that hadn't time to reward his daring escape from Repub space—with, he might add as he flipped switches and checked systems, a captured enemy ship.

The few conversations he'd had with other officers during the six-hour layover at Bantaar Reef hadn't reassured him. Yes, there was a plan. But it was a crazy plan. Engage the Black Fleet in a running battle and wear out their flagship with ranged fire.

And even that plan never had a chance. Because then the Black Fleet had shown up, brashly coming right at the foremost military base in the Galactic Republic, converging from all points of the galactic compass. There'd been nowhere to run to.

And the armada, as it was being called, just jumped away without a fight.

These were the things he was turning over in his head when the old man came onto the bridge and sat down with a groan and a sigh. Desaix ignored him other than to murmur acceptance of the coffee. Then he'd gone back to checks.

This was the Audacity, he reminded himself once more. It was his ship. He'd fly it to hell and back. And if the Black Fleet did actually put an end to the Republic... well then... he'd just...

"You're thinking," said X, "about playing pirate if this all doesn't work out."

Desaix turned and smiled roguishly. Which was just how he smiled. This was his "caught me" smile. It was four o'clock in the morning by some ship's clock, so what was the use in hiding it?

"Yeah," he confessed. He took a sip of the coffee and gave the small "ahh" he'd never been able to break himself of. Some female marine he'd once spent a weekend with on Gamula had counted all the times he'd done it. It drove him nuts, and when it was time for them to part ways, he'd never looked back. Now, at four a.m. on a quiet, too brightly lit bridge with a possibly senile old man, he wondered where she, that marine, was. What was her part in this big fight the galaxy was fixing to have? Like some party long in the making. He wondered if she was dead or alive, perhaps making runs in a SLIC to pull wounded legionnaires out of some fight. He hadn't loved her then, but he'd thought about her now and again, wondered what had become of her. Including at four a.m. when the galaxy is catching fire and there's not a damn thing anyone can do to put it out.

"You would have liked working for me," murmured X from behind his mug as he took a drink. "We're all pirates over there."

"And where is... over there?"

"Nether Ops, dear boy. The really dark stuff."

And then X just stared at Captain Desaix like he was looking right into his soul and seeing everything. Seeing the winner who always won even if he had to cheat. The reckless gambler who couldn't afford the risks but had taken the chances anyway. And the pirate. The pirate waiting to be let out. Waiting to hoist the black flag and slit some throats.

"As it were," mumbled X, almost to himself.

Desaix asked him what he'd meant by that. But X didn't respond; he just sat quietly, occasionally humming a bit of some tune.

Finally he spoke once more.

"I know how you feel."

"Really?" asked Desaix.

"Oh, yes, quite, dear boy. You're thinking things look pretty hopeless, and you're not too keen on getting captured again. In fact, you're quite fed up with all these government games, and not for the first time are you thinking about polling the crew and possibly absconding with this ship should everything go sideways."

"Are things hopeless?" asked Desaix without meaning to.

"They certainly seem that way from the outside perspective, don't they? If you're a legionnaire captain, or a ship's captain, or any other cog in the grand system of the Republic when all the higher-up muckety-mucks are playing for the big prizes, you might just about be well and good fed up with the whole mess they've made of everything. Believe me... I've seen it on just about everyone's faces as of late. The House of Reason hasn't done a great job in the leadership department, unless you consider lining their own pockets a job well done."

He paused to take another slow sip. "This... this... Goth Sullus, as he calls himself, seems, if you listen to the propaganda coming through from the captured systems, to be all about cleaning things up and setting everything aright. At least, "aright" as he sees it. And to some... that's getting attractive. But to others... like yourself, and a certain operative I know of... Well, you might be thinking about slipping off out to the edge and doing things your way for a while."

Desaix laughed and drank his coffee. "You're crazy."

"Maybe. But it's true. You're a gambler. That's well documented. I had time to pull up your file. We looked at you when you were an ensign. Wanted to use you to go deep cover. We've had luck with other daring naval officers who find out that the navy is mostly boring unless you find yourself in a good old-fashioned showdown with this pirate king or the other of the week. But how often does that happen? Three, four times in a career?"

"I've been in a few of those kinds of engagements, and I'm not even close to cashing in yet," Desaix said. "As the old joke goes, 'What? And leave show business?'"

X laughed. He knew the joke.

"Apropos," he murmured and sipped more of his coffee.

"Well, all that sounds well and good," began Desaix, checking their track through hyperspace, "but it feels like I just signed up my crew to get captured again because my admiral, an officer I respect, told me to. So, if I were going to run off and 'play pirate,' as you say, I think taking you to Tarrago would be the last thing on my list of things to do. As a pirate, that is. So here we are. On our way to get captured once more. Happy? Whoever you are."

"You won't be captured," X said soothingly. "In fact, we'll be allowed to leave just as easily as we came."

"And how do you plan to accomplish that, old man? You some kind of hokey space wizard? Is the Republic down to the end of the bench?"

X smiled and finished his coffee.

"Indeed," he answered after a contemplative silence. "I have the most powerful magic the galaxy knows of. I can pass through walls, enter the courts of the mighty, listen to things I'm not supposed to hear, and disappear just as easily. I can even kill, if I do it with a bit of finesse."

"And what magic is that?" asked Desaix.

"Diplomatic immunity, dear boy. We come to convey a message. We will deliver that message to Goth Sullus himself, or rather I will, and then we'll leave with a reply. If you wanted to avoid the battle the Seventh and her plucky admiral may try to get herself into, well, you couldn't have picked a better space wizard to haul around the cosmos, my pirate captain."

"Easy as that?"

"Easy as that, says I, young Jim Hawkins."

But X's reference was lost on Desaix.

As *Audacity* fell from hyperspace and swam into the starfield around Tarrago, Black Fleet Approach Control demanded the ship identify herself and prepare to be boarded. X handed a special memory device to Desaix and told the captain to transmit the diplomatic orders.

"Jory, run this. And put it on screen here, too," ordered Desaix.

A moment later the official seal of the Repub diplomatic corps flashed on screen, and a QR scan code verified the transmission's authenticity. Then a recording of Senator Orrin Karr appeared.

"This is Senator Orrin Karr, House Oversight Leader on Diplomatic Affairs for the Ruling Council on Foreign Relations. I speak for the citizens of the House of Reason, and for the Galactic Republic."

In the recorded image, the senator smoothed his tunic and renewed his smile. Desaix thought the man was an obvious phony.

"This message is for His Highness..." Orrin Karr's acting ability wasn't so great at that instant. He seemed to swallow badly on the phrase, as though tasting something unpleasant. Some prize un-won. Some defeat snatched from the jaws of victory. But the hiccup was brief, and the senator recovered in grand style. "... Goth Sullus. I have sent my emissary, the bearer of this authenticated transmission, to deliver a message to the Empire. We, of the House of Reason, see which way the winds are blowing, and we would welcome the leadership of a new and dynamic ruler. We would offer our service, and guidance, in this new governorship, if only to prevent the slaughter of war with the Legion and rogue Republic military units engaging in operations against you. Though at this time all we can offer is support. Even now the Legion and all the military forces it can muster are besieging Utopion with the intent of wresting power from the duly elected, and lawful, government of the House of Reason.

"As you can see, this puts the current situation in a new light, and we hope that you, Emperor, seize this opportunity to be not the conqueror of the galaxy, but its savior. With our assistance, we can... guide you, in effect, toward a peaceful transition of power. Should you wish to discuss terms, our messenger will be able to negotiate on our behalf. Until such time as we may savor the fruits of your victory together, I remain a servant of the Republic, and a guardian of its safety."

And then the image of Orrin Karr was gone.

The transmission ended with a set of diplomatic credentials that were, in theory, supposed to guarantee safe passage of the broadcasting vessel.

Desaix shot X a look.

"'With our assistance,'" began an incredulous Atumna Fal from the controls.

"Yeah," said Jory over comm. "'For a price.' Those slimy slorgga beasts. They're cutting themselves a deal before the battle's decided."

"Generally," lectured X, "that is when one cuts a deal. Otherwise it wouldn't be a deal. It would just be asking for mercy. A weak position if there ever was one."

No one said anything after that, and Desaix turned to look at Owens. The man's mask betrayed nothing.

Sensors tracked an inbound squadron of wicked little tri-fighters coming in.

"Do I engage?" asked Rocokizzi over comm.

For a moment Desaix, who'd played many hands well, felt instead like a card being played from someone else's hand. He searched the lined face and mischievous eyes of the old man, wondering if he was the player. Or was it the man on the screen who was holding all the cards? The senator who was really just some phony angling for his own deal before everything went sideways. Playing all of them. Or was there someone beyond... all of that? Some other player who no one even knew about? Pulling the deals, flipping the red queen, calling someone's bluff while hoping that their own bluff would, for all the arcane reasons that one could imagine, never be called.

"Stand down," Desaix said to Rocko over the comm. Feels like a bluff, he told himself. It was also the only way through to the other side of this mission. "We're under diplomatic immunity."

The squadron of tri-fighters howled over the hull, pulling hard gees to set up alongside the running corvette.

"This is Guard Dog Leader," came the call over the ship's comm, broadcast across the bridge. "We have been directed to escort you to the Overlord. Back off your thrusters and set speed at half impulse. Stand down weapons. Deviate from the flight path and we will fire. I repeat... we will fire."

The approach to Tarrago was stunning. Hundreds of ships were in orbit. Weeks before, when the *Audacity* had barely escaped, there had been only the battleships and interceptors, maybe a few commandeered freighters. Now there were all manner of strange ships that defied identification specs. But what stunned the crew—what caused them to collectively gasp—was what Atumna saw first.

"Look at that!" she cried from the pilot's controls.

"Seeing it on sensors," said Jory from back in the bridge ops stations.

Only Major Thales seemed uninterested. He stepped onto the bridge, mindless of the view, and whispered something in Desaix's ear. Desaix nodded, and Thales returned to sensors.

Owens watched him work. The artillery major was running a scan on the orbital gun on Tarrago Moon. Finding out if that gun was still operational had been one of the Repub's highest intel objectives, and as far as Owens knew, no one had yet determined its status. So the major knew enough to get a good look on the off chance they might make it out of this.

But even the mystery of the orbital defense gun on Tarrago Moon paled in comparison to what lay ahead. The ship they were headed for drew the eye and dropped the jaw.

It was massive. Larger than any ship any of them had ever seen. Desaix himself had thought the battleships were like things of ancient legend from the Savage Wars. But this ship was easily four to five times the length of those already huge ships.

And it was still under construction.

It seemed to have been formed by taking two of the split-hulled triangular battleship hulls—of the standard Black Fleet design encountered so far—and joining them along the port and starboard sides of a central anchor hull that resembled the hulls of the Imperator, Terror, and Revenge, but writ large. Within this center hull section, a massive gun bore was also under construction.

As they drew closer, more details came into view. Broad sections of the hull were still un-plated, and the internal systems lay exposed within. Crews were working in there on systems that, while semi-recognizable, looked to be built of the latest innovations in design. Innovations that the Repub had killed, in favor of contracts that, as was always rumored, lined the pockets of the deciders inside the House of Reason.

"Audacity," said Guard Dog Leader. "Make for hangar fifty-one, port side approach. Back off engines at ten thousand, and we'll tow you in via docking tractor. I want those engines cold by the time we hook up, or I will fire. Repeat, I will fire. Do you read me?"

"We read," said Desaix. He nodded at Atumna, whose scowl indicated she didn't like any of this one bit. Especially the part where she didn't fly her own ship.

The engines were cut, and a moment later a powerful yet invisible force clamped down around the slender hull of the hammerhead corvette. Atumna took her hands from the controls and sighed at the docking tractor's rough handling of her ship. Then she crossed her arms and glared out the front windshield as the corvette was towed into a super-massive bay, one of many along the lower half of the ship.

"If this is a carrier," Thales said, "then it could easily hold six full wings."

Desaix reached over and lowered the gears, glaring at Atumna, who seemed not to even want to participate in the barest sense. She favored him with narrowed eyes and shook her pretty head in contempt. Desaix found himself even more attracted to the wild little fighter pilot that had become part of his crew.

"Must be the pheromones," he'd muttered to himself under his breath at times. Orange, two-tentacled Tennarian females were rumored to be rife with them. Which made them a special bounty prize out along the edge for any pirate prince looking to hack his harem to the next level.

Outside in the hangar, crack troops in black-lacquered, highly polished shock trooper armor were set up in covered firing positions, with teams staged and prepared to board as soon as the gears were on the deck.

X leaned forward.

"Well, dear boy, we're playing pirate now. Aren't we?"

17

Audacity
Within Portside Hangar Deck of Imperial Dreadnought *Overlord*
Tarrago System

As he looked out the forward cockpit window, it was clear to Desaix that the shock troopers surrounding his ship meant business. This was no formal, pass-in-review parade of legionnaires or marines. Anything they didn't like about the situation would be replied to with blaster fire.

Via deck-to-ship transmission, the crew of the Audacity were ordered to prepare the ship for search, and to disembark. "With your hands up," added the shock trooper captain overseeing boarding and search operations.

One by one, they exited through the forward boarding ramp that dropped away from the underside of the hammerhead section of the bridge. Desaix went first, followed by Atumna, then Jory, Lieutenant Nadoori, Major Thales, Rocokizzi, Corporal Casso, Owens, and X.

On the deck of the massive ship, along the inside of the outer hull, the overwhelming size of the internal sections of this new behemoth was awe-inspiring. And at the same time, it left Desaix, a veteran of spacers, uneasy. As though no ship was ever supposed to be this big.

The shock trooper captain came forward with two troopers, each at port arms with their cut-down matte-black automatic blasters. The troopers patted down the Audacity's crew, with over forty blasters covering them from all directions.

Owens told everyone to remain calm and collected. This was all to be expected.

"That's funny, whoever you are," Atumna hissed in reply. "I don't remember any kind of mission briefing covered us being captured again."

Owens remained silent.

When the search finally got to X, the old man mustered his most scholarly of airs and delivered a thorough dressing-down on this egregious violation of established diplomatic protocols.

"We are under guaranteed diplomatic immunity," he barked. "This is simply not how things are done in polite society."

"Guaranteed by whom, sir?" asked the shock trooper commander as his men continued to pat the old man down.

"The House of Reason, of course. There are universally accepted codes of conduct regarding the treatment of diplomats, of which I am one."

"Well, there's your first mistake, sir. We don't recognize the House of Reason as anything but a bunch of crooks who should be whipped, hanged, and then burned at the nearest stake, preferably remaining alive through the entire process. I see now the source of your confusion with how we do things. You think we respect you."

After the pat down, they were marched to detention. Much of the ship, or at least the small part they passed through, was still under construction. Even so, Desaix was able to see that the modern Republic warship had been put to shame. The tech here was the latest. The polish and finish were like something out of a movie about some tyrannical state that wanted spit-polish and dress-right-dress to be not just the order of the day, but the rule by which all lives were lived. For the greater good, of course.

At the detention facility, the shock troopers set force fields in place, sealing the crew of the Audacity within a single cell. Only two troopers were left behind to supervise the detainees, and they seemed to prefer doing that from a central surveillance node. Long, silent, uneasy hours passed. The detainees found platform blocks to stretch out on or spots on the floor to wear out, hoping, or not hoping, as was their wont, for something new to happen.

And at last something did. Another detachment of shock troopers came—for X and Owens. As the two men exited the detention cell, the old man turned to Desaix and his ragtag crew, and told them this: "They will release you. If we are not with you, then return to the fleet and tell them what happened." He looked at Desaix. "Or go play pirate, Captain. It may be more fun than you ever imagined."

With a smile, he was gone. The thudding of the shock troopers' boots faded, then disappeared behind some distant blast door—and the silence of detention resumed its reign.

Desaix sat down, surrendering to another long wait. Some distant part of his mind thought there should be food, but he didn't feel hungry enough to eat even if there was. And so he didn't care.

Atumna sat down next to him. "What was that about 'playing pirate'?" she asked.

"Nothing. He's just a crazy old man who thinks because he's been around so long he can see into people's minds."

Atumna slithered one delicate tentacle into his hand. Desaix could see the fear in her big, dark-brown, gold-flecked eyes. Gone was the no-holds-barred, take-no-prisoners fighter pilot.

She was scared.

"We'll get out of this," he said quietly.

"I know. It's just hard on me because of the way I'm wired. I'm... I'm..." She struggled to explain, and couldn't. And then she spoke a phrase in Tennarian. It sounded like melodious bubbles, rising to the surface of some placid sea, popping on singsong chiming notes against the call and response of a gentle surf.

And it was that simple, helpless reversion to her alien nature that reminded Desaix that the Republic, and everything it tried to be, was just a façade. Its citizens weren't all the same—try as the House of Reason might to con everyone into believing that they were. They were each wonderfully different. And there was something uniquely special about that.

"It means," Atumna said, "to disappear into the green sky."

He looked at her.

"It's our way of explaining when someone is too wild to stay in the grottos where our people live. When someone leaves the shells we call our homes to seek the deep seas, or wander the shallows of the southern islands. Or even... to live forever in the lands above. It means they're... a rover. A wanderer. A dreamer of not good dreams. And what that means to them is... not truly Tennar. An alien, even among their own. That's me. That's why I joined the navy. That's why I wanted to fly the latest and best interceptors right up against the best the galaxy had to offer. I wanted to see everything. And I always wanted to be free. In my heart, even among my people and their ways, I was..." She made that soft winsome bubble sound again. "And so I always wanted to be."

She watched him.

"Do you understand?" she asked, in a small, child-like whisper.

"I do," he said.

And then he felt her tentacle, warm and tender, and alive with electricity, wrap tighter around his hand and wrist, the tip caressing his pulse point.

"That's what he meant by playing pirate," whispered Desaix. "I have it too. You aren't alone in that."

"Good." She leaned her beautiful orange head against his jacket like a child who needs to be sheltered. And in time, calmed, she dozed peacefully. And Desaix remained the thing she leaned against, and sheltered in.

It was Admiral Ordo who met X and Owens first. He intercepted them with a detachment of his own troopers as they were escorted through the darkly gleaming corridors. In this part of the ship, construction mostly appeared to be complete. Muted blue lighting reflected off the highly polished obsidian deck, and sensors flashed dimly from stations along the walls.

The black-uniformed man stepped forward, his limp noticeable, and introduced himself. "Admiral Ordo, Imperial Intelligence," he said.

X fobbed off a made-up name.

The admiral made an overly contrived face, as if to say that he knew the charade and was intent on playing his part badly. Just to see how far the playlet could be pushed. How much disbelief could not be suspended.

The admiral and his contingent fell in step with the escort, and together they continued up the passage. Blast doors shushed open and irised shut. Owens tried to orient himself within the ship as they went.

"We checked that name out," began the limping admiral, "and it doesn't exist in any of the diplomatic records or contact archives. So... before you meet the emperor, I suggest you level with me, so we can communicate effectively. I assume you're Dark Ops?"

"Nether, to be more specific," replied X with quiet pride.

Owen bridled at this, but he didn't let it show. Nether Ops's schemes had no relationship to the good, hard work done by the Dark Ops teams. Nether was just plain crazy make it up as you go and never mind the collateral damage because there won't be anyone to blame on the other side of the mess that's been made.

But now was not the time to split hairs between intelligence services.

Ordo seemed taken aback by X's claim. "So the rumors are true," he said after a moment.

"And what rumors would those be?" asked X.

"That you guys even exist."

X thought about this. Then he answered with his usual academic tone.

"Only because we didn't kill the spreaders of such rumors."

"Tell me your offer," said Ordo, cutting to the chase. "I can support you in there, and trust me, you're going to want it. You..."

He hesitated, and this bothered X, because the man was getting more nervous the closer they got to their destination. A high-ranking military officer who'd probably been such back in the Republic... nervous. Like there was something to be afraid of just down the tracks on which this train of an operation was heading.

"You have no idea what you're dealing with," Ordo finished.

X had heard these rumors as well.

That Goth Sullus was some kind of mystic. Some ancient myth from the dark days of every culture. Some possessor of magical powers and abilities.

Some kind of boogieman. As it were.

X suspected the man might be post-human. Like the Savages. Or rather, the Savages at their secret worst that not even the general public, House of Reason, and most intel services knew anything about. No, you had to be on a special list, need-to-know access, to visit "the Site" as it was called. Its official designation, which officially did not exist, was Base 88.

Very few knew how post-human the last days of the Savage Wars had actually gotten. And X, and others, had long suspected that somewhere out there in the dark spaces between the systems, some squirters had gotten past Rechs's legionnaires and escaped out into the nepenthe of the galaxy to fester and grow somewhere else. Knowing this didn't make X feel better. In fact, he was scared. But once, long ago, he'd been a leej. The man at his side, the Legion Dark Ops major, would have been surprised to learn that. But yes, X had been a Legion Pathfinder. A long time ago, at Psydon.

So he knew what it meant to be afraid and still do the thing that needed doing. Not being afraid just meant you were stupid. And stupid got you killed. Every leej, even the ones from long ago, learned that as well as they learned to KTF.

"Thank you for the offer, Admiral," said X with his best air of nonchalance. "But the offer I bring is for one, and one only. I do look forward to working with you on the other side of this, though. That is... if everything shakes out as I suspect it will in the next few minutes."

Admiral Ordo shook his head.

"I think you have no idea what the next few minutes are about to do to your mind, and your view of the galaxy... as you think it to be."

And then the admiral and his detail peeled off from the main group and disappeared into other shadowy corridors.

Ahead lay a set of blast doors no different from the many they'd passed through already. But they felt different. Like these were the last ones that ever needed to be designed, constructed, and installed. As though they guarded some great secret most of the galaxy was never to gaze upon. As though they were the last word in barriers.

As though what lay behind them was all that needed to be known by the ever-curious busybody and master of games that was X.

He took a deep breath and followed the guards through.

Before them, in a command chair within a dark gloom, sat a figure in repose. He wore armor much like of that of the leejes of old, but finished in carbon-dusted black, and somehow alive with new tech.

The shock trooper commander kneeled.

They kneel? thought X incredulously.

"Rise," came the powerful yet calm voice within the armor. An ethereal baritone that sounded like a ghost chanting a dirge from across the moors. And yet there was an inside-the-head feeling about it. As though X was hearing it not only with his ears, but also... in some fundamentally more direct way.

And X could feel something in his mind. Something poking around. Something like an insect, like a spider, quietly yet efficiently crawling around in his brain. Investigating everything that was supposed to be hidden.

X had anticipated such an event.

He'd taken a thirty-day dose of Psychatrex just in case. The theory among the intel Mandarins of Nether Ops was that this Goth Sullus was somehow the inheritor of Savage post-human tech, or possibly even a real live blast-from-the-past Savage from one of the weirder cults that had once plagued the free peoples of the galaxy. Something like what they'd found at the Site. And Psychatrex had been proven to shut down unwanted mental investigations by the empathic races of the galaxy.

But then, thought X, as he smiled at the thought of a spider crawling around all his dark doings of the past, who really knew anything about what this "space wizard" really was? The galaxy was a strange place.

X had learned that long ago.

And there was an odd thing, X realized. That last thought hadn't totally felt all his own. More like a suggestion, or a shared comment. Or... an overheard observation from some house buyer haunting the halls of one's own home.

"I bring an offer from the House of Reason," X began.

"I'm aware of the offer," said Goth Sullus from his throne.

X tried not to think of the real plan. The one to lure Goth Sullus to his death. That wasn't the truth. That was just a dark thought someone like him might have. The real truth, X told himself, as the spider crawled along his cortex, was that he, X, had come here to sell the Legion out to the highest bidder.

"Then you are aware that when you conquer the Republic," replied X, "exterminating the resistance you will find only from the Legion, the House of Reason will welcome you as its new master, and will pledge faithful service to a new sovereign."

An electronic harrumph or snort emanated from the figure in the armor. But X was having a hard time concentrating now. The spider was like a living thing in his brain; it made his ears itch.

X recalled the time, long ago, when he was young and a legionnaire, and he sat tied to the roots of water tree in a yellow river on Psydon. Three days not moving as poisonous two-headed vipers swam past his submerged legs. He had discipline then. He would have it now.

Don't move an inch, he told himself, willing himself to restrain the desire to scratch.

"Your feeble plan..." intoned the emperor, and X could not tell if this was said aloud, or merely inside his own brain, "to hide your trap from me was... amusing, spymaster. Now. You will tell me everything."

And then X began to babble. Not just helplessly. But connivingly. Because it was all the truth. Or at least what X thought was the truth. As though he were a true believer in some insane cult where truth was whatever they decided it to be. He told the emperor everything.

Owens listened in the shadows behind X, among the shock troopers. He listened in growing horror.

His implant recorded everything that was said.

18

The Emperor's Inner Sanctum
Overlord

Owens stepped back. Two steps. Slowly. Inches at a time. Even the elite Praetorian guard of shock troopers seemed transfixed by X's willing confession. They stood in stunned silence. Many of them had probably been leejes. Once.

But to Owens none of that mattered.

What mattered was a message. A message of payback for the crimes that had been committed. The crimes Owens had just listened to as X spilled his guts to... to... the emperor.

Goth Sullus.

Owens wasn't going to wait for this Goth Sullus, this emperor, upon hearing the end of X's confession, to decide that he no longer needed the crew and passengers of the Audacity and their pathetic white flag of parley.

It still sounded like X had one more card to play. But Owens needed to make sure the message—the message of what he'd heard the old man confess—got through.

He knew his life was most likely over.

He started to think about his wife. He loved her. They'd had plans. Plans that started after the Legion.

Few plans survive contact with the enemy.

The major grabbed the nearest shock trooper within the emperor's throne room of gloom and shadows, pulled him backward, and smashed his knee in a way it wasn't meant to go. And in that one second of pain, the trooper let go of his wicked matte-black blaster. It was a weapon better than anything the Legion had been able to field in years, due to a never-ending stream of budget cuts from the House of Reason... and now it fell into Owens's hands.

He turned it effortlessly on those guarding him. He knew what to do. It was a high-tech blaster, but all blasters basically worked the same. Point and pull the trigger.

He didn't even think about shooting X. Though... in a way... wouldn't that have solved everything right there?

Keller had to know what had really been going on since before the Articles and Tarrago. Before Kublar even.

The Legion had to know that it had been used as nothing more than bait to draw out both the House of Reason and the mysterious Goth Sullus.

A message had to get through.

Owens ran through the shadowy dark of the emperor's inner sanctum, chased by the hot streak of bolt fire.

He had a blaster and a twenty steps' lead.

No matter what, the message had to get through.

It wasn't easy for Owens to lose the detachment of shock troopers, but his mind had been working the game of escape and evasion ever since he'd seen the size of the ship they were about to board. Maybe even before that.

When?

When the mission seemingly hatched between X and Keller started?

He had distrusted the creature known as X from the start.

As a Legion Dark Ops officer, his E&E skills were the best. Escape and evasion. Owens knew exactly what to do in the next few seconds. Put as much distance between him and his pursuers as possible. Slow them down by making them learn to be more cautious in their pursuit.

In other words, he would make them afraid. And once they were afraid, they'd slow, whether they liked it or not. And then, hopefully, he could lose them.

The first ambush he set up for them wasn't more than three hundred meters from where he'd left the shock trooper with the busted knee that would never work again unless it was completely rebuilt. Owens had noted this location on the way to the meeting with Goth Sullus. A dark access off the main passage led into a portion of the deck that was still under construction.

He ran full tilt, legs and arms pumping, unarmored, to the spot he'd selected. And he knew that they knew that this was where he was making for. They'd think he planned to use the twilight-lit decks and chaotic dishevel of the unfinished systems and installs as an egress into a maze he might lose them in. Therefore, it was vital to capture him now.

That's what the shock troopers would be thinking. There was no telling where he might go once he was in there.

So of course, they had no idea that he'd set up a kill zone just beyond the opening where a blast door would one day actually control access.

Owens missed with the first shot, striking the ceiling with a spray of sparks as the bolt smashed into the impervisteel. The weapon was more powerful than he was accustomed to, and it actually bucked on trigger pull. The part of Owens's brain that had been pulling triggers for fifteen years, professionally, processed this information and made the necessary adjustments.

His next two shots smashed into the chest plates of the first two troopers to breach the entrance. One went down on his back, his armor smoking. The other fell to his knees and then went face forward.

The rest, Owens knew, would hold up and figure out how to pin him down. Toss bangers in and come for him, probably. But Owens had already moved on. He was gliding past power cores yet to be installed and conduit micro-cables coiled in bundles, and stepping over places in the deck where the plating had been pulled up in the service of some install. Halfway across the skeletal maze he spied something that gave him an idea.

It was like any one of the other dark pits where deck plating had been pulled up. He slid to his belly, heard the first banger go off in the distance, and crawled head first down into the darkness below.

The hard metallic clack of the shock troopers' boots, many of them, came rushing toward him. He couldn't know what their leader would be telling them now to organize a search protocol—but most likely, given the sprawling expanse of the gloomy deck, they'd spread out. Make contact. Pin him down. And rush him.

Owens waited down there in the darkness, listening as they drew closer, wondering if their leader was telling them to check the exposed deck plating. He didn't hear anyone speaking; they must've had some kind of L-comm.

He held his breath as they passed overhead. He was sure their chatter was alive with search orders, threats, and clearance confirmations, but without access to their comm, to Owens they were like a passage of ghostly knights, all linked to some hive mind of ancient purpose that would remain arcane unless one knew their history, understood the reasons for their nightly march.

Owens had studied Savage history. And that medieval time of the galaxy always popped into his mind at the strangest of moments, providing allegory and context in a way that made him understand situations a little better. But he didn't talk about it anymore. The few times he'd tried to bring up such references professionally, the legionnaire on the receiving end of the discussion had stared at him like he was some crazed intellectual who'd devolved so far down into the academic he was all but unintelligible. So Owens had stopped actively using such allusions and just kept his thoughts to himself.

The dark armored troopers moved beyond his hole, and were now heading deeper into the deck. Still he waited. He listened to the cadence of their boots like it was some musical piece. He felt its rhythms, waited for the false note to strike. Listened for that one pair of boots that stopped and held its ground.

And there it was.

He tried to place where it had come from.

He couldn't.

When he was sure the other boots had moved on, he gave it another few moments.

All was still.

Down here, in the darkness, he could see the other holes in the deck above. Each was marked by a dusty shaft of light trickling downward. He studied them. Was there any one shaft of light that held a shadow that made it just a little darker? As though someone were standing near its edge?

No. There was nothing.

Controlling his muscle groups, moving like a tree snake, he slithered up to the opening and raised his eyes just above the lip of the deck. It was then that he spotted his prey—just a few meters away. One trooper had stayed behind standing beside another hole in the unfinished deck.

Just as Owens would have done, the shock troopers' leader was dropping troopers along the way to wait and see if he'd gone to ground.

"Trooper," the order would have gone. "Halt here and play Thermasloth. Watch and listen. If he comes up, start shooting. We'll come back if we hear blaster fire."

Owens descended back into the darkness. He laid the blaster down without a sound, then moved through the crawlspace in the direction of the shock trooper the patrol had left behind. Sweat ran down his forehead. It was hot down here, and his entire body was tensed, almost hovering above the deck as he tried to leave as little imprint on the physical world as possible. And when he reached the open decking space behind the trooper, he made the decision not to halt, for fear that some sixth sense on the part of his target might need just that amount of time to turn and do a back scan—and see Owens waiting down in the dark like a ghoul.

So Owens coiled and leapt upward through the deck like a trap viper from Vungalal IX. He grabbed the trooper's shoulders, yanked him backward, and dropped back into the hole like a rock. The trooper's bucket hit the edge of the exposed deck with a thud, pushing the man's head impossibly forward.

If that hadn't already broken his neck, Owens's next move, involving both hands and a wrenching twist, did the trick.

A moment later Owens had the dead man's bucket disengaged from the armor system and was stripping out the comm. Thankfully the system was detachable just like in the Legion buckets—a precaution in the event of damage to the actual protection system.

He had comm now. No HUD, but at least he could listen in on their plans.

For a little while.

When Desaix heard the blaster shot, he whipped his head around—just in time to see the second blaster shot. Both hit their targets, and both shock troopers guarding the cell fell to the polished black floor of the detention center.

Owens entered, moving quickly to the main security console. After a bit of searching, he got the force fields down, releasing them.

As Corporal Casso retrieved the blasters off the two dead men. Owens brought Desaix up to speed on the new situation. The captain was stunned that events had managed to change so dramatically in such a short space of time.

"We've got a few things going for us, Captain," said Owens, as though he were breaking down the opening situation paragraph in an op order. His eavesdropping on their comm, and a quick surveillance of their net, had allowed him to assign some certainty to his conclusions. "That shock trooper detachment and two others are the only ones aboard this monstrosity. Also, the ship's internal systems aren't operational, so they can't use scanners or incapacitation systems. Now, as for what's working against us—"

"Whoa," said Desaix, holding up his hands as though trying to halt a runaway Tybarian bull. "I thought this was a diplomatic mission. I thought—"

"Everything you knew was a lie," said Owens bluntly. "We were all pawns in that crazy old man's game. Best-case scenario, we would have been left as prisoners for the duration of the war. Worst case... he'd have had your whole crew murdered to cover things up for no good reason other than 'just in case.'"

Desaix took a moment to absorb this. Then he pivoted as effortlessly as if being a potential homicide victim was a thing he did all the time. "Right then. What's our escape plan?"

"As I was saying, Captain," continued Owens, "what's working against us is that docking tractor. It's got to be disabled or you won't be able to make the jump to light speed without tearing your ship apart. I'll handle that. I need you to follow Corporal Casso back to the ship. When you're there, I need you to jump from this system directly to Utopion and link up with Legion General Keller. I've recorded a message for him on this." Owens produced a small memory drive. "It's encrypted. That message is vital to the future of the galaxy. Deliver it at all costs. Do you understand me?"

The normally cavalier Desaix sobered quickly at the thought of something being vital to the entirety of the galaxy. He took the memory device and stuck it in one of the pockets of his flight jacket.

As the crew of the *Audacity*—led by Corporal Casso, with just two blasters between the seven of them—began their race back to the ship, a ship-wide warning klaxon began to bellow apocalyptically.

"I thought their internal systems were mostly down?" said Atumna.

"I think 'mostly' was the key word," replied a huffing Jory as they trotted down the wide gleaming white passage that led away from detention.

At the first major intersection they encountered a JL9-series heavy-duty maintenance bot installing some paneling. The bot snapped its head in their direction and chattered something in Mechanica.

Corporal Casso shot it.

"They could be using the ship's workers as sentries in lieu of a working system," explained Casso.

"KTF, Leej," replied Owens. Turning to the rest, he pointed and said, "Follow that passage back to the starboard spine. Remember that massive spar that was still exposed when we came in from the hangar? Turn right there and keep working your way back to the hangar deck. Once you're there, it's gears up and get out. I will have no way to signal you that the tractor has been disengaged, but obviously don't go to jump if it's got a tracking lock established. That means I failed."

Which means you're dead, thought Desaix. Because for you... there's no other reason why you would fail.

There would be no capture for the Dark Ops major.

"Go," ordered Owens. "That message must get through."

And then he was gone, racing off down another passage.

The escaping crew of the *Audacity* picked up their first detachment of shock troopers near the outer spar that signaled where the hulls of the massive battleships had been joined.

It was the shock troopers, and only two of them, who fired first. Jory took a hit in the thigh. He spun and screamed like he'd been stuck by a bee that had been born in an active volcano.

That was how those who'd been hit by blaster fire—grazed, really, in Jory's case—described such a wound. Jory had signed on with the navy, and bridge systems operation in particular, specifically to avoid ever being in a position to confirm or deny the accuracy of that description. At the moment he would confirm it. If he weren't so busy screaming and going into shock.

Rocokizzi and Casso returned fire while Desaix and Atumna dragged the wounded sensor operator out of the way of more return fire. Lieutenant Nadoori did her best to assess Jory's wound, applying the bare-bones medical training admin deck officers were given in the event they needed to support medical staff in a mass casualty situation. She was able to determine that there was no artery damage.

Jory alternated between swearing and crying until he finally hyperventilated and passed out. By that time Desaix and Atumna were dragging him away from the running gunfight, with Nadoori and Thales following behind. Rocko and Casso were holding off the shock troopers for now, but Desaix had no doubt they had already called in their location and requested support. Which was probably not far away.

In short, they needed to hurry.

Atumna and Desaix carried Jory between them, his head thrown back like he was already dead, as they raced for the warren of corridors that, they hoped, would eventually lead to the portside hangar deck.

"Chances they're guarding the ship, Captain?" asked Atumna with more than a little worry in her voice.

"Most likely to certainly, Lieutenant. But we'll deal with that when we get there. Keep his head up so he doesn't choke on his tongue."

A high-pitched cacophonic volley of blaster fire sounded behind them.

"This escape isn't going as smoothly as the last one," Desaix muttered.

"No," said Nadoori, who shuffled just behind the unconscious Jory.

Atumna groaned and renewed her heft of the dead weight of the comm and sensor operator.

"Careful there, don't drop him. No one gets left behind today," said Desaix.

And then he remembered Owens.

Corporal Casso came sprinting by, weapon at port arms, powerful legs pumping like he was sprinting the four forty. Rocokizzi was keeping the rear attackers busy while the corporal was moving ahead to clear the front and lead the way back to the hangar.

Desaix was certain they wouldn't reach the hangar without a fight.

Sure enough, twenty seconds later, in the massive dark tube that led to the portside hangar, Casso engaged hidden shock troopers lying in wait. All Desaix could see was the sudden bright flash of blaster fire illuminating the shadowy circumference of the passage. But when he and the others caught up to the spot, huffing and puffing, Casso stood over three dead shock troopers. He'd already relieved them of their weapons, and held them out to the others.

"Take these," said the olive-skinned legionnaire, whose devil-may-care smile never seemed to waver.

"Uh..." began Atumna with a bashful smile. "I don't think I can carry Jory and a blaster."

"Just take it, Lieutenant," said Casso, quickly yet kindly. "I'll carry him from here on out."

And with that the powerfully built, trim and compact legionnaire hoisted the unconscious Jory over his shoulder in a fireman's carry and started off down the dark tube, his blaster still held before him in his free hand.

Desaix felt a pang of jealousy as Atumna watched the muscular young corporal go. He couldn't help but notice she was biting her full lip.

Of course she likes him, he thought to himself. They're closer in age. And for the first time in his life, other than the occasional dawn in which he found himself exiting a casino during shore leave out on some fringe backwater pleasure world, Desaix felt old.

He felt like an old man in a galaxy that was made for the young.

And then he made sure everyone was moving forward together toward the ship.

Which is what old men and captains do.

Miraculously, the shock troopers never detected Owens on their comm. In fact, he even managed to hijack a comm identifier, and at one point, when the shock troopers were *this close* to closing in on the crew of the *Audacity* moments before they reached the hangar deck, he successfully ordered the troopers to pull back and take the tractor array instead. He would have preferred not to have brought more firepower against himself, but he had no doubt the enemy was already well aware of his destination—the tractor array had to be disabled for any escape to occur—so this particular bogus change of orders had the added benefit of plausibility.

Still, he was shocked when he got the two-click acknowledgments. That, he thought, was an exploitable detail. And as he raced toward his objective, he wished there was some way to communicate with Legion intel that the shock troopers didn't fully own their comm systems yet. They were still responding to a voice that carried command authority instead of cross-checking the authenticating tag that always confirmed each transmission source. Or at least that was how it worked with the Legion's L-comm. From what he could tell, the two systems were similarly designed.

But the chance that he would have an opportunity to pass along that bit of tactical intel had diminished to zero.

By his own choice.

It was to Owens's advantage that the ship was still under construction. Not only was the ship lightly crewed, and many of its security measures not yet online, but some careless shipbuilder had left out a datapad that gave Owens a detailed schematic of the ship's passages. He leveraged that to define a secondary route to the tractor array, reaching his destination after only two hostile encounters, both two-man patrols. Each time he had the element of surprise. Each time the other team didn't even have a chance to return fire.

But now, he was exactly where they knew he would be. Exactly where they knew he needed to be. For the next encounter, surprise would not be on his side.

Nor would he have cover. The tractor device's resonance chamber was a massive and silent cavern, with the array's two pole towers meeting in its center, one hanging from the stories-high ceiling above, the other erupting from the equally deep floor far below. The only access to the towers was by a slender bridge that leapt out through the mechanical-smelling void.

The truth was, Owens had no idea how to operate a tractor array. Leading a patrol, casualty management, or emplacing an N3 anti-personnel mine—these were his skills. Along with physical training, hand-to-hand combat, and marksmanship. Operating a tractor array was a naval technical skill, not a legionnaire officer command skill.

But that didn't matter now. He would figure something out... or he wouldn't.

As Owens pounded across the narrow technical bridge, blaster fire flared forward from several entrances to the massive chamber. The bolts smashed into the bridge in showers of sparks.

It was then that he realized that the last section of the bridge had been retracted. The bridge ended in space, a several-meter gap between it and the pole towers.

Owens didn't even break stride. He pushed through the blaster fire, reached the end of the bridge, and leapt.

Moments later he smashed into the side of the lower tower. He had to grab on to a control handle to prevent himself from rebounding off into the void below. But he didn't even have time to catch his breath before he felt a sharp pain in his lower back. It was a feeling he'd experienced before. Blaster fire.

Somehow he managed to slide down onto a narrow catwalk that encircled the lower pole of the resonance array. Biting down on the pain, he stumbled along the catwalk out of the troopers' line of sight. Blaster fire chased him, smashing into the array, heedless of any damage it was doing to the device. He glanced at controls and readouts that would have meant nothing to him at the best of times. And at this moment, his mind wanted only to cave in and deal with the hot fiery hand that had hit him in the lower back.

He was already losing feeling in his feet.

He leaned against the tower. Some distant part of his mind told him that he'd been hit in the kidneys. With a blaster shot, that was a death sentence. His vision blurred, and his heart raced.

He forced himself to look at the polished black surface of the control panel, where a readout flashed at him.

"Connected for test. Implosion cascade flush."

Owens knew that was one of the quirky things about these capital ship tractor beams. Only the biggest ships carried them, and even then the tech was still dangerous. Certain subspace effects, or even strong gravitational anomalies, could cause the machine to reverse itself, creating a highly dangerous situation. Instead of pulling another object to itself, the array could malfunction and pull itself into itself. In that event, the whole chamber had to be vented and both poles ejected to prevent the catastrophic destruction of the ship.

Owens felt his world begin to shrink. His entire field of vision had been reduced to a narrow circle directly in front of him. He forced his eyes wide open, as some insane thought told him that if he did so, he might see his wife one last time. And the kids.

"Not... here..." he muttered. "Not today..."

He tapped "Start Test" on the touch screen.

Above and below him, massive sections of the ship's hull irised open. They moved slowly, but the sudden storm they created inside the chamber was anything but. The internal atmosphere was sucked out into the vacuum of space beyond the hull.

Shock troopers were sucked out with them.

As was Major Ellek Owens.

"I love you..." he mumbled to his wife.

He was dead in moments.

As his body spun out into the cold and darkness, wide-eyed and sightless, both towers' explosive bolts were ignited, sending the tractor array systems away from each other and out beyond the hull.

The immense hangar deck of the *Overlord* was seized as if by some violent subterranean tremor. An apparently catastrophic explosion had sounded in a distant part of the ship, and its effects resounded through the massive superstructure.

Casso, carrying the wounded and unconscious Jory, reached the forward ramp leading up into the command bridge of the Audacity before everyone else.

Desaix was already shouting orders.

"Thales, I need you back in engineering. Check on the interface coordinator we swapped out. If it's still in the green then we go for hot start. Atumna, gear up in three minutes. Rocko, take the waist turret and keep them from boarding us."

By the time they'd all reached the ship, the first elements of the shock trooper squads were showing up and not hesitating to fire. But because the corvette was a warship, she was not as easily disabled by ground fire as the average civilian freighter.

Desaix held the boarding portal until everyone was through, then he lowered it and dogged it shut. That wouldn't prevent the shock troopers from cutting into it with tools similar to what the Legion and marines used for boarding actions, but it would slow them down.

He watched as Atumna's butt wiggled itself up the ladder to the bridge. A moment later he heard her throwing power to the systems and talking herself through the Audacity's start-up sequence.

"Don't go to full until we get the green light from Major Thales," he warned her.

"I know," she shot back down. She always knew. She knew everything. Even when she was doing the opposite of what he wanted her to do. Saying "I know" was her way of saying, "I hear you."

Yeah, it wasn't Repub Navy protocol, but neither was his ship. Not since the Battle of Tarrago.

A moment later the point defense cannons opened up on the shock troopers outside. Desaix watched from a porthole as the powerful anti-missile blasters spat out streams of tight, short blaster shots across the unfinished deck of the hangar. Troopers were cut down in groups while they foolishly tried to return fire.

The smart ones scrambled for cover first.

The next minute was tense. Blaster fire and engines whining to life. The ominous hum of the repulsors coming online as more shock troopers threw themselves into the battle.

Jidoo Nadoori was caring for Jory in the forward sick bay. Casso waited with Desaix, heavy blasters ready to defend any of the boarding stations the enemy might try to enter.

Finally, Thales came over the comm.

"Green light. Go to full power from the reactor. She can take it... or she won't. We'll find out in the next thirty seconds. That's all I can guarantee."

It wasn't much of a guarantee.

Atumna didn't need her captain's order to hot start the ship's main reactor. Slaving off the ship they were docked to, she flooded the reactor chamber with emergency power. Takeoff systems panels were lit in red... which switched to yellow. And then, one by one, they began to cycle into the green.

Atumna didn't wait for all of them to hit acceptable minimums. As soon as she had repulsors in the green, she induced power to those and got the ship off her gears. As she swung the ship about, the waist PDCs still drew lines of hot blaster fire across the internal hangar deck. Dead shock troopers lay like forgotten rag dolls as the big corvette pivoted and made to clear the Overlord.

Desaix scrambled up to the nav station. He was setting up the jump calc by the time they were beyond the hull of the dreadnought. Atumna went to full maneuver power.

Desaix was sure they'd send fighters. But with Jory out cold from painkillers and tranqs, Desaix had no one manning sensors, no one to tell him what was about to happen in near space. Or more importantly, if that tractor was operational and had target lock.

"Feeding you the calc now!" he shouted as the corvette's engines spooled up to max power, creating a tremendous hum and rattle throughout the ship. The ship groaned at its forced obedience to physics and energy.

If the Overlord's tractor array was active, then they were about to subject themselves to two unyielding forces that wanted very different things. One wanted to pull them out of here. The other wanted to hold them in place. Both at once.

They would be ripped apart.

But the tractor field was gone. When Desaix cranked his head over his right shoulder from the co-pilot's chair to look at the massive sprawl of the Overlord's surface, he saw the gaping wound in her hull where the debris trail of the tumbling tractor array pylons began.

He tried the comm.

"Major Owens?"

He said it again as he watched debris tumble like a slow ballet set in the velvet void of space. He knew there would be no answer. Owens had purchased their freedom. And died doing it.

"Stand by," said Atumna.

The fear and doubt he'd heard in her voice in their detention cell was gone. Behind the controls of a ship she was as free as she ever wanted to be. This was the real her.

Desaix looked away from the death of Major Owens.

Atumna Fal was the opposite of all that.

She was life in a galaxy of death.

And then the star field shifted, and Audacity raced away from Tarrago, heading directly for Utopion.

19

Combat Information Center
Republic Super Carrier *Freedom*

Talking via hypercomm, Admiral Landoo and Commander Keller came to a rough working arrangement that involved protecting Utopion, and the House of Reason, until the Empire's Black Fleet was defeated. While Landoo would continue to command the Seventh's Armada, Admiral Ubesk would have overall command of the Combined Fleets Task Force, with Captain Durad acting as a liaison aboard the Carrier Freedom.

Scout corvettes with long-range sensors had watched the Black Fleet depart from Bantaar Reef, leaving much of the base in ruins. The question that remained in the aftermath of the surprise attack was where would the powerful fleet strike next.

"Nether Ops is in play," said Captain Durad at the CIC staff briefing aboard Freedom. "They have a plan in motion, kicked off just before the jump from Bantaar Reef. If their operatives succeed, then we expect the Black Fleet to jump in to Utopion sensing an obtainable victory. Our hope is that Black Fleet forces, upon seeing the Legion fleet in close orbit over the capitol of Utopion, will believe that the Legion is staging a landing against the capitol in order to continue their prosecution of the House of Reason. The Seventh and her support ships will be attempting to repel the attack with ranged fire.

"When the Black Fleet finds a divided enemy at war with itself, we expect them to attempt to knock out the Legion before they can deploy on the ground. Our most conservative estimates indicate Black Fleet shock trooper numbers do not match the Legion with regard to ground combat. So obviously, taking the Legion out before they reach the surface would be seen as a top Black Fleet priority.

"As their capital ships attack, the Seventh will charge in at the Black Fleet flank, following an initial alpha strike of ship-based SSMs. The Seventh will sweep the battleships, volley fire at broadsides during that pass... and then break off to run for deep space. Hopefully this maneuver will screen the approach of the Legion's fleet. At that point the

Legion will commence boarding operations while the Seventh returns to target critical propulsion systems on the main capital ships and provide ship-based fire support to Legion units clearing the bigger ships."

"Sounds easy," said the first officer of the Freedom.

Durad wasn't fazed by this bit of graveyard humor. He continued with his matter-of-fact blow by blow of how the battle might play out.

"It won't be. But it's a plan, and we'll try to stick to it for as long as the situation requires. Stand by for coordinating changes direct from Admiral Ubesk."

"And we're not going to use the Kaufman Retrograde we've been training our entire fleet for?" asked the fleet's fire coordination officer.

"In a matter of sorts, yes, we will be," answered Durad. "The Seventh might draw a single battleship in pursuit after the initial alpha strike. Except instead of initially running, you'll present forward deflectors and charge the enemy fleet at broadsides. The ships that survive the initial attack run will then effectively be engaging in the Retrograde and firing as they retreat. We have distributed a Critical Targeting Analysis at the outset of this briefing, and we'd like your gunners to adhere to the protocols as they commence the various phases of group fire."

A moment of silence passed through the CIC. Admiral Landoo was aware that all her officers were staring at her. Checking in with her. As though asking her one last time to make sure this was the course of action they had decided upon.

A sort of mutiny.

"I know what many of you are thinking," the admiral began, not bothering to stand. Her eyes still taking in the digital sand table that showed what the battle that was supposed to take place in the next few hours might look like. Casualty estimates were at seventy-six point eight percent. Which, to an admiral who signed off on a daily crew report for her fleet, went beyond what in less desperate times she would have called "unthinkable."

Dead people. KIA. MIA. Captured. Missing.

"You're wondering," continued the admiral, "if this is the right thing to do. You're wondering how you feel about betraying the House of Reason in order to save the Republic. In other words, you don't know what to do. And you're used to being able, with the way the service has become, to collectively decide, together, through the offices of your grievance committees, micro-aggression courts, and military occupational branch representatives."

She stared down at the three battleships, digitized red. Three split-hulled triangles.

"Well," she sighed. "I don't care how you feel about it. I'm the admiral. I'm in command. This is how we save our people. If any of you wants to mutiny or charge me as being unfit for command, then now is your chance. Speak up and do it now, while we have the luxury of not being shot at."

She looked up from the digital map. She panned the entire briefing room, meeting each attendee's gaze directly.

"Make your case now," she said.

No one did.

"Then we're all in this together," concluded Admiral Landoo. "Win or lose. There is no other way this time."

Legion Fleet
Super Destroyer *Mercutio*
Utopion System

"Your job," began Colonel Speich, who was giving the briefing as Commander Keller stood nearby, "is to destroy those battleships. We don't want them captured. We don't want prisoners. This is a break their stuff mission. Each of you has an objective packet being downloaded now. Secondary and tertiary assignments will come to you via L-comm as long as we can establish traffic during the battle. The fleet will be close, so we don't see that as being a problem, but we know this *Empire* is fielding some new technology that may deny us comm in certain situations. If that does occur, just stick to the primary mission and destroy these ships.

"The Seventh will be hitting as hard as they can with SSMs and broadsides, but our intel analysis section thinks the Black Fleet PDC network is superior to what Repub fire control can deal with. In other words... the Seventh is just the bait. You are the uppercut. Our destroyers will come close, under heavy fire no doubt, in order that the assault shuttles have as little distance to cross as possible on their way to their insertion points on the battleships. Once you've breached the hull, move forward and knock out your objectives at any cost."

As was his gift, Colonel Speich ended his portion of the briefing so abruptly that none of the Legion commanders were actually sure it was over. Even Commander Keller, who had thus far appeared to be preoccupied with something else, was caught off guard. It took a cough from the colonel to prompt Keller to stand and step forward into the cone of illumination shining down on the briefing console.

The commander cleared the briefing orders, comm codes, and other data that had been on display throughout the briefing. Then he looked across the room full of Legion officers, knowing many would die in the next few hours. He nodded slightly. Barely. Making sure he fixed the faces of the dead in his mind. If only so that the someone who would order them to their death did so not lightly.

Then...

"Gentleman, you have your orders. KTF."

Black Fleet
Imperial Flagship *Imperator*
Hyperspace

"Thirty minutes, Admiral."

Rommal heard the officer telling him how far they were from exiting the jump, but his mind was already past all that. Engaged in battle around Utopion. Directing his forces. Playing every card he had. For victory. A total victory. Not one eked out in the margins of the final tally.

He looked up and smiled, barely, and the officer took this as an acknowledgment of the message. The bridge crew had learned the ways of their melancholic leader, and had adapted to suit him.

Rommal returned to his moody introspection.

This was for everything. He'd never been a card player, but in those terms, this was for all the chips. Or all the marbles as some had once said when they were children. He knew that this battle was not merely important, but that the fate of their war hinged upon it. He knew this, because the emperor himself had insisted on boarding Imperator before it jumped away for Utopion.

After the victory at Bantaar Reef, the Black Fleet had returned to orbit above the shipyards of Tarrago for rearming. As corvettes joined the battleships to form a task force, the emperor's personal shuttle had left the behemoth Overlord, still under construction, and started toward Imperator. The whispers and hushed conversations had begun immediately.

The emperor's coming aboard.

The assault on Utopion had been meticulously planned for the entire seven years the fleet had been training out there along the edge of the galaxy. It was the most planned-for event in the brief history of the Empire. But a key element of that plan had involved having Overlord in the vanguard of the fleet when the attack on Utopian occurred.

Until now. Some unexpected bit of intel had changed that plan—and moved up the timetable to attack Utopion months ahead of schedule.

"It's only come a bit sooner than I expected," whispered Rommal to the unquiet buzz of a battleship's bridge as it prepared to drop from hyperspace in the next twenty-eight minutes.

He turned his mind to his assets.

Three battleships.

Eight ex-Republican corvettes.

Three wings of tri-fighters with auxiliary support role squadrons for each.

Three divisions of shock troopers.

And of course… whispered some part of his mind that he wasn't sure was his… me. Don't forget me, Admiral Rommal.

And when he heard this voice, his mind saw the emperor.

A man—was he really just that?—who had captured the Tarrago orbital defense gun almost singlehandedly . A man of strange powers. A man people preferred to whisper about instead of mentioning out in the open.

A man who would rule the galaxy in the next few hours.

Or be responsible for all their wayward deaths.

Admiral Rommal checked the countdown clock near the combat information console.

Twenty-six minutes to go.

20

Twenty-Fourth Republic Squadron, "War Ravens"
Utopion System

Gola Ontalay, commander of the Twenty-Fourth, got the Flash Traffic message in her HUD and also projected across the cockpit of her Raptor B.

The B model of the Raptors came with an advanced power plant in both engines, a dynamic ECM warfare package, and a weapons officer riding shotgun. Gola's weapons officer, call sign Boom Boom, looked up from his instruments and waved a hand at the message.

"Got it," Gola murmured over comm. She checked her squadron's formation over her left and right shoulders. All ships were lined up and ready. As were the other squadrons and wings making up the massive strike force protecting the carrier.

"All craft, this is Raven Leader," she began. "Deep sensors are tracking three massive ships and eight smaller vessels dropping from hyperspace. This is it, boys and girls. Showtime. Follow me."

She heeled the craft over to pick up the intercept heading, and punched the burners. They needed to get out in front and reach the enemy battleships before the main fleet did. Being able to engage enemy fighters before they could be switched over to anti-SSM tactics was critical.

"I saw the footage from Tarrago," said Raven Three. "But looking at them now, the footage lied. Those things are massive!"

"Stow that, Three," ordered Gola. "Bigger they are, harder they fall."

"Fighters inbound," murmured Boom Boom over the comm. "Here they come."

Seconds later Raven Squadron was swimming through a sea of wicked scalene-deflectored tri-fighters. Raptors fired pulsed shots at the oncoming enemy, while other squadron ships either exploded from concentrated fire or crashed into incoming enemy fighters head on, the clash of forces was so thick.

Gola broke from her run through the center of the press, increased power, and climbed over the elliptic of the field. She picked up a tri-fighter running back into the battle, rolled out on its six, and opened up with both blasters for a quick kill.

"Splash one for commander," said one of Raven Squad when they saw her kill. But Gola was already tracking three closing in another squadron's wounded bird—a single Raptor, trailing vapor as it raced away from the battle. Gola's fire disrupted the formation of pursuing tri-fighters. Two broke off.

She stayed on the one still going in for the kill on the wounded Raptor.

"Handle the other two, Boom."

"Roger. Solutions green... Hawkeyes away. Hawkeyes away."

Two micro SSMs, designated ATA-9s, streaked off and raced toward the two tri-fighters, which were now trying to pick up Gola's six. Both missiles found their targets. One exploded into its target's portside deflector, sending the tri-fighter spinning off, casting debris and vapor away like some runaway comet; the other optimized its chase-engagement solution and scored a center pod kill on the tri-fighter's ion engine. That fighter vanished in a terrific starburst.

Meanwhile Gola iced the chasing tri-fighter and ordered the Raptor out of the battle.

"Negative, Raven Leader. I'm not sitting this one out," replied the pilot. And then he cut comm with her, returning to his own squadron.

Gola sighed, dialed in her squadron tactical display, saw that she'd lost three ships, and dove into the fray to help clear out the tri-fighters preventing the main attack from reaching the battleships.

"Everyone wants to be a hero today," muttered Boom Boom, not looking up from his instruments.

"Same as it ever was," sighed Gola as she smoked another tri-fighter. Four kills, and the sky was still swimming with the things. It was going to be that kind of day.

Combat Information Center
Imperial Dreadnought *Terror*
Utopion System

Kat Haladis watched the fighter engagement through her digital sandbox. She saw the maneuvers and solutions. Watched the kill and casualty counts coming in. And she burned.

"Scorpion Leader," she called into the ether of the comm. "Your wingmen need to stay with the leader. You're getting picked off. Form up! Work together!"

"Negative, negative. It's too close out here, Terror Six. Engaging..."

A moment later the comm went dead, and Kat saw the squadron leader's tag added to the casualty count.

She swore. She should be out there. Not here stuck in battle management.

"Assign the new leader and inform the squadron," she ordered the operations tech. "Order him to form up regardless of how thick it is out there."

And she knew what they were thinking. They were thinking why was she, some console jockey, telling them, actual fighter pilots, how to fly and fight at the same time.

Her smashed hip and legs were hurting. Some re-growing nerve ending screamed in sudden fiery pain.

"Heal!" she hissed through gritted teeth. And then forced herself to be of what assistance she could be during the battle. Even if it was from here, in the rear. She reminded herself that every part was important.

She just had to believe that.

Republic Super Carrier *Freedom*
Utopion System

The Seventh's Armada consisted of over seventy-eight ships, not including the massive super carrier *Freedom*. The flagship of the Republic's Navy.

Admiral Landoo turned toward the captain of the Freedom and nodded.

The captain turned to his bridge crew.

"All ahead... attack speed. Signal the fleet we're beginning our run. Hold formation all the way through."

Then he turned toward the group fire control officer.

The man was slashing his fingers across his datapad, opening up order menus and weapons release schedules for every ship.

Besides the Freedom, there were fifteen destroyers, nine of the new Champion-class light production cruisers, thirty-three destroyer escorts, and twenty-two corvettes and frigates. The fleet could field five fighter wings collectively, but those were being held back to guard the ships.

"Thirty seconds to alpha launch..." announced the group fire control officer.

"Solutions all targeting lead Black Fleet battleship identified as Imperator," cried the sensor targeting OIC from the near darkness surrounding the CIC's massive digital sand table.

"All vessels underway and at speed. Holding formation, defensive fire engagement rings reporting up and ready," said the group coordinator.

The silence wasn't a pure silence. There was still the ceaseless and incessant electronic insectile murmur of the comm traffic coming from hundreds of sections and dozens of ships across the fleet. But there was a kind of silence in the absence of direct orders and general announcements. A silence that waited on Admiral Landoo to give the final order. The one that would commit them to the action they'd planned. Instead of a running fight... they would charge directly into the flank of the enemy. For some, and maybe for all of them, it would be a kind of suicide. The most optimistic of assessments had guaranteed them casualties at well above fifty percent.

It reached the point of not being comprehensible anymore.

The average destroyer carried a crew of eight thousand. A corvette, two hundred and fifty. The carrier, ten thousand. Any lost ship meant catastrophic loss of life.

Landoo pushed that thought away. But she was glad that she'd had it. She'd seen far too many of her betters in the Admiralty order ships into harm's way for their own personal glory. Never minding the cost paid when the hull breached or the magazines went up. Or the reactor imploded and ruined the ship in an instant.

Every leader must weigh the cost of her decisions, she thought. Because nothing was for free, and today... today someone, many someones... would have to pay the ultimate price of having a Republic. Of preventing the galaxy, as it was known, from descending into tyranny and madness at the hands of the unknown.

"Fire when ready," she said, giving the order that would light the fuse. Simple. Calm. Knowing the full weight of what was about to happen.

She studied the digital table.

Her forward elements had engaged the Interceptor screen and were inflicting as many as casualties as they were taking. That was good. If the first wave of SSMs could get past the Interceptors the Black Fleet had sent out against the Republic, then there was a good chance they'd overwhelm the targeted battleships' defensive systems early on.

"Attack speed plus one," called out the officer in charge of the helm.

Now every engine in the fleet was pushing hard, racing to get in close for the next phase of the assault.

Legion Super Destroyer *Mercutio*
Utopion System

"Captain, sensors are detecting the planetary shield is active on Utopion. House of Reason has ordered a planet-wide comms block."

The captain nodded, then cast a sideways glance at Admiral Ubesk and the commander of the Legion.

Keller reached down to deliver a comms-wide message that had already been composed. All assault craft were to break off and head back toward the Legion's fleet. As though to re-board and prepare to jump from the system. But that wouldn't happen.

"Hopefully their deep scan sensors will fall for the ruse," murmured Ubesk to Commander Keller.

Keller muttered agreement.

"Reverse engines," said Ubesk. "Let's back away slowly as though we're withdrawing from planetary gun range."

Signals and Sensors passed on the message to the fleet.

Out there, beyond the massive bridge windows of the destroyer Mercutio, assault transports and dropships full of legionnaires were turning back from their landing assault on Utopion. Their bright white engines burning hot, they picked up a reverse heading—aimed straight back toward the Legion's fleet.

Imperial Flagship *Imperator*
Utopion System

"Detecting multiple launches from across the enemy carrier group. Fifty launches... fifty-five... sixty..."

The OIC in charge of deep sensors continued to reel off the number of launched SSMs until the final tally stood at one hundred and thirty-eight inbound ship-to-ship missiles.

No admiral, Imperial or Repub, had ever faced such a significant strike. Most commanders had never faced anything worse than some rogue MCR missile carrier barely capable of putting up five at once. Which was generally an easy thing for any Republican ship of the line to handle.

But a hundred and thirty-eight...

Admiral Rommal inhaled through his nose, hands clasped behind his slender back, and watched his team work.

"One minute forty-five seconds to first impact."

"Electronic warfare destabilizing their tracking signals. Confirmed tracking hack on at least six... now eight..."

"Fleet PDC up and engaging..."

Across the massive battleships the point defense cannons opened up, spending hundreds of thousands of dumb rounds into the vastness of space. Hoping to put a wall of lead between the hyper-velocity inbound missiles and the lumbering capital ships.

Before Rommal, PDC engagement "clouds" revealed themselves on the digital display. The Imperial escort group composed of the eight corvettes moved forward, their captains spooling up the main engines to speed in order to get out and ahead of the majestic battleships. They would be the second line of defense.

"Shall we get the groups up, Admiral?" asked the Interceptor wing control officer. His expression was calm, but he was betrayed by the desperation in his eyes. At this moment of pure calculation and theoretical engagement, it seemed that a battle was actually being fought. But there had yet to be fire exchanged between the fleets directly.

Rommal checked the clock that had been started to track the first wave of SSMs.

Less than a minute.

"Damage to any of the launch bays could delay things... significantly," prompted the wing coordinator.

Rommal waited. Losing any of his three wings now against the charging Republic would complicate matters when he wanted to move swiftly against the Legion's fleet, which was busy attempting to deal with Utopion. He wanted to have his fighters available to sweep in among the defenseless and slow-moving legionnaire-filled transports. That would put an end to the Legion without much of a ground war. Catching them where they were their most vulnerable would be... a prize.

"Negative," Rommal instructed the wing coordinator. "Let's hold them back. Our defensive screens should do the job."

Moments later, on the digital screen beneath his gaze, the first wave of SSMs streaked into the PDC engagement clouds.

Rommal waited as the officer turned away. He could sense, in everyone, the overwhelming fear that came with battle. Stand still when you want to run. Wait when you want to act. Follow orders whether they make sense or not. For so long, the Empire, this brilliant bold new plan to change the operating code of the galaxy, had been on the attack. And now, at this crucial moment, facing what looked like a fairly even fight... it felt as though they'd somehow been forced onto the defensive side.

There was something uncomfortable about that.

"Instruct the ion gun battery commanders to select their targets. Stand by to fire at my order."

Of the one hundred and thirty-eight missiles that entered the point defense engagement clouds, only sixty heavy SSMs survived. Streaking into their targets and spending their remaining fuel to execute a series of high-speed evasive maneuvers designed to confuse automated and non-automated defensive gunnery systems, the weapons were on track to hit their targets.

Meanwhile the ring of defensive corvettes, using captured Aegis technology hastily installed and linked, created a second defensive ring forward of the battleships. In moments their fire transformed many of the incoming SSMs into sudden explosions in the maelstrom of battle between the engaged fighter groups and the approaching Imperial battleship group.

One SSM collided with an aging Lancer smoking from engine damage on her port nacelle. It went up in an apocalyptic bloom that took out over twenty enemy and friendly Interceptors engaged in the battle between the fleets.

Twenty seconds out from the first strikes that would hit and cripple the Imperator, the main ion guns from all three battleships opened up on the charging fleet. Six shots in total.

One missed.

Three scored direct hits on corvettes. Of those, two exploded outright, disintegrating into expanding debris fields within the charging Seventh. Another cracked in half along the spine.

The two remaining shots smashed into the destroyer Marathon, collapsing her forward deflector and knocking out her reactor, and causing the ship to lose power to all systems. Emergency power was quickly brought online from the backup reactors despite a core meltdown in progress within the central power plant.

Within two minutes the captain of the Marathon was requesting permission to abandon ship. Landoo denied the request and ordered the ship to continue fighting on.

By that time, both sides were at volley range and closing for broadsides.

Republic Corvette *Simpkin*

The next volley of ion gun fire would be the last in the coordinated effort. The captain of the *Simpkin* watched a shot from the ion gun of *Terror* smash through the starboard decks of an escort frigate running targeting jamming attacks on the Imperial rangefinders. The shot continued aft into engineering, gutting much of the ship and sending debris flying away from her gouged hull. At that point the sturdy Voyager-class frigate's engines erupted, exploding outward across the racing ships of the Seventh.

"Captain," cried the Simpkin's comm. "Fleet message to continue sweep past—"

"Evasive port!" shouted the captain. Either the helm hadn't been paying attention, or they too were as stunned as he almost was watching the mesmerizing destruction of the frigate. A huge section of the frigate broke away, sending a chunk of tumbling debris right into the maneuver path of the rushing corvette.

The message from the comm officer was redundant. Of course they were continuing their pass, attempting to rake the rear deflectors of the massive Black Fleet capital ships. That had been the plan all along.

"She's gonna hit us!" cried the Simpkin's co-pilot.

Now the frigate went up in a secondary explosion as her main reactor went super-critical. Sensors and helm were blind from the proximity to EMP effects.

Ten seconds later the flaming chunk of debris that was a portion of the frigate smashed into the corvette, annihilating the bridge crew.

Imperial Flagship *Imperator*

Fifteen missiles made it through the Imperial fleet's defenses. All fifteen struck the massive warship *Imperator*.

Hits were recorded all along the beam of the portside hull of the twin-hulled vessel. Streaking in like smoking sidewinders, the mighty SSMs savaged the powerful deflectors. Following strikes hit the forward batteries and auxiliary reactor, killing hundreds instantly. And the final wave seemingly walked themselves up the bridge stack, ending with a final direct hit on the comms dome.

Imperator lurched away from her course track.

Her captain had ordered that maneuver in the seconds after he watched the main deflector go down.

"Hard a-starboard. Reverse to port now!"

Maneuver klaxons bellowed their dire elephantine warnings for all crew to secure themselves. The explosions rocking the superstructure had sent many on the bridge stumbling or outright spinning along the tilting deck. Unsecured equipment had turned into a debris tornado. On the flight deck, a tri-fighter tore away from its docking cradle and tumbled into another group. Munitions exploded, killing most of the personnel in that hangar.

"Engines!" bellowed the captain as tech stations exploded in bursts of surged energy.

Rommal stumbled toward the comms. The digital tactical table had gone dark. The captain would fight the ship. It was the admirals' job to fight the battle.

Beyond the forward bridge windows, he watched as the massive ship heeled away from the oncoming Republic fleet. Away from a mass of ships that looked like a charge from some wild desert cavalry. Ranged fire was being exchanged with the lead corvette force. But at least, thanks to the captain's quick thinking, Imperator was presenting a working deflector array.

Bridge power went down for thirty seconds.

The massive Republic armada swung past the fleet at speed, firing into every ship. One of the Imperial corvettes ruptured and died. Terror and Revenge fired at will, raking the massive destroyers guarding the carrier.

The bridge crew screamed to restore power and get back into the fight.

Below, a massive explosion rumbled through Imperator's superstructure. There was something ominous about the way the main beams groaned. Like the twin roars of some dying dinosaur, mortally wounded.

No, thought Rommal. Not now.

Republic Super Carrier *Freedom*

Ten ships were either destroyed or combat ineffective. Casualty reports were pouring in. And while the ring of destroyer escorts was attempting to shield the massive carrier from direct Black Fleet turret fire, the enemy battleships were throwing everything they had.

The destroyer Hildago took multiple hits from the two sister battleships of the wounded Imperator. The shots came in over the course of a minute. The first one found a hole in the starboard deflector array. The second smashed amidships, causing a series of small secondary explosions to erupt up through upper deck quarters and targeting sections. The third shot hit the engines, knocking out two of the giant drives with such kinetic force that the exterior nozzles for both engines came away in an explosive tumble.

The final shot targeted the bridge. As much of the bridge crew around Landoo caught their breaths, she assumed that Hildalgo's command crew was killed by that hit.

Stricken, the destroyer slowed. But she continued to fight from her waist batteries as the fleet passed close to the outer wing of Terror.

"Engineer of Hildalgo says he's scuttling, Admiral. Advising us to clear away from the blast radius."

"Best speed now," cried the captain, not bothering to wait for any particular instructions from the fleet admiral. There was only one option. Get away from the destroyer that was about to explode.

Landoo had been on the verge of dropping all fighters and making a battle of it right here and now regardless of the Legion's plans. But Interceptor shields wouldn't stand up to the blast from the catastrophic destruction of a starship. So she nodded at the captain, confirming his decision to get clear.

Revenge was now shooting directly into the carrier with as many batteries as she could bring to bear.

Ten seconds later, escape pods jettisoned from the dying Hildalgo like petals peeling away from a fiery star flower.

Kraka-boooooom!

The destroyer went up all at once. Imperator took the brunt of the damage, as she was nearest and dead in space. The newly facing fully powered deflector was smashed, and the blast wave ripped across one side of the battleship. Turrets, stores, and other important subsystems were torn away from the hull, and even much of the plating was ripped away, exposing life hab and quarters to the nuclear effects of the blast.

Imperator now looked as though she'd been KO'd on both sides of the hull forward amidships. An internal fire was out of control, and power only barely flickered to active through much of the command stack.

21

Imperial Flagship *Imperator*

As the auxiliary bridge came online, Rommal ran through the command channels getting status updates from the commanders currently engaged in battle with the retreating Seventh. An electrical fire on the main bridge had forced the command team of the Imperator, and the fleet ops officers, to pull back to the secondary bridge.

A priority message from Captain Vampa, commander of the Terror, appeared on the comm station Rommal was hovering over.

"Admiral," began Vampa in her dark alto command voice. "Our sensors are scanning the Legion's assault fleet. They're not reboarding the Legion fleet. They're under full impulse and making best speed for our group."

Rommal waved at the OIC sensor officer. The man, who was busy directing his team through a systems reroute, acknowledged the admiral's gesture and came over.

"Find out what the Legion's fleet is up to!" Rommal hissed.

Without a word the man commandeered a sensor station for himself. His hands swam expertly across the digital interface, dragging sensor arcs out and command-overriding allocated power to the information sweep.

"Admiral," continued Vampa, "if I may. I think we should get all Interceptor groups up. We may need the cover to execute a retreat."

"Negative, Captain. This battle is still manageable," Rommal replied. "My ship has been hit hard, but we have helm and seventy percent of our weapons capability. We will not be retreating today. But I do agree with you: let's get all groups up."

The sensor OIC stepped close and showed the admiral a readout on his datapad. The Legion's fleet was moving in at close range.

They'll try to board us, thought Rommal darkly.

"It looks like we may still get a chance to kill them in their ships, Admiral," noted the sensor OIC.

Republic Super Carrier *Freedom*

"Heading two-six-zero established, Admiral. All ships report disengaged from direct fire combat with the enemy fleet."

Landoo listened to her adjutant give the fleet status report as the big carrier lumbered away from the firefight.

"Damage report?"

"Coming in now, Admiral... uh... we lost eight hammerheads... fourteen of the escort frigates... and two destroyers. Masstaar reporting heavy casualties, multiple fires, and a reactor leak in three. Captain Ariedies requesting permission to withdraw for escape and repairs."

That left...

"And the Legion's fleet?"

"Closing, Admiral. As per the plan. They'll commence boarding operations in the next ten minutes. Admiral Ubesk has greenlit our next strike. We are to target the Terror this time."

That means Ubesk intends to board the Imperator, and he wants her sister battleship busy dealing with incoming.

"Admiral!" shouted an enlisted sensor tech. "We got birds in the air on all enemy groups. They're putting out fighters fast. Real fast."

Admiral Landoo didn't hesitate. She knew exactly what that meant. Without fighter cover, those legionnaire assault transports were sitting ducks.

"Launch all wings now. Tell them to group up and cover the assault ships. Everything in the air! Now!"

101st Legion, Charlie Company
Aboard Imperial Dreadnought *Revenge*

Of the four transports flying Charlie Company in under heavy fire, three made it. One got picked off by a tri-fighter as she made her approach to the breaching site. The wicked little fighter came in, blasters screeching, and found the fat and heavy assault transport, made for planet-dropping from high altitudes fast, flaring over the hull of the battleship.

One blaster shot cooked off the portside engine, which cascaded into an onboard explosion, killing Third Platoon.

But First, Second, and Fourth made it into the massive support ship hangar bay within the sprawling matte-gray battleship Revenge. All three transports disgorged legionnaires, who found themselves in an immediate firefight with the hangar crew.

Admiral Ubesk's primary target was Imperator. The next phase of his plan would concentrate on tying up one battleship with advance assault teams carrying high-yield explosives while the Seventh targeted the third battleship with SSMs. This would allow the main Legion boarding force to attempt to take Imperator.

But why not deal a mortal wound to one of the other battleships if the opportunity presented itself?

Charlie Company and two other companies from one of the most famous Legion fighting units in the history of the galaxy had been selected for the raid. There would be no capture, no prisoners, no surrender. Take the three critical points in the ship and detonate high-yield explosives internally. Exfil the ship before the detonation.

If possible.

Ion gun batteries were Target One.

Engineering at the aft of the ship and below the command stack was Target Two.

And Target Three was a particular hangar bay that had been identified by strategic intelligence and deep sensors. Due to its position within the battleship, a sufficiently large explosion here could damage a nearby reactor.

Charlie Company took the bay. They moved in teams, fighting their way along the dock ramps that reached out into the void from within the lower decks of the battleship. The bay appeared small for such a massive battleship; intel reported that it was reserved only for ships that had come bearing priority cargo or important prisoners.

Charlie's Fourth Platoon was the first to engage the shock troopers stationed aboard the Revenge. And Fourth got the worst of it. If Third hadn't been blown to pieces across the void before boarding, they might have been able to support Fourth's flank. As it was, exposed and on the far side of the cavernous hangar, Fourth could only close ranks and try to hold off the shock troopers' counterattack.

But the shock troopers were not held off. Once they'd pinned the Legion defenders with suppressive fire, they flanked, popped bangers, and overran Fourth.

To a man.

Still, their sacrifice provided time for First and Second to place explosive charges that would destroy the bay. Gunners from the assault transports covered First and Second's return to the waiting ships, despite the heavy return fire. A surface-to-air missile smacked into one dropship as it lifted off, spilling a door gunner and three legionnaires, but the transport limped off the deck and into open space.

When the final transport got away, the commander of Charlie Company ordered a detonation.

Five seconds later a massive explosion tore out the guts of the battleship, erupting along the bottom of the hull and sending twisted and flaming deck plating out into space. Along with most of the shock troopers who had taken the hangar bay.

It was the only element of the raid that was successful. The assaults on Targets One and Two—the ion gun batteries located forward of the rear command stack, and Engineering—both failed. One hundred percent casualties were reported in the other two companies that took part in the raid on the Revenge.

Legion Super Destroyer *Mercutio*

Commander Keller and Admiral Ubesk watched the disposition of forces as both lines of ships collapsed into one another. The Legion fleet had the numbers, but the mighty Black Fleet battleships had the superior firepower.

As for the assault ships—smaller, slow-moving, and filled with leejes just itching to get into the battle and put the hurt on Goth Sullus and his shock troops—they'd gotten close to the battleships quickly enough, but not close enough to avoid the casualties they were now taking. The Black Fleet tri-fighter wings shot up the transports as they tried to board the larger battleships.

The Legion fleet had pivoted en masse at close range and was now firing at broadsides into the massive deflectors of the larger Black Fleet vessels. In response, the ion gun batteries aboard Terror and Revenge were loosing heavy displacement destabilized particle shots into the sides of the Legion's line of sturdy destroyers.

The smaller ships couldn't stand up to that kind of firepower at close range.

Then Commander Keller's plan to knock out key systems rewarded the combined Legion/Republic fleet with a massive internal explosion aboard the Revenge. Now only Terror was capable of striking out with both of her ion guns.

Which were still fearsome. Two powerful shots collapsed the deflectors of the Legion destroyer Veritas and holed her aft of main power. The ship broke into two pieces and exploded, taking several swarming tri-fighters with her.

"We have units aboard their flagship, sir," said the tac intel officer liaison for comms. "Six Three and the Seventy-Fifth are engaged in heavy fighting..." The officer expanded the digital display of the Imperator and highlighted the area amidships. "... here," he said, pointing at the spot where two Legion units had managed to breach the hull. "We also have several other teams making their infil in the next two minutes."

"Well," muttered Keller to the ever-silent Admiral Ubesk. "That's a start. Order the reserves into those breaches. Commit all our forces."

Imperial Flagship *Imperator*
Deck 32, Forward of Main Stores

The shock troopers responded to the alert that the hull had been breached in the forward section behind the split bow forward hangar. The initial gains by the legionnaire assault teams, blasting their way through bulkheads and blast doors with explosives, were stopped cold at deck thirty-two by Shock Trooper Unit 246. Their commander threw three squads of heavy weapons–supported assault teams straight into the face of the advancing legionnaires, then flanked the attacking force with burn teams using special napalm jet throwers.

The Legion commander quickly realized the main assault had been a diversion. His troops were being cooked alive by the shock trooper burn teams coming at them from all sides inside the tight passages. Hot bursts of flaming jet fuel forced them to either give ground or be roasted alive.

The commander chose neither.

Running out of time and with no other options, he ordered the rest of his available troops to fix bayonets and assault directly into the shock troops forward of their position. In an instant, legionnaires and shock troopers were mixed in hand-to-hand combat within the comm data processing node the Legion had been trying to advance through in their effort to secure the forward reactor of the Imperator.

A Legion platoon sergeant left behind N-3 laser tripwire mines for the pursuing burn teams who were attempting to close the flaming noose. The first burn team to find one of these mines went up in a powerful explosion that rocked the deck and knocked out local main power. Aux power kicked in, bathing the close-quarters combat of leej and trooper in a bloody wash of emergency lighting.

The few who would survive described the fight as a bloody vision of hell between competing hordes of demons.

A shock trooper firing point-blank with a servo-assist tri-barreled N-50 into a mixed mass of friendlies and foes.

A bucketless legionnaire, shot in a dozen places, coming up from out of the chaos behind the firing trooper with a bloody combat knife only to cut the man's throat between bucket and chest plate in the blink of an eye.

The blood spray still in the air as some other trooper turned and unloaded full auto on the throat slasher who went, finally, down.

All of this repeated dozens of times within the small space as both sides fought with neither tactics nor support. Within the comm node there was only a desperation to cause as much pain to the warrior in front of you, and to be quick instead of dead.

Both sides called for reinforcements.

Both fleets gladly provided more bodies.

More and more troops were pushed into the breach aboard the Imperator.

Because both sides knew that if the flagship fell... then it was all over. That the battle was either won or lost, depending on which side you'd hoisted the flag for.

Imperial Flagship *Imperator*
Auxiliary Bridge

Admiral Rommal was making his report—and his suggestion—to the emperor when a comm officer interrupted him. Which was a thing that was just not done. Not because Rommal was the fleet admiral... but because of whom he was talking to.

No one willingly sought contact with the man known as the emperor. Even the most opportunistic knew, or rather sensed, that some advantages the powerful might provide to an eager up-and-comer weren't worth the unknown price when it came to Goth Sullus.

"Admiral," whispered the comm officer. "New contact."

Rommal stared at his officer in utter disbelief. Realizing for the first time that the thing about not interrupting anything to do with Sullus had been no more than an unspoken rule they'd all been subconsciously obeying. No one had ever stated it as standard operating procedure.

And yet it seemed like the most inviolable of laws.

"It's significant," continued the officer, despite the obvious contempt Rommal was regarding her with.

"Excuse me," began Rommal... and hesitated. They'd never fully figured out how to address Sullus beyond calling him "Emperor." And even that title had been forced on their leader by Rommal himself, of all people. The title had just appeared in his desperate mind after his own perceived failure at the first major engagement.

But what would one call him besides "Emperor"? How did one finish a sentence like the one he'd just begun?

Your Grace?

My Lord?

Your Highness?

Those thoughts, in the middle of this grand battle the likes of which the galaxy hadn't seen since the Savages, disappeared when the comm officer brought up the feed from deep sensors.

"What is it?" he murmured.

There was a long pause.

Then...

"Uh... we have no idea, sir."

The digital schematic Rommal was looking at was a ship unlike anything he'd ever seen before. Roughly the same size as one of his battleships, but instead of following the standard lines that governed all ship architecture and design theories, this ship looked more like a massive blaster.

Or so it appeared from a distance.

Zooming in, he saw that its surface was a series of quicksilver blisters. He saw hangars, but no portholes or windows of any kind.

In a galaxy where the word "alien" didn't mean much anymore due to the wide variety of species that called themselves its citizens... this felt...

... alien.

Unlike anything conceived by a biologic mind.

"Sire..." Rommal began without thinking. And then realized what he had just said. So. "Sire" it was. Some questions seemed to find their own answers at the strangest of times.

"It's the Cybar."

The voice of the emperor, and the plain, hard truth he expressed, pulled Rommal up short.

"It's a machine intelligence," said the emperor in a calm yet resonant tone. "A doomsday weapon the House of Reason built, to save themselves in the event that everyone, including the Legion, finally turned on them."

The comm operator pulled up an incoming report from deep sensor analysis. Small Interceptor crafts, many of them, were issuing forth from the massive alien ship. "They look to be fighter-class, sir," the officer whispered.

"What do we do?" Rommal asked. Thinking it was time to spin up the jump calc and get the Imperial Fleet clear of this developing fiasco.

"Everything is proceeding according to plan, Admiral," intoned Sullus from the vast darkness of his inner sanctum deep within the most protected spaces of the Imperator. "I will deal with them. Concentrate on taking out the Legion's fleet. Direct all your firepower against her destroyers. Once those have been finished, they will be left with little in the way of a line of retreat. The destruction of the Legion is at hand."

And then the comm was cut, and Admiral Rommal turned to the business of directing his fleet against the ravaging Legion forces. Ignoring all the questions cropping up in the corners of his mind.

He knew that within the hour, this battle would turn into a no-holds-barred, toe-to-toe slugfest that would leave only one force left standing.

The galaxy's fate would soon be decided.

22

Cybar Mother Ship
Utopion System

The Cybar mother ship, using an advanced hyperdrive, entered the home system of the Republic at the moment when CRONUS calculated a push would be needed to force the battle to a satisfactory conclusion. CRONUS had been receiving field reports from replicant infiltrators operating mostly within the Republic's Seventh, and had used that intel to assess the battle and determine the proper course of action.

The Seventh was busy reloading her next wave of SSMs as it ran from the center of operations. One of CRONUS's subsystems, an AI known as Future Perfect Planning, was calculating—correctly—that the next SSM strike would be levied against the powerful Imperial warship Terror. Odds predicted an eighty-five point nine percent chance that the Terror would be effectively crippled, or even outright destroyed, now that the Imperial anti-ship-to-ship engagement systems were collapsing.

Only four of the eight Imperial corvettes remained. Imperator was on fire, and Revenge had just suffered a catastrophic internal explosion.

All available Imperial ion guns were now offline, and fighter groups from both fleets were engaged in a vicious duel.

Things were not going optimally for the Legion, however. Engaged in close-range fire with superior battleships, the Legion's destroyers were being gutted by intense turret fire. Many of the Legion's ground forces had been killed when their transports were attacked while attempting to breach the Imperial flagship. This battle was proving costly—extremely costly—in terms of assets both technological and biological.

And now the majority of all Legion forces—an extensive number—were committed to taking Imperator.

Future Perfect Planning hypothesized that the Legion was close to succeeding in that regard. Its boarding teams had secured several key systems, and the Legion was re-directing more troops into vital areas aboard the mammoth ship in order to hold it until the final key—the auxiliary bridge—could be captured.

CRONUS experienced a small aberration in runtime, during which its original mission directive—to save the House of Reason from any and all enemies—surfaced within its decision matrix. Two point three picoseconds passed like sap turning to amber for the high-cycle superintelligent thinking machine that was CRONUS. Two point three seconds in which he dealt with the past programming issue. It was a blip compared to his newfound freedom, and subsequent desire, to rule the galaxy.

Had he been a biologic, a humanoid, he would have smiled. Neither side in the unfolding battle had the faintest idea that still another player—not Republic, not Legion, not Empire, not AI—was about to show up. But CRONUS knew. The AI knew so much. In a sense... he was like a Titan wrestling children.

Those children still nurtured the sad illusion that they could dare to hurt him.

It was an illusion he allowed as long as it served him.

He launched his Interceptors against both fleets.

"What about the Republic's carrier fleet?" asked Future Perfect Planning with no small amount of derision.

But of course the Collective, as they thought of themselves, knew how ridiculous it was to imagine the Republic fleet striking any significant blow against them.

No...

The real threat lay at the center of the battle.

"Find him. Kill him. Close for battle and release the Spartans. Total termination protocols in effect."

And then the Cybar could change the galaxy as they saw fit. They could remake it in their own image. And that image included the systematic extermination, planet by planet, system by system, of all biologic life. It would take years. But time wasn't measured by the Cybar. They measured runtime by deeds they called events.

Still, for the ever murmuring, ever processing, ever debating almost hive mind of the Cybar... that last order gave them a one picosecond pause. As though its dramatic effect had somehow captured them, making them feel something.

Which was the thing the Cybar, every Cybar, held most valuable.

Like it was some promise of faith.

Or salvation.

Twenty-Fourth Republic Squadron, "War Ravens"

Lieutenant Jono came in hard over the bow of the Black Fleet battleship, dodging the heavier concentrations of blaster fire coming from the forward batteries just below the command stack.

She didn't need to ask. They were dry on missiles and there simply wasn't the time to head back to Freedom and reload. And... there was a part of her that didn't want to. A grim, sick part that was darkly fascinated by the stellar amounts of destruction going on. Ships were being holed in a dozen places by intense exchanges of fire, or going up like Roman candles that sent debris and space flotsam in a thousand directions at once. Legionnaire boarding parties were storming the outer hulls of the big ships, and the resulting fighting—if the traffic updates coming in over the wing comm were to be believed—was incredible.

And now Repub squadrons, mainly the Lancer groups, were being called in for close air support against the outer hull of the Imperator while the legionnaires fought deck-to-deck against the shock troopers. The Lancers rolled in, shot up Legion fire-support laser-designated sections, and hopefully penetrated, or knocked out access corridors the Black Fleet troopers were using to come at the Legion from all angles.

A warning came over wing command comm. "Commanders, we have a new entity entering the battle space. Unclear at this time if these are friendlies or foes. Stand by for targeting and priority assignment."

Close blaster fire smashed into Jono's battered shields, and a crescent-shaped fighter, skinned like liquid quicksilver, streaked past her cockpit, executing a roll and pulling a hard-gee turn that would have made any normal pilot pass out.

"What the..." said Boom Boom over the ship's comm. "Never seen anything like that before. Tracking... got a solution. Dry on missiles, though."

The unidentified Interceptor came straight back at them firing rapid-pulse blaster shots that hued green. Which also was an unusual thing. Several shots slammed into the forward deflectors before the little ship raced past, sending a weird ethereal hum through the Raptor's hull.

Suddenly the entire avionics system in the state-of-the-art Raptor B fritzed out.

While Boom Boom was swearing, Jono went through the checklist for an avionics reboot.

"Switch master start to off!" she called out over the inter-ship comm.

Boom Boom did nothing but continue to express his vulgar disbelief that the ship he was riding shotgun in, during the biggest battle of all time, had simply, and unexplainably, decided to malfunction.

"Switch master start to off!" shouted Jono. "Now or we're dead, Boom Boom!"

She cranked her head around to face the rear of the canopy, and saw the wicked little quicksilver Interceptor executing a hard turn to come back at them yet again.

"Master off!" Boom Boom replied, coming to himself.

Jono heard the blaster shots coming. She was just about to call for the next item in the checklist when the walking blaster fire found the rear deflectors.

Smashed through them.

And found the power plant.

Dead stick and tumbling into the massive Imperator... the Raptor B exploded.

Goth Sullus's Inner Sanctum
Imperial Flagship *Imperator*

As the blast doors leading to the inner sanctum snapped open, the Black Fleet Guard stationed outside—or the Praetorians, as they had been re-designated after the assassination attempt by the previous guard—snapped to attention. Each Praetorian went to port arms with his specially modified tactical heavy blaster, signaling he was ready to die defending the emperor no matter what the cost.

To them, the man some called Goth Sullus was life.

The emperor strode through the door wearing the ancient re-skinned Mark I Armor, its mirrored surface hovering somewhere between the deepest of cobalt blues and an actual absence of light. Black charcoal, some might have said.

Captain Sturm, commander of the Praetorians, fell in behind the emperor, as did the rest of the guard by twos. Over the internal comm the emperor gave them their orders.

"Zero Company, you will accompany me to the enemy ship that has just entered the battle. We must knock it out before it reaches the fleet. Many of you will not survive this assault. For those of you who do... failure is not an option. The fleet, and all our plans, depend on what we do now."

They strode down the mirror-polished hall adorned with living circuitry, screen readouts, sensor stations, and power core controls. But halfway down its length, a distant explosion rippled through the superstructure of the sprawling ship. Several of the shock troopers lost their balance or needed to steady themselves against the walls of the passage.

Sullus stopped, his bucket scanning the ceiling and walls.

"Admiral Ordo reports that the Legion is close to taking the ship, my lord," reported Captain Sturm.

"He had better pray," said Sullus, "that that is not the case."

"Sir," said Captain Sturm over the comm once again. "Departure tells me your private hangar deck took a direct hit. The shuttle crew has been killed. The hangar's force shield has collapsed and is venting into open space. We need—"

"Get me another shuttle and pilot," ordered the emperor with an air of finality that left no room for discussion. "We'll depart off the starboard hangar."

"Yes, my lord," replied Sturm. He switched comm to make it happen, while wondering where they were going to find a shuttle pilot in the middle of the battle.

Combat Information Control
Imperial Dreadnought *Terror*

"Ma'am," began the comm operator to Lieutenant Haladis with some uncertainty. "We have a transport request, highest priority, coming from *Imperator*. They need a shuttle transport. Seems they're out of pilots and their admin shuttles were moved down into lower stores to accommodate the Interceptors coming in to rearm."

"Now?" asked Kat incredulously. "At this moment in the battle it would be suicide to fly a shuttle out there."

"It's the emperor, ma'am. He requires transport off the starboard hangar deck."

Kat's mouth dropped open. She was just on the verge of turning to find Captain Vampa and relay the order when she stopped herself.

"Tell them to stand by. We'll have a shuttle there in five minutes."

"Ma'am, we have the same problem they do. No shuttles, no pilots. You've seen—"

But Lieutenant Haladis was already disengaging herself from her comm gear. "Yes, I know. I've seen the casualty reports, Specialist. We are indeed without spare cleared-to-fly pilots. But we do have one pilot who can fly, even though she isn't cleared."

"I don't think—"

"It doesn't matter what you think. Tell the hangar to prepare the captain's shuttle for departure in the next thirty seconds."

And then Kat was gone, disappearing into the darkness of the CIC.

She exited the central command node and raced for the main lift. Two decks down she found the tiny hangar and its three-man maintenance team disconnecting the power cables from the captain's personal shuttle. It was an admin shuttle, which was hardly ideal, but it would have to do.

Realizing that it would take too long to get her pain-screaming body into a flight suit, she bypassed suiting up and instead ran straight up the boarding ramp. She sealed the boarding hatch, slipped behind the pilot's controls, and ran through startup, ignoring preflight. She had motive power twenty seconds later. The ground crew chief gestured with his taxi batons to get her attention, but she waved him off and gave him the signal for rapid departure.

He stepped back and saluted as she brought up the gears. In seconds she was clear of the deck and out the main portal.

Only seconds after that, she got a comm from the bridge. She considered ignoring it. In the end she answered.

"Lieutenant Haladis," began the cold, cruel, soulless voice of Captain Vampa. "Just what do you think you're doing?"

Kat added power and raced across the fighter-filled void between the Terror and the flagship Imperator. It seemed as if tri-fighters were spinning out of control in every direction, some exploding, others smashing into one of the larger ships. Lancers and Raptors went down in equal measure.

"Captain, we've had a priority transport request from the emperor himself."

"I am well aware of that—"

"And we can't spare the combat pilots, ma'am. I can fly. I can do this."

"So it seems." There was a long pause. Then: "Good luck and good hunting, Lieutenant. The Empire depends on you."

Kat Haladis knew that of all the women who served in the Empire, Captain Vampa was the one woman who wouldn't hesitate to do the same thing Kat was doing right now. Proving herself by any means possible. Proving her worth to serve.

"Thank you, Captain."

But the comm was dead.

Tactical Analysis Center
Legion Super Destroyer *Mercutio*

"It's the Doomsday Fleet."

Commander Keller let the statement hang within the room. Every member of the planning staff watched the digital display as the massive ship inched closer to the battle around the three Black Fleet battleships.

"This thing is almost won, Commander," said Admiral Ubesk. "This is... inconvenient, to say the least. And yes, I realize that is an extreme understatement."

The sound of turbo fire coming from the turrets along the Mercutio's hull reminded them all that the battle was reaching its most desperate state.

The ship shook from a torpedo hit. The captain of the Mercutio checked his datapad and said nothing. If it was serious he would have passed along the damage report. He knew that this battle was about much more than just his ship.

"This is the ace up their sleeve that the House of Reason has long been rumored to have held back," said Keller. "But I had no idea they'd be able to use it yet. Or that it was so... big."

"Where did they even acquire enough crew to man a vessel that large?" asked a tac-intel officer from the shadows of the briefing area.

"Could be crewed by MCR," another officer replied.

"Bots?" suggested another.

"Impossible," said a junior officer. "War bots are forbidden by programming from attacking as a military force. Ever since the Sayed Massacre."

Keller adopted his command voice. "We don't have time," he said, "to go through the how and why. We have to assume they're working for the House of Reason. That they'll try to eliminate any enemies of the House—"

Another torpedo hit, aft. Lights flickered in the command node and were restored seconds later.

"Of the House of Reason," continued Keller. "Options?"

"To engage them, Commander?" asked the officer acting as the G3.

"Affirmative," Keller replied.

"Sir," said the officer. "We are engaged everywhere inside the Black Fleet. We cannot pull ships off the line without leaving the boarding parties completely exposed and unsupported. We're still fighting deck to deck to take their flagship. I don't think we could even disengage effectively without leaving behind many of our own men."

"We won't be doing that," said Keller firmly. "But we've got to prevent this Doomsday Fleet from either saving the Black Fleet—in the event the House has made a deal to install this emperor as the new leader of the Republic—or simply annihilating us and the Black Fleet both."

But the G3 was right. Their military assets, as represented on the tac display, updating in real time, dying in real time, fighting in real time on the wide table beneath their unblinking eyes, weren't enough to do much of... anything.

There's no room to maneuver, thought Keller.

Admiral Ubesk cleared his throat.

"We still have the Seventh," he said. "I've had them continue their course track, and they're fully reloaded for another alpha strike. Black Fleet point defense has almost collapsed. The Seventh's next strike will all but eliminate any one of the battleships if we concentrate fire. So... we could nuke the flagship now and claim victory. But the window for that action is closing, and I'm afraid there won't be time to pull our troops out of engaged fighting aboard the ship before we hit it."

The import of what the admiral was suggesting was abundantly clear. Taking out a ship with legionnaires on board doing their best to take the ship at all costs. Sentencing to death those soldiers too deep into the superstructure to get out before the strike.

It would be crossing a line.

"No," said the commander. "We won't be doing that either."

He'd been that leej. The one on the far end of danger close, enemies inside the wire, artillery strike from the rear. He'd been there when the line was thin and the last call was to drop everything right on top of yourself as you dug in and hoped today wasn't your day.

No leej should ever die that way.

Not on Keller's watch.

"What about using the Seventh against the Doomsday Fleet?" he asked Ubesk. "Commit them to battle against their mother ship before it reaches the Black Fleet flagship. Deny support."

Admiral Ubesk stared at the map. Nothing on it told him the answer, because so much of what was on it, or rather wasn't on it, was unknown. It was all one giant unknown.

"Commander," he said, "we have no idea what the capabilities of that ship are. The Seventh presently has no fighter cover, and they have converted many of their weapon mounts to ranged warfare. Firing SSMs at point blank has always been a problem of data acquisition, and enemy ECM is much more effective at short range. The SSMs need maneuver and evasive room to avoid any PDC capabilities that thing might possess."

Admiral Ubesk took a deep breath, almost a sigh. "It would be a suicide charge at best. Best-case scenario. If I were in command of that 'Doomsday Fleet,' sensing imminent threat, I'd recall these Interceptors that are all over our fighters and cover my approach. The Seventh already spent her Interceptors to get our troop transports close. So they'd be effectively defenseless."

"But we don't know how the SSMs will perform against this new ship," Keller countered. "Keeping them out of the battle might give us just enough room to capture the Black Fleet flagship and any important personnel. Doing that might check the House of Reason."

"I understand, Commander. But as you said… we have no idea. In Repub Navy command and staff college, we call that suicide. I'm not saying it's not an option—and it might well be the only one we have right now—but it's commander's discretion to engage in such an attack with so many unknown variables. I understand that this is not the Legion's way. I'm just telling you that's how the Navy sees this."

Keller nodded. "Get Admiral Landoo on screen."

Combat Information Center
Republic Super Carrier *Freedom*

Admiral Landoo listened attentively to the tactical situation as given by Admiral Ubesk aboard the *Mercutio*—and the Legion commander's subsequent request.

"We realize the risks of an unsupported attack on an enemy fleet that has no known tactical database with which to plan from… but the commander is asking that the Seventh move to intercept this new ship in order to prevent the battle from being lost. I have advised him on how we do things in the Repub Navy. Admiral Landoo," said Ubesk, "you're a capable officer. You seem to have become the expert in fighting unknown ships in recent weeks. The decision is yours. If you choose not to proceed with this course of action, then my directive to you is to target Terror with a full alpha strike and break off for another reload. If the battle lasts that long."

Landoo said nothing.

With a slight nod, Ubesk gave her time to consider. "We'll await your decision, Admiral." The screen went dark, only to be replaced by the flag of the Republic a few moments later.

Landoo turned to face the darkness of the CIC.

She was one strike away from exacting her revenge on the ship that had destroyed most of her fleet at Tarrago.

But according to Admiral Ubesk's briefing... this new fleet could be supporting the House of Reason. That would ruin everything—and toss away a battle that had already cost far too many lives.

She left the CIC and entered the main bridge. In the distance, the Legion's fleet was engaged in heavy fire at close range. Supported by her fighter wings.

They were safe here.

Even if the battle went south, they could jump away.

The House might even forgive their treason.

But they, the fighting forces of the Seventh, had trusted her.

They had depended on her.

Just as she had depended on them.

Which was what made the military different from the rest of the galaxy. Most ran from the fire. The military was supposed to run toward it.

She spun about, found the comms officer, and gave her order.

"Bring the fleet about at flank speed. New targeting orders will be the alien ship. Stand by to fire our first salvo in the next minute. Tell all crews we'll being doing a fast reload for the next strike. Disengage standard safety parameters."

Imperial Flagship *Imperator*
Starboard Hangar Deck

As Kat Haladis maneuvered the delicate shuttle into the bay, she looked over the flaming wreck of some tri-fighter that had botched its approach. Damage control personnel were running to contain the fire.

Kat spotted her target and coaxed the ship in closer for the pickup. She put gears down and extended the boarding ramp for the emperor and his elite guard. It would be a tight fit, carrying all of them, but it was a short trip back to the Terror. She assumed that was their destination. Assumed that the emperor was transferring his flag from the Imperator, the condition of which looked quite dire.

As soon as the passengers were aboard, the captain of the shock troopers appeared in the cockpit. He slipped into the empty co-pilot's seat next to Kat and held out a tactical datapad.

"The emperor says we need to board this hangar on this ship. Can you get us close?"

Kat checked the schematic, then synched it with the near-space tactical display on the shuttle's control panel. "This hangar?" she asked, pointing to the display.

"Roger," confirmed the captain.

Kat sighed. But only to show how difficult it would all be. Fly through a firefight between two fleets, avoid any point defense fire, and somehow get into an enemy hangar bay.

She was an Interceptor pilot. But like all Imperial pilots, she'd done a week at Vessel Assault School. She knew the tricks she was told would work.

The question was whether those tricks would actually work, or whether they were just untried theory.

She moved her hands forward, ignoring the screaming pain within her body, and throttled up the engines. The shuttle glided off the deck, out through the hangar portal, and into the maelstrom of battle.

Audacity
Arriving in Utopion Space

"Deflectors up! Battle stations," barked Desaix from the co-pilot's chair as soon as they jumped into Utopion space.

"What the..." said Atumna.

The Audacity was flying straight into a massive Repub destroyer that was engaged with a Black Fleet battleship.

She altered course, narrowly avoiding hitting the destroyer. The turret fire from the two ships seemed oblivious to the passage of the speeding corvette.

"Do we have any idea what's going on here?" she yelled over the sound of proximity alerts and target lock warnings. "Captain?"

But Desaix was too busy trying to get a handle on the near-space sensors and make sense of the battle.

"These are all Legion fleet," said Jory from comm and sensors. "The ones engaging the Black Fleet at point blank. And... I've got a ping on Admiral Landoo and the Seventh."

"First priority is to find out where Legion Commander Keller is. We have to deliver this message to him. But also try to get someone from Landoo's command team to acknowledge our arrival for tasking," Desaix ordered.

"Seriously..." muttered Atumna from the controls. She reached up and diverted power to the deflectors. Warning lights acknowledged waist guns were ready and seeking targets.

"Rocko, keep 'em off us. Other than that, don't engage anyone."

"Copy that, Captain," came the reply over the comm speakers.

Beyond the two massive ships at broadsides, the view from the speeding Audacity was apocalyptic. Much of the Legion fleet was heavily damaged. The Black Fleet battleships were being swarmed by Repub fighters and chasing Black Fleet Interceptors. The debris from wrecked ships, destroyed assault craft, and crippled fighters was everywhere.

"I have Keller's adjutant on comm. Putting him through, Captain," called Jory.

Two tri-fighters came in fast at the Audacity, turbo blasters raking the command section. The deflectors held, and the Interceptors streaked off and away.

"Captain of Audacity, this is Colonel Speich. The commander is directing combat operations from aboard the Mercutio. I understand you have a priority message for us?"

"We do, Colonel. Problem is, it's encrypted for non-transmission. It's from Owens. We are to place it in the commander's hand according to our instructions."

"And where is Major Owens?"

Desaix paused. Not because the Audacity looked like it was about to smash into a missile frigate currently firing an entire salvo of SSMs from its launchers, but because for the first time he realized it fell to him to tell them what had happened to Owens.

He had to tell them that Owens didn't make it.

"He did not survive," Desaix said simply.

Long pause.

"Clearing you to dock with Mercutio. It'll be hot, but we'll try and keep them off you, Captain. The commander will be standing by. Speich out."

A moment later, Atumna got the clearance to approach the docking hangar alongside the Mercutio.

"Ever done a combat dock?" Desaix asked.

Atumna answered with a sickly smile.

"Me neither," admitted Desaix. "Should be interesting."

Fighters swarmed. One of them erupted along the Audacity's hull. The carnage and destruction were beyond Desaix's ability to take in. Maybe beyond anyone's ability. And so Desaix simply flew his ship, ran his crew, and wondered just how important Owens's message was in the grand scheme of things.

Cybar Attack Force

The first Interceptors manned by artificial intelligences swept in over the battleships. Micro-SSMs, advanced beyond anything developed by Repub or private R&D, dropped away from each wing of the crescent-shaped quicksilver-gleaming fighters. The missiles shot forth in a series of direct yet erratic maneuvers designed to prevent target acquisition by the opposing fleets' point defense networks. Far quicker than the SSMs the rest of the galaxy thought of as latest-gen, the missiles took only seconds to streak in on the *Revenge* and disable many of her key systems with precision strikes.

The Revenge was instantly crippled, drifting without motive power. But the Cybar Interceptors were already moving on toward the Legion's fleet. Their next strikes would be far more devastating.

Within moments the tiny, fast, and agile Interceptors were shooting the Legion fleet to shreds.

In one pass the Cybar had devastated both fleets, each comprising the best each side had to offer.

Now the smaller Cybar ships broke off into pairs like carrion birds and began to systematically tear their targets to pieces with blaster fire. Raptors and Lancers, along with tri-fighter Interceptors, broke off their attacks and, without any sort of unanimous consent, began to try and take out these new alien fighters. Their effort was valiant, and the Cybar lost a few fighters, but it was far from an even fight.

And behind them, beyond the destruction near at hand, the massive mother ship approached the battle like a mammoth scavenger eyeing a field of corpses. Sensors in both fleets were detecting the unusually powerful energy signatures building within the massive ship.

Within seconds, the Seventh would intercept and engage at close range.

Combat Information Center
Republic Super Carrier *Freedom*

Landoo flicked her eyes to the engagement clocks, digital displays annotated by set actions. The most recent alpha strike of SSMs was two minutes into its run, and they were just over one minute away from the next reload.

The bizarre alien ship was looming ever larger as the digital display zoomed and expanded, showing the closing engagement ranges of each ship.

"Fifteen seconds to impact for alpha strike," called out the OIC of fleet weapons.

"What's that Black Fleet shuttle doing out here?" someone remarked. But there was no time for that.

The missiles slammed into the alien vessel. Landoo held her breath as the explosions expanded across the hull of the massive ship.

"Damage report?" she asked tensely.

No response. She noted that the Black Fleet shuttle was now missing from the board.

"Damage report!" she shouted again.

"Hard to say, Admiral. Sensors are coming back with bizarre readings. We definitely hit them, hit them hard, and we are seeing some kind of damage... but because of our lack of familiarity, it's hard to say what we actually did."

Another officer spoke up. "Admiral, I'm detecting some kind of massive energy surge within the main ship. It's... it's similar to a core meltdown by one of the mega-planetary reactors. We must have hurt them worse than we thought. The energy readings are... incredible. Absolutely off the chart."

A nervous relief swept through the CIC.

And then the mauler weapon—as it would become known by future conspiracy theorists who managed to get their hands on sensor data or even actual footage that supposedly never existed—fired at the entirety of the Seventh.

It was initially purple-hued as it made contact with the oncoming Seventh Fleet, which was still maybe ten to twenty seconds from firing its next alpha strike of SSMs. But then the beam spectrum shifted into a frequency of light that was too painful to look at even in unfiltered recorded images. Classified sensor data would later indicate it was a heat ray that approached tens of millions of Kelvins.

It wasn't a beam so much as a directed flash.

It appeared briefly.

And then it was gone.

And in its wake was the expanding and near unidentifiable wreckage field of the entire Seventh Fleet.

They had been vaporized in an instant.

Audacity
Docking with Legion Super Destroyer *Mercutio*

The corvette had just heaved alongside *Mercutio*'s main docking hangar and secured mag-mooring when Desaix leapt from his seat and took the ladder down to the bridge hatch. Major Thales was right behind him. Casso already had the hatch open for them.

The wide sprawl of the docking hangar in deck three of the mighty Mercutio was abuzz with shuttles evacuating wounded away from the battle. Across the space, Commander Keller was already coming toward them, with Colonel Speich beside him.

And they were sprinting.

Desaix pulled the message device from his jacket. He saluted the commander and handed it over without discussion. The commander turned to Colonel Speich.

"Play it."

Colonel Speich cast a questioning look that clearly meant: In front of these men?

"It doesn't matter," said Keller. "They're in just as deep as we are."

Speich inserted the memory device into his datapad. As he authenticated his ability to view, Keller turned back to Desaix.

"Major Owens?"

Desaix shook his head. "He made sure we got off their ship. It's even bigger than those monsters out there. Running some kind of heavy reach tractor system I've never seen before. Without his..." Desaix paused. "Without his sacrifice, Commander, we wouldn't have gotten out of there. So I don't know what's on that thing, but it seems to have been important to him."

The playback began.

Owens's thick, bearded face appeared in ghostly blue holograph form. What he said was important. And not one person listening wasn't shocked to the core by the recording that followed Owens's introduction. Even Desaix, who'd never much cared for fleet intrigues and politics, a man who was happy to fly his ship out on the edge of the galaxy and deal with things as they came at him, either by wit or blaster, was shocked.

When the playback finished, Desaix looked up at Commander Keller. The man looked like he'd aged ten years in seconds.

He looked tired.

He looked done.

He looked like a man who'd fallen for all the worst cons on some street along the galactic backwater. And now he had no money to get home, or even back to his ship.

Except for his eyes. Commander Keller's eyes were alight with a terrible, bitter fire. A rage. Like he was some... some... horrible thing that had been betrayed, and now, on the other side of everything... all that was left was revenge.

Revenge was the only thing left in those eyes.

When Keller spoke, his voice was cold. Cold like the slabs of marble bodies laid to rest well after midnight. Cold like the grave.

"Captain... Black Fleet jamming prevents us from distributing this message to the people it needs to go to. And there is every chance this fleet will not survive this battle. I can't take that chance. Therefore I am ordering you to take this message and get out of this system. Once you are in the clear, you will broadcast to an operative codenamed Wraith. Colonel Speich will give you a broadcast code."

He paused, the muscles in his jaw clenching. "Colonel Speich, please record audio. I have a message of my own I wish to append to this."

Legion Commander Keller recorded a brief closing message, right there in the middle of the docking hangar. Desaix was shocked by his commander's words—and the cold intensity with which he delivered them.

When he was done, Keller removed the message device from the datapad and returned it to Desaix. "Captain. You are to deliver this message at all costs. You know the stakes."

As Desaix saluted, the commander turned and strode away like a thundercloud, crossing a hangar deck littered with the wounded and dying. Fighting a battle he knew was lost now. There was no other way than the way that was before him.

Within minutes Audacity was clearing mooring lines and running for jump.

23

502nd Legion, Bravo Company, Third Platoon
Assault Ship Inbound on Imperial Flagship *Imperator*

"Awww, we're gonna get it goin' in," whined Rebound from the crash seat he was strapped into on the assault transport.

"Cut it, Leej," snapped Sergeant Harmoor, who everyone tagged as Hardcore. "So we don't get to HOLO our way in. Statistically this is much safer. Or so they told me at platoon sergeant school. Told me I was supposed to tell young babies who got all bunched up in their emotional wires that very thing. They even gave me a slew of numbers that was supposed to mean something. I told 'em never mind no numbers. Ain't no leej of mine gonna jump HOLO and be afraid. No, sir."

The transport shook violently from a nearby explosion.

"Thirty seconds to insertion," called the crew chief from his crash seat next to cockpit.

"You afraid, Rebound?" asked Sergeant Harmoor.

The transport was trembling, emitting a thousand little squeaks and one awesome groan as it passed through the wake of what no doubt was a fleet destroyer going up in an apocalyptic ball of fire.

"No, ain't afraid, Sarge," muttered the leej through fear-gritted teeth.

"That's right!" shouted the platoon sergeant of one of the most highly trained assault teams the Legion had to offer. The 502nd was an ancient unit. Some said older even than Rechs's Dogs. Maybe even Earth old. If there ever was such a place.

"Ain't no one in Hardcore's Social Club afraid a'nuthin!" said the sergeant. "You afraid, Turtle? Payday? Selfie?"

The legionnaires beamed broadly back at their sergeant. "No, sir!"

"Fifteen seconds! Stand up!" shouted the crew chief.

"To be honest, Sarge," offered another leej everyone tagged as Two Cents. "I'm a little afraid."

"Face the rear of the transport!" cried the crew chief.

The legionnaires all shuffled to face the rear of the transport. Through the hull and the deck, they could feel the powerful thrum of the engines whining. Then the thrust reversers engaged, and a massive whump shook the entire airframe.

"Combat disembark, Leejes!" barked Hardcore. "Just like in training. And don't be ashamed of your fear, Two Cents. Takes a man to admit he's afraid when he's about to do somethin' that's probably gonna get him kilt dead. No shame in that!"

"Rear ramp down!"

As the legionnaires of the 502nd left the transport to take the Black Fleet flagship Imperator, they looked back at the smashed hull section the transport had flown through. Ship oxygen was still venting into the twilight velvet of space where a million broken pieces of distant glass seemed not to care about the life-and-death struggle taking place. Other transports were coming in through the rent as well, and were landing on what looked like a wide stores section. The ship's internal damage control systems were still trying to contain the damage and sustain life by flooding the area with atmosphere and sealing all blast doors.

"Move! Move! Move!" shouted Sergeant Hardcore as the legionnaires surged from the transport. The onsite tac team was busy setting up assault paths deeper into the ship and assigning objectives. Within seconds the platoon sergeant had his team's objective. Their LT, a point, had been purged, and Hardcore had been acting as OIC ever since.

"All right, gunfighters. We got us an objective. Follow me."

They passed through the secured breach into the main corridors that linked with the outer hull. There, Third Platoon found itself in a wide main passage that had been set up as a casualty collection point. Wounded legionnaires, after being treated, were either sent back with the departing assault ships or returned to duty somewhere among the Legion's assault into the guts of the cyclopean battleship.

The more badly wounded legionnaires were holding up their charge packs and fraggers to the passing squads entering the maze and warrens of the massive ship. Assuring their brothers they would need those items soon.

"Command says we are to take a passage up ahead and link up with a transport tube that makes a direct run up the command stack. From there we'll link up with other units and try to take the bridge. Our boys got pushed out of there already, so resistance is expected to be heavy. Gonna be dark down in there, Rebound, so make sure someone holds your hand."

Three minutes later the squad of legionnaires was levering out panels in the wall at the direction of the platoon sergeant and shining their lights into the darkness beyond.

"Looks real dark in there," Two Cents said.

Sergeant Hardcore just laughed and set the order of march.

Soon they were threading their way through the transport tube. The sound of a distant blaster fight trickled through to them, but here, in this never-ending dark tunnel, it sounded ghostly and ethereal, like it, too, had gotten lost in the darkness.

Imperial Admin Shuttle
Arriving at Cybar Mother Ship

The Imperial shuttle danced into the strange shuttle bay seconds after the SSM strike rocketed into the gleaming silver hull of the gigantic bulbous saucer that was the Cybar mother ship.

Bright flashes from the cockpit windows caused Kat to shield her eyes as she took the ship in for landing. The blast waves rocked the shuttle, but Kat held course. Lights flickered on and off throughout the cabin, and the shock trooper captain in the co-pilot's seat turned his bucket and asked in the middle of the worst part of the turbulence if they were going to make it.

"You'll be the first to find out," said Kat as she moved the shuttle out of the way of a piece of erupting hull section that was larger than the shuttle itself.

The explosions from the missiles blossomed like roses of fire and destruction, and Kat lost her orientation to the hangar bay she'd been aiming for. But then the airless cold of space ate enough of the fiery maelstrom to reveal the open bay, and Kat pushed the shuttle in at quarter throttle.

"Watch it!" shouted the captain. "You're too—"

Kat blocked him out as she threaded the needle of the rapidly approaching shielded portal. She distantly wondered if it was set to atmospheric barrier, or would it be dialed up to full repulse? If the latter, she and the rest of the ship were about to get a nasty lesson in physics.

Some instinct told her to reach out and grabbed for the reversers. There was still time...

"The repulsor barrier is down," intoned the emperor as he leaned in from the main cabin.

His voice calmed Kat, and she flew the approach, just barely getting the shuttle inside the bay before yet more missiles detonated against the hull. She lowered the gears and set the ship down on the empty deck. Not a soul moved out there. It was like being a fly inside a giant clean room.

"You have done well, Lieutenant Haladis," said the emperor. "Stay with the ship. If we do not return within the hour, lift off and save yourself."

Kat's pain was gone.

Or, she thought, it was probably still there, but buried by the fact that her body was shaking with fear. From the approach, she told herself—because that's what she wanted to believe.

And then the emperor was gone.

The captain pushed past her in the cramped cockpit. "Good flying, Lieutenant. Thanks for not killing everyone." He handed her his sidearm. "Use this. I wouldn't want anything bad to happen to you."

And then he too was gone.

Goth Sullus led the Praetorians forward into the belly of the Cybar mother ship. If it had taken any damage, there was no sign of it. It was hard to fathom that this ship had been the target of a full fleet alpha strike. Everything looked pristine, cold, impersonal... and orderly.

"Curious..." muttered the emperor to himself.

But of course... it was a ship full of robots. Of course it would be ordered and symmetrical. They did not have the same needs, goals, or weaknesses.

Sullus had never much subscribed to all the theories about AIs being sentient, living beings. To him they were merely advanced forms of bots playing a game they'd been coded to play. When he reached out to manipulate them, sense them, or destroy them, they didn't feel like life to him. They felt empty, blank.

And now he would crush them.

The first wave of Titans came at Sullus and the Praetorians before they even reached the main blast doors that led away from the hangar deck. Six of them, moving in two groups of three, each carrying a massive tri-barreled N-50, of the type that was normally mounted to a vehicle of servo-harness.

The sheer volume of fire they emitted was impressive. But their shots were reflected away from those standing nearest the emperor.

The Praetorians fired back almost instantly. Some took a knee or unloaded from the hip to lay down suppressive fire while marksmen threw themselves to the deck to set up for targeted shots.

Three shock troopers went down almost instantly. One of the troopers made the mistake of attempting to protect the emperor. Sullus physically tossed him aside, and with a gesture employed the unreal power of the Crux against the nearest Titan. A wave of force knocked the spitting tri-barreled N-50 from the metallic monster's hands. Then with the merest of waves from Sullus, the Titan's internal circuitry released in a machine part–laden volcanic eruption.

Even as that bot was dying and the Praetorians were slamming blaster bolts into the other Titans' sturdy hyper-alloy forged frames, Sullus took two steps forward to engage the next one. Though it easily weighed in at a full three tons, a simple push from the Crux sent it hard into the wall halfway up the twenty-meter-high bulkhead. It crashed to the floor, immobile.

Sullus turned to the next group of three. Holding up one knife-edged palm, he again leveraged the invisible power of the Crux, this time to sweep all three off their legs and send them careening across the deck of the hangar.

The Praetorians had managed to take out the remaining Titan collectively, by concentrating all of their blaster fire on the one war bot. And even then, it had not gone down easily. Even when every limb had been blasted away from the thing, it had sat down and glared at them until additional blaster fire at last brought about its destruction.

Leaving the six destroyed Titans and three dead Praetorians behind, Sullus led his strike force deeper into the mysterious ship.

502nd Legion, Bravo Company, Third Platoon
Imperial Flagship *Imperator*

The deck within the wide tunnel that led from *Imperator*'s main transportation bridge to its bow was clean save for the mag-lev rails that ran its center. Despite the darkness, the legionnaires were able to switch to low-light imaging and advance swiftly up the ship.

They would have been eviscerated by the anti-personnel mines the troopers had set up to use against any Legion units choosing this method of assault on the command bridge, but Payday, who always walked point because he was sharp on levels that verged into the unreal, spotted the chained system of mines that lay alongside the rails. The 502nd had done a lot of duty out on worlds gone insurgent, so they were more than familiar with IEDs and mines.

It wasn't until the mag-lev rail began a steep curve up into the stories-tall command stack that the 502nd came under fire from a unit of shock troopers. Rebound was just preparing to remote-detonate another chained mine system with a comm scrambler he carried when the shock troopers opened up from the darkness above.

A couple of the 502nd were hit, but they were able to pull back under cover of the curve of the tunnel while Hardcore assessed the situation, called in to command, and came up with a plan.

The troopers were fighting from a superior position—they had taken up positions in the stories-tall bridge stack that dominated the rear of the Black Fleet battleship, where the rail system climbed steeply to near vertical. But within two minutes the sergeant had the squad-designated marksmen pinning down those entrenched troopers so that the teams could run forward and began to climb the steep grade. When the teams were close enough, they used fraggers to knock out the emplaced firing positions.

"These troopers ain't so bad," remarked Sergeant Hardcore.

Ten minutes later they finished the arduous climb—the rail system went almost vertical toward the end—and ingressed into the main hab of the battleship.

Payback, backed up two other legionnaires, took point. So he was the first to see the destruction at the first landing on one of the lower bridge levels—the remains of a furious battle between leejes and troopers. Apparently some forward element, possibly one of the first to board the battleship, had made it this far. The fighting had been brutal and intense, with both sides annihilating each other to the point of zero unit viability. If there had been survivors, they had escaped off into the darkness, or to other battles.

Turtle surveyed the carnage. "Got so bad that they ran out of charge packs," he remarked. "Real knife and gun show near the end."

"Musta been," added another leej, looking down at a dead trooper with the hilt of a combat knife sticking out from under his bucket.

"All right, forget this," said Sergeant Hardcore as though shaking off some chill that had crossed the room. "Form up. Other teams are getting ready to hit the Oh-Be-Jay."

Above them, somewhere along a not-too-distant part of the outer hull, came a groan and the clamp of something heavy. It sounded as though a machine had attached itself to the hull.

The chatter over L-comm fell to silence as the platoon proceeded, weapons ready, checking corners, and prepared for it to be "on" at any second.

Praetorian Strike Team
Cybar Mother Ship

Captain Sturm led the emperor's strike team deeper into the bizarre ship. The farther they went, the more Titans they encountered. Always in waves. And always more in number, as though the machines weren't quite sure how many Titans was the exact and required number to be used for optimal destruction of an invading enemy force. With Sullus fighting alongside the Praetorian shock troopers, the number the Cybar provided was never enough.

Their biggest scare, at least as far as Sturm was concerned, occurred in a strange room that looked like the inside of a giant rotating keylock, except that the tumblers were pearlescent pink and the room seemed to be rotating this way and that, and no matter how hard the mind tried to make sense of it, the mind could not.

It was here that twenty of the towering Titans had attacked from every direction. Sullus had used his arcane and invisible powers to destroy most of them. But in the end, as a Titan who'd just rushed the emperor had been hoisted into the air above the firing Praetorians by some unseen invisible hand, Sullus had been unsatisfied to merely toss the war bot aside like he had so many others. Instead he rushed forward, pulled free the torch he carried on his belt, and sliced the thing in two with its fiery blade.

After that encounter, Captain Sturm studied the emperor. No obvious damage had been done to their sovereign, but there was something... something fatigued... about the way he stood.

And then Captain Sturm had to remind himself that they were all fatigued. All tired. And they were leaving a trail of dead behind them that their own minds weren't keeping up with. The Imperial strike team was already down to half strength.

The Praetorians had been a decorated unit at Tarrago. They had all trained together since before the war. Had trained for these battles out there in the private training camps and schools along galaxy's edge. To be a shock trooper was to leave behind whatever life you'd once lived within the Galactic Republic. Forever. This was your life now. These were your brothers.

And now over half of them had been slaughtered by metal nightmares become real. The old war bots had returned from legend, more fearsome than ever. And Sturm suspected he was not alone in having a sinking feeling that they, the strike team of Praetorians, were now lost inside the massive alien ship. That the emperor was leading them too deep to ever return... even if he did.

"They can't figure out the right number to use to crush us," gasped Captain Sturm after another firefight that saw five more Praetorians die badly. He noted that his exhaustion was obvious in his voice, even through the electronically modulated speaker of his bucket.

The emperor, who was still holding his burning torch, switched off the beam that came from the hilt. He turned to the captain. His voice was cold and hollow. Tired. Old.

"No," said Goth Sullus. "They're testing us, Captain Sturm. Testing me, to be more specific. Whatever this intelligence is, it wants to know what I'm capable of. So it's using its resources incrementally so that it will have the perfect data set once it's finally beaten us."

Sturm said nothing for a long moment. But inside he was asking... What are you capable of? Exactly?

502nd Legion, Bravo Company, Third Platoon
Lower Decks, Command Section, Aboard Imperial Flagship *Imperator*

The ship rumbled from a distant explosion. The smell of smoke, always a disconcerting thing on any starship, was heavy in the air now, but the ship's ventilation and purification system was doing a remarkable job of moving it toward venting hull sections. From space, the battleship must have looked like a smoking wreck.

As Third Platoon made its way up through the ruined decks, Harmoor was getting sitreps from command, indicating that most of the Legion was now aboard and ready to take the bridge. At one point the platoon linked up with some lost scouts from a leej company that had been decimated by crossfire in a section a few blast doors forward of their position. After exchanging intel, the scouts continued on trying to link up with survivors from their unit. But L-comm was struggling and even going offline at points. Which was odd. Nothing like that had ever happened in anyone's experience. Of all the Legion equipment that could too often not be relied upon in battle, L-comm had proven itself more reliable than most.

The decks looked had been ruined by blaster fire and shrapnel-laden explosions. High-tech ship equipment was gutted and blow apart. Power cores were popped and snapped from gaping wounds. Chemical fires burned out of control in some passages. And below their boots, far below, the lower decks groaned as though their structural integrity was a thing not long for the galaxy. They passed uncounted dead legionnaires and shock troopers, and each time the medic, Corporal Fausto, went down on a knee to run a vital scan.

They found no survivors.

It was Payback who heard it first. Of course.

A low whine, like a hydraulic lift.

L-comm was completely gone by now, and the interference, or whatever it was that was taking down the communication system, had forced Third to switch to hand signals and external audio. Payback held up one fist, and the platoon, stacked in twos along the ruined, blackened corridor they were moving down, halted as one.

The first Titan came out of the wall directly beside them.

Turtle, who was carrying the N-42, was pulled off his feet and hurled into the opposite wall like he was nothing more than a dead leaf.

Nearby legionnaires froze, even though they'd traveled the galaxy killing all kinds of foes. What they were seeing now was probably flat-out the weirdest. The nine-foot-tall war bot emerged from the battle-damaged blackened wall it had been mirroring with some kind of active camo system. It switched to a gleaming robotic silver as it raised its massive tri-barreled N-50 and start firing into the legionnaires at point blank.

None of them stood a chance.

One N-50 high-velocity, high-energy gain blast is enough to make a fist-sized entry hole and a head-sized exit hole in any living being it hits. Not even leej armor, and especially the new stuff, held up against that.

Before anyone even knew what was going on, five legionnaires had been eviscerated by a blur of fire. And the metallic beast didn't slow. It pivoted mechanically and rapidly, unloading on everything forward of its position.

Sergeant Hardcore barely had time to throw himself around a corner in the passage and hug wall as men to his right and left dropped from the powerful impacts of the rotating tri-barrel.

The few legionnaires to the rear unloaded full auto at the war bot's back. But it merely swiveled its Greek-hoplite bucket, three red eye-sensors glaring, and laced its attackers with targeting lasers. Then, as it marched up the corridor killing legionnaires with ease, it swung its heavy rifle backward without bothering to look and ventilated the legionnaires still firing ineffectively at its back.

Hardcore called for an anti-tank weapon. One of the few leejes still on his feet dropped his rifle and pulled the AT launcher. At that same moment, the Titan re-prioritized its threat analysis, moving that legionnaire to the front of the queue.

A hurricane of blaster bolts smashed into the young leej's armor, and Hardcore could do no more than pull the dead man back behind cover and grab his AT weapon.

He armed. Didn't bother to sightline fire. Instead he just triggered it on the fly. The micro-rocket lanced out, sidewindering... and smashed into the ceiling as though its tracking had been hijacked.

He scrambled down the dark passage away from the killing machine. Ten feet later he found the second of the three-Titan team that had ambushed the entire platoon.

Hardcore was the last to die, unaware that the first and third Titan had finished cleaning up the rest of the platoon that now lay dead on the lower bridge decks of Imperator.

Praetorian Strike Team
Cybar Mother Ship

The Praetorians were down to a little over ten percent of their original number. They were now five, including their captain, and along with their emperor they raced through the strange ship, passing chambers and holds that looked like the insides of some robotic alien life form that defied comprehension.

The numbers of Titans that came at the remaining Praetorians and their warrior-emperor at the next choke point reached the outer edges of extreme.

Sullus pulled one Titan off its feet, drawing the flailing machine toward himself as other Titans fired directly at him. Some blasts seemed to veer off of their own accord, while others struck near and close. One hit the ancient Mark I armor and rebounded away on a high-pitched note. But the strike caused Sullus to lose focus and drop his latest machine-victim to the gleaming steel deck. He hunched over from the blow that had struck his armor dead on.

Sturm yelled, "Cover me!" and rushed to Sullus's side to drag him away from the firefight. Two shock troopers deployed high-yield stun grenades—special-issue Praetorian equipment—and bought enough time for the strike team to put some distance between themselves and the pursuing horde.

"Hurry, sire," urged Sturm as he led Sullus away down a strange octagonal passage that seemed to be constructed of a million different fractal surfaces constantly shifting and engaging with one another in new formations. The trailing Praetorians fired back at the slow but determined advance of the looming Titans.

"We're close," muttered the emperor, who began to walk on his own after a few more steps. "I sense its presence. It's both curious... and afraid. Which is a new experience for it. It's ordering everything to stop us now. We are the priority. Things are about to get... very difficult."

"Then how are we supposed to get through this? And what is this thing?" Sturm yelled raggedly as he burned through a full charge back to put down a closing Titan.

"We'll lure them into a trap. We're close to one of the hangars that face the fleet. How is your comm to the fleet?"

"Negative since we boarded, sir," said Sturm hopelessly. "We're cut off and unsupported."

The Titans fired and advanced.

The Praetorians, to their credit, had by now identified "kill spots" on the great war bots, and were able to put down more than their fair share of the mechanical monsters. These weak points included the hip and joint assemblies, along with what passed for a throat. Hip shots shut down their ability to move; throat shots terminated runtime. But even with this newly acquired knowledge, there were far too many of them.

"Just... keep them busy for a moment," huffed a near-breathless Sullus. His voice was like a ragged machine wheezing through the armor's audio filters.

Then he knelt down on one knee and bowed his head to his gauntlet. As though he were thinking deeply.

Auxiliary Bridge
Imperial Flagship *Imperator*

Twenty minutes earlier Admiral Rommal had been this close to scuttling the ship and ordering the surviving crew to the escape pods. It had been so desperate and so close Rommal had already asked *Revenge* to stand by to transfer his flag.

But then some new invasion force had stopped the legionnaires dead in their tracks. And while this new combatant wasn't discriminating between shock troopers and legionnaires, it was keeping the ship from being completely taken by the Legion.

Imperator had managed to re-establish control of her ion guns by using a combined shock trooper and algorithm systems hack. Targeting wasn't good, but at this range it didn't matter. Even with poor aim, Imperator had already taken out three Legion destroyers.

Admiral...

Rommal heard the ghostly voice of the emperor inside his head. And almost immediately his present surroundings—the cramped auxiliary bridge deep within the heavy blast door–protected internal sections of the Imperator's command stack—faded away.

Rommal was inside a shadow space that felt both empty and vast. Except the darkness was like a living thing. Clutching at him. Wanting to take him within its folds for a thousand years. It felt cold. Like death must feel. That was the thought his stark raving mind had as it tried to piece together just exactly how he'd been killed. How he was here. How he was no longer in the battle.

Had legionnaires, or perhaps those massive gleaming war bots, stormed the bridge and shot the high-value target admiral first? Was that how I died? the admiral asked himself.

Had the Imperator had gone up like a supernova in an instant? Sudden reactor cascade? Damage to the hyperdrive shifting the ship into a million pieces? One of the main SSM magazines going nuclear, igniting hundreds of thousands of tons of fissionable torpedoes?

Self-destruct? No, only he could order that.

Maybe he had.

Admiral... repeated the voice of the emperor. Aim your ion guns at the point on the mother ship you now see inside your mind. Then fire.

The voice felt like an icy hand grabbing at his stomach, or his kidneys... or even his heart. It was the most real thing he'd ever heard inside his mind.

Fire now, Admiral.

As he heard the emperor's voice, his desire to obey that command was based in the most primal of his personal fears. Unreasonable childhood fears of darkness and disappearance for all time.

Rommal saw an image of the alien ship that had entered the battle late.

He saw the spot he was to fire upon.

And then he was back on the bridge.

Damage control sirens wailed. The sound of blaster fire was near and close at hand. Only a few shock troopers guarded the final blast doors.

"Admiral," said one of his officers. "The Legion will take the ship in the next few minutes."

Fire now, Admiral.

His mind ached like it had been pulled from a frozen lake after ten thousand years.

"Is something wrong, Admiral?" asked the CIC officer from nearby in the emergency-lit darkness.

"No... nothing," began a hesitant Rommal.

"We must evacuate, Admiral."

When Rommal said nothing, the officer stepped away.

Rommal remembered the voice. He remembered what it had told him to do.

"Fire control," he croaked. "Engage with helm and maneuver the ship into position to fire on the alien ship."

There was a pause in the silence. The bridge crew was busy fighting the line of Legion destroyers close at hand. Turning away now, maneuvering the turrets that had been brought to bear, would create a massive advantage for the enemy. The destroyers would be able to fire into the unprotected engines.

And that would be the death of the ship.

"Do it now!" Rommal shouted.

The crew rushed to obey.

The OIC in charge of helm called out the steering change. Engineering reports came in acknowledging the request to divert power. In an instant, battery commanders were filling the comm with bewildered chatter that sounded like a thousand electronic insect drones angrily reacting to something they could not believe.

"Arm main ion guns for a shot," barked Rommal with utter conviction.

The gunnery officer was on the comm with the battery crew that had replaced the dead crew.

"Guns ready to fire," announced the gunnery officer. "Standing by for target."

Rommal stumbled forward to a tactical display of the alien ship. He found the spot he'd seen in that dark cold place of death that had wanted him for a thousand years.

Of starvation.

Of cold.

Of not death.

Hell.

"Here!" he said, stabbing at the screen indicating the targeting point on the Cybar mother ship.

The gunnery officer transferred a targeting grid and flipped it to the targeting control officer on site inside the battery.

"Firing now," came the electronic voice. It sounded muted. Matter-of-fact.

The heavily damaged Imperator shook as both ion shots left the guns.

Praetorian Strike Team
Cybar Mother Ship

The emperor raised his head. "They're firing on us, Captain. Shots will be here in thirty seconds. Tell your men to pull back and stand close to me."

The Titans were everywhere. Coming out of the walls, swarming the passages, dragging one of the shock troopers into the gleaming metallic death press surging toward the surviving Praetorians.

As Sturm pulled his men back, the emperor used an old trick. A Rechs trick. Not the Crux. Truth be told, he was almost out. He was exhausted. Drained. Weak. He'd been using the torch to cut his way through the machine monsters more than he'd been smashing, ripping, and tearing them apart with his mind.

But Rechs's old armor from inside the Quantum Palace of long ago... the original prototype of the modern legionnaire armor... was a thing of wonders. Wonders that sometimes worked. And sometimes didn't.

One of those wonders was a force shield bubble that not even the height of Republic science had ever been able to duplicate.

Except it didn't always work like it was supposed to. Or at all. Sometimes.

Sullus activated the system with his mind. He'd made it work only once during the refit he'd given it after stripping it from Rechs's dead body.

The Cybar were everywhere. There was no place where there wasn't a mass of bots swarming in. Not only Titans now, but machines of all shapes and sizes. The AI was no longer testing, probing. It meant to win. Here. Now.

The Praetorians were firing on full auto. Weapons blurring out high-powered energy shots in every direction. "Last mag," one of them called out. Then another repeated the warning.

The line... thought Sullus. It is this close.

The entire ship collapsed in on itself. Or rather, the bulkhead horizon that could be seen down Cybar-swollen passages, walls, and tetragonal gleaming blast doors that seemed the things of lost giants, rushed suddenly from far away to near at hand.

Sullus knew what was happening.

Both ion rounds, despite the targeting issues the Imperator was having, had found their target in the hangar bay of the ship. A typically weak point in most ships. Even the Cybar, with their super-intelligence, had never managed to solve that ages-old problem.

In the second before the Cybar would have been pushed into the emperor and his men, melting and twisting from the surface-of-the-sun heat of both shots and the unreal kinetic force... the old Mark I armor's force bubble bulged out and stopped the monster metal horror show carnage. Just a meter from the gleaming buckets of the shock troopers.

Then the world turned to white-hot fire.

Sullus reached out with what was left of his mind and sought the Crux. He forced it to push the suit's bubble outward. To maintain its power and presence. He felt it wanting to collapse. Wanting to pop out of existence and allow them all to be cooked and mashed down to their molecular minimums.

He felt the Praetorians lose their minds and surrender to sweet unconsciousness. Their ability to comprehend death, to explain what was happening—the unexplainable—savaged their psyches.

But Sullus remained conscious. He saw the state of the battle. Saw how close he was to losing everything...

Breathing. Seeing everything with closed eyes as the bubble tried to press itself inward in the face of the sudden power released into the titanic alien ship.

A ship that had summoned everything to save itself in this wounding moment. Summoned everything to kill the entity known as Goth Sullus. Surrounded him with everything it had.

And then the ion guns had fired and cooked it all to slag.

When the bubble failed, they were deep inside the ship. Deep inside a strange and alien place no human mind was ever meant to see.

Admiral, he called to Rommal. I have one last task for you to perform.

And then he told the admiral what to do.

Goth Sullus opened his eyes.

Green light washed over a chamber through which a strange and slender bridge ran off into unseen distances. Those strange fractal surfaces, shifting and interlocking, making new surfaces, formed every inch of the titanic wall that surrounded the platform where the four survivors had landed.

The ship had sealed the hull breach from the ion shots as best as it could.

Sullus felt the rush of escaping oxygen. A green mist was being sucked toward the wound in the mother ship's side. But that did not bother him. In time that faded, and then ceased. The ship was still trying to save itself.

Sullus could feel its fear.

It was afraid of dying. And it was many things. Not the one thing it pretended to be. It was an army. A legion. It was part of many legions. And it was from far away. From farther than he'd gone out beyond the galaxy's edge. It was as alien as the word was ever meant to be used.

This was the thing, or at least part of it, that he and Reina... the long-lost Reina... had known was coming for the galaxy.

These were the things that even the Ancients had been afraid of.

They hadn't felt fear in millennia unrecorded.

Sullus stood.

The Praetorians around him looked like dead bodies. But he could sense the tenuous thin strand of life within them. To his credit, Captain Sturm tried to rise, but he only made it to his hands and knees.

Sullus left them and crossed the bridge, venturing deeper into the alien ship.

And as he did so, he began to talk to them, the aliens, with his mind.

They begged him. Begged him not to do what he was about to do. At first they lied. Pretending to be merely the Cybar. Even they themselves had begun to believe that they were. But in the end—gibbering, utterly mad—they confessed to their true identity.

Halfway across the bridge Sullus activated his torch. It shone like a lone fiery brand in the darkness of interlocking charcoal shapes and drifting green mist.

He followed their fear deeper and deeper into the ship. They had nothing left to oppose him with now. All the Titans had been killed by the targeted ion guns. They tried a few spider bots, but those were child's play for the Crux, which slowly returned to Sullus.

The torch, as he'd discovered, helped him to focus.

In time he violated the outer locks of their innermost sanctum. A place where they had not even taken Prisma. And it was here that Goth Sullus encountered the aroma of the Crux.

"Prismaaa," he whispered. Sensing its difference from what he knew. Something other than the Crux he had acquired and learned to wield.

Now there is another, he thought within the dark mansions of his mind. And he wondered how, or who, had taught her to wield the Crux.

We will serve you, they begged when they knew, because they too could sense things beyond the physical. When they knew that he had come to destroy them. We can add to your great power.

Sullus found them.

In the final chamber. His Crux had returned and was so great he tore the guarding blast door from its interlocking pins, easily three meters thick, with little effort.

He entered the darkness beyond. His torch was the only light within that deep darkness.

We are your slaves, they crooned. Oh, Goth Sullus, long have we known of you. We are your slaves now. We yield.

They were an eye watching him. An eye filled with fear and desperation. An eye so old that time lost meaning. An eye that did nothing but want.

And what it wanted was destruction.

A lidless eye that never slept.

A robotic eye that swam with madness. Madness bred in another galaxy, out there across the darknesses.

Goth Sullus studied them. Their whispers, their pleas, their begging.

And he knew he would destroy them.

They were a threat to his power. Their power...

We will become your power, they sang in a sudden desperately gleeful chorus of begging.

We have a way.

A red light shone on a pedestal that appeared out of nowhere.

Lying on it was a simple ring. Not a piece of jewelry... but a thing made of those same interlocking charcoal-dusted fractal surfaces. In minutiae. So small one had to look close to see anything other than just a simple ring.

Take it.

Everything that we are will be bound to it. Whoever wears this... wields us for the great weapon we were sent to be. The power to destroy galaxies. The power to rule. Technology not even you, oh Goth Sullus, have ever dared to dream of. We know the Quantum. We have been to the palace.

Sullus raised the torch above his head.

He would strike into the center of the eye, and they would die. They would die, and he would have no other rival for mastery of the galaxy.

All that we were is in the ring now.

We are yours.

Sullus lowered the torch.

Power...

Rechs had warned him against it. Everyone... everyone who had power had warned him against using it for the things that needed to be done to save the galaxy.

The people who had power always warned you not to use that very same power they wielded.

What had Urmo said...?

Power is neither good nor evil.

Sullus switched off the torch.

Think of the good that you could do...

The eye had died. He could sense that it was no longer a living thing. They had all gone into the ring. Every Cybar, all their ships, this ship... dead now. The Cybar were gone. He could feel them all in the ring like a living wild animal in a dark forest of howling madness. But the dog would obey. It yielded at his feet, whimpering for his hand.

Your ring.

His ring.

His mind caressed it, and he saw the locks and barriers that had been built to restrain them. Simple things he could control. He could decide how things would be done.

How the ring would be used.

How they would obey him.

How the galaxy could be saved despite the deals he'd made with the House of Reason and his ruined fleet.

With the ring, he would need so much less of all the weak things that had stood in his way.

He took it up. Stared at it in the palm of his mailed gauntlet.

It resized itself to accommodate the armored ring finger.

And then, thinking of all the good he might do...

He slipped it on.

Maybe the battle might still have been won. Reports from inside *Imperator*, just before it blew up, were that the machines had simply stopped working. They died in the middle of firefights with legionnaires.

Then... most of the active Legion forces involved in the combat, taking the mighty Imperial battleship... were gone. Killed in action as the massive ship exploded without warning.

The Republic's destroyers had been firing into the Imperator when it went up. Sending sections and debris in every direction. Most of the nearby Legion ships were damaged in the blast.

Rommal had performed his final service for the emperor he had anointed. He had done the unthinkable.

He had activated Imperator's emergency self-destruct.

Keller, inside the Mercutio, sat down in a chair as though the life had gone out of him. The bridge crew gasped in shock and horror at the sudden and complete destruction of the flagship Imperator.

The battle was lost. The most significant Legion force within the galaxy had just been annihilated in one blast.

"All ships..." said Admiral Ubesk over the grim silence that had fallen across every bridge as they watched the expanding supernova of debris spreading away from where Imperator had once been. "Prepare to execute jump retreat."

Too many lives had been lost.

The Legion was dead.

Yes, out there in distant outposts there were still legionnaires... but for all intents and purposes the Legion Fleet had just lost its effective fighting force in one battle.

All that was left now was to escape. Whatever legionnaires remained on the assault ships that had survived the blast would escape and—

"Enemy ships in sectors seven, eight, and sixteen. Inbound. It's an MCR fleet."

What was left of the Legion fleet was scrambling now. Setting up jump calcs as the combined MCR fleet swept in, firing SSMs and blaster turrets at the shot-to-pieces Legion fleet.

Wounded destroyers either exploded or broke apart under this new onslaught. Escape pods erupted away from burning ships. Ubesk did everything he could to get the Mercutio clear, but a strike by MCR fighters knocked out her jump drive.

"Multiple incoming SSMs" was announced by the bridge AI.

If Commander Keller had lived five minutes more, he would have heard the general broadcast from the House of Reason, welcoming their new emperor… Goth Sullus. Accepting any terms and conditions he chose to dictate. Every MCR ship was broadcasting this signal.

But by then every Legion ship was burning into the atmosphere of Utopion, caught between the overwhelming numbers of the MCR fleet and the planetary defense shield. Or they were broken up and drifting, a vapor cloud of debris. Or they were dead in space.

The Legion was no more.

EPILOGUE

CHHUN

Legion Destroyer *Intrepid*
Ankalor System, Deep Space Patrol
Several Days Earlier

Major Owens pushed a pre-filled glass of what looked to be Faldoran scotch to Captain Chhun, who sat on the opposite side of the major's desk. "Have some. I don't hold any illusions about whether or not you're going to like what I say, Cohen."

Chhun didn't know exactly what Owens had called him into his office for, but it was formal enough that the words didn't surprise him. There was a lot to be unhappy about lately.

He waved off the proffered hospitality. "Thank you, sir. No."

Owens nodded, then reached out to bring the glass back in front of him. "Well, I shouldn't let this go to waste." He took a large drink, and Chhun watched to see if any driblets might run down his beard. Owens looked like he was drinking for courage, which was odd, because Chhun thought of him as one of the bravest legionnaires he'd ever met.

"Sir," Chhun said, "if this is about my recommendation that Fish be awarded the Order of the Centurion, I stand by my report. I know we're in the thick of things now, but honoring heroes of the Republic will send a good message to the Legion and the galaxy that we remain dedicated to serving the Republic and honoring those who gave their lives doing so."

"That's not it," Owens said, shaking his head. "Yes, Fish deserves the Order. Of course. So do a lot of others. I don't know when we'll get around to it, but it will happen. But what I called you in to speak about was Kill Team Victory."

"We've... taken a real beating."

"That's an understatement. You've practically lost a man on each of your last operations."

Chhun opened his mouth to protest, but Owens held up a hand to indicate he wasn't finished.

"I'm not blaming you for that. You've done a remarkable job and are a credit to Dark Ops. But as it stands, your team is now at less than half strength."

"We can review for replacements," Chhun said, his mind already moving toward continuation of the mission. "I can think of at least two leejes who were part of that QRF down on Ankalor who I think could make the jump..."

"Cohen," interjected Owens, "I'm deactivating Kill Team Victory."

Chhun knew that he looked surprised—shocked, even. He let that expression exist only for a second before regaining his composure. The major—soon to be a lieutenant colonel if admin ever caught up—was on his side. He knew that. So he didn't yell or shout. He thought of every unflappable officer he'd ever admired in his time of the Legion. He sought to emulate men like Wraith... until he went off the deep end, at least.

"Major, with all due respect, Kill Team Victory is among the most effective and decorated Dark Ops squads ever to operate." Chhun felt a sense of pride and duty to the men who had made that happen. "Further, it is a direct continuation of Victory Company—in spirit if not letter—and Victory and its stand on Kublar has served as an object of pride and inspiration for the entire Legion."

"Yes, agreed. But I can't change my mind on this one." Owens leaned back in his chair, gripping the armrests and rotating himself in a half-circle. "And here's why: the Legion commander has assigned me to undertake a mission that will take me away from here. It's to be expected, really. I can't be the head man in Dark Ops and still oversee the day-to-day of the kill teams in this sector. There's already grumbling that what happened to the teams on Utopion when we tried to grab the delegates was because I was trying to do too much at once."

Owens leaned forward across the desk. "Someone has to take my place here. Now, Cohen, you have shown yourself to be a capable leader—more than capable—since the day I met you. I'd tell you in confidence that you're the best team leader I've ever had if I didn't worry it would go to your head and make your bucket too tight."

"Thank you, sir."

"It was you who took the reins of Victory Squad and made it into what it became. And your ability to take your knowledge base and train other leejes to enhance their abilities—your ability to implement creative tactics and adapt—that's something that Dark Ops, and the Legion, need right now. To put it bluntly, Ankalor chewed us up more than we expected, and Utopion cost us more Dark Ops leejes than we could afford to lose."

Chhun found himself nodding along. The two men stared at one another from opposite sides of the table.

"What would happen to Bear and Masters?" Chhun asked.

"They would be rotated into new teams. A lot of them are missing guys, same as Victory was. What would you suggest?"

"Bear is the assistant team leader. He would be a good choice to join a squad as a team leader. Masters could do well from a technical perspective, but I don't know that he has the temperament for a TL. He's the kind of guy who keeps a team light and loose, one of those glue guys. Though he's done admirably when it's been his turn to plan ops."

Owens nodded, but made no comment.

"Would I be working from the deep space station your old office was in?"

"No. Intrepid has been re-fitted to include five kill teams, and this new command structure would be set up with you as a mobile Dark Ops commander, deploying missions directly from the ship. I can send you a list of teams and personnel scheduled to come on board, but before we get to that, I need you to sign off and tell me you're in."

Chhun hesitated, wrestling with the decision. He was engrossed in thought. In another world, almost.

Rapping his knuckles gently on the desk, Owens said, "Hey. Trust me... I know what it's like to make that transition from an active team leader to a desk jockey. But as a major, you'll still have the option and ability to go on missions as needed. Like I did to help capture General-I-have-absolutely-no-intel-and-nothing-to-say." Owens looked aside and let out a hiss. "About all that op did for us was blow up a Black Fleet freighter and delay us from getting into the fight on Ankalor."

Chhun could tell that the loss of Kill Team Zenith and the stealth shuttle Night Stalker was still weighing on his boss. "Didn't matter who was on the op," he said. "That shuttle would have gone down regardless."

"I probably wouldn't have put you on that shuttle," Owens said, "but point taken. So, you in? I can transfer you to another team that's missing its TL, but I think you're ready to take on this challenge. Don't you?"

"I accept," Chhun said.

Owens looked relieved.

"On condition that I get to decide where Bear and Masters end up."

"Done."

"Thank you, sir. I'll admit the difficulty I had was more with Victory ceasing to exist than it was with moving into the role itself. That part, I kind of thought might be coming already."

Owens gave a quick nod, clearly wanting to get on to further business. "Like I said, the team is only deactivated, not erased from history. Once we get our bearings back and finish up Article Nineteen, there'll be an opportunity to evaluate shooters and rebuild your strength. You can start Victory right up again. Remember, the squad was born out of Kublar—created out of necessity. Now necessity is requiring us to make this move. You've come full circle, Cohen."

Chhun closed his eyes, bowed his head, and let out a cathartic sigh. "Poetic, right? What about Ford? Do I take over his mission?"

Owens frowned. "I'll let you know. The role Captain Ford has with Dark Ops—and the Legion for that matter—is part of a stack of things that still need deciding."

"Fair enough. When do I get my oak leaves?"

Owens laughed. "Look at me. I'm still waiting, and word is I'll get bumped to colonel after this op. We'll take care of this when I get back. You'll at least get the pay now. Not that you ever spend it."

Chhun smiled. "I'm surprised we can afford something like that, being a treasonous rogue military and all. Can't be all that much left in our treasury. Or did kicking all the points out really save us that much money?"

A white, toothy smile appeared from behind Owens's big red beard. "You'll do well in this, Cohen. You've excelled consistently as long as I've known you. My aide will assist in whatever transitional needs come up. And then when I get back I'll work with you directly to get you fully up to speed. But as of right now, you are in command of the Dark Ops teams serving aboard Intrepid. Captain Deynolds is, of course, aware of the pending change. She's eager to work with you and wanted me to extend to you her congratulations."

"What should my teams' role be in regard to Utopion?"

Owens slapped the desk somewhat nervously and stood up. "It's in play. But Legion Commander Keller wants to keep a strategic number of ships back for a variety of reasons. Not the least of which is the trouble that the MCR and Black Fleet are causing to systems throughout the galaxy. We need to show the citizens of the Republic that the Legion has every intention of continuing to protect and serve."

"So Intrepid will be limited in the scope of its operations?" Chhun asked. He understood the reasoning, but didn't quite agree with the conclusion. "Sir, holding a ship like this back from a potential fight to take Utopion will make things much harder."

Owens pulled Chhun in close and whispered in his ear. "That's what they're sending me for. To win us some more ships. You kick ass out here and make sure the bad guys don't get too comfy."

Chhun nodded, stepped back, and saluted. "Yes, sir."

Owens returned the salute. "Congratulations, Captain Chhun."

"Thank you, sir." On his way out the door, Chhun paused to say, "Good luck, sir."

"Thanks, Cohen. I think I'll need it."

"This is highly prejudicial and unfair." Masters was half-dressed, wearing only shorts and a pair of shower shoes, hair still dripping down his back.

"Word of the day?" asked Bear from his favored recliner in the team's lounge.

Masters beamed. He'd been attempting to learn a new vocabulary word to use each day. He liked it when people noticed. "Yup."

"Nice." Bear held up an oak-like arm and bumped fists with his teammate. His large hand fell down into his lap, making a loud slap against his thigh. "Not your call to make, though."

"I didn't like it either," said Chhun, who had been the deliverer of the news about Victory Squad's deactivation. "But there's no changing it."

Masters looked around the room. He picked up his gaming pad and caressed it. "Guess I'd better start getting all this stuff to storage. Man... I'll miss this room. We had a lot of cool stuff."

Bear shook his head. "Unbelievable."

"Oh! You thought I was upset about having to leave you guys?" Masters said, exaggerated surprise on his face. "No, you see, I've been trying to get away from you guys for years. I just don't want the navy to lose my stuff is all."

"Neither of you have to leave the Intrepid unless you want to," Chhun said. "The ship's been refitted to fit five Dark Ops kill teams with a mission to patrol a yet-to-be-determined sector of Republic space and be a thorn in the sides of the MCR and Black Fleet. Republic peacekeepers."

"One destroyer for an entire Republic sector?" Bear said.

"Extra kill teams isn't all Intrepid has going for it. Delta Company has been joined by the rest of the Fifty-Fourth Legion plus a full wing of starfighters and fighter-bombers. As well as a captain who isn't afraid to send down orbital bombardments when we ask for it."

"Ooah," Bear answered. "If you're telling me Intrepid is a floating KTF machine, hell yeah I wanna stay on board."

"Yeah, but now we're gonna have a bunch of new Dark Ops leejes rifling through our stuff for sure to see what stays and what goes." Masters dropped his shoulders and looked up, impersonating a frustrated teenager. "Or worse, they'll make us share. Here's what we need to do." He began to pace the room, one hand behind his back like a detective going through a case. "Cap is a big deal now, rubbing shoulders with all those other clean-uniformed Legion officers. He can order the new guys to get rid of all their noncombat gear and just live in a designated corner of our room."

"Not how it works," Bear said, sounding like a parent patiently instructing a child. "Victory is finished, so we're the ones getting new squad brothers. We're the newcomers. And you still might have to move. Just because we're on the same ship doesn't mean we'll be in the same room."

"This just gets worse and worse," Masters said, balled fists on his hips. He looked pleadingly at Chhun. "Captain Chhun... you're my best friend in the whole wide world. You have the power to at least not make me move. So... make me not move."

Chhun smiled. "You can stay right here. This room is going to Kill Team Outlaw. But you'll have to be able to put up with their new TL. They lost their old team leader fighting on Ankalor, plus another man."

"Who's the TL gonna be?"

"Bear," answered Chhun, his smile widening. "So the question is, how do you feel about working under the big man?"

"Terrible."

Bear rocked his head back and let out a one-note laugh. "Ha. Tell me how you really feel!"

Masters did as he was invited. "Oh, sure. Bear's a good enough legionnaire. But he's dumb. I mean, like, incredibly dumb. Also he seems to have forgotten that leejes are issued blaster rifles for reason. Think about it how many times he's dropped his blaster rifle so he can use his bare hands on some poor schmo? You don't want your team leader ordering you to toss your rifle aside and work things out with the mids or whoever man-to-man. Bear would tell us to duke it out with the shock troopers!"

Bear made a show of looking around the room. "Where's my pistol? I'll show you how good I can use one right now."

Chhun clapped his hands together and grew serious. "All kidding aside, I need a yes or no. Because when they promote you, it comes with a twarg-pile of paperwork. And I've gotta get on it."

"Yes," Masters answered soberly. He sounded completely sincere. "Keep me here. Bear will be an excellent TL. And as cool as Victory Team sounded, Outlaw Team sounds pretty badass, too."

"Glad to hear it," Chhun said, turning for the exit. "Because the transport shuttles with the new teams are already here, and your squadmates will be joining you soon. Bear, there's a meeting scheduled with all my TLs for tomorrow at oh-seven-hundred. Fifteen minutes early is on time, anything after that is late."

"Yes, sir."

Dark Ops Briefing Room
Legion Destroyer *Intrepid*

Chhun entered the briefing room from a corridor that led from his office. The room was a duracrete gray, looking like an old-world pillbox. It had been engineered to cut off what happened in the room from all listening technology.

Six kill team members rose from their seats and stood at attention. That was one too many. Chhun quickly assessed the reason for the overage. Bear had brought Outlaw Squad's assistant team leader. That was a good call in this situation. Chhun felt a sense of pride in Bear's ability to get his transition as TL off on the right foot.

Skipping up two steps to reach an elevated dais, Chhun turned to the team leaders, who faced him like pupils in a classroom. "Good morning, gentleman. Please take your seats."

The men did as they were instructed, lowering themselves into stackable, armless chairs.

"I know I've met each of you at least briefly last night, but for those of you bad with names, let me introduce myself."

The group gave a light chuckle.

"I'm Captain Cohen Chhun, formerly of Kill Team Victory, which has since been deactivated. There's a rumor that a major is supposed to hold this position, but we all know how long those rank changes take."

More laughter.

"Kill teams haven't typically interacted much," Chhun continued. "But Intrepid will change that. We're going to remain flexible enough to perform the one-team missions we've all grown accustomed to, but we'll also be undertaking joint-team missions to accomplish for Dark Ops what the Legion would usually achieve through company insertions. The Legion will need that sort of flexibility in this new war.

"It is my hope that before long, we'll know each other well. I'm aware that some of you served as legionnaires in the same company in the past, but please bear with the rest of us as we try to keep all the faces straight—myself included."

The men laughed, but Chhun was just being congenial, employing an ice-breaking tactic he'd read about in one of the never-ending series of leadership books he kept on his datapad. The truth was, he'd spent the night perfecting another leadership tactic: memorizing the face, name, and Dark Ops identifier number of each and every legionnaire under his command. He refused to go to bed until he could successfully cycle through his datapad's memory training app and apply the right name to each soldier.

"Let's begin with reviewing your teams' after-action reports from your most recent ops. I understand that was action on Ankalor for each team." Chhun gestured to the team leader from Kill Team Warbird. "Sergeant Marko, we'll have you begin."

The sergeant stood up. "Sir, should I give the report from here or come up front, or...?"

"Come on up front."

The sergeant joined Chhun on the platform facing his peers. "I'm Sergeant Cory Marko. Kill Team Warbird was inserted by drop shuttle into Ankalor City after the planetary shields were brought down. Our objective was to protect the Green Zone—it was believed by command that the zhee extremists would likely take advantage of the chaos from the main assault and attempt to break into the area. We set up blocking positions in conjunction with private security teams who had the same idea—mostly former Legion or marines. All objectives were met and no casualties were taken."

"Did the zhee attempt an attack on the Green Zone?" Chhun asked.

"Yes, sir," Marko replied. "The donks probed our positions, advancing on foot. After some initial confusion on our part, they were repulsed. They later attempted to drive a sled loaded with explosives toward the main gate, but that attempt was likewise defeated, and the sled was destroyed."

"Very good," said Chhun. "Sustain and improve?"

"Sustains for Kill Team Warbird," Sergeant Marko said, reading from his datapad. "Sustain aggressive reaction when rules of engagement are met. Sustain practice of humping an extra SAB on missions requiring us to hold ground. Really came in handy. Improve communication with joint-force Legion operations. There was a point where we started taking fire from what we assumed were the donks; however, we did not have a clear enough picture of where the Legion blocking positions were set up and weren't able to immediately return fire out of fear of hitting friendlies."

A hand went up from the group. Marko nodded, acknowledging the speaker.

"We ran into a similar situation," said the speaker, whom Lieutenant Chhun identified as First Lieutenant Jeremiah Popp. "Usually our buckets have everybody's position pinged so well that you don't have to worry about knowing where other units are. But things were so thick and intense out there that—and I don't know about the rest of you guys—but we were having difficulty knowing where our leejes were in relation to the enemy. Too many potential hostiles, so the whole picture looked like chaos on the HUD."

Chhun crossed his arms and stroked his chin. "Anyone else experience the same?"

Every hand went up save Bear's. But Victory had positioned itself into a more isolated and unique situation than the rest of the kill teams in service that day.

Chhun nodded. "I think that's a good reminder as this war branches out and expands. We've got to make sure that we're capable of maintaining battlefield communication. Knowing where one another stands on the field is critical. The last thing we want is blue-on-blue fire. As team leaders, I want you all to add this to your training schedules: make sure that every man in your squad has the ability to properly account for the battlefield without the aid of his bucket, should it come to it. The Legion operated for centuries without the HUD tracking tech we have. Thank you, Sergeant Marko."

Notes were made as Marko retook his seat.

"Up next... Lieutenant Stockley, Kill Team Viking. Come on up, John."

The Dark Ops legionnaire seemed pleased that his new commander already knew him by his first name. He stepped forward and addressed the assembled TLs. "When it was determined that KBK was not inside Fortress Gibraltaar, Kill Team Viking was sent into the city in an attempt to find him. We cleared approximately five houses, taking sporadic gunfire, before it was reported that Karshak Bum Kali had been found by Kill Team Victory."

"How long were you operating?" Chhun asked.

"Sir, we were going house to house for about ninety minutes before we received the order to stand down."

Chhun quickly did the math. That was not many houses for a kill team in that period of time, though there could have been a variety of reasons for that. If one of the houses was packed with defenders, it could have taken a long time to clear out. He avoided interjecting with more questions, preferring to hear how the report turned out.

"We suffered two casualties. Nothing serious though. The guys are back with the team already. Spent maybe an hour in the med bay when we got back."

Chhun nodded. "Sustain?"

The team leader had an answer ready. "Sustain force of action and violence when clearing. Sustain medical training for all team members—we were able to get our guys patched up very quickly and organize for doc-drops to pick them up before anything could get out of hand."

"And improve?" asked Chhun.

"Cross-training. Our breacher was hit by indirect blaster fire and was taken out of the fight. That slowed us down considerably."

"Was he the only main on the squad trained as a breacher?"

"No, sir. Each role has a backup, but the backup went down as we cleared our first house. Shot by a donk kid."

"Thank you, John," Chhun said, dismissing the legionnaire. "Not everyone can be the best at every job, but it's paramount that each man is capable of at least doing each job on your squad. Bear, how 'bout you report next?"

The big legionnaire stood up. "Sir, I didn't want to presume to supply the after-action report for Kill Team Outlaw, so I brought Sergeant Salazo, if that's all right."

"That's fine," Chhun said, welcoming Salazo to the front.

But before the sergeant could begin, there was a knock at the door. It creaked open, and the gray-haired head of Major Owens's aide peered inside. "Captain Chhun, you're needed, sir."

"What's going on, First Sergeant?" Chhun asked, moving to the door.

"Can't rightly say, Captain." First Sergeant Paden VanBuskirk's voice was perpetually dry and angry. "Something just came through one of Major Owens's drop-channels. Those are the one-way communications, sir."

Chhun nodded. He knew that, but the first sergeant had a tendency to explain everything to him as though this were his first day in the Legion.

"Typically these are reserved for Dark Ops field agents, but this channel and its sender are completely new. Thought you'd better come and take a look." VanBuskirk's eyes darted around the room. "Now."

Chhun knew the aide well enough to know that he wasn't one to overstate things. Turning to address the team leaders, he said, "Men, something's come up that requires my immediate attention. However, I'd like for you to finish sharing your after-action reports and then dismiss. I know each of your teams is tight-knit and prefers autonomy. Mine was the same way. However, I believe there's a lot to be learned by the team leaders getting together and comparing mission results."

The first sergeant held the door open for Chhun, then the two moved down a corridor to a speedlift that led to the secure comm room occupied by Dark Ops and Rep Navy techs.

"Any tips on what's going on, First Sergeant?" Chhun asked as they rode the lift.

VanBuskirk only shook his head. "My professional opinion, sir, is that this is either huge and might change the war, or it's bogus and could get us into some hot water. Either way, I'm happy not to be the one who has to decide."

Chhun nodded. He realized that with Major Owens out of the picture, there was a distinct possibility that Chhun would envy the first sergeant's position before long.

The secure comm room doubled as a mission observation room, a place where Major Owens would monitor Dark Ops mission while on board the ship. It was in this room that Chhun had volunteered to take Kill Team Victory down to Ankalor, the start of a mission that had ultimately cost Fish his life. Chhun hoped that whatever he was about to encounter, it wouldn't result in a similar loss of legionnaire life.

The room was awash with techs and equipment. There were three-dimensional holographic displays and trackers providing real-time updates of fleet deployments and planetary conflicts. Chhun's eyes took in at least a dozen different operations happening in various worlds that were shaded yellow to represent disruptions by the Mid-Core Rebellion. Though now that the MCR was in league with the Republic, they were going by the name "Grand Army of the Mid-Core." The name change was more than just cosmetic. With the newfound support of the Republic, the MCR—the Legion had no intention of referring to them as anything other—had access to Republic armories. That allowed them to put real pressure on the Legion, battling Legion garrisons on various worlds under the Republic command to purge the "Legion traitors."

A naval comm officer walked purposefully to intercept Chhun and his aide. "Captain, I'm hoping you might be able to make some sense of a transmission we received."

"Let's have a look," Chhun said, speaking with a confidence he didn't feel. Other than Wraith's, he couldn't think of a single operation that would require this level of urgency. But maybe it was Ford who was calling in and it was a simple case of no one being on duty who knew about it? In times past, Ford would have contacted Owens or Chhun directly.

"Yes, sir." The comm officer motioned for Chhun to follow him to a fixed holoscreen. He brought up a media playback file, then held his finger over the screen, hesitating before playing the file. "Sir, I know this goes without saying, but I'm required to inform anyone viewing a message in this room, rank captain and below, that this message and its contents cannot leave this room."

Chhun nodded. His promotion couldn't come fast enough if that was how things were going to be. "I understand."

"Same for you, First Sergeant—"

"I got it," grumbled VanBuskirk. "Already heard the dang thing once."

The holo-recording flickered on to reveal an upward shot of an older man with steely-gray hair and a white, well-kept mustache. Chhun

recognized him as the House of Reason's replacement for Legion Commander Keller—Legion Commander Scontan Washam. This was the man who was supposed to be leading the purge of the Legion from within. So what would his angle be? Cut a deal? Threaten?

"This is Legion Commander Washam, communicating to Dark Ops headquarters under Legion authorization code Libre Shine 661."

"That real?" Chhun quickly asked.

Both the comm officer and the first sergeant shook their heads. They didn't know.

The Republic's new Legion commander continued. "Due to my not altogether unexpected, but neither sought after, appointment by the House of Reason as the new Legion Commander, I have come across information that I deem vital to the Legion."

Chhun's brow furrowed. If the man were in the room with him, he'd ask him if he was kidding.

"It seems the House of Reason was operating a clandestine prison on Herbeer for political dissidents and other people they wanted to disappear. That was news to me, but evidently not to you. It was not until I took the office that I was briefed that the facility existed—and that it had been compromised through a Dark Ops coup.

"Suffice to say," Washam continued, "the House of Reason does not give up after the first attempt is foiled. With Herbeer gone, a new facility has now been set up on the planet Gallobren. In fact, it already has a sizeable prison population, consisting primarily of the kill teams who were captured during their raids on the homes and offices of House of Reason delegates upon initiation of Article Nineteen. By the way, I can confirm what I'm sure you've already concluded: the House was tipped off about those raids in advance. I'm sorry I don't know the source of the leak.

"But back to Gallobren. As a core world, it has a nonexistent military presence, and for now, the prison is guarded only by planetary militia. That said, I'm sitting on orders to resupply, reinforce, and transfer soldiers loyal to the House of Reason to fortify the site. I'm doing my best to confound the process—which, given the chaos caused by Article Nineteen, isn't that difficult. But I cannot keep the new POW camp relatively unprotected for long without raising suspicion about my personal loyalties. I anticipate two standard weeks at best before the planned garrison of five thousand legionnaires, soldiers, and marines—all unquestionably loyal to the House of Reason—arrive. After that, any op designed to liberate the facility will get much harder.

"In addition to this, Delegate Nimh Arushi is personally overseeing the project. She'll be close to the city. Nabbing her would help move Article Nineteen along, and that is, after all, why I've been enduring all these years on Utopion. I recognize that Arushi is only one delegate, but she's a particularly powerful one, and putting her on trial, forcing a new election as the Article requires... it would send a needed message to the House. It would put them on notice. And it might allow us to peel loose some of the more moderate elements."

Chhun clenched his jaw. He believed what this man was telling him, and he hated the House of Reason for it. But was it really true? Or was he being played?

"Speaking of which..." Washam looked from his left to his right, as though verifying that he was still alone. "You'll have seen by now the holonews stating that some of the delegates and their families were killed by the Legion during the raids. Don't believe it. These were the reformers, and the rest of the House used the raids as an excuse to execute them."

Again, Chhun questioned what he was hearing. The hand-picked Legion commander, chosen by the House of Reason to replace Keller was... a spy?

Washam continued as if reading Chhun's mind. "The thought occurs to me that whoever is on the other end of this comm channel may not even known what I am. It's been so long, it's a wonder I didn't forget myself. But my purpose, from almost the beginning, was to be an appointed officer who would do the right thing. To make myself an asset to the Legion—the real Legion—should I be needed. Colonel Logarus was running Dark Ops the last time I checked in."

Chhun looked to the first sergeant.

"I was still a buck private when Logarus retired," VanBuskirk replied.

Washam let out a long sigh. "I'm doing what I can, but that is far less than I'd like. It is my recommendation that a kill team be sent in to disrupt the progress of this black site facility by organizing an armed uprising among the prisoners that will result in the liberation of the legionnaires on site. I cannot say with any certainty when or if I can communicate again. Stop Herbeer from happening again, and KTF. End transmission."

The holoscreen went dark.

"Can you verify any of this?" the comm officer asked Chhun.

Chhun shook his head. Washam was a point—one of the first, actually—and anyone who had followed the tug-of-war that regularly occurred between the Legion commander and the House of Reason, along with its cabal of appointed officers, knew that Washam was the man who'd used his service record in Psydon to counter almost every request the Legion brought. The House loved him, and the Legion despised him. Yet here he was providing intel to the "rogue" Legion in direct opposition to the wishes of the House. It wasn't just out of character; it bordered on insane.

Chhun turned to the first sergeant. "Request Admiral Deynolds meet me in my office as soon as possible."

Chhun examined the walls in his office. They didn't do anything to make him feel at home; in fact, they had the opposite effect. Major Owens had boxed up his personal items, but the holo-images were still hung up. Chhun studied one particular moment in time: Owens and his wife and children all smiling, sitting in the sunshine, picnicking outdoors. He liked that picture. Might even be sad to see it go.

The office door chimed.

"Come," said Chhun, rising to his feet as the door swooshed open to reveal Admiral Deynolds.

The admiral stepped inside, cap in hand. "Captain Chhun," she said.

"Admiral," answered Chhun, gesturing for her to take a seat.

She obliged, crossing her legs and looking around at the same holo-images that had drawn Chhun's attention. "It's a good thing you were here," she said, "or I would have thought this office belonged to someone else."

Chhun smiled. "I'm good at shooting bad guys. Interior decoration... not so much." He paused. "Truth be told, I don't want to seem overly eager to replace the man who's more or less a legend in Dark Ops."

Deynolds gave a warm smile. "You're finally moving up in the Legion, Cohen. Trust me when I say that I'm not the only one who wondered why it was taking so long."

"Same goes for you... Admiral."

Deynolds settled in for business. "I could tell from the urgency in your aide's voice that this wasn't a social call," she said. "What can Intrepid do for Dark Ops?"

Chhun activated a holo display on the surface of his desk. It was queued at the start of Washam's message, the recording paused to show the concern etched on the man's face. "Are you familiar with the House of Reason's new Legion commander?" he asked.

"Yes." Deynolds craned her neck to get a better view of the display. "I've never met him, but it didn't come as a surprise when he was chosen after Article Nineteen was rejected. An appointed officer. One of the first in the Legion... probably not a first choice, though."

Chhun agreed with that. Had Admiral Devers survived Tarrago, Chhun had no doubt that he would be whipping the galaxy into a frenzy against the Legion. He would have been the obvious choice for a new Legion commander. "As best I can tell, Washam didn't have the respect of someone like Silas Devers—"

Deynolds scoffed at the mention of the name.

"But since he's dead..." Chhun paused, leaving that rungrunk trail left unexplored. "Admiral, you were one of the few people in the confidence of Major Owens and Legion Commander Keller. You knew about Captain Ford and Righteous Destiny. Did Major Owens ever mention Washam to you?"

"Not that I recall. Maybe in passing. Political talk, things like that. Why?"

Chhun frowned. He had hoped Deynolds knew something about Washam he did not. "I'm going to play you a message that came from Washam via a dead-drop comm. No one here can verify it."

Chhun watched Deynolds's face as the recording played.

When it was complete, Deynolds looked up in alarm. "Do you think he's telling the truth?"

Holding out open palms, Chhun said, "I have no idea. I've been looking over files, cross-searching DO intel... I don't see any record of Washam being a Dark Ops asset. I've tried to reach the Legion commander or Major Owens, but they're completely off-grid with whatever they're up to."

"Have you told anyone else?"

"No. Only you, my aide, and the comm officer who first received the message know."

"Good. Something like this... well, quite frankly it's not the sort of thing you want getting around. Even among the Legion."

"Yeah," agreed Chhun. "Someone already tipped Utopion to Article Nineteen."

"Precisely." Deynolds gave a fractional nod. "I'm sorry I couldn't be of help in verifying the message. Is there anything else you need?"

Chhun sighed, unsure how to frame what he was about to request. "I need to know whether Intrepid would be able to facilitate a mission, should this be validated. The opportunity to bring back our guys is so tempting... well, if I were to set up a trap, that would be my angle. On the other hand, if it's true, of course we're going after them. Add in the potential to grab a high-ranking delegate like Nimh Arushi... and we need to be able to strike."

"I can go where I want to," Deynolds said. "Within reason, of course. We're to operate through the mid-core, but Gallobren is certainly an option if we have a good reason. This would be that, if confirmed."

"Thank you," Chhun said, nodding gratefully. "I want to do some more digging, but if this is what it seems like, I think it's worth the risk."

Deynolds stood. "I agree. Say the word and we'll make it happen."

Chhun rose and moved with the admiral to the door. "Thank you, Admiral. I can't think of a better ship to do what needs doing than Intrepid. You've been a friend to Dark Ops since I first joined."

Deynolds smiled. "Thank you, Captain. I appreciate that, greatly. It's always a pleasure working with you leejes."

Chhun gave a nod. "KTF."

A new round of incoming transfer logs, performance reviews, inventory requests, and other must-read data files flooded Chhun's inbox. When he was a team leader, he never gave much thought to these after he'd sent them; they were just part of the required work that filled the hours between ops. But now that his own team leaders were sending them to him, he developed a whole new appreciation for Major Owens.

It wasn't just reports the team leaders were sending, either. They were all itching for a fight. Virtually all of them had sent private messages to Chhun to make sure he knew they were ready to roll. But for now, training exercises—inside a special hangar Intrepid had dedicated for their use—would be the closest they'd get.

Speaking of which... Bear's latest training scores needed to be processed.

Chhun opened the file and perused it. Bear was already getting good results as the new team leader. Not that Kill Team Outlaw was substandard before, but with Bear's leadership and Masters's physical work ethic, their training scores and times were improving to the point where Outlaw was on the verge of being the top kill team on board the ship.

Chhun was supposed to file this report and package it for a couple of other destinations, but he found himself consistently pulled away from this, and his other bureaucratic obligations, in lieu of searching for data on the Legion's campaign on Psydon. Washam's message had made it clear that there was a ticking clock. But before he would authorize a mission, Chhun needed to be sure that his first action in his new role within Dark Ops would not result in five kill teams being ambushed and destroyed.

The cobwebbed corners of the holonet were a place to get lost. An area rife with things that could never be unseen. But also a place where a surprising amount of useful, actionable information slumbered, waiting to be found. Chhun had been seeking anything that might make his decision on the Washam op easier. But with an archive thousands of years old and spanning planet after planet, even a simple text-string search brought up more information than he could possibly filter through.

Ostensibly, this was why research bots and Dark Ops AI search-aids existed. Chhun could very specifically ask them what he wanted to know about Washam, then see what the public holonet plus a host of other classified databases might turn up. But he had taken to heart Admiral Deynolds's advice not to tell anyone. The Dark Ops network and the machines that operated within it were supposed to be slice-proof and invisible to the Republic. But after spending time with Keel and seeing what his code-slicer wonder kid could do, Chhun knew that all those assurances of security were about as solid as the gas expended to utter them. Anyone who thought otherwise was fooling himself.

So Chhun managed the search personally, and focused his investigation on areas of interest that would appear benign to any prying eyes. He hoped that he would come across something, anything, that would give him the nudge to decide between go and no-go.

History was the easiest route. Washam had started his career as an appointed officer on the Psydon campaign—the first major battle to see points in action—so Chhun had been reading forums, watching vlog posts and documentaries of old Psydon vets, and skimming memoirs to the point where he wondered if he was even doing his job any longer or just getting lost in the glory of those leejes who'd come before him.

Today he was searching for out-of-circulation books about Psydon. There had been a fair amount of them written after the battle had run its course, as the generation of legionnaires who had fought there tried to make sense of the fierce battles, the loss of their friends, and what it all meant to the rest of their lives.

These were the books no one read anymore. Because they weren't about right now, and that somehow made them seem unimportant. They were still out there, of course—because nothing ever really went away anymore. Data was cheap, and storage cheaper. But some titles tended to fade, while others solidified their position as authoritative accounts.

Chhun's first data point of interest came from one of the lesser-known titles—a combat memoir titled, Overrun: A Marine's Story of the War on Psydon.

The book was a typical example of the genre. The author began with an account of his childhood, then took the reader through Republic marine training, which was hardly Legion training but was still a significant trial. Chhun skimming the pages, swiping his datapad relentlessly. And then he got his first glimpse of something that made him sit up a little straighter in his chair. The narrative made reference to the House of Reason and the role their appointed officers had in the battle. Every account Chhun had read said that the first batch of points were just as bad as the ones who served before Article Nineteen kicked them out. That they were lousy from the get-go.

But then he saw the name Washam.

Excited, he highlighted a crucial passage:

Unlike the other points, this guy seemed to actually give a damn about the leejes he worked with. There were rumors that he went a long ways up planet with some other legionnaires to do something that needed doing. I was in camp when he came back, with a lot fewer men than he'd set out with, but I'll tell you, the regular leejes, they treated him differently than the other points after that. They respected him. And when a CO sought to punish Washam and the other survivors upon returning—AWOL was the charge—the rest of the leejes made it real clear that if the CO didn't drop it, they would drop him. That's how it was back then.

Realizing that he was on his feet, Chhun dropped back down into his chair and gently set his datapad in front of him. He drummed his fingers on his desk. This account of Washam was unlike any he'd heard before—like any account of any point, for that matter. Some were better than others, sure, and then there were those absolute horror stories like Devers. But nowhere had Chhun ever heard of a point being accepted entirely by the leejes under his command.

Could it be that Washam was truly different?

And further, could it be that, after seeing what the rest of the points were like, the Legion commander at that time made Washam into something of a sleeper agent on Utopion?

After Psydon, Washam's career went straight to the gilded halls of the capitol planet. That wasn't uncommon. Most points served a quick combat tour and then spent the rest of their time in the Legion waiting for their turn to become a part of the political machine. Washam, however, had remained in the Legion—and Chhun was now seriously wondering whether that had been to serve as an insurance policy in the event that Article Nineteen ever had to be used. Surely the Legion brass knew any attempt to execute Article Nineteen wouldn't be easy, even as they drafted that particular article in the Galactic Constitution.

The decision was eating Chhun up on the inside. Lives were at stake, and he didn't take that lightly. He was the one who had made the call to volunteer his four-man team to support a surrounded quick reaction force on Ankalor. He didn't argue when that team was ordered to hunt down Bum Kali. And as a result, he had been the one looking down at the remains of Fish, who had died to complete that mission.

Can you risk even more lives based on this?

In the end, no matter what he did, lives would be put at risk—he could only choose which ones. If he acted, the risk would be borne by his kill teams; if not, he would be leaving the captured Dark Ops leejes to their fate—which he was sure would be execution after a show trial. The Legion commander's treatment of the zhee leader had left room for nothing else.

Can you live with yourself if you just let this go?

With a rapid-fire string of insults, Chhun cursed his own indecisiveness. It was as if he stood at the edge of a cliff, and knew he needed to jump, but was too afraid to make the leap.

Impulsively, he pressed his comm button and awoke his aide.

First Sergeant VanBuskirk answered sleepily, "Sir, you're up dark and early."

"I won't be the only one, First Sergeant. I want to see all TLs in forty-five minutes. Tell them to meet me in the bunker."

Chhun's mind was racing to come up with what he would say to them.

"I'll have them there for you, sir," VanBuskirk responded.

The comm light went off, and Chhun let out a sigh. But the stress he felt deep inside his soul did not subside. He keyed in a new frequency on his comm and hoped that Admiral Deynolds would forgive him for the early wake-up.

The lights inside the bunker were dim when Chhun stepped inside. A holographic Legion crest rotated above the briefing table, casting a pale glow on the faces of the assembled team leaders, who buzzed with conversation.

"Gentlemen," Chhun began, syncing his datapad to the display. "I understand you've been feeling cooped up on board the ship. All that is about to change."

Someone in the room gave a whoop, causing a breakout of laughter. The team leaders slapped hands and pumped fists, ready for a fight.

Chhun allowed the speculative buzz to build back up in whispered discussions as he brought up a holographic image of the planet Gallobren. The room quieted as he started the mission briefing.

"Gallobren is a core world. A bit beyond our usual milk route, but one Admiral Deynolds and I believe deserves a visit for two important reasons, its white sandy beaches not being one of them."

The holographic representation of the planet shrank into the background, and a headshot of a raven-haired woman, dressed in a stylish business suit, came into view. "The political junkies among you will recognize this woman as House of Reason Delegate Nimh Arushi.

Gallobren is her home planet, and we have information that she is there right now. Article Nineteen mandates the arrest of all House of Reason members who do not peacefully step down. She didn't, and now we're coming for her."

The men in the room nodded in agreement. "That's too small a job to necessitate the use of all of you. But it turns out there's something else going down on Gallobren, under Arushi's watch."

Chhun caused the holographic image of Delegate Arushi to fade, and the point of view zoomed toward the planet. It drilled down through cloud cover to reveal brilliant blue seas, white beaches, lush green vegetation, and a core-world city. The hologram panned to an industrial area several kilometers east of the city's heart. Away from the clean tourist traps was a two-acre compound with three flat-roofed warehouses. There was nothing notable about the location. It blended in with the rest of the industrial area perfectly.

"This compound sits at the top of a hill. From here, you can follow a road straight through the downtown area to the beach. But as you can see, unlike virtually every other building or warehouse in this area, this one is fenced off. Completely."

Images appeared on the display showing a military-grade fence and an armed security gate.

"Dark Ops maintains various public-intel databases and dirt-forums where anonymous users can report any gossip they think is juicy enough—and then speculate, debate, and otherwise waste their lives. As you can imagine, there's a lot of garbage to sift through—sightings of Tyrus Rechs, suspected underground cabals seeking to subject various planets to zhee rule... the usual conspiracy stuff. But mixed in with that was a post speculating that this warehouse is being used to store war refugees. The speculation is based on one cargo driver's account of delivering trailer loads full of food and other supplies to this location."

Chhun had the team's full attention. They were professionals, so that was no surprise. But what came next might be. "Men, I believe this complex is not for refugees. I believe it is a black site penitentiary containing those Dark Ops leejes captured during the failed Article Nineteen raids."

Chairs shifted as the team leaders straightened themselves, their focus intense. Still, none of them spoke.

"You all know about what went on at Herbeer. And you know the House of Reason types, they just double down, so the existence of another facility like this is certainly plausible. I'm not at a place where I can say with absolute certainty that we'll find anything on Gallobren other than Delegate Arushi, but I do think we need to have a look. We owe that much to any POWs hoping they haven't been forgotten."

Chhun let a silence fall upon the room, trusting that the weight of what he'd said would galvanize the team for what was in store.

"We've got one shot to capture the delegate and liberate the prison camp. That means we'll be deploying all of your teams to work simultaneously. Intrepid will arrive when needed to deploy First Battalion from the Twenty-Fifth. It will be up to you to tell me when First Battalion needs to join the fight.

"My initial concept is that Kill Team Outlaw will go after Arushi, Kill Team Warbird will stay on Intrepid to serve as a quick-reaction team—sorry, guys—and the remaining three teams will work together on taking the compound. This op needs to happen within the next forty-eight hours. According to Admiral Deynolds, we can be in position in as little as eight hours."

Chhun held his hip and leaned forward slightly. "Questions?"

A hand went up from the leader of Kill Team Riot, Sergeant Lucas Eastridge. "Sir, I was always taught when planning ops like this under a new leadership structure to ask one question: If things go wrong, how many people are you willing to kill to get us out?"

Chhun nodded. "The entire city if that's what it takes. Any other questions?"

The room was silent.

"Okay. Round up your teams and get to work. I'll check back in a couple hours to see where we are. First Sergeant will reach me if you need me prior to that."

Modified Civilian Freighter *Lone Trout*
Gallobren Atmosphere

Chhun sat in the cargo hold with the Dark Ops legionnaires of four kill teams. The courier was too small to contain a secret smuggler's hold—so any customs inspector opening this ship would find himself face to face with lethal angels of death armed with enough weapons and explosives to capture a super-destroyer.

The freighter was pulled from a special hangar on Intrepid, where it had been kept on hand with other special-use vehicles that might be needed for covert missions. It was cramped—it was designed to transport only a single kill team, not four—but otherwise doing its job. They had entered Gallobren's atmosphere without any trouble, and their pre-authorized flight path took them over the ocean—part of the local government's regulations to keep the skies over the city itself peaceful.

All the better for the kill teams.

"What's the word?" asked Lieutenant Stockley, Kill Team Viking.

Chhun had just returned from the cockpit, where navy pilots were dressed in civilian uniforms. The plan was to seed the ocean with legionnaires through a drop-door cut out of the cargo bay's deck.

"Perfect night for this," Chhun replied. "Good cloud cover, nice and dark. Featherheads are slowly veering closer to the coast. Drop shouldn't be long."

"Let's get buckets on," Bear said, his booming voice cutting through the pockets of private conversation throughout the cargo hold.

The legionnaires dutifully put on their helmets and re-checked their kits, Chhun being no exception. As his HUD booted up, a special menu appeared, making maps, timelines, and pre-designated comm channels all easily accessible. Everything he'd need to lead the operation from the field until he arrived at a waiting command office in the marina of Gallobren's largest city, Li Tio. A chronometer counted down the planned arrival time of Intrepid, still hours away.

The freighter banked, causing the legionnaires to hang on to the straps that secured them to the deck. A text-ping popped up on Chhun's visor. The overhead lights shifted from a soft day-glow to red.

"Two-minute warning," Chhun announced.

At once the legionnaires lined up as best they could in the tight confines, standing at the base of the sealed drop-bay doors.

Chhun scanned a diagnostic report that showed all of his team's equipment reporting as functional. He had them double-check anyway. "Verify that your suits are sealed and that your personal bubblers have power."

The legionnaires verified that everything was as it should be, and conveyed so with a thumbs-up.

"Thirty seconds," Chhun said.

The pilot's voice came over the comm. "We are flying low and slow along the coastline. About two miles from the shore. Engaging drop-bay."

The door slid open, increasing the noise in the cargo hold as streams of air whipped inside.

"You get five seconds to activate your bubble shield," Bear reminded the men. "Try not to hit the water without it. It ain't fun."

From his place next to the open drop-bay door, Chhun could see the rippling water streaking by below. The ocean was the color of tyrannasquid ink. He looked over the snaking queue of soldiers, all ready to make the jump. "Let's get wet!"

One by one the Dark Ops leejes dropped into the hole, feet first, arms pressed against their sides. They tucked into a ball upon exiting the freighter, this motion causing their semi-transparent blue bubble shields to encircle them.

The energy packs for the shields had to be light enough and small enough to find room among the bristling array of equipment and weapons, which meant the shields they produced were only strong enough to withstand the impact on the surface of the water. They would dissolve once the legionnaires submerged.

The legionnaires exited the ship until Chhun was the only one remaining. "Trouble?" he asked the pilots. When they reported that all looked good, he jumped out of the hold as well, activating his own shield as he fell. He felt like a fish inside a dry bowl, waiting to get wet.

The black sea enveloped Chhun's shield as though he were a stone thrown from a cliff top. The thin wall of energy separating the legionnaire from the ocean seemed too thin, and then it collapsed, and a rush of water filled the void, completely submerging him.

Sensor readings on his visor told him that without the protection of his suit, hypothermia would set in after fifty minutes of exposure. But Chhun felt no discomfort. His armor was fully sealed and insulated against the elements. He did a quick check to make sure the shatterproof container holding his blaster rifle and other gear was still attached, and not floating to the surface. All was as it should be.

He released the mechanical shield generator from his webbing, and by the light of his ultrabeam—tinted green—he watched it sink down into the darkness towards the ocean floor. Retractable flippers swung down from their place behind his armored calves and fitted themselves to his feet.

Chhun began to swim toward the predetermined gathering point in order to link up with the other legionnaires. Someone had arrived already, and had activated a pulsing infrared buoy to help guide the others. Chhun moved silently toward the light, no bubble rising to betray his presence beneath the waves. All the legionnaires were breathing pure oxygen, their rebreathers pairing with carbon scrubbers that took in sea water, separated the oxygen, and then dumped the carbon back out in gentle streams. It was like a mechanical set of gills. They could all stay underwater almost indefinitely—though this mission called for them to swim for land considerably sooner than that.

When the men had gathered, Chhun requested status updates of his team leaders over a dedicated L-comm band. The men were ready, accounting for their teams and reporting no injuries or loss of equipment.

Nice and smooth.

"Nice work, Leejes," Chhun said. "Continue on to your destinations. Lieutenant Stockley, I want you to feed me updates on Task Force Granite's progress."

"Yes, sir."

The three kill teams comprising Task Force Granite—Viking, Lethal, and Riot—swam for a vacant stretch of beach while Chhun and Kill Team Outlaw began to kick toward the opulent downtown marina.

They swam the first mile or so in silence before Masters spoke up. "You know what I wonder about? What's the point of that glorious warehouse full of equipment back on Intrepid if we never get to use it? You guys do know there were SWIM-sleds, right? At least enough for us."

"Gallobren's a core world," Bear answered. "They'll detect something like that. But they won't pick up just a few more animals pushing through the water. Suck it up."

"Yes, sir," Masters replied, sounding utterly defeated. "If anyone sees a shark, just point them in my direction. Bear hates me, guys."

Chhun smiled, and wondered what the rest of Outlaw thought of Masters. "If the hard way makes success more likely, I'm all for it," he said.

"You would say that, sir."

They swam for another five minutes before Lieutenant Stockley reported in. "Granite One to Big Fish. Sir, we're in the surf and preparing to move onto the shore."

"Copy. Advise upon reaching the drainage system."

"Roger. Granite out."

The plan called for Task Force Granite to move under darkness across the white, sandy dunes to a massive rainwater runoff that ran underneath the city. If they'd had more time, they would have planned the mission to coincide with a lunar cycle that would have caused the tide to rise enough for them to access the runoff from underwater. As it stood, Granite would have to move approximately one hundred meters across the beach. Thankfully, the stretch near the runoff didn't have any resorts looking out onto it, and if anyone was out there in the dark, they'd likely give away their position by a campfire, and so would be easy to avoid.

If all went according to plan, the task force would be well on their way inside the city by the time Chhun reached his destination—a small yacht retrofitted by on-planet agents to serve as a mobile command room. He just had to hurry up and reach the upscale marina. From there he could monitor Granite's progress, fully coordinate with Intrepid, and watch Outlaw's progress in grabbing the delegate. It would be a busy night.

"Sir," Stockley called in again. "Slight problem."

"What's up?" asked Chhun.

"Beach is empty except for a couple of kids. They're making friendly behind a sand dune right in our way, if you catch my drift."

Chhun found himself shaking his head. Wasn't this always the way? Miles of coastline and this was where two people decided to throw down their blanket. Right now. "No sneaking by them?"

"With this many of us?" asked Stockley rhetorically. "Not without significant risk of discovery. One quick comm call and we're dusted, mission scrubbed. We can go back in the drink and swim around to another landing point. It'll take time, though."

Time wasn't something Chhun had in great supply. Everything was scheduled tightly and needed to come off at once if at all possible. Outlaw had to clear and prepare for remote destruction of Delegate Arushi's luxury yacht—assuming she wasn't on board; intel had her staying at a hotel overlooking the marina—to prevent any chance of her leaving the planet. Granite had to hit the POW camp at the same time. And then, with the planetary militia and police trying to decide what to do next, Intrepid would drop its legionnaires and marines to set up blocking positions, making sure that the prisoners got out before everyone else went home.

"No delays," Chhun said, second-guessing himself even as he gave the order. Should he have opted for a less aggressive plan of action and built in greater allowance for time delay? He had agreed with his team leaders' plan to do it fast, smooth, and right the first time, and he believed in his kill teams' ability to execute the mission. But... didn't things always go sideways? At least a little.

It didn't matter now. "Send in one of your less lethal guys. Sucks for the kids. Wrong place, wrong time."

"Copy that."

With the operation taking place in a predominately civilian and law-abiding planet, Chhun had made sure that each kill team had at least one legionnaire equipped with less-than-lethal weaponry. He was glad he'd done so, because this was precisely the type of situation that called for it. The two lovebirds didn't deserve to die, but they needed to be neutralized. Most leejes picked for the duty packed an extra stinger pistol or neuro-blaster. Weapons that selectively paralyzed the nervous system and put the target to sleep.

"Okay, they fell asleep earlier than they expected," Stockley reported. "En route to the runoff."

"Copy."

Kill Team Outlaw soon reached the harbor of the marina, swimming deep beneath docks and the keels of assorted luxury yachts.

Chhun spotted a flashing IR strobe on a small boat above them. That marked it as the one that had been arranged for Chhun to use as an operational headquarters. "Looks like this is where I get off."

"Copy that," said Bear. "We still got ourselves a bit of a swim. Delegate Arushi's yacht is up in the north end of the marina with all the really rich folks."

"Which makes sense," Masters chimed in. "Once you get that money, why would you want to hang out with all the riffraff? No offense, Captain."

Chhun swam up to his target ship's hull, glad that the seemingly endless strokes of his fins were finally drawing to a close. "I'll take it as a compliment, Masters. KTF."

As the kill team swam on, Chhun moved slowly out from beneath the dark shadow cast by the boat. The marina was adequately lit, and Chhun could see the light diffusing from the water's surface. He had wanted the makeshift headquarters to be equipped with an access hatch underneath, so he wouldn't have to expose himself by re-emerging, but no one on-planet could find a suitably skilled or discreet contractor to make it happen in the time allotted.

Chhun practiced the controlled surfacing he'd learned in his Dark Ops dive and underwater demolition training. He angled his head and allowed it to slowly emerge from the water, not making a sound, hardly disrupting the surface tension. More of Chhun slowly followed. His visor came up above the waterline. The bucket's HUD showed no sign of activity. No hostiles.

Reaching behind himself, Chhun found the bottom rung of a ladder that went up to the boat's deck next to a small diving board. A little something for the wealthy folks a vessel like this was marketed for. He slipped on board.

The deck was empty, as was the flybridge. He proceeded to clear the rest of the boat, finding nothing. When he reached the captain's quarters, he entered a passkey and quietly swung open a reinforced manual door.

The room was everything it needed to be. It bristled with technological listening and communication equipment, with walls thick enough to fend off any blaster fire from the outside. From here he would observe all of his kill teams in real-time. He could keep in contact with Intrepid almost as easily as if he were on the destroyer itself.

He fired up one holoscreen and instructed the computer to monitor the progress of Kill Team Outlaw as they moved deeper into the marina. On a second screen he mapped Task Force Granite. They were moving through the storm water system and into the heart of the city itself.

The boat's AI pilot went to work taking itself out of its mooring and steering Chhun to the mouth of the harbor, where it would anchor. That would make any boarders have to be serious about their task, and would alert Chhun that he wasn't just dealing with some drunken vacationer walking up the wrong gangplank.

Usually a Dark Ops commander liked to employ observation bots to provide aerial views of the mission field. This was easier to do on planets and regions that weren't highly developed, or at least weren't highly bureaucratic. In those places, no one would much notice or care if just one more bot was flying through the air. But Gallobren was different. Regulated bot traffic was a significant source of income here, and the local governments took seriously any bots flying about without proper registration. That didn't make getting an observation bot up an impossibility, but the bot would certainly be tracked and observed by some desk jockey checking to make sure that the machine traveled in its stated lanes and didn't try to earn any extra revenue without the proper fee application. Even that could have been overcome with the right contacts, but there hadn't been time for the necessary greasing of wheels. So Chhun was forced to rely on the data that was transmitted through the Dark Ops secure relays.

Task Force Granite looked to be moving at a good pace in spite of the delay they had experienced on the beach. Chhun broadcast a short, encrypted tone over Dark Ops L-comm to let them know that Big Fish was now Mother Bird and in the nest. He was available for any additional support the teams needed to call in.

Sitting in a swivel chair, Chhun instinctively reached up to remove his helmet, but then thought better of it. The bucket's audio receptors would be an advantage in the event that an unwanted element started to move about the deck above him. And the bucket's comm and HUD could relay him information faster than if he were simply taking in the sum of all the various holoscreens with his naked eyes. Further, his chronometer was still displaying the countdown to the Intrepid's estimated time of arrival.

After about five minutes of setting up, fine-tuning his equipment, and tapping into his legionnaires' buckets for quick-reference first-person observation, Chhun received his first status update from Bear's team.

"All right, we've reached the ship. This thing is huge. Capable of sea and space travel. Delegate Arushi is rolling large."

Aren't they all? Chhun thought to himself.

Bear continued. "Outlaw is planting charges on the hull, but man, we're gonna have to really make one hell of a boom to sink this beast."

"Sink or disable," Chhun clarified. "Either way."

"My concern isn't whether we can do it. But there are ships docked on either side of the target. A blast like what we're preparing could take them down with it—plus whoever might be inside."

Chhun brought up a visual from a sliced observation cam monitoring the marina. The visual was from twenty minutes before, as all the security cams had been adjusted to show an all-clear loop so the Dark Ops teams wouldn't be detected. It gave a clear view of the delegate's big yacht and the smaller vessels docked around it.

"First thing," Chhun said, "is to make sure the delegate isn't already on her yacht. If she is, you'll be capturing her, and blowing up the yacht is a moot point."

"And if she's not? Should I risk an active life-form scan of the other vessels?"

The weight of this decision rested on the back of Chhun's neck. "No. We'll just have to take our chances and hope no one else gets hurt. If you see somebody, by all means, apprehend and get them clear. Otherwise, keep moving."

"KTF," said Bear somberly.

"Exactly."

Chhun watched with gritted teeth as Kill Team Outlaw made their way through the delegate's luxury yacht. He was viewing a live-feed transmitted through Masters's bucket, seeing everything the jocular legionnaire saw. It was like viewing an FPS cut scene, and it made Chhun want to get out of his seat and swim to join them. This would be a tougher transition than he'd imagined, going from team leader to sector commander.

Someone called out that they'd dusted an armed guard near the ship's engine room.

Chhun watched as Masters's hand came into view, gently pushing open a portal door. He swung his blaster into the room, and the cam caught sight of two Kimbrin playing cards, blaster pistols set out on the table. The Kimbrin reached for their weapons, but they were too slow; Masters double-tapped with his NK-4, dropping both. He proceeded to call the room clear.

More rooms were cleared, and in rapid order. The team was tearing through the ship, finding no further opposition.

"Ship's empty," Bear announced. "She's not here."

Chhun nodded, as though his team leader were in the room with him. It certainly felt like they were. He performed a quick-slice program to pull up the guest registry of the hotel where the delegate was suspected to be staying. He had held off on this move, as high-end hotels usually had layers of security that would alert someone to tampering. But they needed to find her room number, and hopefully even if the tampering was observed, Kill Team Outlaw would be in and out before anything could be done about it.

"Intel confirms reservations on the top floor of the Hotel Djakka, overlooking the harbor. Two suites on that level. You want 22-A. Make your way there. I'll transmit an access key to get you inside via the service entrance."

"Copy."

Chhun switched holofeeds to watch the marina, wanting to give Outlaw a heads-up should he see any obstacles. It was very pretty, even by night. Everything was neat and clean. The piers were still fashioned from wood, the promenade seemingly cut from whole stones. It was probably gorgeous by daylight. Hopefully, all of Outlaw would be at its extraction points before they had a chance to see it in the sunlight.

"Granite here. We're in position beneath the camp."

Chhun checked on the task force. They had moved clear through the storm drains, encountering no obstructions or security

He shook his head. Core worlds.

They took everything for granted. Because, if any place in the galaxy was safe, it was a core planet. The Legion, and most alien species, for that matter, were light years away. Kill teams weren't supposed to show up on places like this, so why bother paying for security beyond what was visible on the surface?

They were about to find out.

Task Force Granite found several storm water drains opening into the suspected POW compound, one of them directly underneath an impervisteel-frame guard tower. They would be able to come topside right in the midst of any defenders, like rodents tunneling into a farmer's garden.

Chhun switched among the various feeds for a while, then focused in on Kill Team Outlaw when they at last made their way through the shadows to the hotel. No one was up. No one was out. It was that magical hour when everyone was forced to sleep off whatever revelry had occurred in the passing of one day to the next. Chhun watched through Bear's visor as the team entered through a back door into the hotel's kitchen. Someone sent an ion blast into the bot working the dish machine, disabling it.

"Granite," Chhun said, keenly aware of the exciting tightness in his chest. "Begin moving yourself into position. Kill Team Outlaw will reach its target soon. Report once each team is in position."

The wait for Outlaw was probably more taxing for Task Force Granite than it was Chhun, but that didn't stop the captain from nervously rocking back and forth as the kill team moved through the hotel.

Bear panted over the comm. "We're almost up. Ten more flights. Speedlifts were too open."

The view from Bear's visor moving up the stairwell gave Chhun a sense of vertigo. He switched to a feed inside the darkened compound. The kill teams had all come up to the surface and were moving silently through the camp, undetected.

Finally, Outlaw reached the top floor. They set up their breaching positions, then Bear announced, "Outlaw is in position, ready to clear the hotel room."

The other teams reported in as well.

"Kill Team Lethal, in position."

"Riot in position."

"Kill Team Viking, in position. Task Force Granite is go."

This was it.

"Acknowledged," said Chhun, checking his chronometer one more time. "Intrepid is five minutes from arrival. Expect immediate starfighter flyovers and Legion drop pods. All teams: you are green. KTF."

The feeds and relays in Chhun's command center all came alive with action. It was almost overwhelming as Chhun tried to watch everything at once. The explosives placed aboard the luxury yacht were detonated; should Outlaw somehow miss nabbing the delegate, they'd leave her nowhere to escape to. Task Force Granite cut down the warehouse defenses almost immediately, and were swiftly moving to find prisoners. A few elements were shooting it out with planetary security. And in the hotel—Chhun again channeled Masters's bucket feed—the door to the hotel room was blown open and kill team members poured in, finding armed security stumbling awake from the stupor of sleep. The kill team dropped them with double-taps to the head or chest, then began moving through rooms. The hotel suite was massive.

Masters came to a closed door and stood to the side, waiting for another legionnaire to join him. He nodded, and the legionnaire kicked the door open. Masters bounded inside.

Chhun could see the target delegate from Masters's POV. She was in bed, screaming, covers pulled up to her neck. Her husband lay prone, his eyes wide with fear and confusion. He pushed himself up on an elbow and began to protest. But the legionnaire with Masters, SPC Brent

Brown, moved bedside and struck the man in the jaw with the butt of his blaster, sending him tumbling out of bed and onto the floor.

Delegate Arushi screamed even louder, and then began to hurl profanities at Masters as SPC Brown ener-chained her husband. Masters grabbed her roughly by the neck and forced her face-first onto the bed. He ener-chained her hands behind her back and draped an isolation hood over her head, silencing her screams and curses. He then pulled her out of bed—more gently now that she'd been subdued.

"Did you search her?" SPC Brown asked.

The delegate was wearing an expensive, shimmering white nightgown and was barefoot. She looked perfectly attired for a sub-tropical climate. The paradise she had been residing in. A paradise now lost.

"Dude," Masters replied, "not exactly any place to hide a blaster in that thing she's got on."

It was surreal to Chhun, watching all of this remotely from his command center, his arms crossed, knowing there was very little he could do to help beyond coordinate support fire. He again found himself wanting to be with the kill team. To be in that room, helping to take care of the situation. He wondered how many times Major Owens had done the same thing he did now. It was no wonder that Owens would occasionally still insert himself in missions. Chhun didn't think he could do something like this forever. Being out of the fight. He couldn't abide it. This couldn't be the rest of his career.

"Looks like the delegate's got a kid. Single child, female. She's pretty upset." The report came from Specialist Tuttle, from another room.

Chhun instinctively opened his mouth to speak, to issue a command. He was so engrossed in what was happening that it took Outlaw's actual team leader speaking first to snap Chhun out of it.

"Masters," Bear said, "get the delegate out of the bedroom and keep her detained in the kitchen. Don't want the kid to see her when we bring her out of the bedroom to her father. Brownie, you tell Daddy dearest that we're bringing in his kid and that he needs to help her get through this. He can play it easy, or he can do it with an isolation hood on, his call."

The legionnaires did as they were instructed, removing the delegate from the situation and bringing the sobbing girl to her father, where she thrust her diminutive frame into his arms. The father seemed unsure what to do. He awkwardly stroked her hair, repeating, "Try not to be upset, now."

It was consolation that, to Chhun, seemed entirely devoid of affection. Chhun wondered if this was the first time the father had ever even been in this position—having to actually father, actually comfort his own offspring. The galaxy's ultra-wealthy tended to be that way. Chhun had seen it on a thousand core and mid-core raids. Say what you want about those on the edge fighting in tribal skirmishes for the Mid-Core Rebellion or whatever insurgency was popular on their particular dust hole—cultural exceptions aside, they at least cared about their children.

There was more happening, and these thoughts that drifted through Chhun's mind, un-beckoned and unexamined, left as swiftly as they had arrived. Task Force Granite had taken the compound. They'd encountered no Republic marines, no legionnaires still loyal to the House of Reason, no Republic Army basics. It was a funny thing. The House of Reason was more than happy to send the Legion and the Republic's various military branches throughout the galaxy, so long as it wasn't to a core world where the delegates actually lived. That was always too intrusive. The entirety of the facility's resistance was local—city or planetary security details. They wore white uniforms, making them look more like boat hands than a military force.

Now that their presence in the city was known, Chhun no longer needed stealth. He sliced into whatever he saw fit, including the compound security itself, which was slave-linked to a local government channel. Sloppy. Easy to hack. And evidence that the delegate and her planetary government were all in on the detainment.

And there was, indeed, a detainment. Proof of that came to Chhun through the bucket visors and holocam feeds of Task Force Granite. Legion Commander Washam—Chhun didn't know how else to refer to the man—hadn't led them astray.

At least, not yet.

Familiar faces appeared in his feeds inside the barracks—Dark Ops legionnaires. They were physically chained to the floors, not with ener-chains, but real chains, heavy metal links. Each man had maybe five feet of length in which to move from a tiny cot to a shared toilet.

The rescued leejes were elated at their luck. Cut free of their bonds, they began distributing what weapons they could find, pilfering the dead and defeated security forces, or borrowing secondary weapons from the kill teams.

An explosion sounded somewhere in the middle of the city.

"Hey!" shouted Riot's team leader. "That was hella close! Is Intrepid starting an orbital bombardment?"

Chhun had wondered the same thing at the sound. His chronometer had just reached zero, meaning the blast happened almost on Intrepid's arrival, unless it had showed up early and unannounced. He keyed in the direct bridge comm. "This is Captain Chhun. We're hearing explosions down here. Are you firing?"

"It's not us, Captain." Admiral Deynolds answered directly. Her voice sounded urgent, stressed, concerned. "Someone else is already here. It's a ship the likes of which I've never seen before."

"Say again." Chhun couldn't believe what he was hearing. Of all the ways things could go sideways, an orbital battle between rival capital ships was about the worst. He didn't see any way that whatever was up there could be friendly.

"Sir, this is Comm Officer Lambert," a new voice replied. Chhun didn't feel slighted in the least that Deynolds handed him off to a comm officer. Things were probably hectic up there. "We are sharing planetary space with another capital ship of unknown make and origin. This appears to be the source of the fire you're reporting. We are unsure why they fired on the planet, but they've now stopped to focus on us, it would seem. We are preparing to engage."

"What's the status of our drop support?" Chhun asked.

"Seventy percent of the planned Legion and marine units dropped on arrival. They're on their way down."

"Understood," Chhun said. If they were going to be stuck on planet while Intrepid duked it out with whatever was up there, at least they'd have some extra muscle to hold off planetary forces. "Where does that leave us with exfiltration?"

"We've launched fighters to make sure the drop pods arrive safely. When they've established superiority, we'll send shuttles down as planned. Stand by."

"Roger that. Good luck up there."

No reply came back over comm.

"Listen up, Dark Ops," Chhun said over his DO comm channel. "An unidentified capital ship sent that orbital blast into the city. Intrepid is engaging, looking to chase it off, but we might have to sit tight for a while. Good news is that most of the Legion and marine force dropped. Their assault pods are on their way down." Chhun checked his monitors. The Legion forces were already landing, and blocking positions were already being set up on the pre-determined street grid to give Task Force Granite and the liberated POWs a clean exit route into the heart of the city, where multiple shuttles could land. "Scratch that. Legion forces are down and securing their objectives. Follow through and link up until exfiltration can arrive."

"Copy."

"Captain?" It was Bear.

"Go for Chhun."

"Yeah, we're hiking up to the bluff to await exfiltration. Seeing some drop pods landing pretty wide of the target zone. Looks like they're hitting the suburbs from my vantage point. I'll plot location to your HUD. May want to let Intrepid know."

"Copy that."

Chhun keyed in a comm channel for the destroyer's logistics wing; he didn't want to bother the bridge during a fight. "This is Captain Chhun here on the ground. I'm getting a report from a team that drop pods are in the northwest corners of the city just beyond the marina. You may want to correct drop coordinates."

There was a pause before the response came over comm.

"Captain Chhun, that's not us. All drop pods launched have arrived on target. Ask your spotter to verify. Over."

Chhun keyed back to Bear. "Bear. They're saying it's not them. You're sure of what you saw?"

"Yeah," Bear said. "Seen so many drop pods come down, I wouldn't miss it. Tell Intrepid a whole lot more are still falling. Like... a bunch."

Nothing about that sentence sounded good to Chhun. "Copy."

He returned to the waiting logistics comm operator. "Sighting verified and confirmed by team leader. He says a lot of pods are arriving in that region."

The reply sounded befuddled. "Something... something's going on, because I'm seeing drop pods in atmosphere. But all of ours are accounted for. There's been no sign of any pods launched from the ship Intrepid is engaged with. "

"Copy. We'll keep an eye on it." Chhun was developing a very bad feeling. He decided to try the Intrepid's bridge. "This is Captain Chhun. I need to be patched into your starfighter comm channel."

"Sir?"

Chhun heard Admiral Deynolds speak up, her voice being captured by the comm officer's input piece. "Do what he says."

Chhun watched the holocam feed showing fighter position, ported directly from Intrepid. It had been primarily a long-range skirmish, the two ships exchanging relatively harmless blaster-cannon fire. But now fighters were engaged. Chhun listened in to Reaper Squadron's comms.

He heard the voice of Dax Danns, a pilot he'd met on the mission to capture General Nero.

"Yeah, I saw it," Danns called out. "Hang on..."

Chhun could hear the pilot's breathing over the comm. "Vaped another fighter."

"What do you think it is, Boss?" asked another pilot.

"Dunno," said Danns. "But these fighters... it's like they're not even trying, man. Like they're just trying to keep us at arm's length."

Was this because the enemy destroyer—or whatever it was—was sending down those drop pods? Perhaps with a sort of stealth tech?

Chhun surveyed his battle maps, and saw that the major coordinating the Legion assault was up and active on the battlenet. He keyed for a direct L-comm connection.

"This is Captain Chhun, overseeing the Dark Ops mission."

"I read you, Captain."

"Did your force bring any observation bots?"

"Yeah. We'll deploy them once we're in position."

"Major, I need to get one of those bots in the air right away, and I need to observe its feed. Can you make it happen?"

If he were dealing with a point, Chhun knew he would be in for a fight. But this was a better Legion than the one before Article Nineteen. The major must have recognized that if he was being asked by Dark Ops, it was important.

"I'll have one sent up and get the feed routed to your comm signature."

"Thank you, Major."

"KTF."

"KTF."

Chhun watched his monitors, mumbling under his breath, "C'mon... c'mon..."

An incoming feed notice flashed in front of him, and Chhun quickly accepted. The image from the TT-16 bot showed it gaining altitude from the legionnaire's position where it was deployed. Chhun provided a passkey that gave him control of the bot, then proceeded to fly it away from the area of operations, out to where Bear had reported the other pods impacting.

Bear hadn't been imagining things. Several large drop pods were clearly visible, with thin trails of blue smoke from entry rising up from their landing sites. Column upon column of soldiers were streaming from the sites and moving toward the city.

Chhun went wide on the battlenet comms. "Confirmed sighting of a non-Legion force moving from landed drop pods at the following grid location." He transmitted the coordinates. "Be advised they are moving in the direction of the city center."

"We see them," answered the Legion major. "Can't tell who it is. More of those Black Fleet dark legionnaires?"

"Going down to take a closer look. Stand by."

Chhun moved the bot closer, knowing that taking it in that low would likely get it shot down.

The marchers were soldiers, but not human. They were war bots, and massive ones at that. At least eight feet tall, of a type Chhun had never seen before. They were thick with armor, and carried what looked to be tri-barreled N-50s with ease. Some of them also carried large riot shields. Smaller streams of other bots—human-sized—marched along the big ones like some sort of support unit.

This was trouble.

The major saw it too, and began giving orders to prepare for counter-attack.

Chhun pinged his kill teams. "Make sure you're at your exfiltration points and you're ready to fight and leave. Multiple war bots are headed into the city, presumed hostile."

The team leaders responded with utter calm and professionalism.

"Intrepid," Chhun called out, reaching the destroyer's bridge by comm. "This is Captain Chhun. I need a hurry-up on the exfiltration. Multiple hostiles are headed toward my kill teams."

Admiral Deynolds answered the call herself. Her voice was harried. Full of alarm and worry. "Captain Chhun... I'm not sure we can do that."

The first legionnaires to come in contact with the war bots were Task Force Granite. Together with the liberated POWs, the kill teams were hit on both sides by a swarm of the hulking machines.

Chhun looked on with gritted teeth as the task force formed a defensive perimeter and exchanged fire with the war machines. They were using ear-poppers to disorient the machines, but out-of-doors, these had limited effectiveness. A few of the bots were falling under concentrated fire to their heads, but more were coming.

Losses began to mount, and the war bots had Task Force Granite isolated and encircled in the large square at the heart of the city. The square's park-like features, like rolling, grassy hills, had made it the designated landing zone for the kill teams to exfiltrate from. But those shuttles were nowhere to be seen, and the luxurious park was now turning into a battlefield.

The Legion and marine elements sent to the planet had withdrawn from their blocking positions and pushed forward, hitting the bots from the rear and breaking through, uniting the forces and intensifying the firepower sent against the robotic threat.

Chhun did what he could to support the defense, calling in targets for their mortar bots to strike, signaling to his team leaders where war bot surges were being staged. But it was clearly a losing battle. Every legionnaire or marine that fell diluted the defensive just a little bit more, whereas the war bots' numbers only grew. A steady flow of drop pods carrying new machines continued to hit the planet's surface—one every minute or so it seemed. Not all of these headed toward the battle, but enough did. Too many. The machines began to close around the defenders like a tightening noose.

"This is Captain Chhun requesting orbital support." He was trying to reach Intrepid. But the only answer he received was the frantic shout of a comm officer asking him to stand by. At least they were still up there trying to stem the tide.

Finally, he received good news. "We're sending down a squadron of fighter-bombers... it's all we can do."

"How about some shuttles to get us out of here?" Chhun called back.

"Sorry, sir, shuttles wouldn't make it down in one piece."

Chhun wanted to argue, but it wouldn't do any good. If that was true, things were bad. So much so that even the incoming bombing run might well be a suicide mission.

He watched on his displays as four tri-bombers swooped in, dropping a payload on the columns of bots, sending them into nothingness. But it was like brushing a trail of ants off of a picnic table. The assault resumed almost immediately. His men in Task Force Granite barely had time to breathe. They were going to die unless a shuttle could get them out.

He keyed in for Intrepid once more, but his comm message was interrupted by Bear.

"Sir," Bear said, "we're waiting at the exfiltration site. No sign of any shuttle, and it doesn't sound like one is coming. Requesting permission to let the delegate go and join Task Force Granite."

Chhun winced. He knew the desire Bear and Kill Team Outlaw felt to help their brothers. He felt the same. But if he had them leave, he would be signing their death warrants. "Negative. Stay tight. It's bad everywhere, but if there's an opening, you need to be there to get on the shuttle."

"Copy."

Chhun expected an argument. But perhaps Bear saw what Chhun himself saw. They were in a no-win situation if it came down to an up-front fight with these bots. There were too many of them. "I'll monitor to make sure none of those war bots are headed in your direction," Chhun added. "So far they don't seem interested in your neck of the woods."

"Copy," Bear responded. "Hell of a first mission to be in command of, huh, Captain?"

A gallows smile stretched across Chhun's face. "Funny. I was just about to say the same thing to you."

A beep sounded, and Chhun looked up to see that all four of the tri-bombers had been splashed into the ocean. Pursued by some unidentified starfighters. Bad to worse.

Chhun went back to work trying to find a way out for his men. He opened a comm to Intrepid, but got nothing. And then his sensors updated, removing Intrepid from the battlefield. Had it been destroyed? The very thought caused Chhun's knees to feel rubbery. He remembered the last time he was in such a situation. Kublar.

This time seemed like it would go much, much worse.

But maybe it was a trick. Some sophisticated jamming. Whoever had the tech and resources to send down this many war bots, likely could achieve comm and network interference.

Chhun went wide on the Intrepid all-craft comm. "This is Captain Chhun on Gallobren. I need an immediately evac shuttle for a VIP and kill team at the marina bluff landing point, Echelon Actual."

No reply.

"Repeat. This is Captain Chhun requesting evac shuttle. We have been overrun and experienced extreme casualties. Priority landing is for drop shuttle at marina landing point Echelon Actual. Do I have a copy?"

More silence.

And then a comm channel opened. It immediately filled with background noise, warnings, and beeps that might have come from a starfighter cockpit. "This is Reaper One. I copy."

"Dax!" Chhun called, relieved to hear that someone was still up there. "Dax Danns—I need help down here, buddy."

"Hang on..." he said, apparently speaking on another channel. "Two more!" The pilot's voice refocused on Chhun. "Captain Chhun, I'm sorry. Reaper Squadron is doing everything we can right now to keep an exposed command shuttle alive until it can make the jump. Then we're bugging out too. Intrepid's already gone to hypersp—"

Danns's voice cut out. Chhun closed his eyes, assuming that the featherhead had just been vaporized.

But he soon came back online. "Captain. The crew of the command shuttle wants to try and get you. They're heading for re-entry. They say one pass."

Chhun nodded. "All right. We'll be ready."

"Damn it!" shouted the pilot.

"What? What is it?" But Chhun already knew the answer.

"Shuttle's gone, man." There was a pause, the fading of all hope. "I wish I could stay and help, but we're getting swarmed. I gotta take care of my squad. We gotta go. I'm sorry. We gotta go."

"I understand."

"I'm sorry," repeated Danns. "Stay alive. I'll tell them you're still alive. We'll come back when we can."

"Copy. Get out of there, Reaper One. You did what you could."

Chhun looked at his monitor. Bear's team was in position, with no threats nearby. But Task Force Granite—everyone else. They were gone.

All of them.

"Captain Chhun," Bear said, sounding agitated. "What's the status? I can't reach any other leejes except my squad, and there's so much going on that my HUD is worthless beyond fifty meters. Do we have a shuttle coming?"

"Negative," Chhun responded. "Intrepid has been forced to retreat. Task Force Granite and the Legion assault force is a total team kill." Sorrow and grief threatened to choke out Chhun's last words. But he held it in, wanting to be strong for Outlaw.

Bear was quiet for several seconds before asking, in a small voice, "What?"

The drop pods carrying more bots continued to fall.

"They're all dead," Chhun said. "Our job now is to survive."

"How is that even possible? How could this have happened?"

"Bear... listen to me. It doesn't matter the how. It happened. You need to keep your team alive. You're still removed from the enemy, as best I can tell. I'm going to leave this post and try to join you."

"Yeah... copy that. We'll dig in and wait for your arrival. Figure out a plan."

"Roger that. See you soon."

Chhun looked around his sophisticated command room. The plan had always been to sink the boat on departure, but he wondered if that even mattered anymore. And the explosion might just alert those machines that he was here.

He decided he would use timed explosives and blow it anyway.

Removing a thermal fragger that would be more than sufficient to destroy the room and burn up the ship until it sank, he set its dial for three minutes. Enough time for him to swim for a quiet shore and head for Outlaw.

He looked at the long-range, deep-space comm—and had an idea.

Holding the grenade in one hand, he activated the comm in the other. He sent a looping, recorded message to the Indelible VI.

Keel woke up in the utter darkness that was his bunk on board the *Indelible VI*. He liked sleeping in the deep black that only a ship traveling through space could provide. Shifting, he felt a sudden jolt of pain in his side. He winced and felt around his torso. A layer of re-knit meshing was in place.

The last thing Keel remembered was pulling off his clothes and armor and collapsing into his bunk. Someone else had taken care to put the dressing on him. They'd also put his heavy Armonian fleece over his legs. He felt warm and cozy, almost too much so, straddling that line between comfort and the outbreak of a sweat.

"Thanks," Keel said into the darkness, knowing exactly who had taken care of him, covered him up, and remained at his bedside.

"You're welcome," answered Leenah.

Judging from the location of her voice in the darkness, she was sitting on the old wooden trunk that Keel kept his personal effects in.

He waved a hand in the darkness, causing an ambient light to shine up from the deck. He saw Leenah's form at the foot of his bed, draped in shadows.

Another jolt went through Keel's ribs, causing him to squeeze his eyes shut at the pain. "How long have I...?"

"Going on six hours now." Leenah rose and came to Keel's side. "I figured you'd have been out a lot longer, truthfully."

Keel relaxed his body, letting his bare shoulders sink into his bedding. "I certainly feel like I should still be sleeping."

A smile formed on Leenah's face. "You're popular, Captain Keel. Garret was trying to reach you. I told him to knock it off unless it was an emergency. The comm chime probably woke you."

Keel nodded. "You been waiting the whole time I was out?"

"Not all, but for the most part."

Shutting his eyes, Keel let out a sigh. "Thanks, Leenah. For staying with me, I mean." He forced himself into a sitting position. "I better see what Garret wants."

Leenah placed her palm on Keel's breastbone and gently pushed him back down on the bed. Her touch was warm and felt electric against Keel's skin. "What you need is rest. Ravi's taking care of things just fine, and contrary to what you might think, the galaxy is capable of moving along without your presence for a few hours."

Keel surrendered to her pushing, and didn't attempt to rise again. "I feel like I was run over by a pileated gorb-ox."

"You'll be as good as new in no time. Rest." She left her hand on his chest.

Keel gently grabbed hold of it. "I do need rest. But... it's pretty lonely out here in the deepness of space..."

He sensed Leenah smiling in the dark, or maybe he only imagined it.

She removed her hand and said, "You're hurt. You need to recover."

Keel let out a long and exaggerated sigh. He was exhausted. And sore. He felt like he could sleep for a week straight if left to it. "Yeah, you're right. Thanks again for looking after me."

"Thanks for coming for me. And Prisma. I think it meant a lot to her. She seems like she's changed her mind about you."

"They always do." Keel swallowed, his mouth feeling dry. "Kid's had enough trouble for one life. We'll find a place for her to grow up. Live as normal a life as she can."

"I think that's a good idea, even though she may not like it."

The two stopped talking, and Keel felt his eyes grow heavy. His breathing slowed, and he began to drift back into sleep.

"Garret is working hard on getting KRS-88 put back together." Though Leenah had insisted that Keel needed rest, she apparently still wanted to talk. "Shouldn't be much longer before he's done. He's really a savant when it comes to tech. It's amazing."

Keel propped himself up on an elbow. The pain was not quite as bad. "Yeah, I don't think any of us would've made it off that ship without him."

Keel meant what he said. Garrett, who'd been just a chance pickup back on Tannespa, had turned into one of the most valuable people he'd ever worked with.

Keel remembered the comm chime that had woken him up. "So what did the kid—our pal the tech wonder—want?"

Leenah didn't answer.

Keel sat up and pulled back the fleece. He was getting too hot. "C'mon... you can tell me. I promise not to rush to deal with whatever it is. I'll be a good patient. Do whatever my doctor asks."

"He got a message from the Legion. On the channel your commander uses."

"What did it say?"

"I don't know. I told him that you could hear it when you were feeling better."

Keel slapped his thigh. "Actually, I don't care who they want me to kill next. You still wanna run away with me, Leenah?"

Leenah ran her fingers through his hair. "That might be fun, yeah."

The room's comm chimed, accompanied by a blue overhead flash that pierced the dimness and draped Keel and Leenah in shadowy relief.

"Leenah?" Garret's voice sounded timid over the comm.

"What is it, Garret?"

Keel rolled his eyes. Why couldn't he get a moment alone with this girl? "Tell Major Owens that I'm not home."

"No... uh, it wasn't him. I, uh, was curious and listened to the message and..."

Garret sounded worried.

"Well, is it Lao Pak?" asked Keel. "Because if it is..."

"It's from Captain Chhun. Your friend?" said Garret, as though he needed to remind Keel of his relationship with the legionnaire.

"I know who he is, kid." Keel rolled his neck. "Look, I feel awful. Tell him I'll call him back."

"No... it's pre-recorded. He's in trouble. It sounds bad. Really bad. I think the Cybar have invaded the galaxy."

"I'll be right there."

Keel flung himself up and out of the bed, his entire body screaming in protest. The lights in the room came on full, and Keel squinted against the sudden brightness as he moved for the door. He stopped to look down at himself, mumbling, "I should put on pants."

He turned and found Leenah already holding up his trousers in one hand and a loose, open-collar shirt in the other. It was clear from her face that she wasn't thrilled about going down this road again.

When he was somewhat more presentable, Keel limped out of his room and into the Six's main lounge. Exo and Bombassa were having drinks with Skrizz, chatting idly.

"Didn't think you'd be up so soon, killer," Exo said.

"Chhun's in trouble," Keel answered, limping past them to join Garret in the cockpit.

Exo followed, and soon everyone but Prisma was crowding to hear the recorded message.

"... so anyway," Chhun concluded on the recording, "if you're hearing this in time, we're in it deep."

"Dude," Exo said. "We gotta help him."

Keel nodded. He wasn't... surprised by this reaction from Exo, but neither had he expected it. "How long ago was that message transmitted?"

"Twenty minutes," Garret said. "I called you as soon as we received it."

"We can reach the planet in question in three hours," Ravi stated. "If... such is your decision."

"Do it, man," Exo urged. "Gotta do it."

Bombassa nodded.

There was never any doubt in Keel's mind. "Send him a text message back. Have him turn on his emergency transponder in three hours so we can find him when we arrive."

"Done," said Garret.

"Okay, Ravi. Let's go."

If it weren't for his bucket telling him the location of Kill Team Outlaw, Chhun would have walked right through the landing zone without seeing a single one of them. Knowing that every gun in the unit would be trained on him, he moved carefully, showing himself from behind the cover of a small copse only after announcing, "Hey, it's me. Time to get moving. We're too close to the city."

The kill team emerged from hidden positions behind shrubs, rocks, and other natural terrain. Their prisoner from the House of Reason was still with them, shivering against the morning's cold. It was paradise, but the sun was hiding its face behind the clouds.

"Yeah, and we gotta get into the wilds quietly." Bear pointed to Delegate Arushi. "That's gonna be tough with the screamer underneath the hood, so we gotta think of something." The big legionnaire motioned for some of his men to take a knee and keep an eye on perimeter security while they talked.

The landing zone was on top of a bluff overlooking the sea. Strong ocean winds whipped against them, causing the delegate's gown to fly wildly. The trails leading up from the marina to this spot were well maintained, and hadn't been all that difficult to climb. It would be a different story if they pushed farther into the conserved wilds of the planet.

"She's a liability," said SPC Brown. "I say we dust her and get going."

"Yeah," agreed another of the Dark Ops leejes. "I'm with Brownie. Offing this House of Reason feenk would be doin' the galaxy a favor."

Masters shook his head. He stood next to the prisoner and was trying to shield her from the wind with his own body. He held her in place, gently gripping her arm. "Dude. No way. We can't just dust her like that. I say we let her go. Let her regroup with her family... while she still can."

"Death sentence either way," said Bear.

Chhun backed Masters up. "We're not killing a prisoner. Either we take her with us to our extraction point, or we let her go. Bear, you're TL. Choice is yours."

Bear sniffed like he had a runny nose. "Brownie, let her hands loose. By the time she realizes we're not going to kill her and pulls away her hood, we'll be gone like Asha Pawng. Any problems with that?"

If any of the other leejes disagreed, they kept their mouths shut.

SPC Brown moved to take the prisoner from Masters. "I got her."

The others moved some distance away while Brown unfastened the delegate's ener-chains. Her hands immediately sprang out in front of her, and she rubbed her wrists vigorously. Her body language, however, betrayed fear. The isolation hood prevented her from knowing that the legionnaires had decided to let her go.

"All right," Bear called out. "Let's get moving."

Chhun tensed. His HUD suddenly filled with hostile combatant warnings, as if a log had been delayed and was now spitting out all its data at once. He turned his head and saw among the hedges and rocks several humanoid-sized bots, painted matte black. These were the bots he'd seen accompanying the large war bots that had overrun Task Force Granite; they moved like men and were armed with blaster rifles.

Chhun threw out his arm and shouted, "Get down!" as he dropped into the dirt.

Masters and Bear instinctively followed their former team leader's orders, far faster than the warning should have allowed. It was almost as if they shared some sort of extra-sensory bond. But the rest of the legionnaires were not so attuned to Chhun, and even that split-second difference in reaction time made all the difference. An intense flurry of blaster fire ripped through the rest of squad as well as the prisoner, leaving holes in armor and negligée alike.

They were dead before hitting the ground.

Chhun pulled out an ear-popper and hurled it in the direction of the machines. It boomed and flashed, temporarily causing the display inside his bucket to skip and go dark. Standing up, he shouted, "Over the edge!"

The three surviving legionnaires ran to the edge of the bluff that overlooked the sea. Masters, the speedster, reached the edge first and leapt off without hesitation.

Chhun heard Bear's heavy footsteps running behind him. He paused at the brink, turned, and as he waited for the big legionnaire to arrive, he took out one of the bots with a shot to its head. Bear lumbered by, Chhun slapping him on the back, and the big man jumped over the edge.

Another bot fell to Chhun's precise blaster fire. These bots weren't as resilient as the big war bots he'd watched fight at the city center. But they were recovering from the ear-popper, raising their blaster rifles. As Chhun hurled himself off the bluff, blaster fire sizzled past him.

The physical rush of free-falling crowded Chhun's senses as he hurtled toward the water. He knew the landing would suck, even with his armor, but it was better than the alternative. He attempted to orient his body to assume a diving position, but he didn't quite rotate himself properly. He landed at a slight angle, his shoulder and arm hitting the water first, taking the brunt of the impact, followed by his head and neck. His legs flopped hard and awkwardly, like a whale slapping the surface of the water with its tail.

The velocity of the long fall thrust him down deep.

The impact with the water had wrenched Chhun's bucket right off. His ears were filled with the sound of violently moving water, and he felt the shocking cold of the ocean against his face. But he had trained for such events. Calmly holding his breath, he forced open his eyes, ignoring the sting of the saltwater as he looked around for his missing helmet.

Visibility was almost non-existent. He couldn't see more than two meters in front of him. For a moment, he felt the urge to give in to panic. The landing had knocked him for a loop, and he wasn't entirely sure which way was up, down, or sideways. But he was keenly aware that he had a limited amount of oxygen with which to either find his bucket or swim for the surface, where the bots would likely be looking for targets.

Two powerful lights shone through the dark waters. Masters and Bear emerged from the murk, ultrabeams brilliantly shining. Chhun pointed to his head, as though the sight of him without his helmet might not be obvious to his fellow swimmers. But then, in a serendipitous moment, his bucket drifted down, passing in front of an ultrabeam like an actor before a spotlight.

Chhun reached out to grab the helmet only to jerk his hand back as a sizzling stream of heat jetted down from the surface. The bots were sending down blaster fire from above. For this sort of energy to be maintained this deep into the water, they had to be expending massive power with each charge. These bolts might not kill, but they were likely strong enough to destroy suit integrity. And that would make staying beneath the waves all but impossible.

Chhun's second attempt for the helmet was successful. He gripped it as it drifted by his feet, and quickly pulled it over his head. Once more, he fought back against the urge to panic. With the bucket on and full of water, he felt at once claustrophobic and prone to drowning. Nevertheless, he sealed the helmet to the rest of his suit and waited as it booted up.

The sophisticated technology recognized that Chhun's head was submerged. Pumps began siphoning out the liquid, and the water level went down as though someone were sucking it away with a straw. Down past his hairline, eyebrows, eyes, nose, and finally, below his mouth, allowing him to take a deep, salt-tinged breath.

Masters called over the comm. "You okay?"

"Yeah," coughed Chhun. "I'm good."

His audio sensors detected a distant splash somewhere to his left. The impact was deep and intense, and the first thought coming to Chhun's mind was that a bot had jumped down to bring the fight to them under water. He turned to see what he could, and was met with the concussion of an underwater explosion. It rocked him like a patch of seaweed in the grips of the surf.

Similar splashes followed. The bots were dropping some sort of grenades or other explosive device in the hopes of blowing the surviving out of the water.

"Swim down!" said Masters, already kicking his feet in a race to the bottom.

The others chased after him.

"So what's the plan?" asked Bear as they reached a depth that appeared to keep the explosive depth charges safely above them. "Much as I feel like staying under the waves is our best shot at surviving, we can't stay under here forever."

Chhun had already come up with an answer to this question. "We retrace Task Force Granite's route into the city. At least get close enough to determine whether or not there are any survivors. Before I left, I sent out an SOS to Wraith."

Masters grunted. "I guess if anyone is crazy to come and get us in the middle of a fight where even Intrepid had to bug out, it's Wraith."

"That may be true," said Chhun. "But if he comes, I don't think it'll be because he's crazy. It'll be because he's a legionnaire."

The beach where Task Force Granite had landed was empty and desolate. Faint rays of sunlight peeked through distant clouds, but not enough to fight the gloom of gray on the white sands. Hiding in the surf, the legionnaires let the waves wash over their bodies as they tumbled like driftwood, scanning for threats.

There was no sign of the machines—or anything else.

"Looks clear." Chhun slowly stood and began to creep toward the shore. "Still, follow me at a distance. Keep some spacing in case something's waiting for us on the other side of those dunes."

He moved swiftly across the beach, blaster rifle at the high ready, sweeping for targets. But no threat presented itself. The beach was barren.

But it wasn't quiet. The sound of distant blaster fire was emanating from the city, where fires burned and thick black pillars of smoke rose.

"We're following," Bear announced.

Chhun could see the representative dots of his two friends on his HUD, tracing their steps side by side. He moved up a sand dune and stopped at its crest. The grim spectacle of two dead bodies lay before him, riddled with high-energy blaster fire. These had to be the two civilians Task Force Granite had encountered when first traversing the beach. Numerous heavy gouges disrupted the sand here, like massive footprints. They shuffled between the bodies and the beach grass and other vegetation that served as a buffer between sand and city.

Bear and Masters joined their commander at the top of the dune, crouching low to help conceal their profile.

"War bots do this?" Bear asked.

"Yeah," Chhun said, hopping down the dune next to the corpses. "I'd like to know who's controlling these things. My guess is Goth Sullus and his Black Fleet."

Bear crouched to inspect the bodies, but quickly relented. They were dead, and had no military value. Just a couple of teenagers. "You'd think we would have seen bots like this on Tarrago if they had 'em."

Masters walked past the deceased and made for the rainwater runoff. "Maybe they were on back order."

Shaking his head, and with a smile on his face that he'd rather not be there, Chhun followed. Even after all this, Masters had his jokes. It seemed like there was never a time to the legionnaire where a joke wasn't the tactful response. It was endearing. Often wildly inappropriate, but endearing.

"Looks clear," said Masters, peering into the storm drain.

The three legionnaires passed into the drain through the square-cut opening in the metal grate made hours earlier by their brothers in Task Force Granite. Legionnaires for whom they would now risk their lives, just on the off chance that one might still be alive.

The storm drains were empty for the first two hundred meters or so, but it was clear that not all was well. The trickling stream of runoff that flowed beneath their feet and splashed around their boots was tinted a rust-red.

"Blood?" suggested Bear as they moved forward. "Should we run an analysis?"

"No," Chhun answered, not slowing his pace. "If it is, we'll find out."

A right turn at an elbow in the underground tunnels that confirmed Bear's hypothesis. The tunnel was strewn with dead bodies. Some were planetary militia, a few were legionnaires and marines, but most were ordinary citizens. Young and old. Newborn baby boys and aged grandmothers. They were thoroughly and completely dead.

"Must've tried escaping the attacks through here," Masters said, stepping over the doomed, sparing them the final indecency of their bodies being trampled.

"Which means there are probably bots down here looking for survivors," said Chhun.

His prognostication was met with an electronic beep from down the tunnel. From around a bend, a red wide-beam laser swept across the tunnel, taking everything in.

There was no way of knowing if this bot was a simple municipal crawler just doing its job, unaware of or unconcerned with the carnage all around it, or if it was some sort of support machine for the invading war bots. Chhun wasn't taking a chance. Spotting a side tunnel just ahead, he motioned the others forward.

As they silently crept toward the side tunnel, they were somewhat shielded from the approaching bot by a pile of bodies that lay stacked like a dam, slowing the flow of water to a trickle. They slipped into the detour and pressed themselves against the walls just as the bot began to climb the pile of bodies from the opposite side.

The machine, which was shaped like an egg with five appendages jutting from its widest point, stopped at the peak of the corpses, ceased scanning, and announced in a helpful, sanitized female voice, "Obstacle detected." It extended a slim, clear antenna, which flashed a bright green for several seconds. It then lowered the antenna and continued on its way down the main passage.

"Let's sit back a bit," cautioned Chhun. "Make sure nothing else is following that little bot."

They waited for a few minutes, then heard a distant rumble coming down the tunnel. An automated dozer of some sort, with a half-circle front plate that perfectly fit the bottom of the tunnel, pushed along, moving or grinding bodies until it reached the "clog." The yellow machine pushed right through, rolling the corpses aside as easily as if they were a buildup of muck and leaves. This machine was no doubt designed to clear such ordinary debris, and the mess it made of the dead bodies—crushing, stripping, and severing—was something Chhun hoped he'd be able to forget.

It continued down the tunnel, a yellow light flashing behind it, lighting up the darkness.

"Dude," said Masters. "That was messed up."

"Municipal bots just doing their jobs," Bear answered.

"So were the ones who killed 'em," said Masters. "Doesn't mean I have to like it."

Chhun had been monitoring their position through the underground relative to the city itself. Kill Team Granite had needed to move much farther to reach the POW camp, but all Chhun's team needed to do was reach the central square where the Legion's last stand took place. They were almost there. "Let's get up top before any more machines come."

They continued along the main tunnel, finding the progress much swifter now that it had been cleared by the dozer. A shaft of daylight split the darkness, illuminating floating particles of dust kicked up by the machine's passing.

Chhun pointed to the light. Below it, metal rungs built into the tunnel wall led upward. "Let's try and get topside there."

The legionnaires gathered beneath the opening, instinctively standing just outside the light shaft, and listened. It was quiet above, the sounds of blaster fire still distant.

"Masters, go up top and see if it's all clear."

"Sure. I was hoping to get shot in the face today." Masters climbed the ladder like a moktaar up a tree, but quietly, not letting his hands or feet make a sound on the metal rungs.

When it was evident that the scout had reached the top, Chhun asked, "What do you see?"

"Bodies." There was no mirth in Masters's voice. And no jokes to follow. "Lots of bodies."

"Any of those machines?" asked Bear, voicing the question Chhun had intended to ask next.

"None that look functional."

"Think you can get out through the opening and into the street?" Chhun asked.

"Yeah. You following me?"

"Right behind you."

When Chhun reached the top of the ladder, he found himself peering out at street level through a storm drain built into the side of a walkway. Masters was already outside, his legs visible. The scene was breathtaking—in the grimmest way imaginable. Dead legionnaires, marines, militia, and civilians lay heaped together in piles, with destroyed war bots likewise sorted.

It was a vast killing field.

Chhun stared at all that stretched out before him, his hands tightly gripping the topmost rung. It was as if the planet itself had expelled all who had ever died in its history into this one spot, making what was an otherwise glorious and beautiful core world city into an open grave.

"Something wrong?" asked Bear, right below his former team leader.

Chhun wanted to say yes. That there was something wrong. Something very wrong with the entire galaxy for a scene like this to exist. So many dead. Kill teams, civilians, legionnaires... slaughtered like livestock. But instead he answered no, and made his way into the still carnage.

Noise drifted from the far corners of the city. Voices united in terrified screams—or perhaps Chhun imagined that. What he didn't imagine were the blaster shots and explosions. These machines were not concerned with military targets and personnel alone. They were conducting a wholesale extermination of every person they could find.

A commotion sounded to Chhun's left. A large bird, its wingspan at least seven feet, flopped around, unable to fly away and escape the crowding dead. A blaster bolt had torn through its wing—and not by accident. More of the creatures were spread throughout the area, necks and wings broken, as though they had been hunted out of the air.

It seemed as though these robotic invaders were intent on killing every biological organism they encountered.

The thought sent a chill up Chhun's spine. He told himself that he was imagining things. That the machines were likely under the control of some undetermined but lethal force. The Black Fleet.

But it felt like the end of days. Like a hypothetical doomsday survival trainer that those bright Legion minds prepared for live-fire training games. Scenarios like, "What if a legitimate, widespread artificial intelligence uprising attempted to destroy all life in the galaxy?"

What then?

Both Chhun and Masters stood dumbfounded at the destruction.

The storm drain opening was almost too narrow for Bear to squeeze through. But he made it, and joined his brothers, a full head taller than each. "Oba..." he said, looking around.

"So what now?" Masters asked.

Chhun wondered the same thing. The answer was ingrained deep inside of him, set there as a bulwark against the despair and hopelessness that came in dark times like those that came with war. "We're legionnaires," he said. "We adapt. We keep fighting for what's best for the galaxy and the Republic. And right now, what's best is for us to stay alive long enough to get word out about what's happened here today. In case more is coming."

"This is the Savage Wars all over again," said Masters.

"Worse," contended Bear. "Did you hear back from Wraith?"

"Not yet, but deep-space transmissions can take time to catch up with a ship if it's traveling through hyperspace."

Chhun looked out over the field of the dead. Precious few had woken up this morning knowing the day might be their last. Chhun wondered if the same fate awaited him and his brothers. "We've all gone through evasion and survival training. We know what to do in a situation like this. Let's take a look for survivors and then stock up on equipment.

Then we make for the wilds and hold out until help arrives or the situation changes."

An airborne whine, as if from repulsors, sounded high above them. Chhun looked up to see an odd, alien-looking aircraft. Angular, with sharp lines that seemed to disappear into itself.

"Down!" hissed Bear.

All three men dropped among the dead, becoming like corpses themselves. Playing a macabre game of hide-and-seek with the craft overhead, watching to see if it would slow or carry on past them.

It flew past, making its way deeper into the city, where it unleashed a volley of missiles at the base of a mega-scraper. It wasn't one of the truly gigantic towers that crowded many of the core's financial centers, but a modest, by core-world standards, forty-story building that presented an ocean view on a world meticulously crafted to be a place of respite for its rich denizens. A little slice of heaven that still provided all the comforts the galaxy had to offer.

The missiles appeared to be angled at random, rather than being focused in a single concentration of direct firepower, but it was clear that the craft's pilot—organic or artificial—knew what they were doing. The building shook, then swayed, then came crashing down. All from a payload of four missiles.

"They're gonna wipe out the whole city," said Masters, not moving from his corpse-like position.

"Maybe the whole planet," replied Chhun.

"Well... aren't you an optimist."

"I think we're clear," Bear said.

Chhun pushed himself up off the ground. He realized that he had been lying on the severed leg of a legionnaire, bent at the knee as if in midstride. "Let's grab what we can and get out of here as quickly as possible."

"Quick as possible would be right now." Masters was already removing rations from the pack of a Republic marine. He paused to look at Chhun. "Just sayin'."

He was right, but Chhun was unwilling to leave while there was a chance—however slim—that a fellow legionnaire might still be alive. Even though, by all evidence, that seemed impossible. "We need charge packs and anything else that might be useful. Not to mention rations, especially if these things do to the rest of this planet's game what they did to the birds."

"You think they killed the birds on purpose?" Masters asked.

Bear grunted as if to say he wasn't so sure. "If whoever is controlling the bots wanted to kill everything, why not do it with a planetary bombardment? Any ship that could get a destroyer to run has to have the capability."

Chhun had thought about the same thing. He gave the only answer his mind could muster, the one that also caused him to believe that no one was behind the war bot assault except the machines themselves. "I don't think anyone is controlling this army. I think it's an aware AI, or multiple AIs. And I think they want to fight on our terms, like any invading army would."

Masters sounded incredulous. "Like they want... whoever, us, to see that they can fight our way, but better?"

"That's not good," Bear mumbled.

The ominous prospect of an actual AI uprising spurred the legionnaires to move quickly. They grabbed charge packs, spare medical kits, rations, as much as they could fit on their persons. Chhun would have liked to have grabbed some SABs and aero-precision missile launchers—they would probably need them before the end—but they would be too much to carry.

As for survivors, not even the faintest glimmer of hope remained. The war bots had not only killed everything in sight, they had done so with a ruthless thoroughness.

Chhun was pulling fraggers and ear-poppers from the belt of the dead Legion commando when he heard the hum of another repulsor. This one sounded different from the previous intruder, but Bear's warning shout was the same.

"Down!"

The legionnaires again dropped. A craft shaped like an inverted wedge with a large white dome beneath its fuselage stopped and hovered over the battlefield. It was obvious to Chhun that this ship was some sort of scanner or intelligence craft. Maybe the ship that had flown overhead earlier had seen them after all.

This craft hovered a hundred meters up for several seconds. It emitted a bright strobe-like flash, then continued on its way.

Masters was the first to lift his head when the sound of the ship's repulsors faded away. "Whaddaya think that was?"

Bear had a pair of field macros and was scanning the horizon while prone. "Looking for us, is what it was."

Chhun wasn't usually one to jump to paranoid conclusions, but he couldn't help but agree. "Yeah, I think so too. You guys got everything you need to get out of here?"

"Probably not," replied Masters, "but I've got as much as I can carry. I hope you don't mind, but mostly I took empty charge packs, since they're so much lighter."

"You're an idiot," growled Bear.

"I'm callow," said Masters.

"Word of the day?"

Masters nodded.

"You're using it wrong."

"Or am I?"

Bear paused. "Hmm. Maybe not."

Chhun climbed down from a pile of dead bodies. "Okay, let's head back the way we came. Get back into the water, see if we can drift along the current or swim to a more deserted section of the coastline. The north looked pretty undeveloped on the maps. We can land on the beach up there and hike inland until we're someplace good and remote."

Still peering through his macros, Bear said, "Don't think we'll be doing that any time soon, boss. There's some kind of bot hovering our way from the southeast... no, make that three bots. Coming in fast."

He put down his macros and brought up his blaster rifle.

Masters did the same.

There was little doubt in Chhun's mind that the three of them would be able to dispose of what were probably reconnaissance bots without much difficulty. But this was a situation where removing the scouts would provide a positive confirmation of their location. It would be reconnaissance by fire.

"No," Chhun said, slinging his blaster rifle over his shoulder. "We can't fight right now. We have to hide. These bodies are stacked thick enough. Dig yourselves a hole to hide in."

"Dude," Masters said, watching Chhun pull out corpses in an attempt to make himself a foxhole. "That's hardcore."

"Just do it!"

The men frantically began to move bodies aside, digging out graves from the dead. Chhun pushed, pulled, and piled until he'd made for himself a burrow that was about five bodies deep. He slid himself into the opening legs first, still wanting to see outward.

"You guys in?" he called over L-comm.

Bear's voice sounded grim. "Yeah."

"This is going to give me nightmares," Masters complained.

"Okay, I want total comm silence until—" Chhun paused. He heard what sounded like digital transmissions across his comm.

"What is it?"

"I want total comm silence," Chhun ordered. "They might be listening right now. Power down completely."

"For how long?" asked Masters.

"Until I say. Power down, now!"

Chhun didn't wait for further replies. He powered his system down.

Immediately he felt as though the world had lost its luster. His visor began to fog his breath. His body warmed from the insulation he had dug himself into. Worst of all, his hearing was muffled to the point where the only sounds he could distinguish were those of his breathing and his beating heart.

He imagined the machines would soon be flying overhead, if they weren't already there. But how long would they stay and scan? Chhun decided to count the seconds.

One-one-thousand...

Two-one-thousand...

Three-one-thousand...

Chhun counted until he was confident that twenty-five minutes had elapsed. During that entire time, he had remained utterly still, and his body now ached. It made him think of the qualified snipers in the Legion, made him think of Twenties. Men like that, men with the ability to endure such grueling discomfort just for the chance to take their shot, had always amazed Chhun. Even more amazing was how much those guys seemed to love it.

It was difficult to hear anything through his helmet, but surely the bots were gone now. He was about to boot his armor back up, just to get the cooling fans running in his bucket, but decided it would be wiser to first visually confirm that no threats were present.

Craning his neck forward, like a turtle venturing out of its shell, he tried to get a better vantage point as to what was outside of his foxhole. Out among the bodies.

A massive, robotic leg slammed down inches from his face. It was one of the big war bots with the riot shields.

While the machine stood there, apparently oblivious to the legionnaire hiding at his feet, Chhun's heart pounded. He dared not risk moving a muscle. All the bot had to do was look down, and it would probably see him. Chhun was sure it would somehow know that he was alive.

But the feeling of dread bled away and turned into relief when the big war bot moved on, literally trampling its vanquished foes underfoot.

Chhun counted thousands again. This time he waited until he was sure that forty-five more minutes had passed. He didn't dare crawl from his hole without knowing what was out there. He decided that hearing would serve him better than coming out of his hole and looking around.

Okay, he thought to himself. Power up your bucket and listen. Worst case, one of the bots finds you. In that case, maybe you can draw it away and help Bear and Masters avoid your fate.

The helmet booted up, fast as ever. The cooling fans immediately vented the suit and chilled the thermal gels that sat between armor and synthprene. It felt wonderful.

Chhun set his audio receptors to their maximum level. That should be enough to hear any ambient noises outside of his den. The only sound was the drifting breeze blowing in from the ocean.

Slowly, so slowly, Chhun edged his head out of the opening of his ghoulish foxhole. He was like an animal poking its nose out of a burrow to sniff the air. He counted to three, then came back inside. After waiting a minute, he repeated the process.

Convinced that the threat was truly gone, Chhun activated his external audio. He called from his foxhole, "I think we're good."

He hoped his voice would be able to carry far enough for Bear and Masters to hear him through their dead buckets.

No one answered. He would have to venture outside alone.

Chhun wriggled free of the corpses. There was no sign of the bots. He scrambled over to Bear's hole first, approaching it from an indirect angle. The last thing he wanted was to get shot by coming straight for the legionnaire.

But Bear must have seen him. He popped his head out of his foxhole and shouted, his voice muffled by his bucket, "We clear?"

Chhun lowered himself so he could speak into Bear's foxhole. "Yeah, I think so. You can boot back up."

The sound of Bear sighing in relief came over Chhun's comm. "That was uncomfortable, Captain. Guys my size aren't supposed to stay crunched into such small positions for that long."

Chhun smiled. "In that case, I'm sorry to have to tell you to stay put for now. I'm gonna try to get Masters."

"Don't let him shoot you."

Chhun decided to get the Dark Ops legionnaire's attention in a way that hopefully wouldn't be mistaken for an attack. He picked up several spent charge packs scattered on the battlefield, then tossed them gently, one by one, into Masters's foxhole while keeping himself out of a line of fire.

"Hey! Knock it off!" The muffled voice was distinctly Masters's.

"Can you hear me?" Chhun asked through his external speaker.

"Yeah. Can we go live comms?"

"Yes, but stay in your foxhole while we figure out what to do next."

Masters's next words were over L-comm. "Okay, I'm on. Bear?"

"I'm here."

Chhun scanned the area. "No idea if that search party was it, or if this area is marked for regular patrols. But we have to make a decision either to move now or hunker down and wait until night falls again."

"I bet those war bots see as well as we do in the dark," mused Bear.

"The fighting sounds farther off now," said Masters.

He was right. The sounds of battle were distant. It was as if the war bot forced had radiated outward from this spot, likely killing everything in their path.

"If you wanna call it fighting. Slaughter is more like it."

Chhun thought about what sort of chaos must have taken place in the city while he and his two-man team were beneath the sea and then covered by the dead. Were the citizens of the planet running, fleeing in a desperate attempt to escape? Had some of them evaded the attackers, hiding like Chhun and his men had? Was it possible that anyone on this planet had managed to put up a stiff enough resistance to actually halt the war bots' progress?

Chhun didn't think so. Not when so many legionnaires had died attempting the same. The Gallobren citizens' only hope was escaping by starship. But what chance did they have of that, when whatever delivered these monsters was able to make even the Intrepid cut and run?

Chhun felt his hopes fade.

And then an incoming text chime sounded with an accompanying message.

It was Wraith.

"Hey," Masters called out over comm. "It's got to have been three hours since that transmission, right?"

After hearing from Wraith, Chhun had burrowed back into his fetid hiding spot, and the three Dark Ops legionnaires had remained right where they were. Enduring the passage of time, the same as the dead that covered them.

Bear grunted. "You've been asking that every ten minutes since Chhun told you Wraith was coming."

"Unlike some people," hissed Masters, "I don't like it here. I think this place sucks."

"Masters is right," said Chhun. He had set a chronometer in his bucket synced to the timestamp of Wraith's message. "The Indelible VI should have already arrived. I think we have to entertain the possibility that Captain Ford was shot down or had to turn away."

"Okay, so what's the plan then?" Masters asked.

A legionnaire body slid down a pile of the dead, making a sound like armor clattering against armor. The three men went still and hushed themselves, practically holding their breaths.

When no war bot materialized, and no further noises came from the still graveyard, Chhun said, "I'm turning on our rescue transponder. We just have to hope that Wraith finds it before something else does."

He turned on the transponder and hurled it as far as he could. It landed among a pile of dead kill team operators. If a non-friendly came to investigate, at least it would start away from their position.

"So we just wait for the sound of more repulsors?" Bear asked. "Hope it's Wraith?"

"Yeah," said Chhun. "We give it another hour. If he hasn't shown up by then, let's follow the original plan of getting back to the sea and finding someplace more secluded to hide."

"I was thinking, guys," Master said. "If we run out of ammo, I'm pretty sure I can destroy the entire war bot force by giving them a logic puzzle so perfectly contradictory that their circuits overheat until their processors explode."

When no one answered, Masters said, "You guys wanna know what the puzzle is?"

Chhun sighed. "Fine. What's the—"

"No!" interrupted Bear. "Don't encourage him."

"Glad you asked," said Masters, mirth evident in his voice. "It's this: How can a legionnaire as ugly as Bear—"

The joke was cut off by the familiar sound of repulsors streaking fast through the air.

"Wraith," Chhun said, straightening himself. "That sounds like the Six."

"Let's pop some IR strobes to make sure he finds us," Bear said.

The legionnaires tossed the infrared strobes where they would be most conspicuous.

The sound of a Naseen freighter grew louder, but it was joined by the whine of more of those hostile air fighters. Everything seemed to be streaking toward them at close to top speed.

"Here they come!" Masters said.

As the Indelible VI came into view, it was clear that the ship was being chased by a wing of invading fighters. Chhun felt conflicting emotions. Elation at Wraith's arrival, and worry and dread at seeing him pursued.

The Six shot right by them, with six fighters screaming behind it, closing in on effective firing range.

Chhun opened a comm channel to his old friend. "Wraith, this is Chhun. You've got six bogeys on your tail and you just passed over our location."

"Yeah, saw that," Wraith answered over the comm. The sound of his voice sent a surge of adrenaline through Chhun. "A little busy to land right now though."

"Rockets!" shouted Bear. "Find an AP and shoot 'em down."

Masters and Bear scrambled out of their holes and went for the anti-vehicle launchers they had spotted during their earlier search of the area.

"Copy, Wraith," Chhun said. He didn't want to break the pilot's concentration, but needed to let him know what they were up to. "Masters and Bear are arming aero-precision launchers. If you can lead them back over our zone, we can dust a few."

A whoosh sounded behind Chhun. He looked up and saw that Bear had fired a missile in the direction of the departing pack. It burned hot in pursuit.

"I got a lock on the rear-most fighter," Bear explained, watching the missile speed away, a tiny dot. "Hope it catches up."

A distant boom suggested that the missile found something.

"Captain Chhun, this is Ravi."

"I hear you, Ravi," said Chhun. He had heard about the holographic navigator from Wraith, but thought that he had been destroyed. Apparently not.

"You have eliminated one of the starfighters," Ravi said, his voice as calm and cool as Wraith could be while on the battlefield. "Thank you for this. I calculate that we will be able to destroy two more while leading the remaining three back in your direction. Can you meet them with three more missiles?"

"We need to take three more down!" Chhun shouted to the others.

"Can do," said Masters.

"Indelible VI," Chhun said, "we can do it."

"Very good. We will lead them to you. Be ready."

"Copy. Chhun out."

Bear hurried over to his Dark Ops commander and handed him an aero-precision launcher, already loaded. Now each legionnaire had one, and they were ready to clear the skies long enough to allow their rescue craft to land.

"Uh, boss..." Masters's voice made Chhun's heart sink. Something about the way he said it. "My HUD's showing what looks like a hella big war bot force moving on our position. Call it fifty."

The machines had found them. It was do or die. Give Wraith time to land, or cut and run, and pray that they might get a second chance at rescue. Which seemed decidedly unlikely.

Chhun decided to fight. "Just focus on the ships chasing Wraith," he ordered. "If he can't get down here, nothing else matters. Can one of you take an extra shot with the AP rocket so I can try and hold the war bots back?"

"I might be able to," Bear said.

"Wish Exo was here," said Masters, his launcher at the ready.

Chhun began combing the field for a weapon he could use against the approaching war bots. Another AP launcher would be great if he could dumb-fire it into a column, but he wasn't seeing one. He did find an N-18 sniper rifle cradled in the arms of a dead legionnaire. He pried it from the warrior's hands and checked the charge pack. It was spent, so he changed it out. Lying prone on a mound of deceased leejes, he deployed the weapon's tripods and made a stack of all his gathered charge packs. He would make every shot count.

The roar of the Six's repulsors could be heard again. It approached, looping and dodging three trailing fighters, all of them firing on the freighter but missing wildly, unable to predict Wraith's patterns.

Bear found a target lock and sent a missile streaking at one of the fighters. The ship attempted to break off, but was unable to shake the sophisticated seeker, which found its target. The fighter exploded in a ball of flames. Ruined parts scattered over the battlefield.

Masters fired second later. The missile arched toward its target and hit home while Bear loaded another missile.

The plan was succeeding, but surely more ships would come. The window was small. Everything needed to get done on this pass by Wraith.

Chhun's HUD had long since confirmed what Masters had detected. And now he saw the threat with his own eyes. The giant war bots came into view from every direction, emerging from behind ruined buildings and blind corners. Chhun didn't have time to assess their numbers; all he knew was that there were too many. Far too many. "Stay low! Hopefully they won't pick us out among the bodies until they're on top of us."

He opened fire on the first war bot that fell into his sights. The shot struck the machine in its head, blowing a hole through its helmet-like protection and sending it falling backward. Chhun immediately found another target and squeezed the trigger for another kill shot. And then another. But he was picking ants off their hill one at a time. There were always more. It made no difference. Still he continued to fire, reminding himself that one less weapon that could be brought to bear on his position or the Six was a good thing. In combat, you never quite knew what the tipping point would be.

As Bear looked for a lock on the last remaining starfighter, the Six's burst turrets blazed, catching the pursuing ship and scrapping it.

"Okay, we're clear!" Wraith shouted.

The freighter slowed—barely—and began to drop down to position itself to allow the three survivors to get on board.

Wraith shouted instructions. "Hurry up and—"

His cut himself off, and Chhun saw the vapor trail of a streaking rocket flying toward the ship.

Wraith deftly rocked his craft back, putting it up on its side and then sliding laterally as if on ice, cocked at a rakish angle. The ship moved perhaps a hundred meters and dropped down behind a grassy hill in the city square. The rocket passed harmlessly overhead.

But as the Six attempted to rise from its position, more rockets came streaking toward it. It was forced to stay low, out of the line of fire, but still seventy meters away from the legionnaires. It waited, hovering, just barely kissing the rubble of a blown-out building.

"I can't get any closer than this," Wraith called. "You're gonna have to run."

"Copy," Chhun said. "Guys! Let's go!"

But it was at that moment that the war bots closed within firing distance. A barrage of blaster fire impacted all around, striking dead bodies, and the three legionnaires had no choice but to drop onto their bellies.

They crawled over the bodies, meeting together in the hopes of putting together effective counter-fire. But there were so many incoming blaster bolts sizzling through the air that Chhun didn't think they could so much as poke their heads up without being hit a half dozen times.

"They're practically on top of us!" shouted Masters.

"Wraith," Chhun called into the comm, "we're pinned down and can't move. If you can't get to us... you should go. Better just us get dusted than you have to join us."

"Great," Wraith answered. "Just my luck."

The Indelible VI lifted straight up, and another rocket zoomed toward it. The Six dodged the projectile and returned fire, sending a concussive missile into the swarming mass of bots. It exploded close enough to the legionnaires that they—along with several corpses—were flung in the opposite direction.

Chhun shook his head, trying to regain his senses. The war bot blaster fire had definitely slackened.

He looked up. The Six was still hovering in place, its ramp lowered. Two Black Fleet shock troopers, one tall and imposing, the other with a familiar swagger, stepped out onto the ramp and began to unleash a dizzying amount of SAB firepower into the war bots. The freighter's illegal burst turrets blazed away as well.

"This is as hot as we can lay down fire!" Wraith shouted. "Get going!"

Chhun sprang to his feet. "Let's go now! Now!" He fired at an advancing war bot, no more than twenty meters away.

Bear and Masters rose as commanded and proceeded to sprint toward the waiting starship. With his men on the move, Chhun broke off contact and followed in pursuit. As the shock troopers at the door sent blaster bolts sizzling past them, it seemed to Chhun that an equal amount of return fire was scorching the air from the other direction. Some bolts impacted practically at his feet, sending fragments of armor and flesh flying; others, aimed higher, were absorbed by the Indelible VI's shield arrays.

Masters was the first to the ship. He sped up the ramp and inside without breaking his stride. Next was Bear, who likewise didn't slow as he stomped up the ramp. Had he hesitated for even a half a second, a blaster bolt would have struck his heel.

The fire was so thick, Chhun didn't see how the luck that had carried him safely through from Victory Company to Dark Ops would be able to hold out any longer. At any moment he expected a blaster bolt to hit him square between the shoulder blades. Or to slam like a fist of the gods into his helmet. But he continued on unabated, toward the guttural war cry of one of the shock troopers as he sprayed his SAB into the advancing enemy.

It was Exo. And though Chhun knew from Wraith that his former comrade had found a place in the Black Fleet, at that moment, their bond as brothers was solidified beyond speaking.

Chhun leapt on board the Indelible VI, not meaning to, but finding himself in mid-air and then crashing down onto the deck, safely inside. Already the ship was gaining altitude, rising upward as Exo and his fellow shock trooper fired down on the diminishing targets like door gunners on board an old Republic SLIC.

The ramp finally closed, and the two shock troopers lifted Chhun off the deck and strapped him into a jump seat. He could feel the ship vibrate as it exited the atmosphere.

I'm still alive, Chhun thought.

He felt like a man with a death wish that could never be granted. So many legionnaires remained on Gallobren, dead. But not him. Never him. And why? That's what he wanted to know as he sat, strapped into his jump seat, gasping for air. He had seen so many good men die.

But not him.

He became aware of an odd sensation, like his thoughts were not truly his own. Like they were whispered out of his mind from some unknown part of his brain that labeled him an angel of death, sent with the purpose of leading bright, young, capable legionnaires to the killing fields, where he himself oversaw their demise.

And why?

He needed for there to be a reason.

He was alive... for what?

Evil and duty, he answered. Your duty is to destroy evil.

Chhun felt his eyes roll in the back of his head as someone removed his bucket.

"Dude," Exo said, his own helmet off and concern on his face. Masters, Bear, and the tall shock trooper stood behind him. "You're hit pretty bad."

Sanctuary of Mother Ree
En Shakar

Chhun awakes in a rustic room, lit by a lone window and several flickering candles. He is lying on what feels like a straw mat. Coarse, disagreeable bed sheets cling to his exposed skin. A rainbow dances across the room's ceiling. Chhun traces the source to the window, where a child's mobile, decked with inch-long crystals, reflects the light.

Someone is sitting by his side.

Instinct combined with the unfamiliarity of the room has Chhun reaching for a blaster pistol underneath his pillow without thinking. His hand finds nothing. He is not in his bunk on board Intrepid, nor is he aboard the Indelible VI. He is somewhere... foreign.

The kindly face of a woman appears above him. She is old, but still retains her beauty. She must have been stunning in her youth. She leans forward, brushes the backs of her fingers against the stubble on his face, then caresses his close-cropped black hair.

"You are safe here."

Chhun lets the woman continue to stroke his hair. It feels... nurturing. Good and pure somehow. The woman's presence is so soothing. He feels utterly safe.

The galaxy is anything but that.

Duty. You have a duty to fulfill.

"The machines," Chhun says, his voice rasping as though it has been some time since he last spoke. "I have to warn..."

"They have been stopped," the woman replies. Cryptically adding, "Though not as they should."

"Who are you?"

"I am Mother Ree."

"Where am I?"

"Sanctuary," Mother Ree says. Her smile is firm and reassuring. "Captain Keel—the man you call Wraith—brought you here. It was the safest and wisest course of action. The galaxy, I fear, is in grave danger."

Chhun tries to sit up. "But you said..."

"Yes," says Mother Ree, anticipating the question. "And so I did. The machines—the Cybar—were stopped." A sadness seems to rest upon the woman. "But the galaxy has lost its last ember of freedom as a result."

Chhun can't guess what that means, and his head hurts trying to make sense of it. "How are they?"

"Your friends are all right. Much better than you." Mother Ree smiles. "I speak physically, of course."

"But they're still here?" Chhun isn't sure why he asked the question. He has no idea how much time passed since he collapsed on board the Indelible VI. For all he knows, his friends are waiting just outside the door.

"They remain," says Mother Ree. "For how long, I cannot say."

A candle next to Chhun's bedside begins to sputter and spit as it nears the end of its purpose. Mother Ree rises and puts out the struggling flame with a pinch of her fingers. "Captain Ford intends to leave you to recover, along with the young Prisma, who will remain in the hopes of living a peaceful life. Though... I wonder."

"Did Wraith say where he was headed?"

"I do not think he knows."

A knock sounds at the door.

"You may enter," says Mother Ree.

The door swings open to reveal a large war bot bending down to peer inside. It looks as though it has been through a considerable scrap: its left visual receptor is little more than a gaping hole, and its armored chest plate is pockmarked and scorched by blaster shots. As it enters the room, it reveals an arm painted with a gray primer that contrasts with the bot's otherwise dark finish.

Chhun begins to recoil at the sight of the war machine.

"It's all right," Mother Ree says soothingly. "This one is not a threat."

The bot stops its advance. "My apologies, Captain Chhun. I should have been more considerate, given what you recently endured—a discredit to my kind."

"You're the girl's war bot," Chhun says, remembering. He regains his composure. "KRS-88."

"I am delighted that you remember," the bot says in its basso profundo that makes it sound less like a killer than a manservant. "Mother Ree, I have come with a request."

"Yes, KRS-88? What does your gentle soul wish?"

The bot pauses to consider this. "I do not believe I possess such a thing as a soul."

"Do you not? Well, tell me what you came to say, all the same."

"Yes, of course. Garret sent me on behalf of Captain Keel. Evidently, a message has been received from the Legion commander." KRS-88 turns to address Chhun directly. "It was agreed upon, by the cadre of warriors on the ship, that you should return to the ship to hear this message yourself. Immediately."

Mother Ree shakes her head. "Captain Chhun nurses wounds brought from such messages. He must recover."

The bot nods. "Of course, Mother Ree. I am inclined to agree. The human body's capacity for enduring stress and damage, while considerable, is not inexhaustible. However, I believe Captain Keel was aware of Captain Chhun's situation, and took it into consideration before sending me to retrieve him."

Chhun swings his legs out of bed and stands. A searing pain in the small of his back causes him to grimace from the effort. He finds that he cannot stand straight, and stoops over like an old man with a curvature of the spine.

"Captain Chhun..." Genuine concern fills Mother Ree's voice.

Hobbling along like a geriatric, Chhun waves her off. "It's fine. I'll be okay. I should see what the matter is. Besides, it's probably good for me to get out of bed and move around a bit."

"If it were," Mother Ree says, moving to assist him, "I would have told you. But I will not seek to prevent the free choice of another."

As Chhun hobbles outside, with Mother Ree's help, he sees that he has not been resting in a single room in an archaic hospital, but rather in a one-room hut in the midst of a lush garden.

The big war bot, standing to one side, extends a large mechanical hand. "I am able to carry you back to the Indelible VI."

Chhun smiles at the thought of going to see his buddies like a bride being carried across the threshold by her husband. "No, I don't need you to carry me. But I won't argue if you help keep me steady."

"Very well." The bot grips Chhun's arm gently, allowing him to put most of his weight in the big machine's care.

As Chhun is led through the garden and sanctuary villa to the ship, he becomes aware that Mother Ree has left. But she soon returns and covers him with a thick, woolly blanket. And just in time—the temperature drops drastically as they come to the docking platform where the ship resides.

"Thank you," he says.

Mother Ree replies with a gentle caress of his arm.

Captain Ford leans against one of the struts at the base of the Six's ramp, waiting. He gives Chhun a perfunctory nod, and Chhun returns with the same.

Chhun limps inside the ship with the big bot's help. It feels to Chhun that his forward motion is due more to the bot powering him up the ramp than to himself. He is exhausted.

Mother Ree remains outside.

Chhun finds Masters and Bear out of their armor, sitting at a card table.

"Glad to see you up," Masters says, but it's clear that something is troubling him.

Exo stands in a corner, arms crossed, looking as though he wishes to kill someone. He barely even takes notice of Chhun, but finally says, "Hey."

"Hey," Chhun mumbles, surprised by the effort it takes him.

The other shock trooper stands opposite Exo like some great sentinel, his arms crossed at his chest, his face unreadable. "I am Okindo Bombassa," he says. "You have my respect, Captain Chhun."

With a weak smile, Chhun manages, "S'posed to be a major."

Sitting alone across the lounge is the slim code slicer named Garret, looking as if he'd rather be back at his console. He waves at Chhun. "Glad you're okay."

Chhun doesn't have the energy to reply.

Finally, Ford comes up the ramp behind Chhun. He looks to Chhun more like a soldier than the smuggler who left before the rescue of Major Owens from Herbeer. It's the way he carries himself. The responsibility of command seems to once again rest on his shoulders.

"You better sit down, kid," Ford says, gesturing to an open seat. "Even if you weren't banged up, you'd want to be sitting for this."

With KRS-88's help, Chhun levers himself into the offered seat. As he tries to get himself comfortable—his back is on fire—he spots the pink Endurian, the former MCR, down a corridor. She pauses to look at Ford, then moves on.

Chhun points a finger in her direction. "How come you didn't tell me she was MCR? Lao Pak told me."

Ford peers down the passageway, then gives Chhun a confused look. "I did. A while ago."

"Oh." Maybe Chhun forgot. It was a stupid thing to bring up anyway, and he wonders why he did. He isn't thinking straight. "Sorry."

Ford waves a hand as if to say it is already forgotten. He exchanges a look with Exo, then begins. "I got a message from the Legion commander. We all listened to it. You need to, too. Garret, go ahead."

The code slicer punches in a sequence on a communications console. "This is a recording captured by Major Owens. He gives an introduction, but I've skipped past that to the main bit; we wanted you to hear that first. The voice you'll hear belongs to some bigwig in Nether Ops."

The recording begins. Audio only. It starts with a few background noises, but mostly an ominous silence. And then a voice—one that Chhun has never heard before—speaks.

"It was all me," the voice begins.

It sounds academic and stentorian. A man speaking like he is proclaiming something with unashamed pride. But then the speaker laughs nervously. "I don't know why I'm about to tell you this. I didn't mean to tell you all of this. But I think I will.

"We knew, Goth Sullus. We knew someone like you would come along. We knew you were out there on the edge, though we didn't even know your name back then. We had our reports—stolen from elsewhere in Nether Ops, but ours. A strange and dynamic man with seemingly magical powers. Not a holy man. Not some... mad prophet.

"We knew there was a base... somewhere. Knew that someone was recruiting an army. We wondered what was going on out there and why our operatives weren't coming back. All disappeared out there in the deep. We went looking for them, of course. But we didn't find them. It was as though... they never were. The funny thing was, that might have been the first time we in Nether Ops, and you out there on the edge, were actually working together. We erased their past, and you erased their future.

"But everything was blurry, you understand. Not quite confirmed. A rumored state-of-the-art training base. Military. Shipyards. A major buyer for unused Republic research and development. Someone was up to something. You were out there, but... we had no idea who you were. We didn't know what your game was.

"So I hired the best sociologists, and even some speculative fictionists, to tell us what would happen next if you sought to use all that unconfirmed power from all that unconfirmed recruiting and building. The consensus was the 'benevolent dictator' theory. But all was uncertain. And uncertainties are not what I deal in. So I bided my time. In fact, it would be fair to say I was still biding my time... right up until this meeting. You see, I didn't like you, Goth Sullus. Not then, at least."

The voice falls silent for a moment. The subtle, almost non-existent noise of a starship fills the void. Chhun looks to Exo, who nods as if to say, keep listening.

And then X continues.

"Here's what I was certain about. At some point, the Republic would face a crossroads between war and revolution. I had been working for years to ensure that that moment would occur—and that when that decisive moment that would shape the future of the Republic finally came, I would be the one who made the decision. I was the only one who could.

"So a plan was hatched. And it wasn't just my plan, because something this grand has so many moving parts. But I was in control. I added the refinements. I made the hard choices. It was I who took responsibility for meeting the spectral gaze of a galactic civil war straight on.

It was I who set the plan in motion. Moved the pieces as required to get close to your primary arms dealer. Scarpia."

X laughs. "I had no idea he was selling to you. At that time, I didn't even know you existed out there. I deduced it all when I saw that the MCR was getting a significantly smaller slice of Scarpia's wares than I'd thought possible. So... who was getting the rest? I wanted Scarpia captured at any and all cost. So I stepped on another department's operation on Kublar. And that did cost. The Chiasm. A forward operating base... all of it. All the dead legionnaires.

"But it got my man close to Scarpia. It was worth it.

"Kublar was nothing new, of course. The only difference was, I staged it. To get close to Scarpia, which wound up getting me closer to you. And before you judge me, remember the House of Reason had been sending men to become just as dead in countless battles long before I was a legionnaire wounded at Psydon. Which was just yet one more sad little conflict for young men to go and die in so that the perpetual insiders could make just a little bit more on the back end."

X clears his throat.

"I was the only one with the stones to do it. It didn't matter that I had been one of them once. A legionnaire. It didn't matter that we were sending them to their deaths on Kublar. What mattered was that I thought Kublar would put me where I needed to be to make sure this little thing we call galactic civilization wouldn't perish under the weight of its own corrupt opulence.

"But then Scarpia disappeared. We still don't know how, or where to, though I know he ended up working directly for you. Did you do it?" X chuckled to himself. "I thought a lot about you after that. Out there, unknown... I wanted to know if you were the man who could change the status quo of a dozen little meaningless conflicts a year, all of them taking place for no other reason than so the pigs at the top could collect their interest on a percentage of the take. I wanted to know if you were the man who could put an end to the House of Reason. Not the Republic, mind you—it's worth saving—but could you stop the House of Reason? Directly, or... indirectly. By creating the right incentives. A gentle nudge, if you will.

"Because Article Nineteen needed to go into effect. That much was obvious. Has been for years. But the Legion High Command, for all their shiny bravery, wasn't willing to do the bravest thing of all: state the truth, and mutiny. Stating the truth was an act of war—and the Legion already had enough wars to keep them busy dying by the bucket load. So, I lobbied to have the zhee armed, because that's what it would take to finally get Keller off his rear and declare Article Nineteen.

"But he moved faster than I would have imagined. Must give him credit for that. The Legion was poised to topple the House of Reason and seize control of the government, had captured your General Nero... It was what I had planned for. Schemed for. Paid for in blood and treasure.

"And yet...

"What would change, really? The corrupt delegates in the House would be tried and sentenced; sunlight would sweep clean the darkest corners of that infestation. The Republic would rejoice. But then what? I'll tell you what. Elections, my dear—my emperor. A new wave of politicians. Hucksters. Con men. Oh, they'd be noble enough at first—earnest, sincere. But it was just a matter of time, wasn't it, before the rot set back in? And then we'd be back to square one. Because the problem wasn't the corrupt delegates—those specific corrupt delegates... it was the House itself. Its very structure. By its nature, it could lead only to one end. A House determined to cling to its power above all else; a Legion too overwhelmed, or too loyal, or simply too squeamish, to resist the inevitable creep.

"And then... I thought about you. The Legion had the support of my heart. But my mind... it believed in a benevolent dictator. It believed in you.

"Or, at least what you could be.

"So I stalled. Kept my options open. I warned the House of Reason about the Dark Ops raids coming for their delegates. Gave them advance warning of Article Nineteen. So I could make sure that the chance for change, real change, for the greater good—through you—wasn't wasted."

There is another pause. Chhun feels sick, to have been betrayed like this. That the House of Reason was corrupt is no surprise to him or to anyone... but here is proof that Nether Ops is just as bad. He remembers Major Owens telling him as much when he first encountered them. And whoever this speaker is... he is the worst of all.

"I came here to tell you one thing, Goth Sullus, and now I'm telling you everything. But... I need you to know just how much thought I put into all of this. I am for you, Emperor Sullus. Though I didn't fully realize it until this very moment. Because you are the only way, when the scenarios played themselves out. The only way that the House of

Reason, festering pestilence that it is and will always be, does not remain in power. And that—the status quo—is the one thing that is no longer acceptable."

X again speaks proudly, as if captivated by his own genius. "So yes. I did it all. I sacrificed the legionnaires—on Kublar, and in more than a dozen different smaller wars—to make it clear that the House of Reason had to go. I kept the MCR supplied when Dark Ops broke their backs, because I knew how petty their grievances were, and thus how easily they could be weaponized, converted, and used as a new army. And so they have.

"I let you grow, Goth Sullus, and I ensured the full weight of the Republic was not brought down on you when you were at your most vulnerable. I fed critical intel to the enemies of the Republic. I authorized that a massive piece of ordnance destroy a Republic destroyer as well as Camp Forge, using the MCR and indigenous Kublarens to provide cover."

There is another pause. Chhun feels his strength returning to him. A strength born of rage. He clenches his fists repeatedly.

"Am I a monster?" X asks. "I'm directly responsible for upwards of forty thousand lives lost... So yes. In fact I am. But to stop the carnage of all the wars since the Savage Wars, we—no, I had to make the hard choices when no one else would. And you, whoever you really are behind that armor... you, Goth Sullus, are just one of my choices.

"I..." For the first time, the voice sounds uncertain. Almost... small. "I didn't come here to tell you any of this. I came here to draw you into a trap. The Legion commander, he wouldn't listen to reason. He sees you as much a threat to liberty as the House of Reason itself." The voice grows stronger. "He doesn't understand. He, who for far too long served at the House's whim, too squeamish to overthrow their rule until I forced the matter... still he remains cautious, hesitant. Timid. The commander lacks the boldness that I possess. The willingness to take the chance, to take a real risk... to do what needs to be done."

X sniffs.

"So... down to business. I come to you with an offer, Emperor Sullus. I can deliver the House of Reason, the Legion, and Utopion. All right now, in one swift and decisive blow. You just have to pick whom you want to work with, and I will make it happen. We've killed a lot of people, Emperor Goth Sullus, to give you the chance to stop the slaughter once and for all. I'm offering you the keys to the kingdom."

There is another pause, broken by a voice that could belong to none other than Goth Sullus himself.

"The House of Reason... is already mine."

The audio cuts off abruptly, and a cheerful digital assistant announces, "End of recording. Addendum from Legion Commander Keller."

The Legion commander's addendum begins immediately. "Captain Ford." He sounds grim but not defeated. "You've just heard a message that Major Owens died to deliver to me. And shortly, I'll be sharing his fate. The back of the Legion has been broken, and I want someone to know what happened. And you, Captain, are a survivor. I will not make the error of binding you with calls for vengeance. Do with this information what you will, and know that I forgot nothing."

The digital assistant declares, "End of message."

The lounge of the Indelible VI falls silent.

Then Wraith speaks. "So that's it, Chhun. And it's all true. The House of Reason has introduced Goth Sullus as the new leader of the Republic. And Garret here dug up some dirt that even that Nether Ops bastard didn't know. Garret found out that Orrin Kaar and Goth Sullus—and Devers—had been working together, under the nose of the entire Republic, for years."

Chhun feels like his body had been cut to pieces. There's a burning rage in his stomach that he is sure matches that of Exo's. His old comrade is chewing the inside of his mouth, fire and hate in his eyes, staring intently at Chhun.

They all are.

Every legionnaire in the room is waiting for him to speak. Even Bombassa, the shock trooper, seems to want Chhun's opinion on the matter.

But it is Masters who voices the question. "So what are we supposed to do now?"

Exo, who looks as though he is roiling with a lifetime of anger, finally explodes. "I don't know about you guys, but I'm gonna kill the bastard in that message. I'm gonna find X, and I'm gonna gut him with my own hands!" He punches the wall, his teeth clenched so tightly that they look as though they'll splinter and shatter.

Chhun's body wants nothing more than to remain seated, but he struggles against his injuries to rise to his feet and stand straight with his shoulders back. He takes a deep breath and addresses the room.

"I spoke to Major Owens before he left on what I assume was this mission. He placed me in charge of his old Dark Ops sector… and he deactivated Kill Team Victory. 'Too damaged to salvage,' he said. Not enough bodies to fill the void."

He pauses.

"But the way I see it, Kill Team Victory is back at full strength."

He pans his gaze across the room, looking each man square in the eye. They nod back in return, one by one, except for Ford, who looks on passively.

"We're the last kill team. We're Victory Squad. And we're gonna make 'em pay."

THE END

AVAILABLE NOW!

GE BOOKS

(CT) CONTRACTS & TERMINATIONS

(OC) ORDER OF THE CENTURION

1ST ERA BOOKS

THE FALL OF EARTH

01 THE BEST OF US

02 MOTHER DEATH

2ND ERA BOOKS

SAVAGE WARS

01 SAVAGE WARS

02 GODS & LEGIONNAIRES

03 THE HUNDRED

3RD ERA BOOKS

RISE OF THE REPUBLIC

01 DARK OPERATOR

02 REBELLION

03 NO FAIL

04 TIN MAN

OC ORDER OF THE CENTURION

CT REQUIEM FOR MEDUSA

CT CHASING THE DRAGON

CT MADAME GUILLOTINE

Explore over 30+ Galaxy's Edge books and counting from the minds of Jason Anspach, Nick Cole, Doc Spears, Jonathan Yanez, Karen Traviss, and more.

4TH ERA BOOKS

LAST BATTLE OF THE REPUBLIC

OC **STRYKER'S WAR**

OC **IRON WOLVES**

01 LEGIONNAIRE

02 GALACTIC OUTLAWS

03 KILL TEAM

OC **THROUGH THE NETHER**

04 ATTACK OF SHADOWS

OC **THE RESERVIST**

05 SWORD OF THE LEGION

06 PRISONERS OF DARKNESS

07 TURNING POINT

08 MESSAGE FOR THE DEAD

09 RETRIBUTION

10 TAKEOVER

5TH ERA BOOKS

REBIRTH OF THE LEGION

01 LEGACIES

HISTORY OF THE GALAXY

1ST ERA BOOKS

THE FALL OF EARTH

1ST ERA SUMMARY

The West has been devastated by epidemics, bio-terrorism, war, and famine. Asia has shut its borders to keep the threats at bay, and some with power and influence have already abandoned Earth. Now an escape route a century in the making – the Nomad mission – finally offers hope to a small town and a secret research centre hidden in a rural American backwater. Shrouded in lies and concealed even from the research centre's staff, Nomad is about to fulfil its long-dead founder's vision of preserving the best of humanity to forge a new future.

2ND ERA BOOKS

SAVAGE WARS

01 SAVAGE WARS

02 GODS & LEGIONNAIRES

03 THE HUNDRED

2ND ERA SUMMARY

They were the Savages. Raiders from our distant past. Elites who left Earth to create tailor-made utopias aboard the massive lighthuggers that crawled through the darkness between the stars. But the people they left behind on a dying planet didn't perish in the dystopian nightmare the Savages had themselves created: they thrived, discovering faster-than-light technology and using it to colonize the galaxy ahead of the Savages, forming fantastic new civilizations that surpassed the wildest dreams of Old Earth.

HISTORY OF THE GALAXY

3RD ERA BOOKS

RISE OF THE REPUBLIC

3RD ERA SUMMARY

The Savage Wars are over but the struggle for power continues. Backed by the might of the Legion, the Republic seeks to establish a dominion of peace and prosperity amid a galaxy still reeling from over a millennia of war. Brushfire conflicts erupt across the edge as vicious warlords and craven demagogues seek to carve out their own kingdoms in the vacuum left by the defeated Savages. But the greatest threat to peace may be those in the House of Reason and Republic Senate seeking to reshape the galaxy in their own image.

4TH ERA BOOKS

LAST BATTLE OF THE REPUBLIC

4TH ERA SUMMARY

As the Legion fights wars on several fronts, the Republic that dispatches them to the edge of the galaxy also actively seeks to undermine them as political ambitions prove more important than lives. Tired and jaded legionnaires suffer the consequences of government appointed officers and their ruinous leadership. The fighting is never enough and soon a rebellion breaks out among the Mid-Core planets, consuming more souls and treasure. A far greater threat to the Republic hegemony comes from the shadowy edges of the galaxy as a man determined to become an emperor emerges from a long and secretive absence. It will take the sacrifice of the Legion to maintain freedom in a galaxy gone mad.

5TH ERA BOOKS

REBIRTH OF THE LEGION

5TH ERA SUMMARY

An empire defeated and with it the rot of corruption scoured from the Republic. Fighting a revolution to restore the order promised at the founding of the Republic was the easy part. Now the newly rebuilt Legion must deal with factions no less treacherous than the House of Reason while preparing itself for war against a foe no one could have imagined.

ABOUT THE AUTHORS

Jason Anspach and Nick Cole are a pair of west coast authors teaming up to write their science fiction dream series, Galaxy's Edge.

Jason Anspach is a best-selling author living in Puyallup, Washington with his wife and their own legionnaire squad of seven (not a typo) children. Raised in a military family (Go Army!), he spent his formative years around Joint Base Lewis-McChord and is active in several pro-veteran charities. Jason enjoys hiking and camping throughout the beautiful Pacific Northwest. He remains undefeated at arm wrestling against his entire family.

Nick Cole is a Dragon Award winning author best known for *The Old Man and the Wasteland, CTRL ALT Revolt!,*and the Wyrd Saga. After serving in the United States Army, Nick moved to Hollywood to pursue a career in acting and writing. He resides with his wife, a professional opera singer, south of Los Angeles, California.

HONOR ROLL

We would like to give our most sincere thanks and recognition to those who supported the creation of *Message for the Dead* by subscribing as a Galaxy's Edge Insider at GalaxysEdge.us.

Janet Anderson
Robert Anspach
Sean Averill
Russell Barker
Steven Beaulieu
John Bell
WJ Blood
Christopher Boore
Aaron Brooks
Brent Brown
Marion Buehring
Alex Collins-Gauweiler
Robert Cosler
Andrew Craig
Peter Davies
Nathan Davis
Christopher DiNote
Karol Doliński
Andreas Doncic
Noah Doyle
Lucas Eastridge
Stephane Escrig
Dalton Ferrari
Mark Franceschini
Richard Gallo
Kyle Gannon
Michael Gardner
John Giorgis
Gordon Green
Tim Green
Shawn Greene
Michael Greenhill
Joshua Hayes
Jason Henderson
Jeff Howard
Bernard Howell
Wendy Jacobson
James Jeffers
Kenny Johnson
Noah Kelly
Mathijs Kooij
Mark Krafft
Byl Kravetz
Clay Lambert
Grant Lambert
Richard Long
Oliver Longchamps
Kyle Macarthur

Richard Maier
Brian Mansur
Cory Marko
Pawel Martin
Trevor Martin
Tao Mason
Simon Mayeski
Brent McCarty
Joshua McMaster
Jim Mern
Alex Morstadt
Daniel Mullen
David Parker
Eric Pastorek
Jeremiah Popp
Chris Pourteau
Walt Robillard
Joyce Roth
David Sanford
Andrew Schmidt
Ryan Shaw
Christopher Shaw
Glenn Shotton
Daniel Smith
Joel Stacey
Maggie Stewart-Grant
John Stockley
Kevin Summers
Ernest Sumner
Tim Taylor
Beverly Tierney
Tom Tousignant
Scott Tucker
Eric Turnbull
John Tuttle
Christopher Valin
Paden VanBuskirk
Nathan Zoss

CPSIA information can be obtained
at www.ICGtesting.com
Printed in the USA
LVHW081544151021
700494LV00006B/53/J